THE NOTHING MEN

DAVID KAZZIE

GRUB CLUB PUBLISHING

ACKNOWLEDGMENTS

To my Advance Reader Team, thank you for your support, encouragement, and feedback. Your contributions are deeply valued.

And to Brady and Ingrid, thank you for the gift of a lifetime.

ISBN-13: 978-1-7331341-2-5

ISBN-10: 1-7331341-2-3

❀ Created with Vellum

As Always, For My Kids

ALSO BY DAVID KAZZIE

THE JACKPOT (2011)

THE IMMUNE SERIES (2015)

THE LIVING (2017)

ANOMALY (2018)

1

They began calling numbers at an ungodly hour, in that sliver of night just before dawn when nothing good happened but bad things often did, not because they had to but because they could.

Ben Sullivan had been dozing since midnight; the fatigue had finally closed in around him like a noose and left him hovering in that thin space between sleep and wakefulness. His body buzzed upon the call of each number, and when he finally heard his own, a loud, drawling NUMBER FOUR, laced with a Southern twang like good barbecue soaked in pepper vinegar, his eyes shot open and his heart began pounding like a coke-fueled hummingbird's. He gently rubbed his eyes, ran his hands across his face, trying to massage some life back into his skin. The fear and stress had carved inside him deep canyons of exhaustion that would soon need to be filled with real sleep, but he didn't have time for that now. He would sleep later.

"Here," Ben called out as he staggered to his feet.

He pulled on the straps of his permanent companion, a

haggard-looking blue backpack he'd carried during law school, now dirty, paper-thin, having lived up to its promised warranty and then some, in situations probably not envisioned by the good people at L.L. Bean. It held a pocketknife, two cans of ravioli, a canteen of water, some toiletries, a thin blanket, and his papers. Its straps had frayed, the zipper barely functioning. In other words, it was just hanging on. Like everything and everyone else.

They were in the parking lot of an abandoned shopping center in Short Pump, an unincorporated suburban community in Henrico County, just west of the city of Richmond, Virginia, camped out in a federal staging area known as the Cage. Years ago, the strip mall had been quilted together from a menu of suburban prerequisites, a mishmash of stand-alone fast-food joints, nail salons, and wireless phone stores. A huge Walmart at the southeastern tip had anchored the development in headier times. Now the one-acre parking lot served as a clearinghouse for government-sponsored job lotteries, swap meets, day-laborer pickups, and all manner of illicit commerce.

The U.S. Department of Reconstruction & Recovery had set up a cattle call in the southwest corner of the sprawling shopping center just outside an old Taco Bell restaurant. About three hundred people were packed into the Cage like hogs and not smelling much better. Portable spotlights ringed the perimeter, blasting the Cage with harsh sodium light from which there was no escape.

Despite the early hour, the air was swollen with humidity; it had been drizzling off and on all night. It was the sort of rain that seemed ready to burst, like an overripe piece of fruit, and wash away the stickiness. It never did, leaving you wanting, the itch unscratched, the sneeze unsneezed. The sky simply perspired, the intermittent drip-

drip-drip of the rain against the asphalt nothing short of maddening.

Ben had been in the Cage for sixteen hours now. It had been his luckiest break yet, finding out about the job fair before word of it had been announced on Freedom One. He'd been one of the first on site, scoring a very low lottery number, which meant that he'd be one of the first considered. The Department made its hires on the spot, and when all the slots were filled, that was that.

Thanks for playing, but you can return to your regularly scheduled programming of starving to death with your families.

The job lotteries, which started at four in the morning, were as organized as anything else these days, which was, to say, not very. They were first announced via Freedom One, the government-controlled communications network and then just as quickly by mouth. Hundreds of people lined up for each lottery, often for just a handful of job openings. Some days there were a dozen jobs; every now and again, you'd stumble across a job fair with thirty. The typical gig involved manual labor – debris cleanup, construction, body removal, the dirty work required after the closest thing to total apocalypse the world had seen since the Black Death killed a third of Europe.

Security was loosely maintained by a small platoon of Volunteers, the new federal security force that had been commissioned after the Panic ended. The lightly trained soldiers kept a disinterested eye on the corral; they usually didn't get involved unless absolutely necessary, and the definition of "absolutely necessary" fluctuated from day to day, from platoon to platoon. The soldiers handed out lottery slips in a first-come, first-serve fashion starting twelve hours before the interviews began. When they ran out of slips, they locked the gates.

A pair of portable chemical toilets constituted the beginning and the end of the government-sponsored amenities, and those were normally rendered unusable within the first hour. Anyone was free to leave the pen, but if you left, you didn't get back in. Abandoned spots fell to those on a waiting list, those ringing the pen like vultures.

As Ben wove through the waiting throngs of nameless, faceless strangers who just wanted to work again, he felt scores of eyes on him, the burning envy, the anguish, the hate of those holding higher lottery numbers, most of whom would leave today with nothing. He didn't begrudge them these feelings because he'd felt them as well, but he wasn't experiencing any survivor's guilt either. You didn't make it far these days by feeling sorry for other people.

The foreman nodded imperceptibly toward Ben before turning and making his way toward the small corrugated trailer at the north end of the cage. Ben hurried to catch up, falling in step behind the man. The foreman was a big fellow with an easy way about him, confident in his place in this new world.

"Your number?" he asked.

Ben handed him the slip of paper, stamped with the numeral 4, which had been issued to him upon his arrival at the camp. The man scanned it with a handheld electronic wand, and the machine emitted a satisfying beep upon confirming that Ben's ticket was genuine.

"You got your papers, right?"

"Yes, right here," he said, unzipping his backpack and removing the folder. He offered his papers toward the man, who simply waved them off.

"Wait until you're inside."

Ben closed the backpack, and they walked in silence as they covered the distance to the doublewide trailer. The aluminum siding glinted under the glare of the floodlights, the familiar U.S. Department of Reconstruction & Recovery logo emblazoned on the side. The ubiquitous seal, which had made its debut a few months after the Panic, consisted of a magnificent bald eagle in the foreground with a bright orange sun peeking out just behind its head. Ben had once wondered how they'd managed to come up with a logo so quickly, and he decided that maybe they'd had one all along, part of a contingency plan that had been drawn up, considered, revised, approved and then stuck in a drawer somewhere.

That is, at least, until they'd been faced with the question of *What the hell do we do now?*

Well, for starters, we've got this kick-ass logo we can use!

To his left stood the ruined shell of the Walmart, the store's marquee still identifiable despite missing both letter A's. A fire had consumed the building at some point, the edges of the doorways blackened with soot, as if smudged by the hands of a child giant. The burned-out chassis of an Army vehicle remained lodged in the front entrance. Its tires were gone, as was the canvas top. The devastation never got easier to look at, stark reminders of those terrible months three years ago when all seemed lost.

The foreman checked his watch as they reached the trailer. The place was quiet but for the rattle of an air-conditioner unit protruding from a side window like a cancerous growth. On the far side of the trailer, two yellow school buses bearing the words U.S. DEPARTMENT OF RECONSTRUCTION & RECOVERY idled in the old drive-thru lane. A pair of soldiers walked the perimeter of the trailer, their rifles gripped tightly in their hands.

"You've got another five minutes or so," he said. He lit a cigarette.

Ben pressed down each of his thumbnails firmly, a nervous tic of his. He took a deep breath and let it out slowly.

"Nervous?" the foreman asked, blowing smoke out through his nostrils.

"Yeah," Ben said. "First time I've made it inside."

"Just try and relax," he said. "They're looking for healthy, stable people for these jobs. There's two dozen openings today. As long as you don't piss yourself in there, you should be fine."

Ben nodded.

"What'd you do before?" the man asked.

"Nothing," he said. "I haven't worked in a while."

"I mean *before* before," the foreman said. "Before the Panic."

Ben tensed.

"Oh, before before," he said. "Right."

Before before, Ben thought. When America had spent its days watching YouTube videos and going to farmers' markets and arguing about climate change.

Before.

"Lawyer," Ben said, hoping the guy would drop this line of discussion. He didn't want to talk about the *Before Before* or the *Time Before That* either. He spent enough time thinking about it. Most days it was all he thought about.

The foreman seemed to find this amusing and began cackling with delight, a big explosive thing that burst out of him, as if Ben had stepped on a laugh mine. He dropped his cigarette to the ground and crushed it with his boot.

"Damn lawyers," he said, a sudden edge to his voice. "Bet you're not used to this kind of cattle call. Golf and cocktail parties and strippers for you lawyer types."

"No, sir," Ben said, his heart clapping against his ribs like a frightened puppy trapped in a cage. He was terrified that he was blowing his chance. "I just want to work."

Just then, the door to the trailer burst open, and a soldier emerged, dragging a thin man behind him. The man's name was Milton; he'd gotten to the site a few moments before Ben and had drawn Ticket No. 3. He was a nervous fellow, twitchy, talking nonstop until the interviews had begun. The soldier, the name Kendrick stitched to his fatigues, had Milton by the lapels of his dirty work shirt. With his M4 rifle slung over his shoulder, Kendrick dragged Milton, who had let his legs go limp and seemed hell-bent on making his eviction from the trailer as complicated as possible, down the steps.

"Hey, fuck you!" Milton was barking, twisting and turning like a child refusing his medicine. "A monkey can do this job! I just want to work! Look at me!"

"No Reds," Kendrick said. "You know the rules."

The soldiers outside rushed over to help their comrade, but before they could get there, Milton cleared his throat and fired a loogie directly into the soldier's face. That was that. With fresh spittle on his face, rife with only-God-knew-what pathogens, Kendrick unslung his rifle and drove the butt of the rifle directly into Milton's stomach, doubling the man over. As Milton struggled back to his feet, moaning, Kendrick rotated the rifle and aimed it directly at him.

"Take this asshole into custody," Kendrick barked. He turned his attention back to Milton. "Get your hands up."

"You ruptured my spleen!"

The foreman took Ben by the arm and the two of them eased away from the scene. Not breathing, not making a sound, Ben stared at the barrel of Kendrick's weapon, a steel snake hovering in the air. They were no more than ten feet away from Milton, just a few steps behind the soldier.

Milton remained rooted to his spot, not giving an inch. He looked each of the three soldiers in the face, and then he swung his gaze over toward Ben. Their eyes locked, and in Milton's, Ben saw nothing. Just a total absence of light and hope and anything that once might have been good and pure in his life. Ben blinked and looked away, focusing his gaze on one of the school buses. This wasn't his problem.

But from the corner of his eye, he saw Milton's shoulders sag, about as perfect a case study in body language as there ever was, a man who'd just watched his very last straw flutter away, a child's helium balloon caught on a thermal and disappearing from sight.

Milton's body tensed, leaning forward ever so slightly, and then he bull-rushed the soldier, a manic howl erupting from the depths. Kendrick squeezed off a short burst from his rifle directly into Milton's chest. It was a little thing, but a terrible thing all the same. A dark stain bloomed on Milton's shirt like a dark flower portending an ominous future. He crashed to the ground in a heap, and he died there in the parking lot of a Taco Bell. Behind him, the crowd buzzed loudly, but they remained docile, conscious of the heavy guns that would be loosed upon them at the slightest provocation.

"Clean this piece of shit up," Kendrick said to his comrades. Then he looked over at Ben and said: "You. Let's go."

Ben could barely move, his eyes locked on Milton's body. He willed himself to take a step forward, and Kendrick searched him, pawing through his bag, confiscating his knife.

"Well, counselor," the foreman said, his voice devoid of emotion, as though he watched soldiers kill unarmed civilians every day. Hey, perhaps he did. He clapped Ben on the shoulder. "You're up."

Ben's knees nearly buckled with fear as he climbed the three steps to the screen door, Kendrick trailing close behind. He took a deep breath and briefly considered hauling ass out of there, but he couldn't. He'd come too far. He'd invested too much. And certainly, he was better prepared than Milton had been.

It was time to push his chips to the center of the table.

2

The chilly air made him shiver, a delicious ripple dancing across his skin that he hadn't felt in ages. The sudden change in temperature, combined with the shock of what he had just seen outside made his stomach flutter.

The trailer was sparsely furnished, small, about twenty feet wide by fifty feet deep. Cheap particle wood paneled the walls, which were bare but for a single propaganda poster bearing the DRR logo mounted on the wall to Ben's left. It featured a smiling little girl wearing a colorful shirt, a bright pink thing dancing with flowers. The words *Winning the Future* were printed in its lower right corner.

"Sit down," a male voice said. "You have your identification documents?"

A middle-aged man sat at a metal desk in the center of the room. The man was rail thin, pale, his lips disturbingly red. A name badge pinned to his short-sleeve shirt identified him as R. KINCAID. His long, thin fingers danced across the keys of a laptop computer, and he seemed decidedly uninterested in the goings-on just outside his front door. Kendrick had disappeared into the background, a stage prop that had served its purpose.

"Yes, sir," Ben said, sitting down in the green plastic chair across from Kincaid.

He removed the folder from his backpack and handed it to the man. Kincaid reviewed the documents slowly and deliberately, one at a time. The passport and social security card were genuine. Ben had retrieved them two years ago, and he guarded the documents with his life. The third card, however, the only card that mattered, was an expert forgery and had come at a heavy price.

Six months after the Panic ended, Congress passed the National Recovery Act, which, in part, mandated the registration of every survivor, both infected and uninfected. It also banned Redeyes, as those who'd been infected with the Orchid virus were known, from having children. Those who had never been infected drew first priority for what little government assistance was available and, with a valid registration card, were eligible to work. Redeyes were currently ineligible to receive benefits, left to fend for themselves, although the Department promised that they would address the plight of the Redeyes in due course.

A thumbnail photograph of Ben took up the left half of the card. The right half was dedicated to Ben's biographical details, including height, weight, hair and eye color, and of course, his antibody status. It was this last field for which he had paid so handsomely, for which he had exhausted his last dollar, the field before R. Kincaid's eyes indicating that his status was Negative.

Ben sat stone still as the bureaucrat scanned his registration card, reminded of the time he'd used a fake ID for the first time. Upon hearing the satisfying beep from the wand, he concealed his relief like he was tossing a blanket over a delicate archeological site. When it came to passing yourself off as someone else, it was all about confidence. As though this review was just a mindless waste of his time. As a bartender, he could detect whether someone was of age within seconds, almost always by the level of interest in his review of the driver's license.

"This job opening we've got, it's not an easy one," Kincaid said, leaning back in his chair and tapping the tips of his slender fingers together.

"Truly, sir, I'd be happy to have any job," Ben said. "I'm ready to work."

Kincaid made a clicking noise with his tongue as he considered his applicant.

"Do you know how many people died during the Panic, Mr. Sullivan?"

It wasn't the question that took Ben by surprise as much as the manner in which Kincaid asked it, flatly, with no emotion. As if he were reading it from a Trivial Pursuit – Apocalypse Edition card and was waiting to see if Ben could earn a little plastic wedge for his wagon-wheel game piece.

Ben didn't know how or whether he was expected to answer. He didn't know the etiquette for discussing the Panic with government officials. Like everyone else, Ben had heard all kinds of casualty figures, presented in every conceivable form – bar graphs, charts, three-dimensional maps created by the Freedom One Network. The actual number didn't really matter all that much, not to know how bad it was. The smell told you that. The rich, deep smell of death, like a hunk of roast beef forgotten in the back of the refrigerator, blanketing the big cities for weeks and months afterwards, getting into everything like rancid cigarette smoke.

"More than one hundred and fifty million Americans, Mr. Sullivan," Kincaid said, breaking the silence. "Half the population. Three billion worldwide."

"Wow," Ben said.

The number didn't surprise Ben in the least, but Kincaid was obviously trying to dazzle him with his grasp of the material.

"I didn't know it was that many."

"Goddamn Reds were nearly the end of us," Kincaid said, as if Ben hadn't been there for it, as though he might have been vacationing on the polar ice caps of Mars while the world had nearly come to an end.

"That they were," Ben agreed. "That they were."

"And now we have to live beside them every day, as if nothing happened," Kincaid said. "No way to know if the infection will come back, if it's just lying dormant."

"Right," Ben said, nodding, trying to maintain his very best poker face. He spent every day wondering that very thing.

"Anyway, I'm going to assign you to a HARD Team," Kincaid said, using a piece of government nomenclature that meant absolutely nothing to Ben.

Kincaid turned to his laptop and began tapping away. The room was quiet but for the clickety-clack of the keyboard and the drone of the air conditioner.

"That's Human Asset Recovery and Disposition," Kincaid said, apparently picking up on Ben's confusion. "We've been using these acronyms so long we forget that the general public might not be familiar with them."

Ben puzzled over this for a moment and then a flash of

heat swept up his back, the words registering with him. A government euphemism for something unspeakably awful.

"What will I be doing?"

"Simply put, more than a hundred million corpses are dotting the American landscape," Kincaid said. "The administration has made the disposal of these remains a national priority. There are HARD teams in every city and state to recover remains and transport them to disposal facilities. It's a long, tedious project. But this country can't fully move beyond the Panic until this matter is attended to."

Ben sensed that Kincaid was reciting a well-memorized script, but his stomach fluttered anyway. In his mind's eye, he saw a three-dimensional map of America, a camera sweeping over the nation, zooming in on hospitals and churches and schools and houses, choked with the bodies of the dead, piled up like firewood in some places, strewn about like debris in others.

"These teams have been working for nearly two years, but we're seeing tremendously high turnover and progress has been slow," Kincaid said. "Not everyone has the stomach for the work."

A ripple of annoyance at that. Kincaid had said it as if he weren't some paper-pushing bureaucrat. Ben wanted to ask Kincaid if he had spent a single moment on a HARD Team but thought better of it.

"You think you can handle it?" asked Kincaid.

"Yes, sir," Ben said. "I used to be a prosecutor. Saw a lot of crime scenes."

"Good," he said. "This job isn't for the faint of heart. Any questions?"

"How does it work?"

"You'll be assigned to a four-man team working a

specific grid here in Henrico County," Kincaid said. "Are you from here?"

"No," Ben said.

That was true. But for his three years in law school here in Richmond, Ben had spent most of his life in North Carolina. He'd moved north after the Panic, deciding to start over where he was an unknown, just another hardcase trying to get by in a world that was like a haunted funhouse version of its former self. Someday, he hoped to reunite with his wife Sarah and son Gavin, but they weren't ready for that yet. They had made it through the Panic without becoming infected, a fact that cleaved Ben from the two people he loved most of all.

"We use standard garbage trucks for collection. Once you've got a full load, you return to Central Processing to offload the cargo. Lather, rinse, repeat. The crematoriums are running twenty-four hours a day."

Cargo. He reminded himself that Kincaid had probably been at this a while, had become desensitized to it all, by necessity. He'd experienced the same thing during his years as a prosecutor because after a while the cases and victims and carnage and ruined lives started to run together and you couldn't even remember the name of the little girl who'd been molested by her grandfather even though you'd promised yourself that you'd never, ever become like that.

"You know how pay and benefits work?"

Ben shook his head. Three years on, the global economy was still a mess, still struggling to recover. No one knew what to do because there was no model for what to do. During those apocalyptic eight months, nearly half of the world's workforce had died or become disabled. Demand for goods and services had dropped significantly, but it was still there, relying on wrecked supply chains. Entire industries had disappeared virtually overnight. Leisure and travel and dining were still things of the past, although the government was trying to push people back into their former lives like they were old clothes that still fit. Other industries had risen in their wake as the corporations rushed in to fill the void. A number of the larger companies had started buying construction and manufacturing interests as the world turned its attention to reconstruction.

"We pay in cash, per truckload, at the end of each day. The more cargo your crew clears, the more you make." Kincaid said. "That's all we can do right now. No benefits. No paid vacation. Twelve-hour shifts. You get one day off per week. You get hurt on the job, you might lose it. Forget worker's comp. You were a lawyer, you said? This is probably blowing your little lawyer mind."

"No, I get it," Ben said. "State of emergency and all that."

"Exactly," Kincaid said. "I know the Act isn't the most popular thing in American history, but I'm sure you know how tough it is out there right now. Welcome aboard."

Kincaid clicked a button on his mouse, and his printer began revving up like an aircraft warming up its engines. Ben stared at the machine, rapt, unable to remember the last time he'd heard a printer warm up. Things that had been lost. The ordinary and mundane. What was once background noise suddenly seemed like black magic. Electricity. Printers. Hell, maybe Kincaid still had a Facebook account!

A moment later, the printer spit out a single sheet of paper. He handed it to Ben, whose fingers trembled as he accepted this passport to a new life.

"You start work immediately," he said. "Captain Kendrick will escort you to the bus, which will take you to Central Processing for orientation. Give this document to the superintendent."

"Thank you," Ben said.

Kendrick led Ben back to the bus; he followed without a word, careful to avoid a misstep when he was so close, so agonizingly close to turning the corner. Because no one was hiring Redeyes.

And Ben was one of them.

3

The first two weeks on the HARD Team were the worst.

Each twelve-hour shift began and ended at the Eastern Henrico Processing Center, as it was officially known in government documents, or the Dump, as it was unofficially and more accurately known. The Department had slapped the facility together in an industrial section of the county's east end, bracketed to the south by a residential neighborhood and the interstate to the north. This particular installation serviced several dozen HARD crews operating in the central Virginia area – the city in the middle, like a baseball, Henrico wrapping around it to the north, west and east, like a glove, and the less-populated counties on the far sides of Henrico and farther south. The crematorium chugged like a steam engine twenty-four hours a day, seven days a week, belching its tragic smoke into the skies.

Ben arrived at the depot each morning at five-thirty, making extra certain he was never late, as tardiness was grounds for immediate termination. The early start really didn't present much of a problem; he suffered from intractable insomnia and slept little at the refugee camp at the Richmond International Raceway about a mile away. He'd pitched a small tent there about a year ago, trying to make a home out of polyester and dangerous, slippery hope.

The scope of the cataclysm was never clearer than when Ben pulled a shift on his HARD crew, scouring each structure for victims, moving door-to-door through neighborhoods and commercial districts like a salesman hawking vinyl siding. Behind every door, in every backyard and two-car garage and shed, tucked into every convenience store and gas station and commercial office park, lay bodies waiting to be reclaimed and placed into eternal rest. There would be no funeral for these people, fate casting them the most meager of final dispositions. Day by day, hour by hour, Ben's crew forded a river of bodies that had no end.

And yet, like anything else that human beings had found themselves subject to during the course of their history, working on the HARD crew became, in time, part of his reality, part of his routine. The Panic, and Ben's role in it, were never far from his mind, and so it wasn't like body recovery had him thinking more about the Panic. Such a thing wasn't possible; it would be like trying to top off an already full fuel tank.

Over time, he began to derive a certain grim satisfaction of doing something productive for every minute of every twelve-hour shift. No down time for the mind to wander. From the time he clocked in until the moment he clocked out, like the wolf and the sheepdog from the old cartoons, he and his crew were studying plats or *en route* to a site or processing bodies.

He grew numb to the grisly nature of the work, the way doctors became immune to the deaths of patients, the way he'd become numb to the horror of crime as a prosecutor. In an unexpected but not unwelcome way, it was a reminder that the Panic was over. There was something cleansing and therapeutic about cleaning up a mess, especially when the chaos that had created the mess had been so horrific.

And in a way, it was penance. Penance for his own terrible contribution to the Panic.

As Kincaid had promised, the turnover rate on the HARD teams was quite high. All but one member of the crew he'd shoved out with on his first day had already washed out, apparently preferring unemployment and possibly starvation to the burden of harvesting bodies. For the past week, though, the rotation had stabilized, leaving Ben as the second-most senior member on his crew.

The senior guy was a beefy guy named Danny Brooks. Rounding out the crew were a young woman named Ellie Campbell and a quiet fellow named Randall Holland. Randall and Ellie were pleasant enough, but Danny gave Ben the creeps. He stank of beer and cigarettes and sweat. Ben pictured him as the kind of guy who spent his pre-apocalypse days beating up his girlfriends and telling racist jokes.

When Ben arrived for work on that Wednesday morning, Ellie was already there in the staging area, pulling on her biohazard suit over her small but athletic frame. Her wire-straight brown hair was pulled back in a tight ponytail. She was about thirty years old, quiet, didn't say much. She seemed content to observe the things going on around them. Every now and again, Ben would catch her watching him and the others, almost studying them. Nothing escaped her keen eye. She didn't engage in small talk, which Ben found rather appealing.

"Morning," Ben said, setting his bag in the cab area of the truck.

"I'm going to grab a cup of coffee," she said without looking up. "Want some?"

He nodded, pleasantly surprised, almost proud of himself. He felt like he had impressed her in some small way, and this, he was embarrassed to say, delighted him immensely. She wandered off in search of their morning brew, leaving him alone to pull on his suit. He tried telling himself that he was nervous around her because he was afraid she'd discover his secret and not because he'd developed a schoolboy crush on her. Just the thought of being attracted to another woman made him feel guilty on so many levels, not the least of which was that he was still technically married. Granted, he hadn't seen Sarah or Gavin in more than a year, and the last time they'd spoken, Sarah had told him that she never wanted to see him again, but it didn't make him feel any less guilty. He missed them terribly, but he respected her wishes. Maybe there were things that you could not undo.

"You want the coffee or not?" she said, her harsh tone quickly breaking him out of his trance.

"Oh," he said, looking up and seeing her fresh, clean face hovering over him. He hadn't heard her come up on him. "Sorry. Just zoned out for a second."

She handed him the Styrofoam cup, and they sat on the back bumper of the truck, enjoying a last few minutes of peace before their day devolved into an endless wave of tragedy washing over them, an ocean delivering its eternal beating to the shoreline. The coffee was actually decent and, even better, high-octane. A single cup had his body buzzing.

"Some job, huh?" he asked.

"I guess," she said.

He tried to think of something else to say, but everything he considered sounded stupid in his head, and he cast them off, one at a time, like a quality control inspector carefully inspecting a new load of widgets rolling by on an assembly line.

"Not a huge fan of the old Double-R," he said, "but you have to admit that it is an important job."

"I suppose," she said.

She looked down at her coffee for a minute and then dumped the contents onto the ground.

"This is harder than I thought it would be," he said.

"Yeah," she replied, finally cracking. "How long you been on this team?"

"Just a week more than you," he said. "Couple folks washed out since I joined."

"It's easy to get rattled," she said. "Gotta find some way to stay sane."

"Got any suggestions?"

She held his gaze for a moment, apparently considering whether to continue this bonding moment.

"I like to be outdoors," she said, breaking the gaze and staring off into the distance. "Away from the city. There's this place off the Appalachian Trail I like to go. The Priest. You ever heard of it?"

Ben shook his head.

"It's really pretty there," she said. "Away from all this. You almost forget how things are now. There's a logbook in the shelter where people write their confessions. It's something else to read them. Especially these days."

A metallic clang interrupted the conversation; Ben looked over to see Danny Brooks banging a golf club against the bumper of the truck.

"Let's go," he called out to them. "This ain't no goddamn Starbucks!"

Ben felt his skin tighten with heat. The man pushed

his every button, the way a child might slide his hand across all the call buttons on an elevator of a very tall building.

"I'll see you on the truck," she said.

AT SIX SHARP, Ben's truck pushed out from the depot, groaning and belching diesel smoke as it headed north on Glenside Drive toward the northern part of the county. The air was sticky, and thick clouds hung over the area like a gray blanket. The atmosphere seemed ripe for a thunderstorm at some point in the morning.

Ben rode shotgun while Danny drove; the newbies rode on the back of the truck. Danny was a heavyset, twitchy man, sporting the look of a guy who considered the easy access to porn as the great achievement of the Internet. Under his suit, he wore jeans and a cutoff t-shirt that accentuated his thick but undefined arms. Ben's dislike of Danny was growing by the hour and was directly proportional to the amount the man talked.

"So we were camping in this trailer park," Danny was saying. "Up the road a piece, actually. And the Reds are swarming around like flies on shit."

Ben hadn't minded the Red moniker prior to meeting Danny Brooks, but hearing it cross the man's lips made it seems ugly and harsh, every bit the slur it had become during the past few months. Ben sat silently as Danny continued his favorite pastime – telling war stories, recounting his brave struggle against the Reds. To hear him tell it, it was as if Brooks himself had neutralized the threat, as though the Orchid virus hadn't simply burned itself out, the human immune system stepping up to the plate, later

than everyone might have liked, perhaps, but just in time
nevertheless.

Ben preferred to look out the window while Danny
rambled on. They turned west onto Staples Mill Road,
which meandered through a mixed residential/commercial
district. This section of the county had flourished after
World War II, when people had first left the city for the
infant suburbs. Middle-class all the way, dominated by
small ranches and Cape Cods on square lots, home to
contractors and factory workers and police officers and
social workers. The kind of neighborhood where someone
was always in violation of one county ordinance or another,
storing junk in the backyard, keeping an old Ford with no
wheels and a decade-old inspection sticker in the front yard,
the weeds growing up into the chassis.

On every block, people went about the business of
rebuilding because when you got right down to it, all disas-
ters were the same, they just came dressed in different
threads.

They passed a billboard, long since commandeered by
the Department, now sporting giant red letters against a
black background:

KNOW THE SIGNS OF AN ACTIVE ORCHID INFECTION!

It amused Ben because it was probably fair to say that
nearly everyone on Earth was pretty well versed in *The Signs
of an Active Orchid Infection*, thank you very much. But it was
a reminder of everyone's ultimate fear. That the virus would
resurface and finish off the job it had nearly completed.
That was why the signs were still there.

"I was hunkered down in this one trailer, right near the
front gate."

Truly, the guy just did not shut up.

"Had this piece of ass with me. So I start picking them off one after the other, easiest turkey shoot ever. Then this dumb bitch I was with, she freaks out and runs out the door, right into their zombie arms. Stupidest damn thing I ever seen. Another few minutes, and we would have been safe. Stupid bitch."

Ben sighed and let it out slowly. This was at least the fourth time that Brooks had told this particular story, and he was tired of it. He was tired of Danny. Every morning, he arrived at work hoping that Danny had had enough, but it wasn't meant to be. Danny had struck Ben as an apocalypse junkie, someone who was happier with the state of the world after the Panic.

"Whaddya think of the new chick?" Danny asked, stealing a peek out of his sideview mirror, where he could see Ellie hanging from the back of the truck, her face impassive.

"They both seem nice," Ben said, in no hurry to wander down Danny's Hall of Planned Sexual Conquests.

"I'd hit it," he offered. Then, slowly, more deliberately, his eyes still glued to the sideview mirror: "I would tear that shit up."

"We're here," Ben said, pointing toward the approaching intersection and desperate to change the subject. Danny slowed the big truck down and turned off Staples Mill Road, one of the main arteries in the county.

Thank God, Ben thought.

THEIR ASSIGNMENT for the week was a subdivision called Fox Ridge, an upper-middle-class neighborhood of about six hundred houses in the northwestern part of the county, home to nearly 2,500 souls when the Panic had hit. A handful of residents had moved back since, but the rest were either dead or gone. The livable houses were occupied by Volunteers or heavily armed squatters, the pain-in-the-ass survivalists who'd made it through the Panic unscathed, or groups of refugees from the big cities, many of which had been devastated during the war.

Fox Ridge hadn't been the swankiest subdivision in the county, but it was still nice, once occupied by successful lawyers and bankers and where some of the moms worked. These folks had driven Acuras and Infinitis here rather than the Range Rovers and Mercedes in the chicer subdivisions off to the west.

The Department had classified Fox Ridge as a Category B site, which meant it anticipated at least one thousand bodies that required processing. A Category A was a big one, at least five thousand bodies to clear. Clearing out the As and Bs was the Department's main priority. They would be here for at least a week.

Working in two-man units, the HARD teams moved from house to house, free to enter any private residence thanks to the sweeping authority granted by the National Recovery Act. The crew conducted a room-to-room search for bodies, wearing the biohazard protection suits and respirators. The sweeps loaded the remains into body bags and carried them out to the curb.

More than a dozen federal lawsuits were pending across the country, claiming that these HARD searches violated the Fourth Amendment right against warrantless searches. And the plaintiffs were probably right, but not a single court had sided with them; the appeals courts, which had been notoriously slow before Armageddon, hadn't spun the wheels of justice any faster afterwards. There hadn't been much of a public outcry, largely because the American people supported anything that would push the Panic into the history books. The motto after the September II terrorist attacks might have been *Never Forget*, but that was decidedly not the case for the Panic. There were no lessons learned, there was no sense of unity, and everyone wanted to forget it as quickly as possible

Ben and Randall cleared six houses in the first hour, hauling sixteen bodies out to the curb. The seventh and final house in the cul de sac was a heavily damaged colonial with a brick façade and a wide driveway that curled around to the back. The lawn was overgrown, rippling in the thick breeze as if it were alive, the neighborhood quiet but for the susurrations of the tall grass.

A badly-decomposed body greeted them at the front door, lying over the threshold, the lower half draped across the front stoop like a picnic blanket. The flesh was long gone, but there was still something more than just skeletal remains, necrotized fibrous tissue still clinging to bone, a ghostly reminder that this had been someone, that this wasn't the bright white plastic skeleton from the high school biology lab. He scooped the remains into one of the body bags and wondered a bit about who this person might have been.

After tying the bag off, he hoisted it onto his shoulder like a sack of potatoes and took it out to the curb.

That was when he heard the scream.

4

B en had been at work when he first heard about the thing that would eventually metastasize into the Panic. It was strange, the way it came back to him with such clarity, right down to the project he'd been working on, the tie he'd been wearing (a yellow silk thing peppered with Brazilian poison dart frogs), to the way one of the fluorescent bulbs in his ceiling was flickering, even how he'd kept meaning to call maintenance and kept right on forgetting.

As had so often been the case back then, he was tucked away in his office at the Raleigh branch of mega-firm Willett & Hall, where he'd spent the previous decade after two years as a prosecutor. It was a Tuesday, mid-March, spring just starting to send out feelers into what had been an unusually harsh winter. At his desk on the sixteenth floor of the Gale Building, he was snacking on a protein bar (cookies and cream, he still remembered the flavor), reviewing a financing document for a client that manufactured computer chips that was in the middle of buying another company that made circuit boards.

He didn't mind the work; it appealed to his analytical mind, the ensuring of the t-crossing and the i-dotting so that the deals withstood the reviews of the various alphabet soup agencies like the Securities and Exchange Commission, the Federal Communications Commission, and the other federal regulatory bodies who thrived on making things needlessly complicated. Who knew why they black-flagged one deal but not another? Probably because someone was on the take. Someone was always on the take. His work probably bored people at cocktail parties who made the mistake of asking him what he did for a living, and on the surface, it probably was boring, but he saw these deals as giant puzzles with many interlocking pieces that had to be set down in the right order.

Plus, they paid him a great deal of money to do it. He'd been elevated to partner two years earlier and had earned an equity share in the firm, which, along with the bonus, pushed his annual salary to within striking distance of half a million dollars, a veritable fortune in a reasonably priced market like Raleigh.

On that particular Tuesday, however, his mind wasn't there, trapped instead in a netherworld between the end of winter and the approaching summer, zeroed in on his upcoming Vegas trip with his college buddies or drifting just over the horizon, once school let out, a week at the Outer Banks with Sarah, Gavin, and her father, a widower. More pedestrian and immediate obligations were bearing down on him as well. He needed to order mulch. Gavin had a soccer tournament that weekend.

He set a thick financing prospectus down on his desk, and ran mindlessly through a series of web pages book-marked on his laptop. The college basketball tournament was just around the corner (and had he known that the tournament would be cancelled after the second week due to an unusual viral outbreak sweeping the nation, he might have pocketed the fifty-dollar entry fee for the office pool, cash that might later have proven useful – *decisions, decisions!*).

In his old life, he'd often failed to recognize those moments that had ended up having great import. A decision to go to this college or to take that job offer. To break up with this girl. To take that flight to Paris. Little decisions, little pebbles dropped into the center of the lake of his life that sent ripples to the far edges of his existence. But in this new post-Panic world, he'd become hyper-aware of all the decisions he had to make, conscious that his life depended on these choices. People literally lived or died by the choices they made these days. He often wondered if he'd be in this mess if he'd made better decisions in the opening days of the Panic, primal, survival-of-the-fittest decisions, back when it might still have made a difference.

He was slightly alarmed when he saw a series of some-what disturbing Tweets rolling through his feed hashtagged #RedFlu. There were reports of a few deaths, of violent behavior in a few cases, supposedly attributable to the delirium and high fever. The Centers for Disease Control had gotten involved but were reporting that the outbreak was localized and not indicative of a wider epidemic.

Decisions, decisions.

The trail of flu-related tweets went cold. Ben promptly forgot about them and went on to read about spring training opening, about Iran rattling its nuclear saber again, about cheap flights to Jamaica if you dropped everything and left that afternoon. He bored quickly, turned his attention back to the big merger and buried himself in his work.

The next day, he flew to Chicago for a meeting with the

client's in-house counsel, a lawyer with whom Ben had been decidedly unimpressed, a forty-hour-a-week guy who kept looking at his watch when their meeting had drifted past the no-no hour of five o'clock. Ben worked and worked, ignoring the news, ignoring Twitter and Facebook and the news sites and only heard chatter about a worsening flu outbreak, the kind of chatter that blended into the background of polite chit-chat, just something to talk about while waiting for a meeting to start or for the elevator to finish its interminable trip from the first floor.

By the time he boarded a flight home at Chicago's O'Hare Airport that Friday night, sipping a gin and tonic, reading a novel, he was blissfully unaware that they were all reaching a tipping point, that things were about to get out of hand, that the entire human race was on a roller coaster approaching the highest point on the track.

BEN FROZE as the scream dialed up in intensity, every muscle pulling tight, like fishing line that had snared something big. He hadn't heard anything like it since the darkest days of the Panic, when every moment of every day had become a bad horror movie that wouldn't end and blood-curdling screams were a dime a dozen. The market had become flooded with them, down to the point that they had no meaning, no real value. Just indicative of another day in hell.

It was piercing, close by, maybe just down the street. It hadn't had a chance to soften in the open air, no chance of editing it for content. Just pure unadulterated terror.

"What the hell was that?" Randall asked, his head swiveling around loosely like a bobblehead doll's. Fear lined the man's face, as if he half-expected to see a herd of Redeyes stumbling down the boulevard, back for an encore presentation. Not that Ben could blame him. The fear was huge inside all of them, with the deep roots of an old oak, stretching its branches everywhere.

Then: AWAAAAAAAAAAGHHHHHHH!

"Shit," Ben said.

He heaved the bag into the back of the truck and set out down the street in a full sprint. The second howl had helped triangulate its place of origin. He ran as fast as his legs would carry him, sucking in huge gobs of warm, humid air that seemed just as likely to drown him as sustain him. At the next intersection, he turned left into a large cul de sac of a half-dozen colonials, their lawns sporting shaggy beards of grass, as if they'd unified in a refusal to shave. Their DRR truck was parked in the middle of the circle, pointed outward, and a handful of bagged remains had been piled haphazardly by one of the driveways. The other houses on this short street had sustained heavy damage and seemed devoid of any human life.

Ben burst through the door, half-expecting to see a gaggle of Reds slaughtering a co-worker in the living room, but the scene was unmolested, as it the family who'd lived here had just stepped out for some ice cream. He was in the foyer, bright from the sunlight streaming in through the skylights, steamy from the lack of air conditioning. Straight ahead was a long hallway, leading toward a galley kitchen.

The sound of a grunt caught his ear. Upstairs. He bolted down the hall and found the stairs at the back of the house. The smell of rotted food and animal droppings, rich and sour, permeated the air. He scanned the kitchen for a weapon, anything that he could use to defend himself. A cast-iron skillet hanging from a pot rack mounted over the island countertop caught his eye. It was glossy and black, shiny with the ghosts of a thousand meals gone by. He grabbed it. His heart throbbing like a redlining engine, he pressed his back to the wall and took the steps gingerly, one at a time.

Then he heard a voice, harsh, cold and dead.

"Fucking bitch!"

Then another grunt. Louder. Clearer. And definitely female. Ellie.

Ben picked up the pace and made it to the landing. The sounds were clearer now, and Ben's fear grew exponentially. Two bodies were stacked to Ben's right, pushed up against the railing, carefully wrapped in bags. He heard another grunt, and then a choked voice coming from his right, the female voice again, pleading, "no, no, no." Ben looked over and saw a door, half-open; beyond, just inside the room, shadows swam against the wall. He eased up to the threshold for a better view. It was a small room, an office or a study. An ornate Oriental rug covered most of the floor, and a large modular desk in the corner anchored the room. A bookcase pushed up against the wall at the edge of the door gave him just a sliver of cover. He poked his head around toward the commotion on the floor.

Danny was holding Ellie to the ground with one arm, his huge hand plastered across her small mouth, and he was trying to shuck his camouflage pants off. Ellie was putting up a stupendous struggle, twisting this way and that, a crazed gazelle pinned under the paw of a lion. But the man had at least a hundred pounds on the diminutive woman, and that was the way it was in this brave new world.

Ben crept up, crouching low behind him, and readied a home run swing of the skillet. As he came up on the attacker's left, he locked eyes with Ellie; the man noticed just in time, just as Ben brought the skillet down, swooping down like a pile driver. The wannabe-rapist shifted just slightly, rolling onto his left flank, and so instead of taking fifteen pounds of cast iron to the skull, the flat bottom of the skillet crashed into his beefy right arm; the skillet slipped out of Ben's grip and thudded to the ground. Danny howled like a wounded bear, rolling over onto his back and then up to his feet. Terror swelled inside Ben as he realized how quickly the big man had moved.

Ellie rolled onto her stomach and staggered to her feet, but Ben kept his primary focus on the injured and extremely pissed off man.

"You just made a big mistake," he said, his breathing shallow and ragged.

He shuffled to his right, circling around Ben like a shark moving in for the kill. Then he charged, his shoulder low, crashing into Ben's midsection like a freight train. The men rolled to the floor in a heap, and Ben knew instantly he was in an enormous amount of trouble. Ellie leapt onto Danny's back, raining down punches, but Danny was too big, too strong, too fueled with rage. He bucked her off like she was a rookie rodeo cowboy, and he concentrated his attack on Ben.

Flat on his back, Ben was defenseless as Danny slammed a closed fist against the side of his head. The room fractured in front of him, and a rush of nausea washed over him. Strangely, he pictured the videos games of his youth, the health bar in the top corner of the screen illustrating how much more punishment his character would be able to take. As his consciousness faded, he saw Zelda, he saw Street Fighter, he saw Karate Champ. Another punch like that, and the bar would slide to empty, and that would be it for Ben Sullivan.

GAME OVER! GAME OVER!

There was nothing he could do; he pulled his arms up over his face and waited for the final blow.

Then Danny suddenly stopped.

He leapt off of Ben like he was on fire, squealing like a frightened child, backpedaling toward the door. He pointed an accusatory finger at Ben, as though he hadn't been the one guilty of a brutal attempted rape.

"Jesus Christ!" he bellowed.

He turned toward Ellie, who now held the skillet.

"Look at him," he said to her. "He's a fuckin' Red!"

This was enough to swing her attention from her attacker to Ben. Danny shivered and wiped his hands on his filthy pants.

"I'm OK," he muttered to himself. "I'm OK, I'm OK, I'm OK."

A vanity mirror was mounted on the wall to Ben's right; he turned his head toward it and saw what had spooked Danny so badly. One of his bunkers, the black-market lenses he used to cover the sclera in each of his eyes, had popped out. And staring back at Ben in that dusty mirror was a single fiery red eye, a deep shade of crimson that meant only one thing. The gift that never stopped giving. The telltale sign that he'd been infected with the Orchid virus. He stared at himself in the mirror, and the memories came flooding back, pouring into his brain like raw sewage, polluting and infecting the fragile ecosystem of peace he'd managed to build in the last couple of weeks.

Then he heard a loud *thunk*, not dissimilar to the sound of a baseball coming off an aluminum bat. He tore his gaze from the mirror just in time to see Danny stagger forward like a boxer who'd taken a haymaker to the jaw. Standing just beyond him was Ellie, the skillet in her hands.

"You crazy bitch!" he cried, cradling the back of his head with his hands. Ben hadn't seen her deliver the blow, so he didn't know how much damage she'd done, how much danger they were still in. The three of them stood there, eyeing each other, three points of a constellation of fear and confusion and fury. Danny's gaze bounced from Ellie to Ben and back again. Ben prayed that she'd rattled the man enough that he'd just split, that he was too dumb and afraid of becoming infected that he'd just run away and leave them alone. He couldn't remember an occasion that he'd been thankful for his infection.

First time for everything.

"Fuck this," he said between gritted teeth. "I'm out of here."

He slipped out of the room without another word and banged down the stairs like a drunken dinosaur. A moment later, the truck revved up and groaned down the quiet street.

Ben took one step to the door and then paused at the threshold.

"Are you OK?" he asked without looking back.

"Fine," she said. "You?"

"I'll live," he said.

"He's going to report you, you know," she said.

His shoulders sagged.

"I know," Ben said.

It still hurt to hear her say it.

They stood silently, his back to her. He could feel her eyes boring in on him, and he could almost read her thoughts. What atrocities had he committed? What monstrous things had he done? Had he really been unable to stop himself? How was that possible? Cancer didn't do that to you. AIDS didn't do that to you. Not even Ebola did that to you. With Ebola, you just died painfully and miserably.

"Thanks," she said. "I was in a lot of trouble there."

"Don't mention it. Are you OK?"

"No real damage done," she said. "Go on. Get out of here before they come looking for you."

5

About a year before he had joined the HARD Team, Ben had stumbled upon a bottle of Pappy Van Winkle bourbon whiskey while on a supply run in Winston-Salem, North Carolina, where he spent a few months squatting in an abandoned single-wide trailer. Booze was tough to find after the Panic, as many of the breweries, distilleries, and vineyards had gone offline and were slow to restart; not surprisingly, alcohol was in high demand and actively traded on the black market.

He hoped to open it when he'd returned home to his wife and son, when Sarah and Gavin were ready to put the past behind them and let Ben back into their lives. But as time went by and that prospect became less and less likely, the sealed bottle became a reminder of things that had once been possible but were no longer. Selling it for food was probably the wisest course of action, but he had been unwilling to do so.

You never knew when the occasion would call for it.

Losing his job on the HARD team turned out to be such an occasion.

And since he didn't have much else to do, it made the days at the Richmond International Raceway refugee camp in the eastern part of Henrico County a little more bearable. It had been a week since the incident with Ellie, and he'd spent most of it pleasantly buzzed on the aforementioned bourbon.

The camp was crowded but relatively well-organized. It was home to approximately a thousand men, women, and children who, like Ben, had survived infection with the Orchid virus.

The camp had been born during the lawless days following the Panic, when the Redeyes discovered how hostile the world was going to be to them, one that didn't care that they'd once been mothers and fathers, sisters and brothers, doctors, firemen, police officers, decorated war veterans, housewives, drug dealers or bank robbers. Eye color had replaced skin color as the currency for discrimination. The camp even had a governing body of sorts, a council that managed to maintain order among the camp's residents and cottage industries that had popped up during its lifecycle.

Tents were set up in a grid pattern in the raceway's infield, some fifty across. Clean water and food were at a premium, the most in-demand items on a robust black market. Every week or two, the Department would throw the camp a bone and drop off a few hundred cases of water and Meals Ready to Eat, which invariably led to fights and other assorted lunacy. Crime was a problem, but it was dealt with swiftly and severely. Redeyes had little tolerance for their own kind perpetrating crimes against one another, and this alone seemed to foster a certain détente in the camp.

It was early June now, and central Virginia was baking under a heat wave, as if the region didn't have enough problems to deal with. The days were unbearable, the air like steaming chowder, and so Ben spent most of his waking hours huddled in his tent drinking, napping, or re-reading the few paperback novels he'd collected during his wanderings. Evenings, he did his best to socialize with his tent neighbors, not because he felt any particular attachment to them, but because it was in his best interest to remain friendly with his fellow Redeyes.

Ben had given up trying to find a house months ago; occupied homes made easy targets for bandits, and besides, there weren't that many to be had anyway. A fifty-percent reduction in population had not made finding permanent shelter any easier. The war had devastated many urban areas on the coasts and in the Midwest; millions of refugees from Boston, New York, and Philadelphia had streamed toward the smaller cities and more temperate climes in the south. Many neighborhoods, the ones not occupied by Volunteers, had fallen under gang control and weren't safe.

The nights were the worst. It was the worst cliché possible, but when after the last bit of twilight had been rubbed away, Ben's mind filled in the space left empty by the darkness. It was natural selection up there, the strongest memories pushing out the other ones, leaving them alone to lord over his gray matter. Even when he'd been working body disposal, his sleep came in small bursts, twenty or thirty minutes at a time, whatever his body needed to keep functioning, before the memories and the nightmares crept back in like mold.

Ben was reading an old Larry McMurtry novel, waiting for a can of ravioli to heat up. His food supply was running low; this was his third meal noshing off the same can. Tonight's supper would be it for this can, leaving Ben with one can of tuna and a protein bar until he could restock his supplies. Even worse, he was getting near the end of the whiskey. He had a steady buzz going, which helped keep his mind off the pressing issue of where exactly he would locate these supplies. The cash from his time on the HARD team was running low; they paid a pittance, and he hadn't collected his pay for his final day.

Around him, the camp had started to stir. This was the time of day that worried Ben the most. Although it was generally safer here than in the world beyond, safety was a relative thing these days. The troublemakers came out at sunset, after the heat of the day abated, full of piss and vinegar like cooped-up first-graders. Usually drunk, generally dissatisfied with their new station in life.

He sat in a small camp chair outside his tent and ate his tiny portion of ravioli, which stopped the hunger shakes but left him still ravenous. His tent was on the outer perimeter, near the racetrack's steeply banked third turn. It was a rowdier section of the camp, home to a string of men and women in their twenties and thirties, young enough to cause trouble, their station in life exacerbated by the fact that they were old enough to have been settled in life when the Panic exploded around them. The air was ripe with a symphony of aromas - marijuana, body odor, urine. Ben's neighbor, a short, stout man, was smoking a joint with the diameter of a Cuban cigar. Ben didn't know his name.

"Wanna hit?" he asked.

He was thin and his skin was loose and gray, leaving him with an unhealthy pallor. He'd shared his sad tale with Ben at some point, but eventually, they all started to run together. Crazy news stories, bad shit happened, infection. The saddest three-act play in the world.

"No," Ben said. That was sort of a lie. He did want a hit, very badly in fact, but he was still a little too wigged out to swap saliva with a fellow Red. He'd been lucky to emerge from the Panic without any severe infections; he'd heard horror stories of fellow Redeyes contracting hepatitis, HIV, tuberculosis, and every other conceivable infection, viral, bacterial and fungal, and he didn't want to push his luck any farther than it had already been pushed.

"What are you, some kinda pussy?"

Ben ignored him, turning his attention to activity brewing several tents down; a woman was yelling at two men he didn't recognize, two guys who didn't quite fit in. They looked clean, well-fed, healthy. Just by looking normal, they stood out. They moved from one refugee to another until a flock of index fingers began pointing in his direction.

Shit, he thought mildly. They'd tracked him down.

But strangely, escape wasn't the first thing that crossed his mind. He sat there and watched them approach, equally relieved and disappointed in himself. Where was his goddamn survival instinct? Where was his fight, his goddamn spunk? And yet, it felt good not to run. All he'd done was run.

He locked eyes with them, and they knew they'd found their man.

"You Sullivan?" asked the first one.

He nodded.

"Why don't we step inside?"

BEN HAD NEVER HAD GUESTS, and it seemed especially silly that three grown men had wedged themselves into his small tent, sitting with their legs criss-crossed before them. He felt self-conscious, but his visitors didn't seem to care about their environs.

"My name is Luke Coleman," the first man said. He gestured toward his partner. "This is my associate, George Laprade."

Coleman was a regular-looking guy, the kind you'd see while sitting in traffic, when you'd glance over to the late-model sedan inching along the freeway with you, checking his phone or listening to Howard Stern on satellite radio. His partner George fit the generally accepted definition of muscle. He wore black jeans, a tight black T-shirt, and wraparound sunglasses.

"How do you know my name?" Ben asked.

"I believe you know my sister," Coleman said.

"Your sister?"

"Ellie Campbell," he said.

The woman from the HARD Team. Fear prickled his skin like a bad sunburn. Had Ellie told them that he was the one who had attacked her? Had she gotten the names confused? Were they just here to kill him? Vigilante justice for an attempted rape? He'd survived the Orchid virus only to come down with a deadly case of Mistaken Identity.

"She told me what you did," Coleman said. He removed his hand from his pocket, sending Ben in full retreat to the back of the tent. He tried to speak, defend himself, but the words were lodged in his throat, trapped in a quicksand of fear.

"I can't tell you how thankful I am," Coleman said, holding his hand out.

Ben was stunned. He couldn't remember the last time someone had offered to shake his hand. A simple societal nicety, taken for granted until it had all but disappeared during the Panic. Social distancing, they called it in the early days of the outbreak, when people were still having a hard time comprehending the fact that their neighbors might try to murder them.

He took the man's hand, reminding himself to go hard with the grip, make sure the guy didn't think that Ben was a sponge-wristed loser. Strength. Confidence. Things that Ben wanted other people to think he had, even if he didn't. They shook for a moment.

The other man, Laprade, lit a cigarette. It was a bit ballsy of him, but Ben suspected that was kind of the point. Marking territory. The cigarette smoke burned his eyes, and Ben wished he had the balls to ask him to extinguish the cigarette, a Bruce-Willis-in-Die-Hard kind of moment, but he chose to let it go.

"I'm just glad I could help," Ben said, his voice cracking like a thirteen-year-old boy in the throes of puberty. Great. So much for the firm handshake.

"Me, too," Coleman said. "Me too. Ellie's all the family I've got. Do you mind if I call you Ben?"

Another territory marker.

"Sure, Luke," Ben said. He had to score points somehow.

"You can call me Mr. Laprade," the big man said, expelling smoke from his nostrils like an ornery dragon.

"Don't mind him," Coleman said, waving Laprade off.

Ben again glanced at Laprade, who continued to smoke. The orange dot of the cigarette tip brightened as he took a drag from the filter.

"How is she?" Ben asked.

"She's pretty tough," he said. "She was rattled, but she'll be fine. Which is more than I can say for that waste of space."

Ben's eyebrows rocked upwards.

"His uncle's a Department bigwig. They know what

happened. They just wouldn't have done anything about it. They'd blame us for the Kennedy assassination if they could."

"Us?"

Coleman peeled off his sunglasses and held up Ben's lantern. The white light illuminated Coleman's red eyes. They shined red and bold, as if Luke Coleman were proud of the mark that made him and Ben and millions of others pariahs.

"April sixth," Coleman said. "You?"

"May," Ben said. "May sixteenth."

"When did you recover?" Luke asked.

"Late July," Ben said.

"Yeah, ten weeks was the average."

"I guess," Ben said. "I haven't really done a survey."

"So you've had a rough go of it," Coleman said.

"Par for the course, wouldn't you say?"

"Yeah. Yeah, that's true." Coleman said. "But it doesn't have to be that way."

"What do you mean?"

"Well, that's why we're here," Coleman said. "My sister vouched for you, and that's good enough for me."

"You know, I didn't really get to know her all that well," Ben said. "I kind of kept to myself, for obvious reasons."

"She's good at reading people," Coleman said.

"Wait, is she-" Ben paused. He pointed an accusatory finger at Coleman and then back at himself in a conspiratorial pantomime.

"No," he said. "She was never infected."

"Oh," Ben said. "So why are you here?"

"We have a proposition for you," Luke said.

Ben stood silently, still on guard, still unsure what was happening.

"We're with a group called the Haven."

"And what is that?" Ben asked.

"I'd say we're like a family, but that would come across a little hokey, wouldn't it?"

"Yeah," Ben said. "Like drink-the-Kool-Aid kind of hokey."

"Believe me, I thought the same thing."

"So what's this proposition?"

"We'd like to invite you for a visit."

"For what? A keg party?"

"We have a place out in the country," Luke said. "People like you and me. Just Reds."

Ben's heart raced. For months, an emptiness had been growing inside him, like someone had been carving out a little bit at a time the thing that had made him who he was. His soul, the part of him that mattered, was vanishing, leaving ruin and waste behind. And this simple statement, from a man he did not know, had been the cold glass of water to slake his thirst.

"No commitments," he said. "Just come out and let us repay you for what you did."

Ben turned the offer over in his mind like an appraiser examining a Ming vase. He chewed on his lower lip, his gaze ping-ponging between Luke and Laprade.

"Let me ask you this," Luke said. "What do you think of the Department?"

"R & R?"

"Do the other ones matter?" he asked, a sudden sharpness in his voice, like he'd just traded out a dull blade from his razor for a new one.

"No, I guess not," Ben said, a wave of fright washing over him. "I mean, I think the government got dealt a pretty shitty hand."

"That they did," Luke said. "No argument there. But do you enjoy being treated like a second-class citizen? For something that wasn't your fault?"

The memories started poking their way into the edges of his mind.

"No," he said, his voice soft, a whisper.

"Do you like the fact that there are two Americas?" Luke asked. "One for them, one for us?"

"No," he said, his voice even softer now. He was looking down at his shoes, unable to look at Luke in the face. He didn't want to look up and see those red eyes again; that would just remind him of that terrible summer.

"And you shouldn't, Ben," Luke said, his voice soft and warm and encouraging again. "You shouldn't."

Ben nodded, his head still down. Tears dripped silently from his cheeks. In the silence of the tent, he could hear them splashing against the hard-packed ground.

Way to go, big guy! Weeping in front of two men you've just met. That'll convince them of your hearty and hale.

He wiped a hand over his face and cleared his throat.

"We're not animals, Ben," Luke said, his voice ramping back up in intensity, like a lathered-up preacher. Ben felt like he was being hypnotized. "We deserve better. We deserve a life."

Ben was nodding his head with each word. He hadn't even been aware he was doing it, and he thought about church and the way a minister swept up his parishioners in an ecclesiastical funnel cloud, thundering away about sin and temptation and God and Jesus and everlasting life that awaited the faithful.

"How about we take a little ride?"

6

L uke and George waited outside while Ben packed up his tent. Despite having spent nearly a year here, there wasn't much to take. A flashlight here. A can of tuna over there. As he packed, Ben considered this twist of fate, this fork in the road. He didn't know where this new road would carry him, but he could always hope that he was headed somewhere better. After all, it couldn't be much worse than his current lot in life.

Somewhere better. A concept ever out of reach, reinforced by Freedom One's daily propaganda efforts. Reconstruction updates. Stories of economic recovery. A glimmer here. A spark there. A big, bright, shiny NEW AMERICA was waiting for all of them, just around the next bend. He'd certainly watched his share of television when he could; there had been that need to believe that someone was at the wheel, that things were in motion, that adults were in charge. But eventually, he realized that there was nothing new under the government-sponsored media sun; it was going to be a long hard slog until it wasn't anymore.

After giving the tent one final lookover, Ben joined Luke

and Laprade outside. It was getting dark. Thin clouds streamed across the sky, the crescent moon breaking through like the smile of a pretty girl at a crowded party.

"You ready?" Luke asked.

"I guess so."

His time at this camp was done. They made their way through the infield, winding their way through the maze of tightly bunched tents. As he had back at the job lottery, Ben felt the stares of his campmates, but he found himself not caring. He hadn't made the world the way it was. Any of them would do what he was doing.

A black Ford Explorer was parked on an access road on the complex's western perimeter. The Department's logo emblazoned on the driver's side door. He stopped suddenly.

"What's wrong?" Luke asked. He followed Ben's gaze. "Oh, that. Yeah, this comes in handy."

"You stole it?"

"Not exactly," Luke said. "Rest assured, it'll get the job done."

The trio piled into the car, Laprade at the wheel, Ben in the back seat, and they set off down Laburnum Avenue, once a busy artery connecting the city to the airport in the eastern part of the metro area. Ben sat quietly in the back as the landscape rushed by. He'd gone to law school in Richmond, before moving to North Carolina to start his career. It was a long enough stay that it now resembled a demented funhouse version of a place he'd once known very well. Even three years later, it was still dizzying to see the devastation, the ruined buildings.

They passed a bowling alley, one he'd frequented during his third year of law school. It became a tradition, he and his buddies sloshing through half a dozen pitchers of icy cold Budweiser on Tuesday nights while betting five dollars a game. He'd actually developed some aptitude for the game, regularly breaking two hundred; he'd even considered buying his own ball. But then he graduated and met Sarah while studying for the bar exam and he couldn't remember the last time he'd even gone bowling.

The façade of the building had been blown away, twisted rebar and cables and broken concrete still exposed like ruined entrails. Sandbags ringed the parking lot. Skeletal remains lay draped over a low brick wall in front of the building. A goddamn bowling alley. It reminded him how insane this war had been, how it had been fought on every front, how it had been fought not for oil or food or religion, but for their very survival. War at its most elemental. There were no cease-fires, no backroom negotiations, no compromises, just five months of all-out war and death and destruction until it was over.

The bowling alley faded behind them but ahead lay more of the same. They passed a gas station offering unleaded for $13.59 a gallon, down from its peak at about sixteen bucks. At the peak of the war effort, the government had prohibited the private use of fuel, saving it for the massive military operations underway in every corner of the continental United States. But many of the pipelines had sustained heavy damage, and even after the war, there weren't enough truckers still alive to transport what fuel remained. Globally, the price of crude oil had zoomed to three hundred dollars a barrel. A number of surviving members of Congress had called on the President to simply carpet-bomb the OPEC nations out of spite. Eventually, the country had dipped into the Strategic Petroleum Reserves, which had stabilized the prices.

"Put this on," Luke said, flinging something into Ben's lap once they'd reached cruising speed on Interstate 64. Ben held the object up to the ambient moonlight. It was a ski mask, the eyeholes stitched closed with scrap fabric. He pulled it on, his heart pounding as the world went dark around him. He hated to put it on, to surrender one of his senses, but the die was already cast. He was already at their mercy; wearing a ski mask for the duration of the trip wasn't going to affect his non-existent bargaining position one way or another.

He leaned back in his seat and settled in for the ride, loosing a yawn. He was tired. So very tired. The rhythmic hum of the highway finally wrapped its arms around Ben and pulled him down into a deep, dreamless sleep.

BEN WOKE up to the sound of the Explorer chunking along an unpaved stretch of road, pitching and yawing its way in the darkness.

"Where are we?" Ben asked, blowing a lungful of warm air into his cupped hands and rubbing them together.

"Home," Luke said. "You can take off the mask."

He peeled it off his head and tossed it on the seat next to him. He leaned forward in his seat to get a better look, but he could see no farther than the sweep of the headlights. The road was wide, well-traveled, bisecting a sprawling expanse of farmland to his right and a thick forest of oak and pine to his left. A light rain was falling; every few seconds, the intermittent wipers swept across the windshield. The dashboard was lit up like a spaceship. It was cold in the car, and Ben, wearing only shorts and a t-shirt, shivered in its stale chill.

Luke wasn't forthcoming with any additional details, so he sat back and leaned his head against the window. The rain started to pick up, and with it came a corresponding increase in the squeak of the wiper blades. Ben started to feel a tincture of regret slowly working through him like an intravenous drip. Things hadn't been peachy keen back at the Raceway, but at least he had been at the helm of his own ship. Now he'd entrusted his future to other people, people he did not know, and worse, people whose agenda he did not know. He didn't even know where he was. Something so elemental, so basic, that you took it for granted until you were riding with two guys who might very well be casting you as the city boy in their backwoods revival production of *Deliverance.*

How had things gotten so far off track?

Were things so bad that he'd simply signed up for the first cult he'd come across? He felt like an Iowa farm girl stepping off a cross-country bus in downtown Los Angeles with a head full of movie posters and A-list parties and then two weeks later signing up with a production company, something with a suggestive name like Electric Skin Video, agreeing to do a little soft-core work, no penetration or anything like that, just something to pay the bills until a better opportunity presented itself.

On the other hand, it had been a long year. He was out of food, out of money, out of options. He'd raided as many empty houses as he could, looking for dry cereal, canned goods, bottled water, anything that he could use, and that had worked for a while. But, of course, he wasn't the only one with that idea, and the pickings grew slimmer with each passing week. Even when he'd had a job, hyper-inflation had chewed up the mileage he was getting out of his dollars, the way a dirty gas line sucked away a car's fuel efficiency. Simply waltzing into a supermarket with a fistful of coupons just wasn't an option anymore. The distribution channels that had kept America fat and fed had collapsed during the Panic, bearing out the pessimistic forecasts that the country, for all its bounty, had been just one major disaster away from mass starvation.

A few months before he'd found the camp at the raceway, he'd hooked up with a nomadic group of a dozen Redeyes, moving from town to town, relying on handouts from churches, mosques, temples, and other charitable organizations. He was not surprised that the megachurches turned their backs on the needy. Once, during a particularly barren stretch, the three children in the group, all orphans, all under the age of ten, kept asking Ben when they would find some food.

I'm hungry, Benny.

Yeah, we're hungry.

Yeah.

He had no answer for them, other than soon, soon, they would find something to eat soon. But they hadn't, and two weeks into their starvation diet, Kelsey, the nine-year-old, died. She passed in her sleep; she simply did not wake up. She was about the same age as Gavin. The group dissolved shortly after that.

And much as he couldn't handle facing his friends and family again any more than they could handle dealing with the monster in the family, the loneliness had started to wear on him. No better way to alienate your loved one than by trying to tear them to pieces. He'd been alone, looking for something that was lost, except there would be no happy ending because that thing would never be found unless they could all somehow shove the planet into a time machine and zip backward three years.

As the truck pierced deeper into the dark countryside, Ben thought about his neighbors in the tent city. Some had been friendly, others aloof, others simply certifiably insane, but he hadn't bothered learning a single name. It had been easier to work in knowing glances and wide berths. Orchid wasn't a disease that they organized five-kilometer races for. No one was running with a race bib bearing his name. People didn't gather to celebrate Orchid's eradication or the miraculous recovery of its victims.

Maybe he should have gotten to know his fellow Redeyes, but Ben didn't want to think about what had happened, and getting together with other Reds would require talking about it because what the hell else were they going to talk about? The Iowa caucuses? Global warming? Duke basketball?

"We're almost there," Luke said, snapping Ben out of his trance.

White light glowed softly in the distance, off to his right, a shining beacon in the center of all that dark land. Electricity. Electricity was still at a premium in many places, a few hours a day at best, and in some ways, Ben had come to see it as a liability, a gigantic blinking sign that said, *PLEASE ROB AND MURDER ME!* His disdain for artificial light didn't make him impervious to danger, of course, he was under no illusion of that, but lighted houses were easy targets. It was simple math, really; far more houses were dark than were lit up. As the saying went, the bad guys didn't want to kill, rape, or rob *you*. They just wanted to kill, rape or rob someone. And bad guys didn't like hassle any more than the average person.

Despite the warm glow ahead, he was still totally lost, stripped of any sense of direction, which, he decided, was a pretty good metaphor for the current state of his life. As they drew closer, the scene began to sharpen, and the primordial ooze of light began to take form. A moment later,

Luke decelerated and turned right onto a hidden drive. The road, flanked by magnolias, narrowed here, and as their destination grew in the windshield, Ben felt a spike of warmth up his back. His breathing became ragged and shallow, and he could feel his blood pulsing in every single extremity.

"Relax, Ben," Luke said. "There's nothing to worry about."

The main house came into view a moment later. Antebellum-style, reminiscent of the ones Ben knew from Southern literature, enormous, roughly the size of one of Saturn's moons. Marble columns lining the façade gave it an imposing, castle-like feel, inaccessible to the common man. Huge oaks, full grown at the time of the Civil War, provided an additional layer of natural defense. Beyond the main house were a half dozen or so additional smaller guesthouses, the pawns to the queen of this very southern chessboard.

As the Explorer looped onto the main circular driveway fronting the house, Ben could see that as big as the house was, it was but a drop in the bucket of acreage. The house itself was brightly lit, as though it were ready to host a New Year's Eve party for the ages, but rather than warmth, the glow exuded a sense of alarm and anger. A middle finger to a world that had gone dark in so many places. It was disarming to see a place so well-kept, so manicured, somehow immune to the disaster that had swept the globe, as if such things were beneath it.

And all these thoughts he was having, Ben realized, were exactly the point.

As Luke brought the Explorer to a stop, Ben pulled his backpack close to him, a buoy in a sea of confused *What-TheHellHaveIGottenMyselfInto*? He alighted from the car and joined the men as they climbed the steps and slipped past the giant columns that made Ben think of a prison for giants.

"Welcome to the Haven," Luke said.

THE HOUSE WAS EVEN LARGER than Ben had anticipated. A formal staircase, wide at the bottom and narrowing toward the top like a giant pouf of swept-up hair, greeted them in the foyer. To his right was a formal dining room, its layout tucked just out of view, the type of room Ben always imagined for men with money to sit and plot.

"We've got a room for you upstairs," Luke said.

Now THAT seemed a little weird. Sort of presumptuous, to be quite honest.

"You guys haven't even bought me dinner," he said, hoping to break the awkwardness he suddenly felt.

Luke laughed, and Ben relaxed a little. It was the right kind of laugh, the kind that told him that Luke got the joke.

"There's no point in trying to hide it," Luke said, holding out his arms in an *aw-shucks* sort of pose. "We're trying to recruit you. Your first night here, you get the deluxe package."

"Recruit me for what?"

"We'll get to all that tomorrow," Luke said. "When was the last time you had a good night's sleep?"

Ben rubbed his chin as he considered the question, the never-ending struggle of the past year weighing heavily on his mind. Before the Panic, he had been keenly aware that he had never experienced hard times. He would think about his elderly relatives talking about eating soup that they'd wrung from the sweat of their handkerchiefs or the *pro bono* clients he'd once represented to meet the firm's requirement that its attorneys "give back," and he'd wonder if he had the resourcefulness to get by the way some of his clients did. Those that had made it through the Panic had probably been a lot better equipped to handle the aftermath than people who lived in four-thousand-square-foot homes and drove Range Rovers.

Before the Panic, Ben had never gone to war, had never seen a man die. He'd never lived in poverty or gone to bed with an empty stomach. He'd never been deprived the basic necessities, and although he knew it was a combination of hard work and luck, the good fortune of having been born in the U.S. in the late twentieth century, to parents who worked hard and had good jobs, of having worked hard himself to get through college and law school, he had once felt guilty that he'd never truly had to find out if he had the goods to survive when all those things were stripped away. He didn't feel that way anymore.

Now he wished he could go back and slap the shit out of his pre-Panic self. No more guilt over not having suffered in the first part of his life, he'd given at the office, thanks. Suffering sucked. That's why they called it suffering!

"It's been a while," he said. He took a deep breath and let it out slowly.

"Look, I remember my first night here," Luke said. "On your own all that time, feeling all alone, that you're just this big sack of nothing, feeling like the monster that everyone thinks you are. And then all of a sudden, someone's offering you a warm bed, a roof over your head, and it all seems like someone's gonna slip you a roofie."

Ben nodded.

"Relax," Luke said. "That's all behind you."

7

Ben woke up with a start, awash in the feeling that something was amiss, out of place. The coolness of the sheets, the cushion of the pillow, the feeling of warmth that spread through him like a good shot of whisky. Things that had grown harder to recall as time had gone by, like the fading signal from an AM radio station as you cruised down the interstate on a hot summer night. He felt refreshed, cleaned out. He sat up and stretched, still wearing the clothes he'd arrived in. He checked his watch and was stunned to see that it was nearly three in the afternoon. As he stared at the digital readout, the events of the previous night swirled back into focus. Luke, the Haven, the promise of the motive underlying his invite to this place.

They hadn't lingered upon their arrival at the house. The downstairs was quiet but peaceful, the air cool and redolent with a hint of garlic or oregano, like someone had been at work on a hearty tomato sauce. Luke commented that Ben looked dead on his feet, and this was something that he couldn't disagree with. They led him to a small guest room on the third floor and told him they'd see him in the morning. Ben had locked the door behind them; it gave him a small measure of security, whether imagined or not remained to be seen. He'd planned to explore his new environs but just wanted to sit down for a second, just one minute on that comfy-looking bed and before he knew it, he was out, buried by the sandman.

The bed was small, a twin, but comfortable. Crisp sheets with a high thread count, a down comforter, a soft pillow under his head. The rest of the room followed the same design - minimalist but top of the line all the way. Someone had spent a lot of time decorating it and maintaining it. It seemed to be a theme common throughout the house, that this place was immune to the way the world was now.

A small flat-panel television was mounted in the corner of the room; a remote control lay on the night table. Dare he dream? He rested his thumb on the volume button, ready to cut the sound at a moment's notice. His index finger snaked forward for a smooch with the power button, and the screen flickered to life. There it was, he thought, the only show in town. Freedom One. Its logo, a disembodied hand holding a flaming torch, shined in the right corner of the screen.

Ben watched a few minutes of the broadcast, a fluff piece about an elementary school re-opening in Joliet, Illinois, an hour outside of Chicago. The reporter, an attractive blonde in her late twenties, was standing in front of the school, the camera drawn in tight on her, probably so the audience couldn't see the devastation that lay beyond. A throng of students crowded in behind her.

"The students and staff of Lincoln Elementary have been waiting for this day for a long time," she said, tucking a tendril of her flaxen hair behind her ear. "And when the school opens its doors on Monday, they will be more than ready to start a new chapter in their lives.

"Cassandra Blue, reporting for Freedom One, live in Joliet, Illinois."

The picture cut back to the Freedom One studio, where an anchor moved onto another feel-good story. As he switched off the television, Ben couldn't help but wonder how many Redeye children would be in that class on Monday. At least he was an adult, he had some coping mechanisms that he could fall back on. He couldn't imagine having gone through the experience as a child. He remembered the little girl who had died in her sleep. Kelsey.

He did a lap of the room, poking around the drawers, peeking in the closets before stepping into the on-suite bathroom. Sitting on top of the toilet was a thick green bath towel and matching washcloth. A variety of hotel-sized toiletries were lined up on the sink like little soldiers ready to go to war for him. Even more surprising, he found a set of clean clothes, shorts, a collared shirt, even a new pair of socks.

The pristine nature of everything made him self-conscious of his own appearance, the grime on him so thick it was like his own ozone layer. There was no way he was going to let this opportunity slip away, and within a minute, he was standing in the claw tub, under the heavy blast of the shower head. He let the hot water run and run and run over him, until his skin reddened, until he was way past what constituted polite in terms of how long to shower in someone else's house.

After his shower, he made his way through each remaining toiletry, through the toothpaste, the mouthwash, the deodorant, until he finally felt human again. It was amazing, the effect a simple thing like a shower could have. After dropping the new clothes on the bed, he sat down on the edge and leaned over, holding his head in his hands. As he sat there, trying to regain his bearings, he heard the murmur of voices behind him. At first, he thought he'd imagined it, and going crazy wasn't something he put past himself, but as he primed his ears, he realized it was coming from outside.

Still wrapped in the bath towel, he drifted over to the window and peeked behind the thick curtain draped across the glass. He was looking south across a wide expanse of lush greenery. A red barn stood a few hundred yards clear of the house, surrounded by what seemed like miles of fencing. A horse galloped lazily along the fence line. Like a postcard. If you wanted one mailed to you from the apocalypse.

As pastoral as that little picture was, it was the scene closer to the house that captured Ben's attention. A backyard barbecue was underway. To his right, almost out of his field of view, a pit-style grill shimmered. The mere sight of the smoke billowing from the vents made his mouth water. Two men stood watch over it, both holding beer bottles. He just stared at the grill, the cloudy puffs of smoke curling skyward, and thought about what might be sizzling away under the lid, keeping quiet, for the moment, its wonderful secret. Real food. Not from a can.

Ben took a deep breath and gave his head a quick shake. Amazing, he thought, that he could be distracted by something so simple. Inch-thick ribeyes, seared on the outside, juicy and pink inside. Or perhaps thick, juicy Italian sausages, the skin split just so, the fat bubbling up out from the depths and filling the air with the pungent tickle of fennel-

Dammit, Ben, snap out of it! Acting like you've never eaten before. Christ.

He swung his gaze back across the yard. About twenty people were scattered about, some drinking beer, others eating from paper plates. A few were clumped together at the picnic tables that had been set up under a large white tent. The normalcy of the scene, the absolute unremarkable nature of it all, was jarring.

He scanned the group for Luke or even Laprade, looking for anything familiar, something to which he could anchor himself. After a panicked moment, he spotted Luke chatting with an attractive young woman holding a toddler. At that precise moment, Luke, perhaps feeling the hairs on his neck standing up, looked up at Ben's window. Ben froze and stood unmoving as they made eye contact; Luke delivered just the barest of nods, which did not seem the slightest bit ominous or threatening. Ben returned the nod, unsure whether Luke had even seen him in the first place or if he was just imagining it, and closed the curtain.

He got dressed and headed downstairs.

It was like nibbling on a dread-and-excitement swirlie cone, the feeling of the first day of school, the same sensation he remembered from his single days on those rare occasions a young lady would invite him back to her apartment for a nightcap. As he made his way through the sunroom at the back of the house, the final threshold between his old life and whatever lay ahead, he reminded himself that he was docked now with people like him, all compatible pieces of software, who knew what it was like. From that fact alone, he took solace, without even thinking about what the main server's primary agenda was, because to think about that was too much to grasp right now.

He locked onto Luke right away, tracking him down like a heat-seeking missile; he did not like feeling dependent on the man, but there it was. Not much different than his old life. If you were at a party where you only knew one person, you naturally gravitated toward him. The fact that he was now at a barbecue with a collection of mass killers, albeit unintentional ones, didn't make that any different.

"Hey, sleepyhead!" Luke said upon spotting him. His cheeks were flushed, and there was a slight hitch in his speech, suggesting that the bottle of beer dangling from his fingers wasn't his first one of the day. And Luke was nothing if not a happy drunk. He showed Ben around like a new puppy, barreling from one group to the next. A lot of hand-shaking and *nice-to-meet-yous* and *that-was-a-hell-of-a-thing-you-dids* until his head was spinning and he felt the early signs of a headache, the way rough surf pounding the beach preceded a wanker of a hurricane blowing ashore.

He met Manuel Camacho, a wireless phone salesman who'd helped reunite lost children with their parents, and Janet Rusnak, a certified public accountant who'd fought the Redeyes in Arlington before she'd been bitten and the Reds gutted Washington, D.C. He met Floyd Agnew, a shifty type that Ben couldn't quite get a handle on, and Mary Carroll, a schoolteacher who'd killed her entire family. Each had their own story of woe, tales they seemed to have no problem sharing freely.

After a solid half hour of this, he finally sat down with an icy cold bottle of beer and a paper plate – the fancy thick one, not the flimsy one with the scalloped edges – full of food and took a deep breath. He was a few beers in, liquid courage he'd needed while hearing his new friends' Tales of the Apocalypse. Even with his head buzzing, it had been a lot to take in, a flash flood of tragedy, one story told a thousand different ways, because when you got right down to it, they were all the same story.

The smells wafting from the plate made him dizzy with hunger; home-cooked meals had been few and far between. He gorged on barbecue chicken and baked beans and a spicy Italian sausage and pepper sandwich, on the good kind of roll that didn't split and fracture under the weight of the filling and told you that even this little detail mattered.

They hadn't pushed him to share his own story, which he'd appreciated, even as he suspected that was a calculated maneuver they used on newcomers. After all, they didn't want to freak anyone out on the first day with the equivalent of telling your blind date you were in love with her before the check came.

By and large, though, he liked almost everyone, and on occasion, he would almost forget that he was one of them and begin to pity their lot in life and then it would snap back like a rubber band. But more than anything, it felt good to be with other Redeyes doing something more than merely staying alive. It felt good to be with them and to feel human again. It felt good to be with others who knew what it was like, who knew what waited for him in dreams when he lay down to sleep at night.

He sat alone at the end of a heavy wooden picnic table, drinking his beer, eating his hot sausage sandwich.

AS THE PARTY WOUND DOWN, Ben slipped away for a tour of the grounds. He sensed eyes on him with each step he took. They were watching him, trying to gauge what he thought of their little summer camp, but they left him alone. The heat was still immense, pressing down on him like a heavy blanket. The sun dipped low in the sky, its fiery orange-red light spilling across the sky like an overturned can of paint.

Ben came up on a cornerpoint of white fencing, stretching away to the west and south. The land undulated like a gentle ocean of green, shimmery and hazy in the falling twilight. Horses, black and brown and chestnut, lazily wandered the fields, presumably unconcerned with the turn that humanity had taken. Ben leaned against the wood, propping his foot up on the lower railing, and took another pull from the beer. He was unmistakably buzzed now, long past the point that he could volunteer for designated driver duty, but he felt good, alert. And even though evening was settling in, he'd only been awake for about four hours. No wonder he felt so good!

As he polished off the last of the beer, he sensed movement behind him. He didn't move, maintained his position at the fence. He was comfortable leaning up against the strong wood.

"I hope we haven't scared you off," said the interloper.

There was a steeliness in the man's voice, one that told Ben that he was here with a belly full of food, a solid beer buzz, and a cool pillow on which to lay his head thanks to this man's say so. Ben turned to face the newcomer. He wore a tan linen suit, a robin egg blue handkerchief tucked just so in the breast pocket. He looked to be in his early sixties, deeply tanned, his hair neat and sprayed into place, sporting a touch of grey at the sides so appropriate and so regal that it didn't seem natural. And, not surprisingly, his eyes swam with that deep crimson red.

"Not at all," Ben said.

"Did you get something to eat?"

"More than my share."

"Aw, that's nonsense, son," the man said. "I'm a big believer in a hearty meal. Good for the soul, my mama used to say."

"It was delicious."

Stuffed to the gills, Ben patted his stomach, suddenly eager to show this man how much he appreciated his generosity.

"I'm Calvin Thompson," the man said, extending his hand to Ben. "This is my family's homeplace, and I'm damn happy to have you here. I'm sorry I hadn't had a chance to meet you yet."

"A pleasure," Ben said, shaking the man's hand, doing his level best to resist hugging the man like he was his long-lost birth father.

"I'm sure you've got a million questions," Thompson said. "The first of which, I imagine, is what the hell are you doing here, right?"

"The thought had crossed my mind, yes, sir."

He smiled, revealing twin rows of gleaming teeth, their stark whiteness amplified by the man's red eyes.

"You know, I've come to enjoy these peepers," Thompson said, chuckling to himself. "I always had boring brown eyes. These, though, these are something else. Anyway, enough of an old man's vanity. We've brought you here because I think we can help each other. As you know, we all have something in common here."

Ben nodded.

He held up a finger, slipping his free hand inside his jacket pocket. A moment later, it re-emerged with a pair of very fine-looking cigars.

"Care for one?"

"Sure."

Thompson paused momentarily while he cut and lit the cigars with a small butane torch lighter. Ben puffed on his, blowing out clouds of smoke before the cigar finally caught. They smoked in silence for a while.

"I love this time of day," Thompson said. "Funny thing. I used to get eaten alive by mosquitoes. Got so bad I couldn't come out at dusk."

Ben perked up at this.

"Yeah," Ben said. "Me too. Sometimes my bites would swell up so bad they'd get infected."

"And now-"

The revelation hummed through Ben like fork tines on crystal.

"I never get bitten at all," Ben said with a sense of wonder. "I had noticed that."

"I'd say we've earned at least that parting gift," Thompson said. "Wouldn't you?"

Ben shrugged. It was a gift he'd gladly exchange. He'd roll around naked in his shaggy, steaming backyard, right at dusk, to live in a world where the Panic had never happened. It made him wonder what the virus had done to him to ward off the world's most eager bloodsuckers.

"Anyway, Ben," Thompson said, changing gears like a sports car, his presence and personality a huge engine overwhelming the conversation. "I hope, after hearing what I have to say, that you'll want to stay on with us."

"And if I don't want to stay?"

"We'll put the blindfold back on and take you back whence you came," he said. "Your basic money-back guarantee. The meal and the hot shower are yours to keep. But this is a one-time only offer. You say no, you won't be invited back."

Ben nodded as he took a long puff from the cigar. He didn't know anything about cigars, his experience with them limited to bachelor parties and drunken convenience store runs, but even he could tell this was a good one. It was smooth and rich, the perfect cap to what had been the best day he'd had in a long time.

"Fair enough," Ben said.

In the distance, the faintest rumble of thunder.

"I was infected pretty early on," Thompson said. "March twentieth. I got scratched on an Amtrak shuttle down from Washington, D.C. Son of a bitch had been acting weird the whole trip. Sweating, bloodshot eyes, twitching. That was before anyone knew what was going on. He bit half a dozen people before an off-duty police officer shot him, right there on the train. Never seen anything like it."

He paused to take a breath, and they enjoyed another cigar-centered intermission.

"Anyway, he got me pretty good, took a chunk outta my bicep, and I ended up in a hospital in Fredericksburg. Forget the virus, I damn near died from a bacterial infection. And I attacked two doctors before they managed to strap me down with restraints and flood my sorry ass with antibiotics. See, at the time, they thought my behavior was related to the bacterial infection – high fever, delirium. They knocked out the bacterial infection after a couple days. So there I was strapped down, getting IV fluids, trying my god-damndest to get free so I could, you know..."

His voice trailed off, and Ben looked off to the horizon. The stories, they never got easier to hear. What they had become.

"Anyway, long story short, I made it back here," he said. "I'm a widower, and my son's grown, living in Paris when the Panic hit. Still don't know if he's alive. As the outbreak wound down, I realized that we'd become public enemy number one."

His voice was getting louder with each word, as if they'd

crossed over into the badlands of his mind, the place where things mattered.

"We're the biggest refugee crisis-slash-public health threat-slash-medical-miracle the world has ever seen," he went on. "We can't get jobs, benefits, places to live, you know how it is. We're goddamn radioactive."

"Radioactive," Ben repeated. "That's a pretty good way of putting it."

"Two hundred years of human rights progress went right out the window," he said wistfully, his voice softening like winds dying down after a vicious storm. "It's a broken world. A world that's still afraid of us. They see our eyes, they think about the Panic, and they wonder whether we're going to snap again and finish off the job.

"Anyway, what I'm getting at," he said, "is that we'd like for you to stay on with us. Make this your new home. You'll be safe here."

"In exchange for what?"

"What, you a lawyer?" he asked, dropping the 'r' in that Southern way.

"Matter of fact, I was," Ben said.

"Figures. Always looking for the catch."

"Old habits die hard."

"Well, you'd help us build our community," Thompson said. "There's only about twenty of us right now – in fact, you'd make number twenty-two – and I reckon we got room for a couple hundred more. I've got a lot of land and a lot of money. My whole life, I wondered what my purpose was, and God never saw fit to show me until I recovered from the infection. Turns out it was this.

"But we've got a lot of work ahead of us if we're going to turn this into a permanent home for all of us," he continued. "Security, fresh water, food, electricity. I've been doing a lot

of research into the old communes, how those places oper-
ated, which has got to be the great irony of my life. I was a
kid in the 1970s, and I hated hippies, thought they were a
drain on society. Figured they were looking for ways to avoid
the real world. Well, here I am fifty years later, and I'm
looking to do the same thing."

Ben yawned, a big sloppy one that got away from him,
and he flushed with embarrassment. Ben silently cursed
himself, but there was nothing he could do. The yawn had
been yawned.

"Excuse me," he said.

"Please," Calvin said, holding up a hand. "I know how
exhausted you must be. It'll take more than one night in my
house to make up for all the sleep I'm sure you've lost."

"Thank you."

"Anyway, everyone around here has a job, except for the
few children, and we're working on starting school for
them," he said. "Luke will take you on as an apprentice. He's
taken a shine to you. You'll start in the fields, and as you
prove yourself, you can move up in the hierarchy. I'm pretty
good at reading people, and I think you could have a bright
future here. People will look up to you. Eventually, I'll want
to have a governing body of some kind. This won't be a
utopia forever."

"Am I ever allowed to leave?" Ben asked, chuckling.

"Of course," Thompson said.

Ben took a deep breath and let it out slowly.

"Eventually, that is."

Ben's next breath caught in his throat.

"We have to be very careful about security. We're pretty
off the beaten path, but this isn't a public shelter. We have a
very strict protocol about leaving the grounds. Unauthorized absences will result in expulsion from the community.

Besides, it's important to us that our new members have a chance to acclimate themselves, get to know other people."

"I see," Ben said.

Ben's dozen years as a lawyer had embedded in him a healthy skepticism of many things, including, but not limited to, nearly every word anyone said. Unlike Thompson, he didn't rely on gut feelings too much, so instead, he took a more utilitarian approach and simply assumed that everyone was lying about something.

"What if I change my mind a week from now, two weeks from now?" Ben asked.

The question seemed to take Thompson by surprise, as if no one had ever asked it before. As though he'd never contemplated the possibility that someone might decide that life out there, beyond the borders of the Haven, was preferable to their insulated existence here. Thompson froze, just for an instant, long enough to make Ben wonder whether he was making it up as he went along, looking for an answer that would satisfy this desperate newcomer. Ben suspected that the promise of food and shelter and safety had been more than enough to convince a wide-eyed guest to sign on the dotted line. He had the very strong sense that Mr. Calvin Thompson expected everyone to say yes, and that this was a permanent arrangement.

"Same deal," Thompson said finally, breaking the brief but awkward silence. "Blindfold. A ride back to wherever you were picked up. And you never see us again. But I'm proud to say that no one has turned down my offer yet, and no one has changed their mind."

"What's to stop me from taking off in the middle of the night?" Ben asked.

Thompson smiled, a jolly-looking grin that reminded Ben of a sparkly rock, which if you pulled it up, would reveal maggots and centipedes and other terrifying creepy-crawlies underneath.

"We're a long way from anything out here, son."

Ben rubbed his chin as he considered this, his hand scraping across the ever-present stubble. He gazed out over the fields and the thick forest, and realized with just a touch of morbidity that it would make a good place to dump bodies of people who hadn't been swayed by Thompson's offer.

He glanced back toward the main house, where things were still hopping. A few torches had been lit, and someone had fired up a boom box. Formless music filled the air, and he thought about the other side of the coin. Was he being too suspicious? Why wouldn't Redeyes want to stick together? Wouldn't a place like this make sense? There were probably communities like this popping up all over the place. Millions of Reds were roaming the countryside, scared, hungry, alone.

Perhaps he was just having a hard time accepting that the rest of his life would be flavored by the Panic. He was making the mistake of thinking of himself as a special little flower. Poor little Ben. So the Panic would dominate the rest of his life. At least he had a life. So many didn't. Billions lay dead in houses and schools and hospitals and bowling alleys and shacks and tenements around the world.

"When do I need to let you know by?" he asked finally.

"I'd appreciate an answer by noon tomorrow," Thompson said. The warmth in his voice had evaporated like a puddle of seawater, leaving behind the salty, shrewd businessman Ben suspected Thompson once had been. "If you turn us down, I've got other candidates to consider. But I hope you'll say yes, Ben."

Classic! Ben thought. *Addressing me by name directly. Making it all personal. Making me feel all warm and cozy.*

"Just come by my private study," he said. "Someone will point you in the right direction. Enjoy the rest of the evening."

Thompson headed back to the party without shaking Ben's hand. Ben watched the man walk away, like a rescue ship steaming away from a crippled boat.

•

8

I n the end, it hadn't been a very difficult decision at all. It wasn't like he had other offers on the table, other communes banging down his door, or really any other options at all. The ease of it, the way it seemed that there was only one correct choice, surprised him. After Thompson had taken his leave of him, Ben watched the sunset over the farm and then retired to his room. He expected to be up all night, tossing and turning, wrestling with this grave decision, but he'd been out as soon as his head hit the pillow. He slept even harder and more soundly than he had on his first night, and when he woke up, he felt new, fresh, and dare he say it, home. And so at noon on his second full day at the Haven, he sat with Thompson in his study, clinking glasses of scotch with the man and accepting his offer to become part of their "family," as Thompson described it.

Like all rookies, Ben started in the fields, working from sunup to sundown for the rest of that summer, harvesting vegetables and fruits, weeding, mulching and fertilizing. The work involved in feeding two dozen people without the assistance of a supermarket was gargantuan, more than he'd ever fathomed. By the time he joined the work crew, the crops were in full bloom. Luke, who'd grown up with Ellie on a farm in southwest Virginia, was in charge of the farming operations, and Ben worked hard to impress him. Not because of any particular desire to become a master farmer, but because he figured it would be the quickest ticket out of the fields and into more responsibility. He occasionally felt guilty for thinking in this way, given that Thompson had opened his home to him, kept him fed, sheltered, and so on, and he sometimes wondered why he couldn't just be happy with his good fortune. Millions of people would trade spots with him in a second. But if there were other jobs to be had, he could do those too. Ambition didn't care about the state of the world.

He was assigned to a small guest cottage northwest of the main house, which he shared with four men, all of whom worked in the fields. Ben shared a room with a former consultant named Marc Basnight, a pleasant enough fellow who kept to himself and read fantasy novels in his spare time. He was plagued by bad dreams; this Ben knew because he'd wake up during the night to find Marc sitting on the edge of his bed, his head in his hands, taking slow, deep breaths. Ben never spoke to him about it because seriously, what was there to say? He knew what lay behind the curtains of slumber. You didn't go through what they had gone through without a little scarring. Post-traumatic stress disorder, the ironic gift that kept on giving to those that had been the cause of all the trauma in the first place.

One night in late October, Ben was at the main house,

reading in the modest library. It had been a bad day in the fields; something had gotten into the pumpkins and ruined about two hundred of them, leaving tempers short among the field crew. Everyone had retired for the night, but Ben was restless, couldn't sleep. A little after midnight, he gave up, threw on a light jacket and made his way to the main house. The air was clear and cold and, instead of relaxing him, infused him with a jolt of energy. Fall had definitely arrived.

Ben chose *The Stand* to whittle away the insomnia. He had read Stephen King's post-apocalyptic opus in college, and it had quickly become one of his favorites. As he thumbed through the familiar pages, he read the story with a sense of aching nostalgia for a time when, he was embarrassed to admit, he'd been intrigued by the prospect of surviving an apocalypse. He never quite understood why he believed he would be among the tiny fraction of survivors, or why he thought he'd become some important figure in a post-apocalyptic wasteland. Knowing his luck, had he been a character in the novel, he'd have died before the public-at-large even knew what was going on, or if he did manage to survive the initial plague, he'd have succumbed to food poisoning. But there it was. Every man believed in his own potential greatness, greatness was that was being suppressed, held down by society and circumstance. Life, the ultimate restrictor plate. And now that he had survived an apocalypse, albeit not as complete as King's vision but scarier, what with the neighbors slaughtering each other and all, he was ashamed by his naiveté.

It was well after two in the morning when his eyelids grew heavy. Finally. The days in the fields were hard enough with a good night's sleep. He got up from the reading chair to re-shelve the massive hardcover novel and head back to his room. He scanned the other titles and made a point to read something different next time, perhaps a previously unread piece of fiction that might stretch his mind and his horizons.

As he passed through the main foyer on his way to the front door, he heard a ruckus from somewhere deep inside the house, and he froze. At first, he couldn't quite make it out, but as he stood there, not breathing, his hand on the doorknob, he realized it was the sound of people talking.

No, strike that.

People arguing, three or four of them. Loudly. The cacophony came from everywhere and nowhere at the same time, bursting through the old house, echoing against the walls, seeping through the floors. Although he couldn't quite discern the words being said, he tried to distill the emotions from the tone, the way a wine connoisseur might detect hints of fruits and cheeses in a new bottle of Pinot. Anger, mostly. A slight hint of fear, perhaps.

A dozen people living in relatively close quarters, you were bound to have disagreements from time to time. This didn't concern him. This was none of his business. A lovers' quarrel. Perhaps even a love triangle, even. But his legs wouldn't move, and his ears primed themselves, working harder and harder to pick up the discussion, as if part of him knew that if he didn't learn more, it would just eat at him for the rest of the night, the rest of the week, the rest of however long his stay here proved to be.

Letting go of the doorknob, he sighed and crept toward the darkened corridor behind the stairs, his best guess for the voices' origin. He stepped gingerly, staying close to the wall, where he hoped the floor was tighter and the creaking would keep to a minimum. Old houses like this creaked all the time, he told himself. Part of their old South charm, a stubborn old grandfather's worn-out joints.

He made his way past the stairs, down a small hallway that fed into a longer corridor that ran the width of the house. A series of doors lay opposite the base of the stairs, almost all shut tight, dark and ominous like approaching storm clouds. All but one. The fourth door down, nearly beyond Ben's vantage point, was cracked just so, revealing a sliver of dim light spilling out. His heart was pounding in his ears now; his mouth had dried out like overcooked meat, and he could barely keep his legs underneath him.

The voices hadn't gotten any louder, but they'd maintained the same pitch that had initially drawn Ben's attention in the first place, as though they'd found a new equilibrium, a new status quo. There were at least four people in the room, three men and one or two women. He recognized Luke and Thompson instantly; Luke lived in the main house with Thompson. The other voices were familiar to him, but he couldn't definitively match them up with their owners. If he had to guess, Floyd and Carrie. He hadn't really gotten to know them at all, although he suspected they had a little bit of a thing going, and they were quite close to Calvin.

He stole a quick glance over his shoulder, back toward the main foyer, making sure that no one was spying on him spying on other people. Seeing nothing, he turned his attention back to the late-night get-together and focused on picking up slivers of conversation, words or phrases that might clue him in as to what was going on. He crouched down low, leaning in toward the wall, hoping the acoustics of the building would amplify the discussion a little. Words lacking context registered in his mind, and it was virtually impossible to match words to voices.

"...next week..."

"Department..."

"Mercury..."

"...traceable..."

"...willing to take that risk..."

Laughter.

"...never..."

The longer he listened, the more confused he became. Each word or phrase was like a piece to a puzzle whose ultimate destiny he did not know. It was maddening. Information was coming at him rapid-fire now, and the earlier bits were slipping away from him, despite his best efforts to harness everything into a mental net he could sort through later, as though he were panning for gold.

And then he heard it. A solitary word that tied the others together, the word that served the foundation for the entire discussion.

"...bomb..."

The word took his breath away, like a punch in the stomach. The discussion went suddenly silent, as if someone had muted a television. His heart fluttered madly, and a single bead of sweat traced an icy trail down his back. Had they heard him? Did one of them have that inscrutable itch of an unknown presence eavesdropping?

He retreated down the hallway, staying in his crouch and keeping his back pressed against the wall. His head rotated from side to side, as though on a swivel, searching for any sign that his presence had been detected. A door screeched open, but he didn't hear any footsteps.

As he drew near the end of the corridor, the front door came into view. The foyer was empty, dimly lit by the chandelier hanging from the ceiling. He rotated his body into a sprinter's crouch, ducking low at the base of the stairs. From there, he could see into the library, which was, mercifully, empty. He didn't know what he would say if someone confronted him, and the more he tried to push the thoughts away, the more this worst-case scenario ran through his mind. A worrier by nature, he thought it was ironic that he hadn't been a big enough worrier. If he had been, then maybe he wouldn't have become infected in the first place.

"I'm sure it was nothing," one of the voices said behind him. Luke.

"I've lived here my whole life," a sharp voice replied. Thompson. "I know the creaks in this goddamn house. Check the first floor."

Bootheels echoed through the corridor as Luke searched for the eavesdropper.

Before Luke had a chance to turn the corner down the main corridor, Ben broke for the door and opened it just wide enough to slip out onto the country porch, where the night seemed preternaturally quiet. He considered making a run for it, but there was nothing but open ground between here and his cottage.

Think, dammit, think!

The panic was huge inside him, now, like an earthquake threatening to crack his foundation. He heard voices in the foyer behind him, and he knew it was time to act. The air was heavy and still. No cicadas. No hooting of owls. He leapt from the porch to the sidewalk below, trying to recall if the night was always this quiet at two-fifteen in the morning, or if he should consider this a very bad omen.

Omen, he decided. If he were proven wrong later, so be it.

He curled around the side of the house and took refuge behind a large azalea bush that gave him an unobstructed view of the house, just as the door opened and Luke trailed out behind him. A channel of moonlight stretched from the house to the edge of the driveway like a silvery river, but Ben's hiding spot was shrouded in darkness. Luke scanned the property, perhaps thinking that the intruder had fled. Relief flooded through Ben when Luke ducked back in the house. He knew he didn't have time to celebrate his victory. Luke was likely going back for a flashlight or worse, reinforcements.

But it bought him the time he needed. He sprinted through the night, terrified that the moonlight would spotlight him like a suspect under the unforgiving glare of a police helicopter. The only sound was the susurration of the shin-high grass as he knifed across the grounds.

HE LAY awake in bed all night, his heart racing, his brain trying to maintain order, the unemotional scientist attempting to make sense of what he'd heard. He started with the word "bomb" and worked backwards. Perhaps it had been a metaphor. Metaphorically, things went off like bombs all the time. But he pieced that word with the other phrases he'd heard, like a rudimentary NSA computer scouring Internet chatter, hunting for terrorist plots, to try and sketch the big picture, and he didn't like what he was coming up with.

What did he know about these people, really? Had he signed up with a terrorist group? Was he in the early stages of the indoctrination? Was that the *more responsibility* that Thompson had talked about that evening when they were watching the horses? They hated the government, of course, but who didn't? Even those who hadn't been infected had to live in this brave new world of checkpoints and a catalog of civil rights that was being drawn down upon like a dwindling bank account.

He could run away. He'd made it on his own for a long time before signing on here. He could survive. He could make a new life for himself. So what if he didn't know where he was? It wasn't like he had anywhere to be. It didn't matter if it took him a day or a week or even a month. Such was the life of a post-apocalyptic refugee. But would they hunt him down?

Something else was at work, as well, something he didn't necessarily want to admit at the top of his consciousness. Because if it wasn't there, he'd have packed his bag and kept on keeping on, right on out the back door. There wouldn't be any of this ridiculous pacing, like a pathetic teenage boy trying to muster up the courage to call a pretty girl for the first time. These were his people. The world had left them behind.

Sleep eluded him, and so Ben was wide awake when the first explosion ripped across the grounds about an hour before dawn.

9

B en hoped it was thunder. But he knew instantly that was a pipe dream. It had been too close, too immediate, and there had been no wind or rain, no heat lightning flickering in the distance, no atmospheric foreplay to suggest a tempest was imminent. And if it wasn't thunder, then it was big trouble. He made a beeline for the window; he ducked low and peeked through the curtain, looking southeast toward the main house over the pitched roof of his house's front porch.

"Marc, wake up!" Ben called out over his shoulder. His roommate grunted something unintelligible in reply.

A second explosion boomed across the farm, and a corona of fire bloomed from the roof of the main house. Now the place was ablaze, flames pouring from the upstairs windows. He did not think anyone could survive such a holocaust. Sitting there at the center of this dark farm, the fiery structure looked like a star going red giant. A sloppy, disorganized mess of shouts and screams sprayed the grounds and the deep guttural roar of engine sounds shattered the stillness of night.

"Shit," he whispered.

As Ben turned away from the window, his mind running in a million different directions (*a ruptured gas line? Was anyone hurt? Was this house on fire?*), he noticed movement out of the corner of his eye. Two figures, clad in dark clothing, illuminated by the flames, firing on the rear of the house with guns. Ben trained his eyes on the pair for a moment, long enough to confirm his initial assessment. They had automatic weapons, the barrels spitting their tiny tongues of flame.

He rushed over to Marc's bed and shook the man awake.

"We gotta get out of here," Ben hissed, scanning the bedroom for something he could use as a weapon. There was an old golf bag in the corner; he grabbed the antique driver and inched his way to the door. Gently, he touched his hand to the doorknob and found it cool to the touch. A giant sigh whooshed through his lips, and he began to turn the knob when he heard footsteps coming up the stairs. Those were followed by the crack of splintering wood from the next room over. Screams and a burst of gunfire. Then the pitched howl of the dying.

"What was that?" Marc barked behind him.

Ben's face tightened with frustration. Guy hadn't said two words in six weeks, and he chose that moment to become chatty. He considered their options. Priority one was getting clear of the house. If the house wasn't on fire yet, it likely soon would be. As he neared a decision, he felt the knob turn in his hand, and his bowels turned to water. Someone else was trying to get in.

Instantly, he let go and sidestepped to the wall on the side of the hinges as it swung open. As the figure stepped in the room, he reared back with the club, as clumsily and ungracefully as he had during his days hitting the links with his law school buddies, when he'd been far more interested in throwing back a few beers and pathetically flirting with the beer cart girl. He stepped into the swing and connected with the face of their would-be killer. The club head crashed squarely into the intruder's face and broke loose; it ricocheted against the wall and clattered to the floor.

The man stumbled backwards with a pained grunt. As he crashed backwards to the ground, his gun roared once, indiscriminately spraying a mist of hot lead into the room, the way an automatic air freshener dispensed compressed lilac. Ben dropped into a crouch and covered his head with his hands. Then the barrage stopped, replaced by a low moaning sound behind him. The upper half of Marc's body lay draped over the side of the bed. By the light of the moon streaming in through the window, Ben could see dark stains on Marc's white t-shirt, blooming rapidly like activated yeast. The poor guy had taken several rounds in the torso.

Ben had to get out of here, but trying to escape through the house proper would be too risky.

The roof!

After a single deep breath, he launched himself from his crouch onto the bed, vaulting over Marc and then down to the floor. He paused, trying to control his breathing and heart rate as much as he was trying to gather information. For a moment, silence. Then, the tinkling of glass and a loud whoosh, like oxygen being sucked out of an airlock. More screams, these closer, encased, coming from inside the house.

Time to go, Sullivan, time to go!

Using the club shaft he was still carrying, Ben stabbed at the large plate glass window, which spider-webbed and then shattered into a dozen pieces with a satisfying tinkle. He grabbed his blue backpack, which he kept under the bed, and slung the straps over his shoulders. Then he swiped the edges of the window frame clear of any renegade shards and eased his way through the opening onto the roof, keeping low so that no one would spot him.

Now he had a clear vista of the mayhem stretched out before him, a demonic child's diorama in a shoebox from hell. Fiery fingers had punched through virtually every window of the main house and curled up, grasping the home's upper floors in a clenched fist of flame. Unseen glass shattering, invisible joists crackling and splintering. He counted at least three bodies strewn in the yard, and another three black-clad figures stalking the perimeter of the house.

As the fire consumed the stately building, gooseflesh popped up all over his skin and he felt sweat bead at the base of his neck. Despite the humidity and the heat that the fire was kicking off, he felt icy cold, and he began to see the things he wished he wouldn't ever have to see again, the things he wished he'd never had to see in the first place.

BEN FIRST REALIZED that something was not right about a week after he got back from Chicago, just before things had bubbled over like an unattended pot left over a hot burner. He'd been out for a weekend run through a large park on the west side of Raleigh. Sarah and Gavin were visiting her father Walt, a widower, at his cabin in the hinterlands of Caroline County, about thirty miles north of Richmond. Ben was swamped with work, and this Saturday afternoon jog would have to do as his break for the day. The balance of the day promised a painful discovery project and Chinese takeout for dinner.

After circling the gravel path that followed the perimeter of the park, he had picked his way up a steep hill into its interior, home to skinny trees, thick bramble and narrow trails. At the center of the hill, his legs and lungs burning, a loud moaning sound stopped him dead in his tracks. It was a warm spring day, the air ripe with birdsong, but the moan overwhelmed the sounds of the new season. Ben froze. He looked around frantically, every fiber of his being urging him to run like hell. He remembered that very clearly, how urgently the flight response had tugged on him, like a small child dragging a parent down an aisle in a toy store. But it sounded like someone needed help.

Another moan, and with this second bit of data, Ben triangulated its source a little better. It was behind him on the trail; again, a deep, primal drive inside him, its engine burning as hot as he'd ever felt, to light out of there as if the trees around him might rise up and swallow him if he lingered here too long. He retraced his steps, doubling back about fifty yards when he saw him.

A man lay prone at the edge of the trail, on his side, the lower half of his body hidden by thick brush and ivy. Blood was smeared across his face and arms like war paint, and after a moment, Ben saw why – the man had been impaled on a large tree branch that was protruding from his stomach. He was pulling himself along the ground, and he didn't seem to be aware of Ben's presence. A wide trail of blood curled deeper into the brush, a red carpet into hell.

"You wait right there," Ben said to the man, feeling dizzy. His body was trying to cool down from his three-mile run, but the sight of the grievously wounded man had sent Ben's heart into overdrive, and he was trembling from the shock of what he was seeing. "I'm going for help."

The man turned his head slowly and looked up at Ben,

giving him his first look at those glorious red peepers that would become familiar to all of them. Startled, Ben jumped backward, and just in time as it turned out; the man lunged, as best as he could, and snapped his jaws at Ben's leg but capturing air instead. For a single surreal second, Ben stood there, stunned by the fact that this man had just tried to bite him. The man continued thrashing about in the weeds like a wounded animal.

Ben fled down the trail like all the demons of hell were chasing him. He found a police officer patrolling the park on his mountain bike and reported what he'd seen. Cocaine or bath salts, that was the only explanation. An ambulance was dispatched to the scene, but by the time the crew reached the man, he was already dead. Ben was there at the base of the trail when the paramedics had hauled the man's body out on a stretcher, the white sheet covering it soaked with blood.

Only later would he realize that he'd just seen the Orchid virus in action for the first time.

BEN CREPT to the edge of the roof and peeked down, his mind cycling through one memory of the Panic after another, like a rehearsal dinner slideshow of a happy couple the night before the big day. Another cluster of mystery guests, sweeping around the perimeter of the guesthouse, perhaps wondering what had become of their fallen colleague. Ben was running out of time; they'd find him soon enough. It looked to be about a thirty-foot drop to the ground below. A row of boxwoods fronted the porch, but landing in them wasn't particularly appealing. Just then, he spotted movement below.

A lone gunman had broken off from the pack and had taken up sentry just outside the front door, his gun trained toward the house to mow down anyone trying to escape the building. Easy pickings. Rage roared through Ben; these monsters were just massacring them, and there was nothing he could do about it. He eyed the gunman, who stood stone still in a perfect firing stance. His feet shoulder-width apart, his shoulders square. Christ, he was even wearing night-vision goggles, as if he'd somehow miss someone staggering out the door in a desperate panic. Then it hit him. The man was standing perfectly still, like a statue. A fall-breaking statue.

Before he had a chance to overthink it, he heard voices behind him.

"In here!" one man called out. "On the roof!"

Taking two steps back, he did one quick calculation, trying to estimate how much lift he needed to clear the boxwoods and hit his intended target. As the staccato burst of the machine gun split the night, he sprinted for the edge and pushed off from the roof like a basketball player in a dunk contest. The ground rushed up at him so quickly it took his breath away, as if no time had elapsed at all.

Ben's one-hundred-seventy-five-pound frame crashed into the cherry-picking gunman like a wrecking ball. His kinetic energy dissipated, Ben somersaulted to the open ground, wincing as his body rolled across the grass like tumbleweed. He came to a stop on his back, breathing hard, looking up into the night, a film of clouds covering the sky like a cataract. His left shoulder burned, and he suspected it was separated. The ring and pinkie finger of his left hand were busted to hell too, quivering, and he couldn't bend them a millimeter without a grenade of pain exploding through his hand. Probably broken, he thought. All in all, however, he was in reasonably good shape given the risk he'd just taken.

"There he is!" a voice boomed from above.

The gunmen had spotted him.

A burst of gunfire chewed up the ground next to him, close enough that clods of dirt sprayed his face. He surveyed the scene quickly, calculating an escape route. His human trampoline lay motionless about ten yards away, his hips wrenched to one side at an obscene angle. The gun had landed in between the men, almost equidistant to each of them. A gun would sure as hell come in handy, even if his experience with them had largely been limited to first-person shooter video games and a few visits to the local gun range.

The house was at the edge of the property, near the tree line. The killers on the roof opened fire in earnest, and Ben bolted west across the front yard, carving as serpentine a path as he could without sacrificing speed.

Behind him, up on high, the shooters continued firing on him, trying to bring him down like a runaway deer. He ran as fast as his legs could carry him, as hard as his lungs would let him without exploding in his chest like overinflated balloons. Tears streamed down his cheeks, a weird byproduct of fear and terror and adrenaline swirling together inside him, pushing, pushing, pushing him along. The trees seemed so far away, looming large in the darkness, shadowy giants that might save his life, if he could just make it there, he was never going to make it, any second now, a hot slug would tear into his back or his head and that would be that. He wondered if it would be quick, just a burst of light, or if he would crash to the ground and die slowly.

And then there they were, the giant oaks and maples crowded together in an arboreal dance party. He plunged into their welcome darkness, the black night becoming blacker still as he pierced the heart of the forest. Low-hanging branches scratched at his face like skeletal arms reaching out to grab him.

Then, just as he felt like he was in the clear, slowing his crazed flight to a slow jog, as his heart began downshifting into something resembling a normal rhythm, he stumbled over something. Something big. And something alive.

10

A s Ben fell, his balance shot to hell, he crashed into the trunk of a large oak and froze, afraid to move, afraid not to move. His first thought was that he'd stumbled over a bear, which were not uncommon in rural Virginia. He scanned the ground carefully, waiting for his eyes to adjust, but it was so goddamn dark out here. It was like working a television antenna and only picking up snow. He could just barely make out the prone outline of a figure on the ground, larger than any small woodland creature.

A bear. It had to be a bear.

Then the bear spoke.

"Whozat?" asked a voice drizzled with pain and discomfort.

Jesus. Someone else had made it out here. Someone from the compound.

As his eyes adjusted to the darkness, like a camera lens focusing in on its subject, Ben took one careful step forward toward the person. He or she sounded badly injured, but fear continued to ripple through him. Staying out of arm's reach, he knelt down for a better look.

"It's Ben," he whispered. "I can't see your face. Are you hurt?"

"Ben," the voice whispered back. Panting. "It's Calvin. I'm shot."

"Can you move?" Ben asked.

"No," Calvin Thompson said.

"What happened?"

"They found us," he said.

Ben was perplexed. His head was spinning from the events, he hadn't even had time to process who might have been behind the attack.

"Who did?"

Just then, the moon slid out from behind a layer of clouds, spilling a little light into the small clearing where Calvin's flight from the house had ended. Ben was able to see how badly the man was injured. His face was pale, the color of milk gone bad, and sweat had matted down his hair to his forehead. Red stains bloomed across his shirt like a rosebush. It was hard to tell how many bullets he'd taken, but he'd been hit at least three times. His breathing was shallow, his chest rising and falling rapidly.

"Man, who do you think," he replied, a shade of disappointment in his voice despite his grievous injuries. He grunted. "The fuckin' Department."

"Why would they do this?"

"Because I have something they want."

"What?"

Calvin said something, but his voice had dropped below the audible stage. Another sound caught Ben's attention, coming from somewhere near the tree line where he'd entered the woods. As he scanned the dark woods, he felt Calvin's hand on his wrist, tugging at Ben with as much strength as he could muster. Ben drew down closer, turning his left ear toward the man's lips.

"Tranquility," Calvin said, so softly that Ben wasn't sure he'd heard him correctly. "You have to stop tranquility."

With that, Calvin's grip on his wrist failed and his lifeless hand fell to the ground. The sound he'd heard in the darkness ramped up in intensity, becoming clearer with each passing second. The gunmen were after him, that much was certain. He had no idea what Calvin was talking about, what he wanted Ben to do.

Stop tranquility?

What the hell was he talking about?

The sounds of men rustling through the trees, barking orders to one another were becoming too much to ignore. Ben did the only thing he could think of. He patted Calvin's pockets for anything useful, finding a bolt of cash and a small flashlight. He felt a twinge of embarrassment and shame; it wasn't the first time he'd looted a body, but he'd never quite gotten used to it, no matter how integral to his survival it might be.

He shoved the money and the flashlight into his pockets and fled through the woods.

FOLLOWING the light of the moon, he ran until he puked, and then he ran some more, running until he puked again. He had no idea if he was making any progress or if he was just running in circles, but he'd shaken his pursuers, and so when his legs felt like spaghetti, he took refuge in the shadow of a huge oak, which towered majestically over the other trees, its dominance over its brethren so complete it might as well have been wearing a garish ring and waited for the tiny saplings to kiss its wooden fingers.

Terror made for good fuel, but too much of it ruined the engine.

As dawn broke, he hitched a ride with a long-haired hippie couple driving a pickup, banging down a rural two-lane highway, and uninterested in whether he was Red or Pure. He rode in the bed of the pickup, taking stock of his situation. The woods had thinned out quite a bit around him, and the sky had just begun to lighten in the east. His body was spackled with fatigue and he was thirsty. In short, he had a whole slew of new problems that would need addressing in short order, or he wouldn't be around to figure out what the hell had happened back at the farm.

The farm already seemed like a lifetime ago – could it have been just last night that he'd eaten roasted chicken and grilled vegetables and washed it down with Virginia wine?

Calvin's message rattled around his head like a can of beans that had popped loose from a grocery bag on the way home from the grocery store.

You have to stop tranquility.

What did it mean?

Did he even care?

Had he been living with terrorists?

Were they after him?

What the hell was he supposed to do now?

Hate crimes against Reds were commonplace, but those were typically the work of angry drunks, pissed off at their lot in life, pissed off at the state of the world, and there had never been an easier target than a Red. The attack on the Haven, though, was something else entirely. Had it been a Department raid, as Thompson had said with his last few breaths? Had they sniffed out Thompson's plot, the one that Ben had stumbled on in the main house?

Ben's mind wandered through a jungle of pop-culture conspiracy theories that had been popular before the Panic. The location of Area 51 or 9/11 *was an inside job* or *those weren't really students, they were crisis actors.*

And the Panic!

Lo, the conspiracy theories that had emerged from the Panic! There were as many theories as to its origin, lifecycle and coda as there were people on the planet. The government had never issued any official statement about the origin of the Orchid virus, a failure the public had never forgiven. Ben wasn't sure it mattered, because truthfully, what difference would it have made to know now? Either way, three billion people were dead, and the human race had been set back a hundred years.

Before the government had seized the airwaves and the internet, a conservative cable news channel had declared the virus the work of Muslim extremists, whereas its liberal counterpart had branded it a byproduct of climate change, a pathogen getting all warm and cozy in places it had never previously reached. This had amused Ben; the sky had been falling but the political chess pieces were moved across the board in their predictable fashion.

Climate change and jihadist extremists were the most popular theories, but they certainly were not the only ones. Before things had gotten really bad, social media had popped with all manner of theories – that the virus was extraterrestrial, that it was a mutated version of the rabies virus, that it was a bioweapon designed to create supersoldiers, that the government had intentionally released the virus as some misguided method of population control, that it was a precursor to Rapture.

The raid was still fresh in his mind, and he felt a pit in his heart about the slaughter of his comrades, about the death of Calvin Thompson, the way he'd gripped Ben's wrist as his life ebbed away, like the tide drifting out to sea. Calvin Thompson had taken him in, protected him, provided for him when no one else had. The world had changed, and it was never again going to be like it was, at least not in Ben's lifetime. And if he was going to make it out there, he was going to need people like Calvin and Luke and Laprade, people like him, people who knew what it was like to feel the stares, to be yelled at and spit on and told to go to hell and that was for starters.

And yet he cursed them. He had almost died because of them, because of their schemes and their plans and their plots. Who knew what kind of mayhem they'd planned to unleash? How many innocent people might have died if their plan had come to fruition? A thought crept out of the dank darkness in his mind like a mushroom. What if *Tranquility* was a Department plan to shut down the Haven? What if delivering the message to Ellie would restart the engine of the plot, put back on track what the Department had successfully derailed?

He was disgusted with himself. All his life, he'd prided himself on being too smart to be taken in, too streetwise and cynical to be hoodwinked. He attributed that characteristic to, ironically, his late parents' maddening naiveté. Even as a teenager, Ben had vowed he'd never let anyone get the better of him, brainwash him, and yet here he'd spent the last six weeks, just sucking down Red Kool-Aid without a second thought. Living on a commune! Picking vegetables and singing Kumbaya all the live-long day. He would have laughed if it hadn't been his own reality.

His parents had been quiet folks who saw the good in

everything and everyone, no matter how often they were taken advantage of, no matter how often this relative or that supposed friend screwed them over. His father Roy had been a deacon at their church, his mother Diana a beloved Sunday school teacher, both as well-meaningly gullible as the day was long. They had died a year apart while Ben was in law school; his mother from cancer, and his father from what could only be described as a broken heart. Ben missed them terribly, but he was glad that they hadn't lived to see the Panic. The thought of his mother watching the world unravel like a cheap sweater was almost more than he could bear. He could just picture her, glued to the confusing and terrifying news coverage in the early days, giving her husband Roy worried glances, refusing to discuss the matter in front of Ben as though he were still a little boy. He couldn't even entertain the thought of them becoming infected; it was such a ludicrous thing, no less ridiculous than the idea of his seventy-year-old mother working as a stripper.

His father, Roy, would have been offended by it all, this monstrous thing invading their lives, the orderly existence he'd created for himself, from his fastidious work as an accountant for a national tire chain to the way he wore a tie every day of his life until the day he died to his painstaking devotion to the church. Ben thought about the church he'd attended as a boy, and wondered what his father would have thought about the great cataclysm that had befallen them. A terrible judgment, a reckoning, a recalibration.

What would he have thought of the Reds? Perhaps that was God's true test, how humanity treated Ben and those like him. An extra-credit test in forgiveness. What about the Haven? Certainly they didn't seem themselves as terrorists. No one ever thought of himself as a terrorist. You called yourself a freedom fighter or rebel or revolutionary. No price was too great to pay for the cause. That's what he had overheard that night in the main house. These people had plans to undo and unfix and delay and obfuscate, as though the world didn't have enough shit to deal with.

A steady rain began to fall as the pickup truck continued east toward the breaking dawn. Ben curled up against the truck bed, trying to stay dry, unsure what he was supposed to do next.

11

B en ordered another tequila, his fifth of the night, adding to a tab that was quickly exhausting his financial resources. As he waited for the bartender, he lit a cigarette and took a long drag. One benefit of the Panic? You could smoke inside bars again. Put that one in the Silver Lining column! The good people in Richmond, Virginia must have been thrilled by this development; after years of decline, smoking was *en vogue* again. People needed their vices, and the tobacco industry was happy to provide. Tobacco was easy to grow; many companies had invested heavily in the crop, and demand had never been higher.

He was perched on a bar stool at a hole-in-the-wall on the east side of Richmond called The Doorknob, one of the many speakeasys that had popped up after the Panic. The Doorknob was housed in the bar area of an abandoned Applebee's. No jalapeno poppers or boneless wings or crab-meat quesadillas at this place. Just stale crackers, moldy cheese and a limited selection of bottom-shelf liquor, run by a stinking hulk of a man named Aaron. No beer, nothing like the icy coolers back at the Haven, where you might enjoy a cold one while watching the sun go down over the distant mountains. This was a place for serious drinking, where a patron wouldn't look twice if he saw a public execution.

He had been here for hours, efficiently blowing through the cash that he'd rifled from Calvin Thompson's pockets. Already he'd eaten two plates of cheese and crackers, five dollars a plate, and he gave only the briefest of thoughts as to why he was pissing away the money he would desperately miss the next day.

The bartender poured the liquor into Ben's shot glass, stopping only when the tequila had splashed over the rim and onto the cherrywood bartop. After sweeping up Ben's five-dollar bill, he quickly mopped up the spillage with a dirty hand towel and then turned his attention to another patron clamoring for a drink.

It was nearly midnight, and the place was full despite the nationwide dusk-to-dawn curfew that had been in effect for nearly three years. Kerosene lamps lit the bar area, but the rest of the place remained dark as a black hole because there was no point in using good fuel to light up the path to the bathroom. Central air was still a thing of the past here, and the air was thick and stale, like a sauna rotting from the inside out.

Ben threw back the shot, which crisped the back of his throat like a welder's torch, and scanned the dimly lit bar area. A pair of Volunteers occupied a small table in the back corner, conspicuous in their urban camouflage uniforms, their standard-issue M4s close at hand. So not only did The Doorknob make no attempt to hide its operation from the Department or its stormtroopers, it catered to it as well.

Then a thought struck him, and he felt foolish for not having considered it before – these soldiers were almost certainly engaged in a little secondary employment, strictly off the books, running a protection racket. The Knob greased their pockets, and these soldiers provided security. And it gave them a perfect cover; if things went south, they could simply claim that they'd uncovered this illegal bar and were about to bust it up when everything had gone to hell.

He didn't see any other Reds in the bar – he'd gotten pretty good at picking them out. Even if they were wearing bunkers, most couldn't hide the shame shining on their faces as like a blinking neon sign. Ben knew what they were thinking about, and that could be unnerving. He certainly took no strength from their shared experience.

These customers were good clean folk, untouched by the dread plague. Made sense, actually. Those who had never been infected were more likely to be living a normal life, or at least a decent enough facsimile of one. Maybe not an exact duplicate, run through a fancy photocopier, but something mimeographed, where just enough of the original showed up to reveal what it had been like before. They probably had jobs, perhaps they still lived in their same homes. And if had a little extra scratch on the side, what else were you going to spend it on these days? Courtside seats to the Knicks? None of the four major professional sports had resumed operations yet, and it was unclear when or if they would start again. After all, most of the athletes were dead.

His cash was running low, but he was no closer to nailing down a permanent living arrangement. He desperately wanted to go home to Sarah and Gavin, but she had made it clear that he was not welcome. Sarah. They had met when he was in law school and she was a senior at the University of Richmond. She was finishing a degree in marketing and had secured a job with a firm in Chapel Hill. He missed her to his core; when he thought about her, his chest tightened. Her face was always in his mind, her brown eyes, her light brown hair that always smelled like vanilla.

As good a time to drink as any. He might have a wicked hangover the next morning, but for now, it was working. Five shots, and things didn't seem so bad. Booze was just as useful during the apocalypse as it had been back in college.

It had been almost a week since the attack on the Haven. The encounter with the dying Calvin Thompson was stuck on a loop in his head, playing over and over the way children watched the same movie ad infinitum.

You have to stop tranquility.

Five words that didn't mean a whole hell of a lot to Ben. Truth be told, as time had widened the gulf between the present and that terrible fiery night, they were becoming five words he didn't really care about all that much. Probably just the fragmented, disjointed thoughts of a brain on its last legs, like a computer on its last legs spitting out nonsensical garbage.

If it was all just gobbledygook, though, why did Ben keep coming around on it?

As he contemplated the issue again, he felt a sharp jab in his right shoulder blade. He glanced back at the intrusion of his personal space, assuming that it had been an inadvertent bump from someone struggling to snare the bartender's attention, and then turned his attention back to the empty shot glass before him.

He was wrong.

A second poke, this one stronger and leaving no doubt that he was the intended target of the thick finger jabbing him. His heart thumping, he looked up into the moonishly round face of an angry-looking man, reeking of liquor and sweat, eyeing him the way a predator stared down its prey. He wore jeans and a flannel shirt, which would have been a ridiculous fashion choice for late summer even if the air conditioning had actually been working.

"I know you," the man said, and not in a way that suggested they'd once been high school teammates and wouldn't it be nice to throw back a few drinks and talk about the good old days.

Ben was careful to engage the man cordially, thinking that it would vent the pressure building between them like a balloon pushed to its limit.

"Actually, I'm not sure we've met," Ben said, extending his hand. "Ben."

The man swiped Ben's hand away and took another step closer. Ben pressed his back against the bar, scanning his memory banks for any clue as to the man's identity. His brain cycled through its catalog of faces but was unable to find a match.

"Oh, we've met," the man said.

"OK," Ben replied, his voice sharpening, his systems on high alert now.

"I seen what you done," the man said, wiping a hand across his brow. "I seen what you done."

A stab of heat in Ben's midsection, spreading out to his extremities. There was only one thing this man could be talking about. Somewhere along the line, this man had seen Ben while he was infected. Somewhere back in Raleigh.

They eyed each other for a long moment. The anger rose in the man like the core temperature in a wounded nuclear reactor. This was bad, very bad, and he began scanning his surroundings, anxious to find an escape route. Hoping to buy some goodwill, he thumped the wood with the knuckles of his left hand.

"How about I buy you a drink?" Ben asked.

"Think you can just come in here like nothing happened?" the man said, ignoring Ben's offer.

"I don't want any trouble," Ben said, sliding off his seat, bringing to light the significant size difference between him and his new friend. Ben was laying at least six inches and a hundred pounds to the man. He tried easing around him, but the man stepped in line with him at each turn, as though they were engaged in a choreographed routine.

"Where you running off to, big man?" he said, his voice high-pitched now, coated with a film of terrible glee, as though he'd been hoping and praying for a moment like this. Then he turned to the crowd and proclaimed loudly:

"We got a Red in here with us tonight!"

His statement silenced the idle chit-chat like a smoker stamping out a cigarette with his heel.

"I gotta go," Ben said, making one more attempt to get out the corner he'd been pinned into. He became acutely aware of the silence, of the stares, the palpable sensation that the temperature in the room had dropped ten degrees in an instant.

With that, the pair's uneasy détente came to a quick end. Flannel Shirt shoved Ben hard in the chest, sending him careening toward the bar. His feet tangled with the legs of the barstool, and he lost his balance, landing squarely on his ass with as much grace as a baby elephant. A chorus of nervous laughs rippled through the bar as the confrontation began to draw an audience. Ben's face was hot with shame; the crowd was turning on him.

Feeling naked and defenseless, he scrambled off the ground as quickly as he could, but before he could regain his footing, the man's boot connected with his right flank. The impact stole his breath away, as though he'd been sucked into a vacuum, and he crashed back down to the ground on his side. Flannel Shirt closed in on him like a lion, pulling him off the ground by the lapel of his shirt. As his attacker brought him up to eye level, Ben swung wildly, his right fist crashing against the side of Flannel Shirt's head.

The impact didn't do much damage, not by a long shot, but it did cause Flannel Shirt to release his grip on Ben, just long enough for him to break free. Ben grabbed a bar stool and held it up in between himself and Flannel Shirt; all he needed was a leather whip, and he could double as a lion tamer. His right side was on fire; his torso radiated with pain at even the slightest movement.

A crowd closed in, forming a semi-circle around the combatants, titillated by the prospect of a Red getting the ever-living snot beaten out of him. Ben retreated against the bar, taking little solace in the feeling of the wood at his back. As he looked out at the crowd, he felt the full weight of dozens of eyeballs staring him down, seeing in him the symbol of all that was wrong with the world, of all that was wrong with their lives. The two Volunteers lingered at the edge of the crowd, just watching.

So that's how it was going to be.

These soldiers weren't going to intervene on Ben's behalf, not when they had a Redeye in their midst, not when the clientele was unified in a single purpose. Volunteers were no bigger fans of Redeyes than Flannel Shirt was. Hell, a good old-fashioned lynching might be good for morale!

And, of course, he still had Flannel Shirt to deal with.

He was probably going to die here; he'd fall victim to this mob, and the Volunteers would just drag his body out of here once the crowd had had its way with him, taking out all its frustrations, and deliver him to Eastern Henrico Processing Center. A good sort of group therapy, a come-to-Jesus moment for all of them, and maybe that night they could all sleep a little better, a little more deeply, with that itch that had been nagging at all of them for months scratched. Because people like Ben didn't deserve to be treated any differently than Ben had treated others when he was infected.

Flannel Shirt took another step closer to Ben, and with him, the crowd, forming an ever-tightening noose of anger around his proverbial neck. He gripped the edge of the bar stool tightly, his thumb stroking the worn wood of the seat, still warm from when he'd been sitting on it. The crowd's murmurs were increasing in intensity, a film of anger forming on the surface the way a crust hardened on a steak cooking on a hot grill.

He was out of time. If he was going to do something, it had to be now. Lowering his hands to the legs of the stool, he rotated the upper half of his body ninety degrees and snapped around like an Olympic shot-putter, wincing as he did so, flinging the bar stool into the maw of the crowd with as much force as he could muster. A hush dropped over the crowd, as though time had suddenly frozen for everyone in the bar, their collective fates about to be determined by the projectile's ultimate destination.

The stool spun wildly through the air and crashed into a spectator, a thin, greasy-haired man at the front of the mob, like a bowling ball crashing into a pristine triangle of pins. This man stumbled backwards into the throng behind him, setting off a chain reaction of flying elbows and knees and broken glass.

Ben's science classes came rushing back at him. Potential energy. Kinetic energy. Bodies in motion. Bodies at rest.

Entropy. Chaos. The entire place had become a powder keg, and his bar stool had been the match.

In the moment it took him to blink his eyes, the crowd exploded like a star going supernova. He stood ramrod still for a moment, part of him shocked that his gambit had worked, another part unsure of what he was supposed to do next. He hadn't thought things out beyond *Step 1: Throw Barstool.*

Things broke down quickly from there, a little microcosm of the world at large. The buffer between him and the crowd dissolved instantly, and he found himself in the middle of a pulsing, stinking mass of people. He bounced around like a pinball, covering his head with one hand and throwing wild punches with the other. His fist occasionally found purchase, connecting with a random shoulder or abdomen, but usually he found himself slicing through empty air. Grunts of pain and exertion peppered the air and a steady stream of obscenities flowed through the crowd like a river. The tinkle of glass shattering and crack of splintering wood added to the symphony, *A Riot in D Minor.*

Ben concentrated on making his way to the exit, surprised at how difficult it was to stay on task, how easy it was to let himself get swept up into the mob, as though he'd become a part of this living, breathing organism. And it scared him. Because it reminded him of those terrible weeks during the Panic, when he'd roamed the streets of Raleigh, one single driving thought powering his engine. His entire existence subordinate to the pathogen that had hijacked his programming.

He stayed low to the ground, absorbing glancing blows to his ribs and shoulders, but nothing too serious, nothing that knocked him off course. He began to feel a lightness in his step as the exit came into view.

He was going to make it. He was going to make it. He was going-

Then pain shot through the side of his head, so intense that his field of vision filled with white light, as bright as the sun. It staggered him. It was like being drunk and hungover at the same time. His brain was still issuing its order to retreat, but his body wasn't responding the way it was supposed to. He grabbed a table edge to steady himself, but his legs felt weak, rubbery, as if the floor itself was a giant sponge. Behind him, the riot continued unabated, so he paused to take a breath, to regain his bearings. A moment later, something heavy and hard crashed into the small of his back, and he dropped to the ground.

As his view on the world faded out, like watching night descend across the land through a darkening window, he heard two gunshots ring out.

12

B en's father had died the summer after his second year in law school, joining his mother, who had passed a year earlier. After the funeral, distraught, depressed, angry, Ben found solace in a bottle of Virginia Gentleman, drinking roughly a dozen shots in the span of about an hour. A few minutes of retching into his toilet, his head hanging just over the rim, had likely saved him from a severe case of alcohol poisoning, but it did nothing to abate the nuclear hangover that was waiting for him the next morning. His arms were wrapped tightly around the base of the toilet, as though it was the only thing keeping the room from spinning. He would go on to have other hangovers, some terrible ones even, but no pain or misery he'd ever experienced matched the breadth and depth of the misery he'd felt the morning after his father's funeral.

Until today.

He was awake, but he kept his eyes closed; the effort required to open them seemed too gargantuan to take on right now. He became aware of a dull ache in his side, and he recalled Flannel Shirt's boot in his ribcage when it had just been the two of them, dancing their intimate dance, before everything had gone straight to hell.

He raised a hand to the side of his head, careful not to move too quickly and disturb the fragile equilibrium he'd achieved, the room spinning in conjunction with the rotation of the earth – no faster, no slower. He absently tugged at his tangled locks; his hair was quite long, longer than it had ever been. Close haircuts had been all the rage during the Panic. The shorter your hair, the harder it was for a Redeye to grab hold of you. Long hair had become a luxury humanity simply could not afford. It had been a tough thing to adjust to, Ben remembered thinking, the way they'd all begun to look alike, so utilitarian, devices simply programmed to survive.

Sarah, who'd never worn her hair long anyway, had gone with a cute bob, but she refused to take the clippers to her head, her argument being that if a Red was close enough to grab what little hair she did have, another inch closer to her skull wasn't going to matter much. He wondered if she'd let it grow out again; the last time he'd seen her, it was still short, as if she wasn't quite sure to declare the Redeye threat over. He liked having it long now because it meant that hair length was no longer a matter of life and death.

Just above his left ear, Ben felt a sticky crust, like dried syrup, and the spot was tender to the touch. The souvenir from the heavy blow he'd felt just before the world had blinked out, like a television whose power cord had been suddenly yanked from the wall. He suspected a concussion; he was lucky he'd managed to wake up at all.

He pulled in a deep breath, hoping a hit of fresh oxygen would make him feel better, but instead, he was greeted with the sour stench of piss and stale body odor, a pungent combination that made him gag. He rolled over on his side, the sudden movement throwing his equilibrium off even more, and he began retching. The sound echoed through his dim environs.

He sat up, drawing his knees into his chest, wrapping his arms around his folded legs. It was not completely dark, and his eyes quickly adjusted to the lack of ambient light. A quick scan of his surroundings delivered the intel he needed. A jail cell, a small one from the looks of it. The door was narrow, the dark grey bars roughly eight inches apart.

There was a splash of weak light at the foot of the cell, a tired yellow finger reaching out from some hidden location. It was deathly quiet. Terror soaked every fiber of his being at the prospect of being abandoned here, wherever the hell here happened to be. Images of a long, drawn-out death from dehydration flickered through his mind, and he wondered if he would ever look at anything again without following the thread to its most extreme, most horrifying outcome. It was difficult not to, after all, because the world had indeed followed the thread to its most horrifying extreme. You didn't come out the other side of the Panic without a healthy dose of doomsaying.

"Hello?" he called out. His voice echoed through the empty silence.

Silence at first. Then, rustles of something familiar. The clearing of a throat and the sharp slap of a hardback book being closed, as though its reader was annoyed at the interruption but would not be remiss in his duty. A book, Ben thought. That sounded nice. A cup of coffee and a new novel sounded pretty fantastic right now.

His ears pricked up at the sound of footsteps approaching, and his heart began to pound. A figure wearing the familiar urban camouflage of the Volunteers came into view, silhouetted by the light in the hallway. Ben wasn't in just any jail cell. He was in federal custody, a guest of the Department. He wasn't sure if this was good or bad news.

"Good morning, Mr. Sullivan," the voice said, distinctly female, even more distinctly hard-edged, all military. A male Volunteer accompanied her.

"Can I get some water please?" he said, the words sticking on his parched tongue.

"Later," she said, with such force it felt like she'd fired the word at him from the sidearm strapped to her hip. She seemed neither corrupt nor dim-witted, and this worried him.

"I'm Lieutenant Porter. Mr. Sullivan, you've been charged with incitement of a riot, use of false registration documents, and impersonating a non-infected person in contravention of the laws, peace and dignity of the citizens of the United States."

"Impersonating a non-infected person?" he said, incredulous, and yet feeling quite guilty even though he wasn't quite sure what he was feeling guilty about.

"You'll appear before a Department magistrate day after tomorrow," she said. "If you are found guilty, you will be remanded to the custody of the Department."

Ben stared at her shell-shocked, as though he'd just been involved in a terrible car crash and was just starting to piece together his recollection of what had just happened. He'd heard her, he'd understood each of the words tumbling from her lips, but they seemed to make no sense. A trial? Incitement? False documents?

"I don't understand," he said. "Day after tomorrow? What am I charged with again?"

"Incitement of a riot, use of false registration documents, and impersonating a non-infected person."

"How am I supposed to prepare a defense in two days?"

"I do not make the rules, Mr. Sullivan," the lieutenant said.

"Do I get a lawyer?" he asked. This was his first encounter with justice system since the Panic, and he couldn't believe how little he knew about it.

"No."

"Are you fucking kidding me?"

"Everything I have explained to you is in accordance with the National Recovery Act,"

"The National Recovery Act," he repeated in disbelief.

She turned to her colleague.

"Private Harris, can you acknowledge that I have advised the defendant of his rights pursuant to the National Recovery Act?"

"Ma'am, yes, ma'am," said the private.

"Can I at least have my water now?"

"Your daily meal will be served at 1900 hours. Lights out at 2100 hours."

"I'd like a lawyer," Ben said.

"You have been advised of your rights pursuant to the National Recovery Act."

"This is bullshit," Ben said, the panic loose in his chest like a runaway train. "What the hell happened to due process?"

"Do you understand your rights as I've read them to you?" Lt. Porter asked.

Lieutenant Porter was just a component in a larger machine, programmed to do her job the way an engine powered an automobile without asking whether it was worth the lives of American soldiers to ensure the continued flow of oil from the Middle East.

"What about the others from the bar?" he asked. "The guy that started it?"

"Do you understand your rights as I've read them to you?"

"Fine," he said. "Whatever."

Porter turned on her heel and marched back down the hall, leaving Ben alone once again.

THE DAILY MEAL arrived promptly at 1900 hours. Private Harris delivered the tray, mechanically setting it in the metal drawer that traversed a track connecting the two panes of the cell doors.

"Chow time," the soldier said, the way he might have said it to his dog.

Ben considered flipping the tray over, Cool-Hand-Luke style, sending the food flying into the young private's face, but he was too hungry. He needed his strength for whatever lay ahead, and skipping his only meal of the day was probably not a good strategic move. He retrieved the tray and sat cross-legged on his bedroll, setting his dinner on his lap. Harris stood awkwardly in front of the cell, as though he were a pizza delivery guy waiting for a tip, so Ben simply ignored him.

The meal before him appeared to meet some federal requirement that its consumer not die after eating it, but that was about all. The entrée consisted of a square filet of unidentifiable meat about the size of a deck of cards, gray, tough and cooked to within an inch of its life, perhaps inside a clothes dryer. It could have been anything. A side of thick gruel that might have been instant mashed potatoes or coagulated bull semen accompanied the protein. Lastly, a roll of some kind, an abomination of breadmaking, so rock-hard he was surprised they allowed him to have it, lest he use it as a weapon.

He cleaned his plate, ignoring the taste, using the runny side item to soften up the bread. It was better than nothing; he'd had worse. Millions of people out there would have traded places with him in a second for just a few bites of the meal he was now choking down. After he'd downed the last bite, washing it down with the small lukewarm bottle of a salty energy drink, he set the tray back in the drawer and assessed his situation.

This upcoming trial did not sound promising. He'd heard rumors about the Department crackdowns, about the new and improved criminal justice system that had evolved since the Panic, but he hadn't seen anything firsthand, preferring to fly under the radar. The Department had assumed jurisdiction over all criminal offenses nationwide, absorbing into its fold the various battered local law enforcement agencies, but it gave local personnel wide discretion to punish offenses in their bailiwicks. Criminal cases were processed quickly and efficiently, a display of Department strength.

It was a byproduct of the national emergency the President had declared in April of that year. Congress followed suit, quickly repealing the Posse Comitatus Act, which had barred the U.S. military from operating inside the country, as the Redeyes began overwhelming local law enforcement and state national guards. Habeas corpus was suspended, which allowed authorities to detain and hold anyone it deemed a threat without due process. Hundreds of thousands of people had died or disappeared in government custody.

There was discussion of holding a constitutional convention to suspend certain constitutional rights until the

President terminated the national emergency declaration, but the idea fizzled as the outbreak receded later that summer. And in the end, it didn't really matter; there was more than one way to skin your rights. The National Recovery Act gave the government sweeping powers in the interest of protecting the nation from total collapse. The feds seized the airwaves, the internet, lumber companies, steel mills, waste removal companies, farms, utilities, anything it might need to rebuild the wounded country. America's status as a functioning democracy had all but disappeared, and it was unlikely to return to its pre-Panic days anytime soon.

Ben turned his attention back to the problem at hand. Escape seemed unlikely. He didn't know where he was, and he hadn't detected any system weakness he could exploit. And who was he fooling anyway? Was he going to overpower the guards? Tunnel out of his cell like Andy Dufresne in *The Shawshank Redemption*? No, he needed another way.

And then it came to him, all wrapped up and shiny, a wonderful present, that last one under the Christmas tree, toward the back, that thing you'd desperately wanted but had resigned yourself to not getting until your mom mentioned offhand that it looked like there was one more for you, right there behind the tree. He stepped up to the cell door, wrapping his fingers around the cold steel bars, ready to cash in his most valuable chip, quite possibly his get-out-of-jail-free card.

"Lieutenant Porter!"

13

Agent Alexander Whitmore grimaced as the prisoner thrashed and bucked against the cannon of water. He'd been waterboarded himself as part of his CIA training many years ago, the idea being that agents needed to experience it themselves before they could be trusted to do it to another person. He knew what it felt like; he would confess to anything after a minute. But it never got easier to witness.

The blast of water seemed endless, as if an ocean itself had become a weapon, firing bitingly cold water into your eyes, your nose, your throat, triggering a hacking, exploding cough as your lungs did their level best to keep the water from drowning you while taking in enough oxygen to keep you from passing out. It felt like you were being held underwater by an invisible hand, pushing you down, just shy of the surface, just shy of all the sweet life-giving air a guy could want. And just as your consciousness started to fade, it would stop, and your body will pull back from the brink, sucking in the air, desperate to stay alive just a little bit longer.

Whitmore gestured to the young dopey-faced Volunteer holding the hose to shut off the water. The prisoner, Ben Sullivan, relaxed and sucked in gobs of dank, humid air. Sullivan was racked out on a long, narrow table, on his back, his head hanging over the edge. He was trembling from the cold and wetness; his arms were above his head, burning and aching with fatigue, held in place by a series of ropes suspended from the ceiling. It stank down here, reeking of sweat and urine, but it was air, sweet breathable air, and anything was better than the hose, Satan's water gun. Next to the hose, the air was as welcome as a warm Pacific breeze. It wouldn't take long for Whitmore to get what he wanted from this man. Thank God.

Waterboarding was worse than people realized. Way worse.

Sullivan struggled to catch his breath, an endeavor made all the more difficult by the terrifying prospect of another round with the hose. He was naked, as exposed as the day he'd been born. He opened his eyes to a dark gloom, surrounded by a pair of Volunteers and an impassive-looking man wearing a dark suit. Whitmore hadn't even asked him anything yet.

"What do you want?" he asked finally, his voice sounding meek and broken.

Whitmore stepped forward, his features sharpening a bit as he leaned in close to Ben. His face was hard and devoid of warmth, like an arctic landscape. His suit was crisp, his shirt pressed, his necktie looking like he'd Windsored the ever-living shit out of it. He wore wire-rim glasses, and his hair was coiffed just so, not a single strand out of place. Nothing about Whitmore was out of place. He demanded perfection of himself in all things. Order in the chaos of the world.

"Mr. Sullivan," he said, grasping Ben's chin in the V between his thumb and index finger. "I'm Agent Whitmore. I'm with the Department of Reconstruction & Recovery."

Ben's eyes widened with terror.

"I'm going to ask you some questions," he said. "Believe me when I say that it's in your best interest to answer me truthfully and completely. Don't leave anything out, no matter how minor a detail you think it is. Do you understand?"

Ben nodded again. Whitmore knew the man understood, as surely as he'd understood anything in his life. He was going to tell them everything, truthfully and completely, just as Whitmore had requested. No detail would be left out. That was the power of the water cannon.

"Good. See, I just need to make sure you're not here to pull a fast one on us. Smart guy like you, doesn't fit the part, the kind of guy who could just really lead us down the primrose path."

Ben shook his head forcefully.

"Is anyone else from the Haven still alive?"

"I don't know," Ben said. "I don't think so."

"Are there other Havens?"

"I don't know," he said. "I never heard any discussion about any other Havens."

"When was the attack scheduled?"

"They didn't tell me," Ben said. "I was eavesdropping on the meeting where I heard the attack being discussed, but I think they heard me, and I ran off."

Whitmore glanced over at someone, just out of sight, and nodded his head.

The laser-like beam of water crashed into his face, and it felt like a gallon was forced down his throat before he could get his mouth closed. Sullivan held his breath tight, holding it, holding it, until his head started to swim from the effects of the oxygen deprivation, and just before passed out, the water stopped. He heaved once, and then turned his head just in time to vomit sour water all over the cold concrete floor. The stench of puke hung in the chill air.

"Mr. Sullivan, perhaps I wasn't clear. I want to know what you know."

"I swear, I don't know anything!" he pleaded, his voice growing desperate.

"What do you know about the Haven?" Whitmore asked.

"I was there," Ben said, his nose running, his head lolling to one side. "I worked in the fields, farming, that kind of thing. I didn't really get to know anyone. They just wanted to have a place where they weren't treated like shit."

"How long were you there?"

"About six weeks."

"How did you end up there?"

"I helped a woman who was in trouble," Ben said. "When I was on a HARD team. Her brother was in the group. He invited me to join them."

"Who was the woman?"

"I don't know," Ben said,

Whitmore paused, his face blank.

"How did they find you?"

"At the camp. I guess they followed me."

"Of course, the camps. Breeding grounds for trouble. And you just went along with them?"

"I was having a hard time," he said. "I was out of food and money. I had nowhere to go. I didn't know what they were up to."

"I see," Whitmore said.

There was a pause in the discussion, two boxers retreating to their corners. Still no emotion from Whitmore.

He wasn't sure if he believed all, some, or none of Ben's story.

"Have you ever heard of Mongoose?"

Ben shook his head, his brow furrowed in confusion.

"Emerald?"

Another pause, followed by: "No."

"Tranquility?"

"No," he said.

"Roadrunner?"

"No."

"Are you sure about that?"

"Yes. I'm sure."

Whitmore nodded again, and the prisoner braced himself for the liquid assault, his body locking up like he was about to take a punch from Mike Tyson in his prime. As he twisted and writhed around the table, straining against the rope restraints until he felt them cut into his wrists and ankles, screaming and hacking, Whitmore shut his eyes tight and waited for it to pass. He reminded himself why he was doing this. He reminded himself what he had lost.

"Are you sure?"

"Yes, I swear to God, I'm sure!"

"Very good."

Whitmore turned and walked out. A Volunteer undid the restraints and threw him a ratty orange jumpsuit before following Whitmore, leaving Ben alone in the dark, dank room. He pulled it on quickly, desperate to beat back the chill that was seeping into his bones, down into his core.

BEN WAS flat on his back, one arm tucked behind his head, when he became aware of the fact that his arm had fallen asleep. The word *Tranquility* kept cycling through his mind like that familiar piece of luggage that passes by on the conveyor belt a dozen times before you spot your own. They had asked him about it. Why had he lied about that? It was his biggest bargaining chip. And yet he covered it up, like protecting an injured part of the body from further harm.

He'd been back in his cell for hours, and the place had been as silent as a tomb. No other visitors, no one to check on his well-being. They could just leave him here until he rotted away, and no one would say boo. He had no lawyer, no family members, no one would even know he was gone. He was an un-person, a nothing man. Oh, sure, there were some pro-Redeye groups out there, those that had clung to the idea of equal rights for all after the Panic had died down. They filed amicus briefs in various lawsuits alleging all manner violations of the constitutional rights of the Reds, but it was more window dressing than anything else. Nothing changed, and nothing was likely to change in the near future.

How had things turned to shit so quickly?

He couldn't believe how badly he'd played his hand, how poorly he had misjudged his captors. All these months, his life had felt like it was happening to someone else, as if he hadn't been hated and reviled by the world around him. Surely they didn't see him that way. He was an upstanding member of the community, a husband, a father, and it would just be a matter of time before they saw him that way again. And what better way to do that than to let them know that he was one of them, that he was on their side!

But he knew instantly that it had been a terrible miscalculation on his part. It felt wrong, so wrong, like a musical note struck in discord, and it played out in just that manner. After telling Lieutenant Porter that he had information about the Haven, angry soldiers had whisked him out of his cell and brought to this God-forsaken hellhole. How long had he been here? It seemed like hours or even days. But it probably hadn't been that long, he realized. The horror and the misery of the water cannon had made time stretch like putty.

The interrogation ran through his mind again like an old movie. They had actually asked him about *Tranquility*. A buzz of energy had coursed through Ben as Whitmore enunciated the word, as though he had touched a live wire. He didn't know why he had said no. It was unexplainable, a sudden protective instinct for that simple word washing over him, the way a mother might hide a child from an abusive father home from a three-day bender. He hadn't intended to protect Ellie, he hadn't intended to protect anyone. All of a sudden, he was keenly aware of how much he wanted to keep her name out of this. The depth of this conviction surprised him a little; after all, he didn't really know Ellie all that well. He hadn't even seen her since that fateful day. And yet here he was, lying for her.

The left side of his brain was making all kinds of rational arguments, that he could just tell Whitmore what Thompson had told him in the woods, and that should be enough to buy him some goodwill. But as he lay there, he became aware that it was going to take more than just the hose to get him to give it up. A lot more. Clearly, Calvin Thompson's final words had been those of someone still in control of his faculties. Tranquility was a thing, a real thing, a precious thing. Precious to the Haven, precious to Mr. Whitmore, and, by extension, precious to Ben.

With no frame of reference, time began to dissolve around him like the memory of dream that was fading. At some point, they'd deliver his meal and that would orient him like a temporal compass, and for that brief moment he would know his place in the world, even if that place in the world was limited to dinnertime in this cell. He felt alone, adrift, and his eyelids began to grow heavy in the stifling humidity.

The sound of the cell door disengaging startling him awake from a deep sleep. He sat up and gave his head a hard shake to clear the cobwebs. Porter and Harris were waiting for him at the precipice, their rifles slung over their shoulders.

"Let's go," said Harris. Acne had done a number on his face, leaving it as pockmarked as the surface of the moon.

"Where?" asked Ben.

"No talking," said Porter, looking as hard and mean as ever. "Cuff him."

She trained her M4 rifle on Ben while the kid slapped on the cuffs and the leg irons. He held her gaze the whole time, part of him furious, part of him amused by the Hannibal Lecter treatment he was getting. They already hated him, so it was probably to his advantage that they feared him a little too. It was a mean thing to think, but he hoped that returning her gaze with his flaming red eyes reminded her of the terrible things that she'd seen during the Panic, that it unsettled her, that maybe she wouldn't sleep well tonight, and she could curse his name while dry swallowing a sleeping pill.

They led him through the bowels of the facility to a sally port, which had once been used to load and unload prisoners from transport vans that delivered them to other correctional facilities or to their court dates in other jurisdictions. It was still dark out, probably coming up on dawn. It was cool but not cold, just a hint of humidity hanging in the air. Instantly, he scanned the area for an escape route, and he chuckled softly to himself; every prisoner who came through here had undoubtedly done the same thing.

The driver of the van idling at the curb smoked a cigarette silently. When he saw his passengers arrive, he pitched the smoke through the window. The half-smoked cigarette tumbled end over end, showering the inky pre-dawn darkness with a cascade of sparks.

Ben's escorts loaded him into the rear of the van. Harris took the seat next to him, Porter on the bench directly across. The driver's compartment was separated by a thick metal screen, and he filed that bit of information away for later, in the event he developed the balls to make an escape attempt. The more he thought about it, the more he thought about *Tranquility*, the more important it seemed to be.

"Roll out," Porter said, turning her head toward the driver.

They pulled away from the curb, destination unknown.

14

Sunrise was still an hour away, but the night had made its final turn for the break of dawn. They rode in silence down Route 288, one of the few crossings of the James River that was still intact. Traffic was light. Twenty minutes later, the driver took the exit for Route 60, a major artery running through Chesterfield County, a suburban community just south of the city of Richmond. The area had seen heavy fighting during the Panic; the Virginia National Guard had worked tirelessly to keep Route 60 open as a supply line running east-west through the heart of Virginia. It had been an important front in the struggle to protect Washington, D.C. from the Redeyes.

They had arrived at what had once been the State Police headquarters, now converted into a regional command post for the Department. The van passed through two sets of black gates, waved through each by a heavily armed Volunteer, before pulling up to the rear entrance of the steel and glass complex.

As Ben alighted from the van, the pointed shove of a rifle in his back caused him to lose his balance and stumble to his knees. The other soldiers laughed at him, and his face flush with embarrassment.

"A little weak in the knees? Human flesh levels running low?" said one of the Volunteers.

"Hey, we got your favorite for dinner!" barked another. "Dead dog. I scraped it up off the Turnpike myself."

The laughter erupted like they were watching a stand-up comedy festival. Tears welled up in his eyes, but he would be damned if he was going to let these assholes see him cry. He wiped his face quickly with his shackled arms just as two soldiers shoved him along inside the double doors.

They took him down a darkened corridor and up a narrow staircase to an observation area; it looked down on a large open room with dozens of workstations facing toward three large screens on a curved wall. Waiting for him was his new friend, Agent Whitmore. His suit looked as fresh and crisp as ever, the knot in his necktie still perfect. He was sipping coffee from an Oceanic Airlines mug. Ben's stomach turned to liquid, and he could almost feel the sting of the water in his face again, in his nostrils, blasting his eyeballs so hard it felt like they would pop straight out of his head.

"Nice to see you again, Mr. Sullivan," Whitmore said, as though he was greeting an old friend.

Ben stared at him dumbfounded. That he'd spent an hour torturing Ben seemed to have no lasting effect on the man.

"What am I doing here?" Ben asked.

Whitmore smiled broadly, a huge grin spreading across his face like someone plastering a pat of shiny butter across a piece of toast.

"We've been having a lot of problems with insurgent groups," Whitmore said. He paused and took a long sip of his coffee. "It was meeting with you that gave me the idea for solving this problem once and for all. In a way, your country owes you an enormous debt."

Ben felt a sudden emptiness chewing through his soul like a puppy left alone with a tennis shoe.

"Coffee?" Whitmore asked.

"No," Ben muttered mindlessly, shaking his head as the screens flickered to life, depicting what appeared to be real-time satellite shots of the Eastern Seaboard. In the upper corner of the middle screen, the current time ticked away. The words *Live Feed* blinked slowly.

5:31:17 AM

The screens flickered again, this time zooming in on a more localized shot, this one in the mid-Atlantic region; another flicker, and it was obvious the satellite was centering on the Richmond area. Another zoom-in, this one tightening in on a large camp, Ben's former home at the Richmond International Raceway.

They watched the screen quietly until the ringing of an unseen phone broke the silence. Whitmore removed a wireless phone from his pocket and answered it.

"Whitmore," he said.

Ben eavesdropped as he stared at the screens.

"You have a green light," Whitmore said after a moment. He terminated the call and slid the phone back into his jacket pocket.

Whitmore caught Ben staring at him and gave him a wink.

"You know, these camps really have become a hotbed for terrorist activity," Whitmore said.

Ben hoped and prayed that his gut was wrong, that he really didn't know what was coming, that Whitmore had some other endgame in mind, because there were few things he hated more than being right about something that he didn't want to be right about. In college, he had suspected a girlfriend was cheating on him, and he hadn't had any empirical evidence supporting such a suspicion, nary a thread, but when she had finally confessed to him what had happened while he was gone for the summer, he remembered how unsurprised he'd been. Devastated, sure, the emotional equivalent of her having fed him into a wood-chipper. But surprised? Not for a second.

"The screen on the far right is a body camera view," Whitmore said. "Mounted on the helmet of the team leader. This will give us a first-person view of the mission."

On this screen, Ben looked into the camouflaged faces of a dozen Volunteers, all wearing body armor, armed to the teeth. They were in the cargo area of an armored personnel carrier. As the scene unfolded, his respiration deteriorated into shallow, ragged gasps.

"This middle screen, directly ahead of us, will give us a wide shot of the mission," Whitmore continued. "This way we can get a bird's-eye view of everything. That'll be nice, don't you think?"

This was an aerial view, from a considerable height, but one that gave a clear shot of the satellite's intended target – a wide clearing, dotted with a number of manmade structures. In the corner of the screen, Ben could see an object rapidly approaching the camp. The personnel carrier.

"Here we go," Whitmore said, clapping Ben on the shoulder.

Ben recoiled at the touch, disgusted by even the slightest suggestion that he and Whitmore were in on this together.

What did you do, Ben?

He could hear his father's voice echoing in his head

when he'd come home from work to learn from his mother that Ben had gotten in trouble yet again.

His eyes flickered from screen to screen, the pit in his stomach deepening as the Volunteers' vehicle drew closer into the camp.

"I used to get a lot of ear infections as a kid," Whitmore said. "Every week, back in the doctor's office for another bottle of amoxicillin. The liquid just would never drain out of my ears. So just as soon as we got one infection knocked out, the bacteria would start breeding again, just a little bit stronger than the generation that had just been wiped out."

Ben's gaze was riveted on the monitors as Whitmore continued his stroll down memory lane.

"These camps have become dangerous," Mr. Whitmore said. "Breeding grounds. Just like my poor little ears. What you have to do is get rid of the stagnant liquid. That's why every kid under the age of ten's got those little ear tubes. You've got to get rid of the liquid."

Ben glanced over at Whitmore to show that he was still listening, that he was still engaged.

"You catch my drift?" Whitmore asked.

A brain-damaged donkey would catch your drift, you monster.

The armored carrier pulled up just outside the unmarked perimeter of the camp, and two dozen Volunteers in riot gear poured out, their rifles unslung and ready for business.

"Jesus, you're not going to-?" Ben asked, his voice breaking.

"What do you think I am, some kind of monster?" Whitmore said. "Of course not. It's just that these camps are no good for your kind. If everyone is in the same shitty boat, maybe it's the boat that's the problem. It's just a self-perpetuating cycle of misery. You need to get out, re-integrate your-selves into society."

His voice was dripping with condescension.

"You know that won't work."

"So I should just let these camps be? And take the chance that we don't find the next Haven in time?"

"It's all many of them have," Ben said, turning to face Whitmore, almost pleading with him, hating himself for it.

"Well, they're going to have to find something else," Whitmore said, his tone the verbal equivalent of a blast door falling shut.

The discussion was over. Not that it had ever really begun. Ben turned his attention back to the twin movie-sized screens, focusing on the wide aerial shot. He couldn't bear to watch it from the team leader's remarkably clear helmet cam. It was awful in its immediacy and clarity. Wasn't it just terrific that so much technology had survived the apocalypse!

The soldiers had split into smaller fireteams of four and were spreading through the camp like viruses. The first team to reach a tent began tapping the frame with the butts of their weapons, and although there was no audio, it was obvious that they'd begun shouting at the residents of the tent.

A moment later, a heavyset woman emerged, a baby on her hip, another one squirreled away just behind her. A thin man followed her out, yelling as the soldier shooed him away. When the tent was clear, two Volunteers wrecked it and then tossed something on top of it. Ben's heart splin-tered like a crystal vase as the tent, the only home this little family had, erupted in a miniature holocaust. The incen-diary device burned hot and fast until the tent and all its contents were nothing but a smoky mess.

"See?" Whitmore said. "That baby right there? We don't know how the virus is going to affect it. That kid alone right there could restart this whole mess. We just don't know, Mr. Sullivan. We just don't know."

The evictions continued for two hours. It was a slow-developing car crash, and Ben was unable to look away. The crowd of refugees grew steadily as each tent was reduced to a charred pile of rubble, a balloon of humanity being rapidly inflated. Ben wondered how much more the balloon could take before it exploded.

"This country is safer thanks to you," Whitmore said.

Ben gagged, and warm bile crept up his throat, burning him from the inside out. He felt hot, his body coated with a thin sheen of cold sweat, but he shivered uncontrollably as the destruction of the camp continued before him.

And then it happened.

He could almost feel the balloon burst onscreen. A group of men, less than half a dozen, rushed the soldiers, approaching from the cover of a small outbuilding on the northwest side of the camp. One was firing a pistol wildly, belying the experience of a marksman who had taken up a gun for the first time earlier that day. He missed badly. Two Volunteers opened up on the erstwhile rebellion with their M4 rifles. The men had no chance, exposed, mostly unarmed, and the Volunteers shredded them into bloody ribbons.

"Dammit," muttered Whitmore.

The remaining Volunteers formed a perimeter around the remaining residents, about a hundred or so, many of whom immediately raised their hands toward the sky. Others rushed up to check on the fallen camp residents. Ben focused on a skinny child, maybe six years old, his malnourished arms pointed skyward, and he couldn't take it anymore. He turned in his chair, away from Whitmore, and buried his face in his right hand. Suddenly, he felt a sharp pain as Whitmore wrenched him by the ear and turned his head back toward the screen.

"You're going to watch this," he said, his voice encased in ice. "I did not want this to happen. But you're such a threat to us. You're a threat to yourselves. You're a threat to everything."

Ben searched for an appropriate retort, something that would put Whitmore in his place, make Ben feel better about himself, but he couldn't. The well was dry. He sat in silence as the soldiers searched the surviving residents and sent them on their way. They drifted away from the camp-site in small groups of twos and threes, wandering off into the bright morning, carrying all the weight of the world on their shoulders.

"There are hundreds of these camps across the country," Whitmore said. "Possibly thousands. And they are just little Petri dishes of trouble. It was your report that convinced the Secretary to liberate these camps." He put air quotes around the word 'liberate,' a gesture that Ben found slightly horrifying.

He turned his eyes back to the screen. The ruins of the camp were virtually deserted but for a handful of soldiers scavenging the infield for anything useful that might have been left behind. After a few minutes of this, the soldiers loaded back into the back of the carrier, and it chugged away from the campsite. The bodies lay where they fell; the picture was clear enough that Ben could see the dark red blood soaking the grass.

"What'll happen to the bodies?"

"We'll leave it for a HARD unit. You know all about those, right, big guy?" he said casually, clapping Ben on the shoulder, as though he were talking about an overflowing garbage can, waiting for the trash truck to swing by and make its weekly collection.

"What now?" Ben said. He said it almost as much to himself as he said it to Whitmore.

"I've been thinking about that," Whitmore said. "To be honest, I'm not real crazy with the idea of giving you food and shelter while you kick back in that little condo of yours."

Ben smiled stupidly at Whitmore's joke, assuming that the man had never spent the night in a claustrophobic room infused with the essence of urine, its walls lacquered with fecal matter. Why was he smiling? Did he think the joke was funny?

"Yes," Whitmore said, clapping his hands together with a single sharp crack. "I think it'd be better for you to be out with your people."

Whitmore flashed a smile of his own, cold and dead, bearing as much sincerity as a viper.

"And don't worry, we'll make sure everyone knows that you were the one who helped the Department, that because of you, these camps are being dissolved," Whitmore said. "We'll get it out in time for the Freedom One News tonight. Your picture will be all over the F-One Network! You're going to be famous, my friend."

A monster to the uninfected. A traitor to the Reds.

An enemy of two states!

More struggle. More misery. More drifting through the nightmare that would never end, like a sailboat lost at sea, its mast snapped, its navigation systems fried. What the hell was the point? Then he realized that was the point. Whitmore wanted to draw out his suffering, make sure Ben knew how little they thought of him and those like him. Divide and conquer. They'd be scattered across the country, unable even to take solace or draw any strength from their shared misery. And now he would be alone, a pariah, a Judas, a Benedict Arnold.

Whitmore stood and gestured toward the Volunteer guarding the observation room, and Ben took this as his signal to take his leave of this terrible place. He put Whitmore and the Department out of his mind because they were already part of his past. He said nothing as the Volunteer guided him down the narrow staircase toward the main hall, the barrel of his rifle tickling his back.

He thought about saying something, a profound statement that might make him feel better about himself, about his recognition of the evil inherent in this shitty new world. But there was nothing to say, nothing that would change anything or make things better. His big fat mouth had already done enough damage, and all at once, he felt stupid, naïve, guilty and awash with shame. His mind was seized with the faces of the men who'd charged the Volunteers, and he imagined what they would have thought if they knew it had been one of their own that had brought this hell to their door.

Along the way, they passed other Volunteers and Department staffers, and he could feel their eyes boring in on in him, smiles of satisfaction on their faces, like they knew what he had done, how badly he'd screwed himself, how he'd just become famous in the very worst way.

They arrived at the double doors through which he'd entered the building, where another heavily armed Volunteer was waiting. Outside, the day was gloomy and dim, the sky a sea of angry roiling clouds.

Just then Ben remembered he didn't have his blue backpack, his constant companion of the past year. His meager food supply, his water purification tablets, his blanket, his everything. He turned suddenly, feeling an icy grip of panic around his throat.

"My stuff!" he exclaimed, the words slick with desperation. "Where's my backpack?"

Whitmore eyed him the way a lion might stare at its prey on the savannah.

"Right," Whitmore said. "Your backpack."

The two Volunteers suppressed chuckles. The whole scene stank of the high school archetype, the quarterback of the football team, his two lackeys at his side, giving the academic overachiever, the dork, the business. All they needed was a trashcan to stuff Ben into, and the picture would be complete.

"Just messing with you," Whitmore said. "Of course we'll get it for you. We know how precious these things are to people in your situation."

"You're an asshole," Ben said.

"It's on its way down here," he said, ignoring Ben's jab.

A few minutes later, a third soldier delivered the backpack to Whitmore, who then handed it over to Ben.

"Wouldn't want you to leave without this," Whitmore said. He gestured to one of the soldiers. "See him to the outer gates. Take care, Mr. Sullivan."

Ben watched him go, taking his perfectly knotted tie and inexplicably pressed suit with him, strutting down the hallway like he was on a Milan runway. When he reached the stairwell, he looked back over his shoulder at Ben. Their eyes locked, and right there, Ben felt a rage build inside him, not quite like the manic fury coursing through his veins while in the grips of the infection, but not terribly dissimilar from it. Whereas the Orchid-induced rage had been random, scattered, like grains of sand on a beach, this one had a laser focus, a cruise missile locked on its target.

He looked like he couldn't wait to get back inside and tell his Department buddies about this great prank he pulled on the piece of shit Red out there while they shared cigars and brandy and eighteen-year-old hookers and the other accoutrements and spoils of being the head jerkoffs in charge.

Like, yeah, I thought he was going to cry when I told him he wasn't getting it back! I mean, you should've seen it! Priceless! Fucking priceless!

More than anything that he'd wanted in his whole life, Ben wanted to kill Mr. Whitmore.

15

Ben spent that night in a badly damaged sporting goods store about three miles west of the Department command post. Before settling in for the evening, he inspected the site carefully for squatters, the way a small boy might examine his bedroom for monsters. Then he constructed a makeshift bedroll from the remnants of singed and scarred cardboard boxes, quite possibly the most pathetic-looking thing he'd ever laid eyes on. He found an old painter's blanket balled up in the corner, so worn it was nearly transparent in spots. Still it was better than nothing, and when a cold front pushed through in the dead of night, sending the temperatures dropped into the low forties, leaving him shivering and awake, he was happy to have it. Sleep eluded him for most of the night, and he longed for the safety and comfort of the Haven, cursing himself for even thinking about selling them out, even posthumously.

The little sleep he got was fitful, and he was wide awake as the sun began its climb into the sky, sending tongues of orange light over the rooftops. Ben was cloudy with fatigue, his eyes gritty, like they were full of sand. He was exhausted and afraid, wondering when the shoe would drop on Whitmore's promise to expose him to the world as a turncoat. The fear and anxiety eroded the rage he'd been feeling like an ocean chewing away at the beach, and he'd never felt more alone. Even the very idea of killing Whitmore seemed ridiculous, the ranting of a crazy person, the way one might briefly think about killing a driver who'd cut you off in traffic.

He peeked out onto a rapidly brightening Midlothian Turnpike. A few cars motored by, but gasoline was still running more than thirteen bucks a gallon, keeping vehicle traffic was still way down. Traffic patterns had fundamentally changed in the last three years, and rush hour was a thing of the past. On the plus side, the air seemed a bit cleaner, especially now that the smell of human decay was starting to fade.

The roads themselves were in bad shape, pockmarked with potholes, really starting to show the signs of neglect with very little money to maintain them. Tax revenue had dropped precipitously; it was a terrible Catch-22 they were all in. The government couldn't fix the infrastructure without tax revenue; businesses couldn't generate revenue without a functional infrastructure. Pockets of survivors made their way along the edge of the highway, trying to eke out another day.

Tranquility.

It was all he had left.

Ironic, too, given that he was feeling anything but tranquil.

The word continued to have no meaning for him, but had been important to Calvin Thompson, and it sure as hell had been important to Whitmore. He went over Whitmore's quiz and tried to recall all the code words he'd been grilled on. Roadrunner. Emerald. A third one that had drifted beyond the tractor beam of his memory banks.

A code name for the attack he'd heard them planning? A place? A person? Plant, animal, mineral?

Ben massaged his temples with his thumb and middle finger, dreaming of a cup of coffee. Nothing fancy, just a good old-fashioned cup in his oversized Cleveland Indians mug. That sent him down a mental highway toward an exit marked Baseball. Under normal circumstances, the first game of the World Series would be imminent. It was weird not having baseball anymore. Not that he watched much of it, a few innings here and there when he had a chance, but he always liked having it on. It seemed like the appropriate background for life, the routine of the season, day after day, a game that seemed so simple on the surface but maddeningly complex when you scratched beneath the surface. A good metaphor for something, he thought, but he didn't know what that something was.

Tranquility.

The word continued to nibble away at him like a robin pecking away at a bird feeder. Ellie might know what to do with the information. At the very least, she would be better equipped to take action than he was. Besides, what the hell else was he going to do?

Before he set off, he scoured the store in the light of day, see if he could salvage anything for this new phase of his life. This store had once been home to a variety of gear that would have been tremendously useful in a post-apocalyptic world. Camping gear. Clothes. Weapons. Backpacks. Energy bars. Water bottles. And in a fully post-apocalyptic world, emptied of most of its population, Ben might have stumbled across a place like this that hadn't been picked clean. But his was a near-apocalyptic world, and places like this had long been stripped to the bone. He wandered among the displays and racks, so barren it looked like a new business awaiting its first delivery truck. Even the cardboard boxes were gone.

He drifted back to the storeroom, where he'd spent the night, and poked through the debris, finding nothing. He was just about to give up when he spotted a small door tucked away at the back of the storeroom, the kind that might lead to Narnia. It was half-blocked by a rack of metal shelving and the door was locked tight. The paint was old, flaking. A dark stain on the door caught his eye, and he leaned in for a closer look. It was dried blood, concentrated around the doorknob, a small rust-brown handprint. Ben gave the doorknob a quick jiggle, scanning the room for anything that might help him pick the lock.

There was an old paint can in the corner of the storeroom; he gave it a quick shake to test its weight. It was still heavy, the can's seal tight. The paint inside had long since congealed. Using it as a battering ram, he reared the can back and slammed it into the lock, hoping that the years of disrepair had weakened the wood. He smiled as the wood gave way, splintering under the heavy impact of his makeshift mace. After a couple more blows, the door splintered clear of the lock and swung open.

The door creaked on its hinges in the morning quiet, a sound that was still creepy even after all the creepy shit he'd seen. That was a creepy sound with staying power. The air was musty and sour with mildew and dust and who knew what else. Ben's heart thrummed in his chest as he stood at the threshold of the small door. A dim haze of light greeted him; there must have been a window back there, and his spirits soared. A window meant that this was more than just a closet, and the fact that the room had been undisturbed meant that there might be something worth salvaging inside. He waited for his eyes to adjust and then, when he was convinced he could navigate the room with something short of total blindness, he edged his way inside.

THE SULLIVANS LIVED in a subdivision called Cortlandt Farms, a sprawling subdivision of about eight hundred houses on the north side of Raleigh, home to doctors, lawyers, bankers, all manner of folk who had done what they were supposed to do, who had studied hard and worked hard and had been in the right places at the right times at the critical moments in their lives.

The neighborhood was dotted with bright, spacious homes. Kids rode their bikes and played at each other's houses. Yards were meticulously maintained and greener than nature could ever manage on its own. A never-ending arms race of bigger and bigger grills was constantly underway, and when the weather was nice, the evening air was redolent with the scent of inch-thick ribeyes or marinated chicken sizzling on cast-iron grates. It was a lively neighborhood with an active social life, progressive dinners and parties marking Independence Day, Halloween, Christmas.

The Panic had hit during a glorious springtime in central North Carolina. High pressure was locked in over the area, delivering beautiful day after beautiful day as the world descended into chaos. The air was clear and bright and the buildings shimmered against the clear blue sky. The night skies were black and moonless, and as the power grids started failing, the starshine grew brighter and stronger. Every night, after Gavin was in bed, he and Sarah would take a break from their preparations and look skyward. The stars shone down like a million specks of diamond scattered across a velvet blanket. They kept Gavin as isolated as they could, not lying to him exactly, but downplaying the extent of the ever-deepening horror as the Orchid virus spread unchecked.

It had happened quickly, so quickly that no one was quite sure where exactly the outbreak had originated, and the initial response had been flat-footed. The Centers for Disease Control in Atlanta was a popular suspect, with many believing that the virus had escaped the CDC's Level 4 labs, where the feds kept their nastiest bugs. Others believed the outbreak had started at Fort Detrick in Maryland, where the U.S. Army Medical Research Institute for Infectious Disease was supposed to be working on ways to protect the nation from biological attack. The conspiracy theorists (and who was to say they hadn't been right) went insane on the Internet, before it had gone down in mid-April, claiming that the military had developed a serum to create supersoldiers and then left a vial of it on the subway or some crazy shit like that.

In the end, it hadn't really mattered a whole lot, because once the virus was loose, it spread like a wildfire in drought-stricken grasslands. States began closing their borders and exercising dominion over their military bases.

Even now, more than two years after the last documented case of Orchid, scientists still didn't understand much about the virus. The incubation period was short, the virus' victims remaining asymptomatic for only one to three hours. Then the body temperature would skyrocket to one hundred and five degrees, give or take a tenth or two, where it remained for the balance of the symptomatic period. Orchid triggered violent behavior in its hosts after the asymptomatic period ended, but no one knew what the basic foundation of it was. Infected persons spread the virus through bites and scratches, but unlike the undead zombies of pop culture, Reds did not eat their victims. Blood tests of Reds captured alive early on revealed huge spikes in adrenalin and noradrenalin, and interviews with them revealed that they believed that every living creature they encountered presented an immediate threat to their lives and that they had no choice but to attack first. That they remembered their actions was the worst part of it. Suicide had become a significant public health crisis. Thousands of Redeyes had taken their own lives since, as many as several hundred a day.

No one had been able to explain conclusively why the Reds didn't attack each other, although some posited that the impossibly high levels of adrenalin made them virtually invisible to one another and that they only attacked living things whose adrenalin levels were wildly disproportionate to their own. Again, these were merely theories; nothing had been proven. No one knew why Redeyes flocked together and attacked in swarms.

Ben's house sat in a cul-de-sac, the second one in from the right. It was a three-thousand-square-foot colonial that they'd owned for four years, purchased when he'd made partner, when Gavin was eight. He'd loved the house from the moment they'd set eyes on it, just as they'd been about to give up the house search and fire their agent after seeing fifty houses and hating every one. The yard was a bit of a pain in the ass to maintain, a good two hours to mow, and their plans for an organic vegetable garden had never quite gotten off the ground; after all, who enjoyed spending three months working to get a dozen cherry tomatoes? Other than that, the house was everything they'd hoped it would be. It was home.

By early April, the Sullivan house was well fortified, the fruits of Ben's and Sarah's labors, hours upon hours of boarding up windows and doors, digging a long ditch around the perimeter of the house, sleeping in shifts so someone could be awake at all times. But it had become a citadel, a place they may well die in. In the early days, neighbors had joined forces and built blockades at the subdivision's two vehicular access points, but squabbling erupted as people argued about this one pulling their weight or that one dicking around and in the end, of course, it all fell apart anyway when Greg Brown, the medical supply salesman down the street became symptomatic inside the safe zone. He ended up infecting every member of his family.

Ben and his neighbor Carlos had shot the five members of the Brown family when they had swarmed Ben's house. Ben had never killed anyone before that day, and he would kill many more people before all was said and done. He had shot fifteen-year-old Katie Brown first and then her brother and mother; Carlos had shot the patriarch, Greg Brown, and the youngest Brown, Lydia, who was all of seven years old. There was little time to dwell on the horror of what he had done because just like that, they were onto the next thing they had to do to stay alive.

By mid-April, it was simply too dangerous to do anything but try and survive. Schools had closed. The sound of machine gun fire crackled all day; helicopter gunships swept the skies, bombarding Redeyes swarms, making a whole lot of noise and busting up a lot of buildings but accomplishing precisely squat. The calendar had become meaningless because every day was the same. Eat. Drink. Kill. Survive. Sleep. And they were alone. By the end of April, the old ways of life were over. Tens of millions of

Americans were infected and in many places around the country, it was all-out war, a battle against an enemy unlike anything encountered in the history of human conflict. The Redeyes had no organization to speak of, no command and control. They had no strategic objective other than to kill every living thing in their path. Their morale was never broken. They showed no fear because they felt none. There were no supply lines to cut, no intelligence to be obtained via espionage. And the worst thing, the thing that made the Reds most dangerous of all was that they did not care if they won or lost because to them it was not a war to win or lose; it was simply what they were.

And their ranks swelled exponentially, by the day, by the hour, by the minute. A single bite, scratch, or exposure to infected blood, saliva, or any other bodily fluid was more than enough to transmit the virus. And how the streets flowed with blood, the final act in the great play that was humanity, from the time *Homo sapiens* took its first steps through the time of the Romans and Charlemagne and the Dark Ages and the Black Death and the Inquisition and the bloody birth of nationalism to a pair of World Wars and the Holocaust to the cold war and the war on terror, all blinking neon arrows pointing toward this moment.

"Let's just go," Sarah had said one night after Gavin was asleep for the night. They had just finished taking inventory. The water would run out in two days, the food in four.

"Don't think that's a good idea," Ben said. "We'll be safer here."

"We're not safe here!" she snapped, loud enough that Gavin began to stir.

She had looked so beautiful right then, he recalled, her face gaunt and tired and dirty, a mama bear who would do anything to protect her cub. He could not believe that it had come to this. That their 'til-death-do-us-part had come up on them so quickly and so horrifyingly.

"This?" she said, gesturing at their fortified encampment. "This is for show. They will get in here, and they will kill us! We need to get to the goddamn camps."

She was talking about the refugee camps that the Federal Emergency Management Agency was planning to set up around the country. But they weren't scheduled to open until mid-May at the earliest, if they opened at all.

But Ben had been stubborn.

"We're safe here," he'd said forcefully, so much so that he'd seen her recoil, maybe even feel a little afraid of him. He didn't want to leave because once they left he felt that there would be nowhere else to go, no other step they could take. They'd be abandoning ship for a shaky future on the road, where only God knew what horrors were awaiting them. But as the calendar flipped to May, and the water ran dry and the cupboard emptied out, Sarah was ready to hightail it out of there and take their chances on the road. The prospect of Redeyes surrounding them was bad enough, and now they were facing the twin specters of starvation and dehydration. But there was still no reliable news about safe zones. In Ben's mind, out there, they were as good as dead.

Finally, they had struck a deal. Ben would venture out on one more supply run, and if he came up empty, they would hit the road. Every day since he had recovered, he wondered how things might have been different if he hadn't gone on that supply run.

IT WAS BIGGER THAN A CLOSET, but not by much. Just above

Ben's head was the cool metal of ductwork and wiring running across the length of the low ceiling. A long table in the corner of the room was covered in assorted gear that might prove useful. As he hustled over to inspect it, his right foot caught on something, and he toppled forward toward the cold concrete, he braced his fall with his hands; they buzzed with pain as they smacked the floor. Wincing, he turned back to see what he'd tripped on, and he quickly forgot about the pain..

Four bodies, all decayed enough to make any sort of identification impossible. The size of the bodies and their orientation, however, left little doubt about what Ben had found. Two adult skeletons, their backs up against the wall, each holding a smaller skeleton on their laps. A handgun lay a few feet away from the larger body's hand. The three smaller bodies were entwined in an embrace. The mother had held them while their father had shot them.

Ben looked dumbly at the scene before him, his mind already going through its paces, trying to imagine how bad it must have gotten before this man had murdered his family and turned the gun on himself. His subconscious began filling in the gaps, caulking in the space constituting the things he did not know, and he could see them here, hoping to ride out the storm, realizing they never would. Perhaps there'd been a herd of Reds outside, scratching and clawing to get in.

Tears welled up in the beds of his eyes, overflowing like rain-swollen ponds. He wiped them away with the backs of his hands and set back to exploring the room. He and Sarah had had this discussion. If there was nowhere to go, nowhere to run, he wouldn't let the Redeyes get to them. She made him swear to it, and he did. It was why this partic-ular scene had affected him so badly. He'd seen countless thousands of bodies in the past year, of men, women, and children, more than anyone would ever imagine seeing in a million lifetimes, way past the point that it had any impact, long rendering him immune to the shock of mass death. His mind on auto-pilot, he retrieved the gun and tucked it into the waistband of his pants. He did it almost reflexively. When you found something of value, you took it first and decided later whether it was worth keeping.

There was a large backpack stashed in the corner, new and heavy with supplies. He looked back at the deceased family, closed his eyes in thanks, and lugged the backpack out into the storage room to get a better look at it. The pack was everything he could've hoped for and more. A brand-new internal frame hiking pack, constructed of nylon and polyester, waterproof and spacious. He even liked the color, red with grey trim, and he smiled a little at that, that he was still thinking about something as inane as the color.

He unzipped the main compartment, where the news was even better. Two large bottles of water, water purification tablets, a few MREs, a crank radio, a first-aid kit, heavy-duty flashlight, clean clothes, and other sundry items. He carefully re-packed the items and searched the smaller compartments, where he found more useful goodies. Waterproof matches. An envelope of cash. He eyed his old blue pack, thinking how it had been such a faithful friend to him all this time, and he decided he couldn't bear to leave it behind. He cleaned out its contents, rolled it up tight, and stuck it deep in the bowels of his new pack.

He cried again, breaking down this time right there in the back room, not holding anything back, his whole body racked with sobs; he was painfully aware of the pathetic sounds of his desperate wails and yet he couldn't stop himself as he thought about his lot in life, about the family in the storeroom, about the lot of the world in general, all these things barreling down on him like a F-5 tornado tearing up the Kansas heartland.

Tranquility.

Ellie Coleman.

This was his new mission.

After clearing his mind with a few deep breaths, he strapped the backpack on, picked his way to the front of the store and stepped outside toward his destiny.

16

T here was only one lead to follow, and so Ben had followed it.

Ben had hiked north along Route 288, which connected Chesterfield County to Henrico, the same county he had worked during his stint on the HARD Team. It took him half a day to cover the fourteen miles, but the weather was ideal. Temperature in the high forties. The sun felt good on his neck. It was a good walk because for once he felt like he had purpose, wind in his sails. He took the exit ramp onto Interstate 64 westbound, toward the mountains, and poked out a thumb. A mile up the road, a pickup truck pulled over and waited as Ben jogged up alongside it.

A bit of luck for Ben. The driver was a Redeye. The man was tall, a tangle of long limbs enveloping the steering wheel.

"Where you headed?" he asked.

"Nelson County."

"Hop in," he said. "Name's Paul."

"Ben. I can give you some money for gas."

"Don't sweat it," he said. "We gotta look out for each other. I can get you as far as Staunton."

"Perfect," replied Ben. "I really appreciate it. You sure I can't pitch in?"

"Just having someone willing to sit here without giving me side-eye is payment enough."

Ben chuckled sadly.

Paul eased back onto the interstate as Ben buckled his seatbelt. The man was quiet, tapping the steering wheel to some tune in his head. The color of their eyes was all the conversation they needed to have. Just two guys trying to make it in this brave new world. An unspoken bond between them all.

Two hours later, Paul dropped Ben off at a gas station inside the Staunton city limits. Ben leaned into the open window and tossed a twenty-dollar bill on the seat.

"Thanks, brother."

"Good luck to you," said the man.

Ben nodded, and they shook hands.

With that, Paul drove off toward his own story. The car receded into the distance, the sun flashing off the roof. When it was out of view, Ben continued south on foot, stopping at a general store and burning the last of his cash on supplies. He bought two large bottles of water, a bag of cashews, and energy bars. The proprietor eyed him suspiciously as he rang up Ben's items but said nothing.

He made it halfway to the mountain before it got too dark to continue; he spent the night in an abandoned farmhouse. He was exhausted and slept deeply and dreamlessly in the cupola of the barn. The temperature dropped into the thirties overnight; the parka helped keep things survivable if not bearable. There were no animals or people around.

He was up and walking with the dawn, connecting with

Route 56 at Steeles Tavern. By the time he made it to the parking lot for Maintop Mountain, the sun was at its peak. According to the dilapidated sign, Priest Mountain lay about three miles to the east. Located in the Blue Ridge Mountains in Nelson County, the Priest was a four-thousand-foot peak; hikers reached it from the Appalachian Trail near Route 56.

After a short break for a snack and some water, he hiked eastward to the foot of the mountain and began climbing. It wasn't terribly steep, but he was all alone; hiking wasn't the hip activity it had once been. There was plenty of walking back down in the real world. The trail had not been maintained during these past couple years and he got lost several times. But he finally made it to the peak around three in the afternoon.

The shelter was abandoned, the wood rotting. The ceiling had crumbled away in spots, but the confessional book was still there, just as Ellie said it would be. It was thick, much longer than he expected it would be. He spent the afternoon reading through it. The confessions ran the gamut from the silly to the horrific. Near the back, he began to see confessions dated after the Panic.

I'm sorry for what I did. I couldn't help it.

We told him she could not come back. We're too afraid she might relapse.

The last one was dated three weeks ago.

His eyes welling with tears, he staggered back outside to the edge of the cliff. He sat there for the rest of the afternoon. From this vista in the Shenandoah Valley, fall was redecorating the place like an enthusiastic new homeowner, adding splashes of color here and there, cooling things off after a long hot summer. Because who didn't like the crisp afternoons of autumn, the air tangy with the smell of burning leaves, the feel of a comfortable sweater that felt just right? These were good things, and in another life, he'd have welcomed the afternoon chill.

No one came.

He read the confessional book again the next day, and still no one came. Five days and nights came and went and now he was staring down the dark barrel of another night on the mountain, his supplies exhausted, his body weak, and hope unable to replenish either. Hope could be a stupid, naïve thing. There were probably millions of people out there right now, clinging to hope like a life raft, waiting for a rescue that for many would never come. Why did he think he'd be any different? He wasn't the hero of anyone's story. He was just another sad sack who'd caught shitty cards in history's saddest poker game. Hope was simultaneously humanity's curse and blessing because it kept people going until the bitter, bitter end.

If this didn't pan out, that would be it. He'd be a ship without a port, carrying cargo that would never reach its destination. It would mean that his story had ended, like a creek petering out during a drought, until the bed was cracked and dry. The prospect frightened him more than he cared to admit, and so he tried not to think about it. Until the trail actually did go cold, it wasn't cold. It meant there was hope, a goal, a potential paradigm shift. Another road to travel.

Hope.

The sun was setting again.

It was low in the sky, spilling its oranges and reds across the sky like a child who's knocked over his fingerpaints. Ben sat at the rock's edge, huddled under the thermal blanket that had been in the pack, wondering how far the mercury would drop that night, wondering if he would survive the night. He'd already spent so many bone-shatteringly cold nights up here, some three thousand feet above sea level, and that was after all that time on the road. Darkness was rapidly approaching; he was dreading it, wishing there was some way he could slow the sun's descent below the horizon. Spread out before him were the serpentine trails of the Shenandoah Park, looking dark and ominous, like a circulatory system about to blow out.

The rock formations cast long shadows across the network of trails, a perfect synergy of creepiness, as though the elements had worked together to make this as scary a place as possible at night. He hadn't seen a soul since he'd arrived on the mountain, and that was fine with him. These days, Mom's ancient edict to not talk to strangers took on a whole new meaning, especially in areas where the Department's reach did not extend. There were lawless lands out here, places in the shadows. Not places like the Haven, but something else entirely. True danger. Ben had heard stories in the camps about these mysterious outposts beyond the Department's reach. Rape, murder, human trafficking, especially of Redeyes. The most dangerous neighborhoods in America were no longer found in the inner city.

Ellie Campbell had been right. The view was breathtaking, hard and pure and unmolested. As though this was the way the world was supposed to be. Ellie had said this place, untouched by war and death, made her feel normal again, and it reminded her of why she needed to carry on in this new world. And it seemed so dangerously convenient that he'd latched onto that bit of Ellie Trivia, because it kept hope alive and flickering, a single pinpoint of light in the growing darkness. Hope was sneaky that way, always finding a way to weasel its way back into things, make him think that there was time for one more play, one Hail Mary pass down the field.

He really knew very little about Ellie, where she lived, whether she was even still alive, but he had still hiked for days into the desolate lonely heart of Virginia, following hope, that cruelest of mistresses. The only thing that kept him from simply accepting the fact that this was a suicide mission, that he would perish out here, was that simple hope he could deliver the message about Tranquility, whatever it was. If he could do something, he could avoid failing yet again, yet again, the way that he'd failed Carlos at the baseball complex, the way that he'd totally and utterly failed Sarah and Gavin.

There was no Plan B.

He was so cold.

He'd failed again. Of all the poor decisions he'd made in his life, he'd saved the worst one for last. And this was the decision that was going to kill him. Had he really thought that he would find her here? For all he knew, she'd given up these little sojourns because she worked seventy hours a week on the HARD team, and maybe she didn't feel like traipsing across the badlands of Virginia for a quick view of these ancient rock formations. Or, knowing his luck, she did still come up here, but she'd taken off hours before he arrived. She'd be back in a week, just in time to find his corpse worked over by the vultures and the foxes and raccoons that called this place home, and she would wonder what had happened, what had he been doing here.

He felt bad for her.

"Tranquility," he said aloud, and he jumped, startled by the sound of his voice, weak and scratchy, like a grumpy nursing home resident, his last bit of alertness fleeing the scene.

An idea popped into his head, but it was like a housefly buzzing around the kitchen. He couldn't calm his mind long enough to grab a hold of it. He tried to sit very still and focus his thoughts, as though he were holding a rolled-up magazine over the little fly, ready to pounce. When he thought he had the idea locked in his sights, dropped the mental hammer, but it slipped away from him, the way the fly simply seemed to vanish when you'd just missed squishing it.

Stupid.

He ran his tongue across his lips and found them dry and cracked. His water had run out; he tried to remember how long the human body could survive without water. Three days? Four? It wasn't like he was expending a lot of energy up here, and it wasn't warm at all, so if he was dying of thirst, he was doing it slowly. Just more time to go insane before he died! Perhaps that was a blessing. Maybe he would be too crazy to be afraid.

He thought about the Internet, about how, once upon a time, he could just run a simple search for "how long can you survive without water" and his shiny laptop would spit out six hundred websites, each with a slightly different answer. He recalled its insidious way of eating up time, the way you'd look up and two hours had gone by when all you'd meant to do was write a single e-mail, the way it fragmented your thinking process, not unlike what was happening to him here on the mountain.

Sarah and Gavin. Were they still living in the house? What had it been like for them after he'd become infected? Whenever he considered this, he'd bump up across the mental equivalent of a ROAD CLOSED sign. Perhaps it was simply a matter of self-preservation. His mind wouldn't let him see the things that might fracture it, that might prove to be its unraveling. So there were no images of Reds swarming the house, pinning them down while they hid, wide-eyed with horror and misery and fear until they were over-whelmed and infected like him. He dug deeper, farther back, to happier times, his mind downloaded old images, cached away for future use. Of weeknight dinners and soccer games and a trip to the emergency room when Gavin had fallen off his bike and fractured his elbow.

He yawned; sleep was sneaking up on him again, a thief in the night, and he worked to fight it off, knowing what happened to folks who laid down in the cold, just for a minute. His eyelids felt heavy and gritty. He wanted to take a nap. He could sleep. He could do that. What the hell was he fighting to stay awake for, anyway? He pushed the thought out of his mind, quickly, the way one might escort an embarrassing dinner guest to the door. He was just talking about a little nap here.

He wasn't that far gone now, was he? After all he'd been through? But the idea seemed more and more appealing, the benefits outweighing the risk. Like an alcoholic thinking he can handle just one drink, hey it's my kid's graduation, I've been sober six months, what's the harm in a glass of champagne?

Time crumbled around him, and before long he was only able to distinguish night and day, and then grew fuzzy, as he wasn't quite sure if he were asleep or awake or whether he was even alive at all, until everything ceased to have any meaning at all.

SHORTLY AFTER NINE in the morning on the last day of his old life, Ben and his neighbor Carlos Farmer, a software engineer, headed out on the last supply run he and Sarah had agreed on. It was the sixteenth of May; the situation was growing more dire with each passing day, and news reports were becoming increasingly unreliable. One morning, there was a report that the military had dropped a tactical nuclear weapon on Chicago; that afternoon, he'd heard that FEMA had constructed massive refugee camps there. But he listened as often as he could, just in case there was wheat in the chaff of rumor and panic. But news outlets were still run by human beings just as scared as everyone else. Nothing made sense.

As the morning crept by, Ben and Carlos drifted farther and farther afield, the distance they were willing to venture from home in direct correlation to their level of desperation. Shortly past ten, they stumbled across the area's Little League complex, a huge sprawling tract of manicured grass with a dozen fields and a sparkling indoor facility that was one of Raleigh's crown jewels. It was abandoned, the grass in the outfield looking shaggy and unkempt, like an invalid relative who'd been forgotten about. A handful of bodies lay scattered about the outfield, but they ignored them. By then, dead bodies had embedded themselves into the fabric of daily life, like traffic or ringing cell phones.

Ben scanned the building with a pair of binoculars and found it to be remarkably intact. Cars were still parked in front, their windshields intact, the sunshine winking back at them like a pretty girl smiling from across a crowded bar.

"What do you think?" Carlos had asked.

"Worth checking out," Ben said. "We need the supplies."

"Hey, we need to talk."

"What about?" Ben replied absently, his focus still on the building.

"This is it for us," Carlos said suddenly, exhaling slowly, as if it had been something he'd been holding in for a while. "We're gonna try and make it to one of the safe zones."

Ben wiped his hand across his cheek, suddenly aware of the thick stubble that had grown in, his face as neglected as the baseball fields before him. Sarah had reminded him of their deal just as he left that morning. This was it. If they didn't come back with at least a week's worth of supplies, they would be on the road by noon.

"Yeah, I hear you, brother," he'd said, and he still chuckled about that one, that things had reached the point where he was calling his next-door neighbor, the guy he'd maybe exchanged a hundred words with before the Panic 'brother.' He didn't want Carlos to leave; they'd become a good team, looking out for each other. He was cautious, smart, and fair.

"We should go together," Carlos said. "The six of us."

Carlos and his wife Lisa had a six-year-old daughter named Cassie.

"Let's deal with this later," Ben said.

Carlos nodded.

They drew their weapons and hustled across the four fields, easing to a stop in the parking lot. The sun beat down hard on Ben's neck as they ran. They searched the cars first, starting with the six unlocked ones first, finding a few choice bits. A flashlight. Half a pack of cigarettes. Matches. A six-pack of bottled water. Those went into Ben's blue backpack. He debated breaking the windows on the locked cars but worried about drawing attention from Reds or uninfected bandits. From the cover of an abandoned SUV, they watched the building, silent, unmoving, a sleeping monster sunning itself. In the distance, the crackle of automatic weapons.

"Still want to do this?" Carlos asked.

"Not really," he replied. "But the pickings are getting slim."

His gut was telling him that they should skedaddle right then and there, that it was all about to go south. But he didn't listen. At the critical moment in his life, when all the useless layers of polite living had been scraped away like old paint, leaving his true self behind, he'd ignored his own personal emergency broadcast system the same way he'd used to mute it on television when that terrible screech would interrupt a basketball game or that reality dating show that he and Sarah had enjoyed watching and mocking together.

"In and out," Ben said.

Carlos nodded firmly, his eyes set on the front doors. He drew it open slowly, training his weapon on the dim corridor just beyond the doors shimmering in the late spring sun. Ben crouched down and shuffled inside. His gun was up, his heart thudding away crazily in his chest. Behind him, the door squealed shut as Carlos followed him inside.

The reception desk's shadow ensconced the room in a gray gloom. A long dark corridor stretched away to the left, down to a large utility room. The staff had stored bottled water and snacks for the baseball camps held at the facility; if there were any extra supplies lying around, they would be down that way.

But it was dark, and fear tightened around his airway like a python. He couldn't remember the last time he'd felt this skittish on a supply run, as if they were blowing through their hourglass of good fortune, the tiny grains of sand slipping away with each passing day. He took a deep breath, tried to relax, and that was when the pod of Redeyes attacked. The glass behind them shattered; three of them were fighting their way in, a fourth one lay face down, her body impaled on large shards of glass from the door.

Carlos opened fire first, his fusillade wildly off the mark.

The first two Redeyes were on him in seconds, and he crumpled to the ground under their assault, curling into a ball, throwing his hands over his head. The violence was pure and huge, like a star exploding. The first Red, a teenage boy dressed in a soccer jersey and dirty boxer shorts, wrapped his skinny fingers around Carlos's throat and slammed his head into the ground like it was a wrecking ball. The second one, a middle-aged woman with a chunk of cheek torn out, the wound deep enough to expose her jawbone, leapt onto Carlos's torso and bit into his face while Carlos tried desperately but fruitlessly to wriggle free as she held on like a rodeo cowboy.

The third Red came at Ben like a heat-seeking missile locked onto its target. She was an attractive young woman, in her mid-twenties, dressed in tight athletic shorts and a bikini top. Her hair was tied off in a ponytail; her fresh face was tanned and unlined and relatively unscathed, as though she'd only recently become infected. Ben got one shot off, one good shot that buried itself into the girl's midsection, but it was too late. Before the bullet brought her down, her hands, radiating with heat, gripped his right arm like a vise. He twisted away from her, but he couldn't break her grip or her singular focus to kill, despite outweighing her by at least fifty pounds

Even as Ben struggled against the girl's relentless onslaught, he could hear her cohorts tearing Carlos apart. Ben's neighbor and friend had screamed only once, a guttural howl cut short when his head had hit the concrete floor hard enough to crack his skull, a thick, splintering sound. But nothing distracted the girl from her goal of ending Ben's life. He couldn't believe how much energy he'd expended to keep her teeth away from his arm, how hard it was to do the one thing he had to do stay alive.

As he swung his left arm wildly, raining blow after blow against the side of her head, he began to form a plan. He had to get out of the building before the other two turned their attention toward Ben as well. His blows were landing, but she simply would not let go. Then it came to him. He rushed the gaping hole in the ruined double doors, aiming for the post, hoping the impact would jar her loose just as he broke free of the building.

He crashed through the opening, twisting counterclockwise as the girl slammed into the post, and for a wondrous moment, he was free. Her grip came loose, and he turned to flee. As he did so, he slipped on the carpet of broken glass left behind by the Redeyes' breach of the door, his right foot sliding out behind him. It all happened in slow motion. He looked back over his shoulder just in time to see the girl sink her teeth into his exposed right heel, just below the cuff of his pant leg. It was like a pinch at first, not totally unpleasant, followed by the sensation of meat being torn from a T-bone.

Time slowed down, and a deep, wondrous calm washed over Ben like a summer rainshower. For that moment, that brief instant, he was free, and he wasn't afraid anymore. All the struggle and the terror and misery, the endless battle to stay alive was now behind him. Then the moment passed and the reality of what had happened slammed into him like a drunk driver running a red light. She'd BITTEN him, this cute little thing upon whom his gaze might have lingered if he'd seen her at the gym had bitten him and dropped a gigantic viral bomb in his leg, and now he was going to become one of THEM. She let go of him briefly, perhaps to get a better grip on him. As she turned over, he kicked at her hard with his wounded leg. His foot caught her square in the throat; and her windpipe crumpled like a cheap cardboard box. She flopped over on her back, clawing at her neck, unable to draw in a breath, and he watched her for a moment with the pride only the victor in mortal combat can feel. Low guttural sounds emanated from her throat as she suffocated to death in the vestibule.

And then he remembered what she had done, and he was having a hard time breathing himself. He staggered to his feet and stumbled out into the parking lot, acutely aware of the burning sensation in his calf. Made his way across the lot and onto the baseball diamonds, where he thought about his own playing days when he'd been a boy. He ran and ran and ran, until finally, he had to stop, right at home plate on the main field, where he bent over and vomited. As his body bucked and heaved, he had a hard time focusing on anything but the bite, but the terrible gift that the pixie had just given him. He ran some more, deep into a thicket of pines across the street from the complex, stopping only when his stomach began to roil again, and he paused at the base of a tall pine, placing his hand on the cool, rough bark of the trunk.

In the shadow of the trees, where the air was cool and fragrant like an eternal Christmas tree lot, he screamed. A long, deep howl, drawing from the capped wells of every mistake he'd ever made, every regret he'd ever had, every wrong he'd ever committed, combining together into the biggest fuck-up of his life. It filled his ears, echoing through the trees, which stood quietly as they had for two hundred years, decidedly uninterested in the affairs of one Ben Sullivan, whose existence on the planet had been but a tiny insignificant thing and was now over. It was like his brain was reformatting itself, deleting years of old files and memories and images that he wasn't going to be needing anymore.

Why had they gone inside that building? Were they that desperate? They hadn't needed to go in there, had they? No, it was his own carelessness, his own stupid laziness. Carlos's announcement had distracted him. He cried, his mind simply cycling through its basest emotions, looking for one that might calm him down before he totally snapped and broke with reality. He wept like he'd never wept before. The sobs were huge and uncontrollable, His body shivered, as if he'd stepped out of a hot shower on a frigid morning.

As he cried, he twisted his foot on its instep to check the wound. The girl had torn out a small hunk of flesh from the calf, like a golfer leaving a divot in the fairway. Blood had smeared across his lower leg, soaking into his right sock and sneaker. Reflexively, he pressed a hand against the ruined flesh, and he watched as the still-flowing blood seeped through his fingers, like water breaking through a failed dam. And that's what had happened. His personal dam, the one he'd built up against this shitty world around them had failed, and the monsters were breaking through.

Home. He had to get home. Sarah was a nurse and could amputate his leg below the knee before the virus took hold. It could work. They had to try, right? They had to try. He checked his surroundings; he was less than three miles from the house. He could be there within thirty to forty-five minutes. Still within the asymptomatic window. Then Sarah could get to work. It would be awful, of course, bloody and horrific and awful, but she would do it because the alternative was Ben turning into one of them.

The tears stopped after a bit because he was too physically exhausted to create any more.

His legs gave out on him, and his body crumpled to the base of its trunk. He sat there in the woods. He ran his hands through the loose soil around him, squeezing clumps of the dark dirt, feeling its damp chill against his fingers. Around him, the trees were alive with birdsong, the air rich with the scent of pine, and he was reminded of his childhood home in mid-December as the smell of the Christmas tree had begun permeating everything. Just another day on planet Earth. His last day.

He ran.

A SCRAPING NOISE BEHIND him broke his trance. He'd become so accustomed to the silence, thick and heavy, that it sounded like a gunshot, but he wasn't alarmed. He wondered if that was because he'd finally reached the point of no return, that whatever was going to happen was going to happen. The die was cast.

A hooded figure on the trail, small in build, eyeing him carefully. He had no idea if this person meant him harm, but he was not afraid.

"Ben," she said.

"Hi," he said. He started laughing. It sounded stupid and wonderful at the same time. He didn't know why he was laughing. Maybe a sign of clarity. Or insanity.

"You're famous."

Then he passed out.

17

Ellie spent their first thirty minutes together warming him back up. She pressed handwarmers in his palms and fed him soup from her insulated container. When he stopped shivering, they started back for the car. Ben's time on the mountain had weakened him, and he had to take frequent rest breaks as they covered the rocky, undulating trail back down the mountain and to the trail that fed back to the parking lot. His mind felt foggy, cloudy; he would not have survived another night on the mountain. He hadn't noticed how out of it he was until he saw her in action, as he'd had nothing to compare it to. If you're the only person in the room, you look perfectly sane.

She seemed strong, clear of mind, clear of purpose. She encouraged him gently, placed her hand on the small of his back as they negotiated particularly tricky stretches of trail. At one point, he stumbled over a thick partially exposed tree root and crashed to the ground in a heap. Despite his weakened condition, he felt hot with shame.

"Let's take a break here for a minute," she said. He searched her tone for a hint of judgment or disappointment, the way a food critic might linger over a bite to note a particular spice or herb, but found none.

"How long have you been out here?" she asked. She handed him a water bottle from her pack. He took it and sat down on a rounded boulder on the edge of the trail.

"A few days," he said.

He cracked open the bottle and took a long pull. The water was pure bliss against his dry, chapped lips, and he didn't care that the water's chill made him shiver even harder than he already was. He was badly dehydrated; his body absorbed the water like a dry sponge.

"I kind of lost track of time."

"How long were you planning to wait? I mean, I'm guessing you were waiting for me, right, or did I just embarrass myself?"

"As long as I could. I don't have anywhere else to go."

He finished the bottle with another long pull and tossed it to the ground.

"Really?" she said sharply. "We don't have enough problems we've got to keep polluting?"

He looked up at her with a flush of embarrassment, as though he was a kid who'd just been stealing cigarettes from his mother's purse. She held out her hand; he bent over, picked up the bottle and handed it to her. She tucked the bottle back into her pack without a word.

"You know, I almost didn't come up here today," she said.

"Still on the crew?"

"Yes," she said. "It was a bad week. We found, um..."

She stopped and took a deep breath.

"Anyway," she said after gathering her thoughts and deciding to keep them locked down. "It was a bad week. I was just going to sleep it off, but I couldn't sleep."

"Lucky for me," he said.

"Indeed."

"What did you mean when you said I was famous?"

"They plastered your face all over the news broadcasts, the story being that it was your tip that led to the camps being dissolved."

Ben sighed deeply.

"So dumb of me. I really thought they were planning an attack."

"You sure you weren't just looking out for number one?"

He looked down at his shoes.

"I don't know. Maybe."

"So you were there that night," she said. "At the farm."

"Yeah," he said. The images from the night came flooding back. The flames consuming the house like a fiery demon, the sound of the automatic weapons shattering the still night.

"We weren't quite sure about that," she said. "We didn't know if you'd decided to stay or go."

"Did Luke make it?"

She shook her head.

"I'm sorry."

"Me too," she said. "He was a good man. Better than that lunatic Thompson."

He looked over at her, puzzled, and she must have picked up on his confusion.

"It's not that we didn't agree on the big picture," she said. "It's just that..."

Her voice trailed off.

"He took a lot of unnecessary chances."

"Why did they do it?" Ben asked.

"There are things you didn't know about the Haven," she said.

"Like what?"

"Like its real purpose."

She laughed softly.

"Doesn't that sound all conspiratorial and mysterious?"

Ben smiled.

"This is a war, Ben. Not every person who was infected hates the Department, and not every uninfected person loves it. People are choosing sides."

"Okay."

"For the most part, though, the world is lined up against you," she continued. She said it matter-of-factly, without judgment or passion. "But you knew that."

He nodded.

"Hate crimes are commonplace, and the Department does nothing. The Volunteers do nothing. A dozen Reds are murdered every day. The world just turns the other cheek."

Her voice cracked a little at the end of the sentence.

"Couple weeks ago, this seventeen-year-old kid got jumped by a mob down in Virginia Beach. He was panhandling for food for himself and his sister. They dragged him into an alley and beat him to death. When they were done with him, he looked like roadkill."

Ben simply shook his head in disgust.

"Before the attack on the Haven," she went on, changing the subject, "we'd become the point group for a growing band of freedom fighters, if you will," she said. "The world is in bad shape, and the Department is just making things worse. Everything they do is designed to perpetuate this so-called state of emergency. They want the world to think that those who were infected will be dangerous until the end of time. You see the signs, right?"

Ben nodded, thinking about the DRR signs plastered all over the place.

AVOIDING ORCHID TESTING IS A CRIME

"You know why they do that? They're trying to scare people into thinking the virus is just waiting to come back."

"Well, we don't know that we won't relapse," Ben said. "I worry about it all the time."

"It's bullshit," she said. "That's what they want you to think. It's been almost three years since the last documented case of Orchid. What better way to scare people into obedience than to make them think that they themselves are the potential problem?"

"I'd never thought of it that way," he said. "But why? To what end?"

"Want to hear something crazy?"

"Sure," he said, even as he wasn't sure that he wanted to hear it at all.

"Every day, people turn themselves in, claiming that they're experiencing Orchid symptoms. They want to be good little citizens, and they support the Department efforts to maintain order. There's an Unauthorized Pregnancy Reporting Hotline. That's why they're always showing footage from the Panic on that goddamn network."

The virus had been devastating to babies in utero. The jury was still out on the effect of the virus on babies conceived after the mothers had recovered, the women's bodies still lit up with Orchid antibodies. No one knew if the virus would someday activate in the children or if they would be immune. For that reason, the government had banned reproduction in cases where one of the would-be parents was Orchid-positive and mandated termination of Orchid pregnancies. The penalties for violating the Unauthorized Pregnancy Control Act were severe indeed. In a remarkable reversal, the American Civil Liberties Union had taken up the pro-life mantle, arguing that the UPCA was unconstitutional and that the government could not order someone to undergo an abortion.

"Freedom One," she said softly, her voice coated with contempt and sarcasm as she said the words.

"They call it a tribute to the victims," she said, her voice hardening now. "I mean, really, we need to see footage of Redeyes killing people to properly memorialize the victims?"

She was getting revved up now, her voice taking an edge like a freshly sharpened knife.

"But again, to what end?" Ben asked. "What's the point?"

She smiled, a sad grin that spread across her face. He realized how pretty she was, and he immediately felt uncomfortable for thinking it.

"The Secretary has an incredible amount of power, and she and her cabal love having that power. Jesus, even the President is basically her bitch. I wish it were more complicated than that. But it's not. Remember how loud everything had gotten before the Panic, how polarized everything was? Conservatives versus liberals, that whole song and dance?"

Ben nodded.

"Well, that's all over with," she said. "No cable news wars. No protests or marches. Democracy, free society, it's a pain in the ass to maintain. A million different moving parts. Now the power is concentrated in even fewer people than it was before the Panic. People are just happy to be told what to do because in their minds, anything is better than we went through. It's the oldest trick in the book. When the people are scared, they'll listen to anyone that promises them and provides them stability."

An owl hooted in the distance, and Ellie turned her head toward the sound.

"We should get going."

〜

THEY MADE it back to the truck just as night had leached the last bit of light from the sky. Ellie had parked in a small scenic overlook cutout, providing a panoramic view of the park. Months of neglect had left the parking area overgrown with weeds as nature had begun to reclaim what was rightfully hers. That had been an interesting phenomenon; with a radically reduced population, many lawns and gardens and parks had gone unattended and had begun to devolve into their natural state. He wondered what the world would look like a decade from now.

She handed him a thermos of coffee. He drank it greedily and with scant regard for the skin on the roof of his mouth, which the hot liquid promptly sheared off. He didn't care. The chill had sunk deep into his core.

She started up the truck and a moment later, they were on the move, bouncing down the narrow dirt road. She drove fast, her handling of the Jeep pure and true. After about a mile, the trail intersected with the main road; she turned left and raced north into the darkness.

Their discussion had left his head swimming, Ellie pulling the curtain back on the way the world was now. He'd been so caught up in his own existence, the universe of Ben, that he hadn't had a lot of time to think about the larger picture. As brutal as Whitmore's destruction of the camp had been, it hadn't been all that surprising. What scared him was the notion that the government wanted to keep things this way, and worse, that the people were content with this new status quo. He thought about his son Gavin growing up in a world like this.

Calvin's last words suddenly came back to him. Jesus! How could he be so stupid? The *raison d'etre* for his trip to the mountain! It reminded him of one of the first cases he'd worked on as a new lawyer. He'd glossed over an important internal memorandum they'd obtained during discovery, one that devastated their opponent's position. He was so inexperienced, only schooled in the theory of law, not the actual day-to-day practice, that he had not yet learned that good lawyering was often nothing more than good-old-fashioned detective work. And had his supervisor read him the riot act on that one. He spent the next six months working ninety hours a week, fueled by high-octane terror that he'd be shown the door.

"I saw Calvin right before he died," he said. "He'd been shot, and he was just barely conscious. He did manage to say something just before he died."

She slammed on the brakes, and he felt even dumber now for not having already told her about Calvin's statement. The Jeep fishtailed and stopped in the middle of the road. The headlights cut a channel of white light into the pitch blackness.

"What was it?" she asked. She wasted no time inquiring why he hadn't mentioned it already. Another glimpse into the no-bullshit persona of Ellie Campbell.

"It was just six words," he said. "Tranquility. You have to stop tranquility."

"Was that it?" she asked.

"He died right after that, so I don't know if that was the entire message or if there was more to it. I didn't think anything of it at first. He was in pretty bad shape when I found him, so I thought it was just gibberish."

"But you don't think so anymore."

"No. The guy from the Department asked me about it. They mixed it in with other code words, asking me if I'd ever heard of it. I'd never heard the others, but I figure they were decoys, control words, so they could differentiate my response when I heard it."

She was staring at him, her eyes wide and fearful and yet full of focus.

"Now it makes sense," she said.

"What?"

"Why the Department branded you as a traitor to the Reds," she said.

"Why?" Ben asked. He was completely mystified. "Why not just leave me to rot? Or just put a bullet in my head?"

"It's hard for you to connect with anyone," she replied. "Maybe they did see you as a rebel, someone who might start a new movement now that the Haven is gone. Maybe they were afraid you'd become a martyr. But now that you've betrayed the Reds, you're no longer a threat. To be honest, they probably think you do know something about Tranquility but let you go anyway."

"But isn't that a huge risk?"

"Yeah," she said, tapping her lips with her index finger. "It does seem a little strange that they would let you go.

Ben felt self-conscious; a seed of suspicion had been planted in Ellie's mind.

"If I was really working for them," he said, "they probably wouldn't have outed me on the news."

"True," she said.

But she didn't seem entirely convinced.

"But you're right," he said. "They must have some hedge."

"When they let you go, how did that go down?"

Ben thought for a moment, pinching his lower lip.

"It was right after they'd busted up the camp," he said. "This Department asshole Whitmore was busting my balls about it, telling me how he was going to make me a star. I was terrified, to be honest. Nowhere to go, nothing to my name. I thought they were going to send me out with nothing but the clothes on-"

Lightbulb.

"Oh, shit," he muttered.

"What?" she asked.

Ben spun around in his seat and began digging through his new backpack, pawing his way to the bottom, where he'd jammed his trusty blue companion, a relic of his old life, a memento he hadn't been able to part with. As Ellie watched, he palpated the old pack's outer shell, the way a doctor might feel for a strange growth, *feeling, feeling, feeling, there*! Just inside the outer seam, near the bottom of the pack.

"Son of a bitch," he said.

"What is it?"

"Feel the bottom here," he said, holding out the base of the pack.

Ellie felt around for a few seconds before she felt it.

"What is it?"

"You have a pocketknife or anything like that?"

She did, and a minute later, Ben was cutting into the seam of the bag.

"Someone sewed this up," he said, pausing to examine his work. The stitching around the object was noticeably different than the original work.

He kept at it. Once his fingers had purchase, he peeled back the outer skin of the pack. *There.* A tiny cylinder in a pouch, sewn right into the dead space between the blue nylon shell and body of the pack.

"It's a goddamn tracking device," he said.

"Wow."

"What do you think?"

"A backup plan. Just in case their plan to discredit you didn't work."

"What should we do with it?"

"Smash it to bits," she said. "They probably figured you'd find it eventually."

"Yeah," he said. "No, wait. It's still transmitting, right? As long as it keeps transmitting, they won't know I've discovered it. I'll just leave it somewhere."

"How about now?"

Ben considered this. On one hand, he wanted to get rid of it immediately, sever any connection that remained between him and Whitmore. On the other hand, if they just chucked it in the woods, the Department would know in a heartbeat that he'd found it. It might be in their best interest for Whitmore to think he was still surreptitiously tracking him.

"Yeah. That'll buy us some time. Out here in the woods, they may even think you've hooked up with another Haven."

"Agreed."

He powered down the window and flung out the transmitter. It disappeared into thicket of tall grasses along the side of the road. A moment later, they were cruising back down the road.

"For the past couple of months," Ellie said, "we've been hearing chatter that the Department has some big operation in the works. I was actually supposed to come back to the farm that following day. Calvin didn't know much, but he seemed pretty confident that it was going to happen soon.

"When I heard about the raid, I figured he was right."

"What do you think it might be?"

"One popular theory is the commission of tribunals to hold Redeyes accountable for their actions during the infection period."

"Are you kidding me?"

"No, I am not," she said. "There's actually pretty big support for it. People have been clamoring for some kind of justice for the victims for months. People are still having a hard time accepting that all this death and mayhem was just a result of people not feeling very good."

Ben's teeth ground together, so tightly he could feel the muscles around his jaw line constrict. He could picture being hauled into some kangaroo court dressed in an orange jumpsuit, his arms and legs in chains, the outcome predetermined.

"What a bunch of bullshit," he whispered.

"I know," she said gently. "Not everyone supports the idea."

"How would such a circus even work?" he asked.

"Just like a criminal court is what I've heard," she said. "Even if they arrest and imprison just a fraction of those who committed 'Orchid-related incidents,' they believe that will help make the public happy."

"Orchid-related incidents?" he repeated, his voice dripping with sarcasm. "This Department sure does like its euphemisms."

"Don't they though?" she said, laughing briefly, a rich giggle full of joy and happiness, if just for a short while.

There it was.

The laugh he'd grown so enamored with during their short time working on the HARD team, the one he didn't think he'd ever get a chance to hear again. They were quiet a moment, as if they both realized they'd just had a nice moment and didn't want to spoil it with more discussion about the Department, about the challenges that lay ahead.

These brief respites from reality were hard to come by, and when you stumbled across one, you treated it with reverence and care. This had been the world left behind when the Panic started, and this is the world you want to get back again. Because if it weren't for these kind of moments, for the promise of more of these kinds of moments, than really, was there any point in fighting the Department? What difference did it make whether they dismantled every last refugee camp in the United States and they all vanished into history, the proof that humanity had been a terrible mistake, and the world was setting things right again, moving on without it. Because really, the world would go on, with or without humanity. If the planet had a preference, it would probably choose without. Such had been the legacy of mankind.

Ellie was the first to break the silence.

"I won't let that happen to you," she said.

"And what about Tranquility?"

"It could be nothing. It could be everything. That's what we need to find out. Soon."

18

They stuck to back roads in Ellie's Jeep, one of the old boxy ones, bouncing along the cratered asphalt. The interior was a washed-out gray, the upholstery torn and sections of it hanging down from the roof like party streamers. Despite its cosmetic flaws, however, its soul was intact, its engine pure and strong, the vehicle still tight.

It was almost noon, the sun high in the sky, the air clear and clean on this early October afternoon, a preview of the coming fall. The leaves had begun making their annual suicide plunges to the earth below. It had been a hot dry summer, and as such, the leaves were brightly colored. His head pressed against the cool glass of the passenger side window.

"So what now?" Ben asked.

The trees whipped by as they cut through the interior of Virginia; if he let his eyes un-focus just a bit, it seemed like they were in a tunnel of green.

"We need a place to hole up," she said. "And we need to figure out what Tranquility means."

Part of him, the small part that still didn't want any part of this fight, recoiled at that, like he'd inadvertently touched a hot stove. This wasn't his fight. He'd stumbled into the Haven by dumb luck as much as anything. He certainly hadn't helped the cause. And most importantly, he had fulfilled his obligation to deliver Calvin's message to Ellie. His conscience was clear. And his family was his primary responsibility. Nothing was more important than repairing the damage in the family unit. He could try going home again. If he could just show Sarah that there was nothing to fear, then maybe there would be some hope of reconciliation. If he could show her that he was, once again, the man she'd married, the father to her son.

And if that didn't work, he could just disappear, melt into the background of America, live out his days with some modicum of peace and dignity. Really couldn't ask for much else. Maybe he could find a job somewhere, somewhere hard and tough where people didn't want to live, apocalypse or no apocalypse.

But then he remembered how the Volunteers had destroyed that camp and the smug look on Whitmore's face as it had happened. The way he had ordered the camp leveled, as casually as a maitre'd directing his wait staff to clear an unkempt table for new patrons. It was always going to be this way for the Redeyes. Kept under the Department's thumb, used as propaganda to keep the population in line, the way you told children old fables designed to keep them well-behaved. Like it or not, this *was* his fight. Whitmore had certainly made it Ben's fight.

"How did Calvin even know Tranquility was even a thing?" Ben asked.

"We had someone inside the Department," she said. "I didn't know much, just that the person wasn't very high up.

He could snoop a little, maybe overhear things he wasn't supposed to hear, but that was about it."

She'd answered without pause or hesitation. Sharing one of her most critical bits of intelligence with him. For all she knew, Ben had cut a deal with the Department on the condition that he deliver the rest of the Haven, the last of the loose threads that needed to be snipped. When doctors went after a cancerous tumor, they excised all of it; they didn't leave anything behind. And so it would be with the Department. The Haven constituted a threat, one that could metastasize, and it had to be completely and utterly destroyed.

"And you don't know who it is?"

"No," she said. "Calvin called him Mercury. I begged Calvin to tell me or my brother who it was, in case something happened to him, but he wouldn't hear it. He claimed he had given Mercury his word. Honestly, I think he just liked the idea of knowing something the rest of us didn't."

Ben considered this, and they sat in silence as they continued east, traversing the gently rolling hills. The landscape was still green and lush, like an older woman hanging onto her looks with all her might.

"It doesn't matter anyway," she said, sighing as she said it. It was as if a balloon had deflated inside her, letting out a little bit of her essence, her hope.

"Why do you say that?"

"Mercury is probably dead," she said. "Obviously, they knew Calvin knew something about Tranquility. Probably wouldn't take them very long to figure out where the information had come from."

"Probably, you say. But you don't know for certain."

"No, I guess not."

"Maybe he got wise and went underground."

"I suppose that's possible."

"How did they interact with each other?"

"Calvin would leave him a signal."

"Where?"

"Calvin still had a little apartment he kept in D.C.," Ellie said. "Mercury lived there. Whenever he wanted to meet with Mercury, he left a chalk mark on the mailbox out front. They had this system worked out so they knew when to meet based on when he left the mark. I took that to mean that he checked the mailbox every day, probably at the same time.

"We could try to make contact with him," Ben said. "Maybe he's got more information about Tranquility."

"You really want to get involved with all this?"

"Look, I just can't take it anymore," Ben said. "What the hell else do I have to do? You're right. They're never going to let us live a normal life. They're just hellbent on driving us all into the ground. Reconstruction and Recovery, my ass."

A match had been struck against the dried-out husk of his soul, its contents desiccated, ignored, left to wither away to cosmic ash. He could feel it rising up in him, like a pot of water starting to boil, its contents starting to froth and swirl around. It felt different than what he'd been feeling the last few months, what he thought had been anger. That had been more self-pity, a metaphorical and half-hearted middle finger at the way things were. This, though, was different. *This* was anger. Some good old-fashioned, time to shove-it-up-someone's-ass anger. He took a deep breath and let it out slowly, like a pressurized canister venting off gas to relieve the building pressure.

He pointed at a pack of cigarettes lying on the console and asked: "You mind if I have one?"

"Be my guest."

He stuck one between his lips and punched in the cigarette lighter.

"I've just been stumbling around for the past few months," he said. "Thinking I was going to figure things out, maybe that if I just waited long enough, everything would go back to the way they were."

The lighter popped free from the cigarette adapter with a loud snap. He lit the cigarette and powered down his window to vent the smoke. The first drag burned his throat and made his eyes water and he tried to remember the last time he'd smoked a cigarette. Probably a poker game or night out with the boys a few weeks before the Panic. It seemed like such an unnecessary vice, a relic of a bygone era.

He let out a long plume of smoke and banged the inside of the doorframe with a clenched fist. The muted thud echoed through the quiet cabin of the Jeep. His hand stung, but it felt good. It felt good to feel something. His act of violence against the car door did not seem to faze Ellie Campbell, as though she'd been expecting it. She said nothing.

"They're no good," he said. "They've made this disaster their own personal playground. And you say people are just going along with it."

"Fear and ignorance," she said. "They're powerful motivators. People want to feel safe again. It hasn't been that long since the world was normal. In many ways, people are like you. They're just waiting for things to go back to the way they were. And the truth is, for many people, they feel like it's right there. They see construction vehicles and soldiers and they watch F-One every night. They see stories about new schools and hospitals and think we're right back where we were before the Panic, but the fact is we're years away from going back to the way things were. The damage was too great, too personal, too intimate to simply undo with brooms and sandbags and ribbon-cuttings. It might take a couple generations. Maybe our grandkids can have the world we once had. And this constant promise that a new day is just over the horizon simply keeps people calm and collected. No one wants to rock the boat the world might be getting ready to turn a corner."

"I'll tell you something else," she continued. "The Department has stepped up its crackdowns on civil rights. They want to keep things copacetic as they push this narrative that we're getting back to the way things were. And of course, they hang the threat of relapse over everyone's head."

"Of course," Ben said.

"It's the ultimate weapon. It keeps everyone suspicious of each other, watching each other for the first hint of infection. The Department has a phone bank set up to field reports of symptomatic behavior from the public. From what I hear, the phones ring off the hook."

"Pretty goddamn brilliant," Ben said.

"No one said they were stupid."

"And you think this Tranquility is just going to be more of the same?"

"No. I think it's going to be worse."

Ben took a drag from his cigarette.

"We need to stop it then," he said. "Somehow we need to figure out what it is and shut it down."

"What we need is a place to hole up."

"Leave that to me."

～

BEN TOOK the wheel for the second half of the trip while Ellie napped; he avoided the interstates, which kept them clear of the Department checkpoints but doubled the length of the trip. As the sun began to set, he negotiated the narrow, winding roads that ambled through a heavily wooded section of rural Caroline County, about an hour northeast of Richmond, twisting through huge expanses of trees, their skeletal branches stretching across the road like oversized Halloween props. Every now and again, a car would pass them headed southbound, the wink of sun glinting off the approaching windshield. He watched each car as it zoomed by, feeling the slight push of the draft as the cars passed each other, and wondered where it was headed, who was driving it, what their story was.

At a familiar billboard for a local truck stop, Ben slowed down and turned onto Route 815, a partially paved afterthought. Ellie sighed and sat up, taking in her surroundings.

"You get some sleep?" he asked.

She yawned.

"Didn't realize how tired I was." She rubbed a hand against the side of her neck and winced. "Great. Just what I need. Freaking stiff neck."

"We're almost there."

She took in her new surroundings as the road sloped downwards toward the large clearing in which the cabin was nestled. Fall was in full swing here, the leaves a kaleidoscope of oranges, yellows and reds, and for a moment, everything felt normal. Just for a moment. He tried to hold it in his mind like a snapshot, something to remind him that their world wasn't always littered with three billion corpses, that families made weekend trips to the mountains to look at the leaves and then capped off the night with a trip to the local pizza joint, the one serving up the big floppy slices that you folded in half to eat.

"Where are we going?" she asked.

"My father-in-law still lives out here," he said. "I need to see him."

The house came into a view a moment later. Ben's heart fluttered as he craned his neck to see whether Sarah's car was here, but Walter's pickup truck was the only vehicle in the driveway. He was slightly relieved that she wasn't here, but part of him was disappointed. He wanted to see them so desperately. Ben didn't know if it was the time of the day or the way the sun was draping its soft beams of light and splash of gold across the roof or if he was just flat-out losing his mind. It reminded him of their good visits here, when Walter would entertain Gavin and he and Sarah could hike in the woods and he would make his chili and they would play board games after dinner.

He puttered down the gravel driveway and rolled to a stop at the back of the house. Walter Clark was standing in middle of the yard, his arm curled around a large rake, watching his visitors pull in. Large, dome-shaped piles of leaves were scattered throughout the yard like bunkers, just begging for a mischievous five-year-old to scamper through and undo two hours' worth of work in a few seconds. The man was a cipher; it was hard to get a read on what he was thinking as his Redeye son-in-law invaded his solitary existence out here in the woods.

The engine ticked and hissed as it cooled down, Ben thought about all that had transpired since his last visit here. It was December, and he'd only seen them once, a few days after he recovered from his infection. He'd come here, begging Walter to facilitate a meeting, which he had agreed to do. It took weeks to get Sarah to agree to the meeting; at the last second, she had changed her mind and chose not to come. Sarah and Gavin had been too afraid to even be in the same room with him.

In the end, Walter told him that while he felt badly for Ben, Sarah and Gavin had to be his main priority. He would prefer that Ben not come around again, but he'd left the door open, saying that if he really had no other place to go, if it was a matter of life and death, he wouldn't turn him away. Ben had honored that request, but he would be cashing in that chip today.

"You planning on getting out of the car?" Ellie asked, her voice warm but firm.

He glanced over at her, nearly forgetting that she was there at all.

"Yeah. Sorry."

They alighted from the car in tandem, like a pair of TV detectives arriving at a crime scene. It was warm out, the air pregnant with humidity. The clouds were swollen and purplish, like a bruise against the sky. Ben approached Walter while Ellie lagged behind, parking herself in the V of the open door. Her elbow propped on the roof, she rested her chin behind her arm, concealing the lower half of her face.

He was conscious of how he walked, as though Walter would judge him on the way he moved, as if he were wearing the answers to any of the questions that his father-in-law might have for him on his shirt.

They sized each other up for a moment, not a long one, but long enough to make him worry that he wouldn't be welcome here. That as deep as Walter Clarke's reserves of patience might once have been, he'd finally run out of the stuff.

"Been a long time," Walter said.

Ben cut his eyes away, too embarrassed to hold the man's gaze.

"Yes, sir. It has."

Walt paused to wipe his brow with and handkerchief, letting loose a long sigh.

"What brings you by?"

"I can't see them," he said. "I know that. But you're the next best thing."

He tilted his head enough and looked over Ben's shoulder toward Ellie.

"Who's your friend?"

"Her name's Ellie. Listen, Walt, it's not what it—"

Walt held his palm up, cutting Ben off.

"None of my business," he said.

Ben looked around.

"Have you seen them?" Ben asked.

"'Bout a week ago."

His heart swelled and shattered simultaneously. He closed his eyes and he could see them, Gavin running loose in the yard, Sarah sitting in the old wooden rocker on the porch reading a book.

"How are they? How's Gavin?"

"Oh, you know," he said. He swatted at an insect lazily buzzing about them.

"No. I don't know." Ben said.

Walter wiped his brow with the back of his forearm.

"Gavin's having a hard time with all this. He doesn't sleep well. Sarah says he still has nightmares. He's taken to sleeping next to her. He's embarrassed, doesn't want to talk about it, but if he's alone in the dark, his mind, well, it just gets away from him."

Bad dreams. A parting gift for everyone who'd survived the Panic, something to remember it by. But Ben had convinced himself that his son had been immune to all that, that somehow, this thirteen-year-old boy had emerged from the Panic none worse for the wear. Kids were adaptable they said. They bounce back, they're tougher than you think. Their brains weren't completely formed, and so new experiences didn't clash with firmly set beliefs and fears and prejudices and so on, they didn't cause that wild internal conflict. He'd just roll with the punches.

Total bullshit.

Because guess what, Sullivan? All those times you told him there was no such thing monsters, well, turns out that was a big steaming pile of lies!

So here's the deal, son o' mine, light of my life, heir to my suburban throne. I know we spent your ninth birthday playing mini-golf and hitting the batting cage, and really, that was fantastic, but we've got a really special surprise for your tenth! You're gonna be fighting to stay alive. Oh, and most of your friends will be dead. Happy birthday!

"God, I want to see them so badly."

Walt was shaking his head even before Ben had finished his sentence.

"They're not ready," Walt said. "Gavin's not ready."

The memory of their first meeting was still as painful as the actual meeting had been. The looks, the stares, the silence. Standing in his bathroom, the one he'd re-tiled with his own hands, he'd felt like a stranger, an intruder.. His reflection in the mirror betrayed the battle his body had waged for months. The gaunt face, the sunken cheeks, the red eyes. He looked like a demonic heroin addict. No wonder Gavin had refused to hug him. Wouldn't even do the elaborate high-five they'd done since Gavin had started kindergarten.

Slap, slap, up fist, down fist, fist bump!

"It's just going to take a little more time."

Ben huffed loudly, deliberately. He wanted to see Gavin, even as he felt like he was about to go too far and exhaust the patience of the only host he was likely to see in the near future.

Reel it in, he told himself. Blowing your top is just going to make things worse.

He sighed again, this time softly, showing his assent to Walt's pronouncement.

"She can have the spare room," Walter said, gesturing toward Sarah. "You crash on the couch."

This was a big moment. Ben had no idea how Walt would react to seeing him; inviting them to stay was a huge step forward. It let Ben imagine a future with Sarah and Gavin in it, however briefly.

"How about some introductions?" Walt suggested. "I think I've been rude enough to my guest."

Ben waved her over, and she approached slowly, cautiously, and at first glance, he wrote it off to shyness. But as he watched, catching the firmness set in her jaw, the eyes sweeping the yard, he realized it was more than that. Her guard was up. She was in a new place and outnumbered. People were a lot less friendly than they'd once been, and nobody took anything for granted anymore. This made him aware of how trusting she'd been of him.

"Pleasure to meet you, miss," Walt said. "Walter Clark."

"Ellie Campbell," she replied, dipping her head toward him. "Nice to meet you."

They didn't shake hands, a social mores that had gone the way of the dodo during the early days of the Panic when the government had warned everybody to minimize social contact. The ritual stuck, and the handshake had largely been relegated to a historical footnote. Maybe it would come back. Maybe not. Who knew anything anymore?

Ben looked for something to say, but the well was dry, and so the three of them stood there quietly. A rumble of thunder to the west stepped in like an anxious dinner hosts whose guests weren't hitting it off. They all looked up at the sky in time to catch a bolt of lightning split the gray sky.

"We should probably head inside." Walt said.

19

F at raindrops spattered the ground as Ben and Ellie
detoured back to the car for their belongings; the
thunder increased in frequency and duration until
it was almost a constant roll. The skies opened up just as
they slipped inside the house. Fierce rain thrashed the roof
and windows as they set their small packs down in the foyer.
Walt was standing at a large bay window at the back of the
home, working on a pipe.

The air was rich with the smell of pipe smoke, which
seemed classy to Ben. A reminder of days gone by. The
living room was sunken, the furniture arranged around a
huge fireplace. It was barren and dark now, but a small stack
of firewood stood at the ready just at the edge. In its maw,
Ben saw roaring fires of old, the weekend trips, the holiday
dinners, and he forced himself to close that door, pushing it
shut before all of his old demons poured out and overwhelmed him.

Ben showed Ellie to the spare bedroom, just off the main
room. It was sparsely furnished, just a twin bed in the

corner and an old wooden rolltop desk pushed up under the room's single window. The desk was open, revealing neat stacks of papers and old paperbacks sporting a healthy film of dust. A bright yellow sweatshirt lying on the end of the bed caught his eye. It was Gavin's. He pressed it to his nose and inhaled its scent, hoping to pick up the smell of Sarah's laundry detergent or Gavin's soap, something of his essence that had been left behind. He knew Ellie was watching him, but he didn't care. If this was as close as he could get to his son, shame be damned.

"So this will be your room," he said, keeping his back to her. "Bathroom's down the hall."

"I appreciate your bringing me here," she said softly.

"It's the least I can do," he said, tucking the sweatshirt under his arm and turning to face her. "That time at the farm meant a lot to me."

"I guess the shoe is on the other foot now," she said.

"I guess."

He absently rubbed a sleeve of the sweatshirt, worn thin by Gavin's bony elbows.

"It's hard being here."

He chuckled aloud.

"What's so funny?" she asked.

"Doesn't that sound like the worst cliché ever?"

"I don't think so. It sounds pretty reasonable to me."

DINNER CONSISTED OF BAKED BEANS, corn and ham warmed over steno burners. Canned food was nothing to get excited about, but it tasted a hell of a lot better after it had been heated up, providing at least the illusion of a home-cooked meal. Except during his time at the Haven, most of Ben's meals since the Panic had started life in a can. He'd become quite the connoisseur of a can-based diet; just as important, he knew which cans to avoid, which ones might be harboring botulism spores.

Ellie and Ben set the table while Walt tended to the food. They sat at the small kitchen table as thunder and lightning lashed the house. Gusty winds blew curtains of rains across the roof and the windows. Ben felt a bit isolated here, alone in the woods, but there wasn't much that could be done about that. Walt had guns, and that was going to have to do. Even though he'd been infected, he had to remind himself that the Panic was over. Those terrible days, the fear, the horror, as the world had disintegrated around them like a child's sandcastle at high tide, were still fresh in his mind.

"Thank you for hosting us," Ellie said after they'd sat down. It was after nine, the house dark but for the soft, warm glow of the few lanterns that Walt had lit. Times like these, Ben was reminded how much they had lost, how different the world was.

"Glad to have you," Walt said, nodding toward his guest and then looking pointedly at Ben. "Never turned my back on family, not going to start now."

"Still, it's very kind of you," she replied. "You don't see it much these days."

"Well, it's a tough old world," Walt said. "Can't blame folks for looking out for themselves."

Ben wondered how much of that barb was directed toward him. He swirled a chunk of ham in a small puddle of baked bean sauce and took a bite. The beans were hot but good.

"So what's your story?" Walt asked Ellie.

"What do you mean?"

"How'd you end up with this yahoo?" he asked, pointing a fork toward his son-in-law.

"We met in the camps," Ben volunteered. He wasn't sure how much Ellie wanted to disclose about their relationship, about the Haven, about where they might be headed next. He was surprised by how easily he'd served up the lie, especially to a man to whom he owed so much. Why wouldn't he just tell him the truth?

"What were you doing in the camps?" he asked. "You obviously weren't infected."

Now Ben felt like a liar and a fool. Trying to put one over on Walter was rarely a successful proposition.

"What makes you say that? I might have a particularly good set of bunkers in."

"Oh, you get pretty good at telling folks apart after a while."

She was quiet a moment. Walter was no fool.

"You're right, I wasn't infected. My brother was. Our family's gone. After he recovered, we decided to stick together. We had nowhere to go, as our hometown had been disinfected."

Disinfected.

The word still made Ben shudder.

By late May, more than 100 million Americans had been infected with the Orchid virus, and although as many as one-third had been killed in the conflagration, the Reds had overrun many cities in the Northeast, the Midwest and on the West Coast. The war was being lost, so military commanders began carpet-bombing urban areas in a last-ditch effort to neutralize the threat. Efforts to preserve infrastructure were abandoned, and the war effort shifted to exterminating the Redeye threat at all costs.

The blitzkriegs had driven refugees out of the big cities toward the smaller ones that hadn't fallen under Redeye control, to the extent they controlled anything. Redeyes roamed in packs, a behavioral quirk that the government attributed to their survival-first programming, clustered together like metastasizing cancer cells and devastating the fleeing hordes of the uninfected. Many urban areas had been overrun, leaving the military with very few options. Disinfection was designed to eliminate huge numbers of Redeyes in short order, but it came at a terrible cost, including uninfected refugees who'd been trapped when the bombs began to fall.

She glanced at Ben quickly and cut her eyes back to Walt.

"Where's your brother now?" Walt asked.

"We've had some problems with the Department," she said, her eyes shiny and wet. "They killed him."

"I'm very sorry for your loss."

Ben looked down at his lap, where his fingers were engaged in a fidgety dance of shame and embarrassment. Here he was, placing his trust in Ellie, but he was lying to the only man, perhaps in the world, that he actually had good reason to trust.

"Walt, there's more to the story," he said, looking up from his hand. He heard the resolve in his own voice, and it surprised him because it had been a long time since he'd felt this kind of resolve about anything. Even his decision to begin searching for Ellie had been based mainly on the lack of any other options, sort of like his decision to go to law school.

Now Walt threw his own glance toward Ben. He could

feel Ellie's eyes on him, and he wondered what she was thinking. Had his admission of deception begun tearing asunder their new relationship, still as fragile as an embryo? He didn't know, but he had to take the chance. He couldn't keep Walt in the dark and expect to bridge the gap between him and his lost family. Walt leaned back in his chair and tented his fingers at the base of his chin.

"I didn't just tip off the Department about the Haven," he said. "I was there the night of the raid. I was there when her brother died. I thought they were planning a terrorist attack."

He felt stupid just saying the words. Two years watching the Department turn the country into a totalitarian police state and he'd sided with them, thinking it would help him turn the corner. Only after meeting the likes of Mr. Whitmore had he realized that he was just a thing to them, a device, a gear in the machine that was the Department. A disposable tool.

Walt started to say something but stopped, covering himself by tapping a clenched fist to his lips. Ben had known Walt long enough to know that he was simply sparing Ben's feelings, that he didn't need to say anything at all, that he hadn't needed to say, "Ben, you're a smart guy, just what the hell were you thinking?"

"Well, what now?" he asked.

"We think the Department is planning a big operation in the coming weeks," he said. "We need access to their headquarters in Washington so we can figure it out. I know you're no fan of the Department and I thought-"

"Thought what?" he snapped suddenly, his voice hardening like it had been flash frozen. "Thought you could get me arrested? Thought you could throw away everything based on your hunch? As it is, I'm taking a hell of a risk having you here."

Shame spilled into his cheeks. It was like he'd been slapped in the face. This he hadn't anticipated at all. Maybe he'd been fooling himself about what they could accomplish. Maybe the Department had embedded itself into this new world too deeply for anyone to change things on his own, and this was the way it was going to be. So even if they could figure out what Tranquility was in time to make a difference, a new Tranquility would be up and running in no time.

"No, I just thought..."

"You're unbelievable," Walt said. "I open my home to you, and you lie to me. Selfish prick."

Walt got up and stormed away.

TIME STRETCHED OUT LIKE PUTTY, and by two in the morning, Ben felt like he had been tossing and turning for days. Part of him thought about Ellie, but much of that involved his mind processing the five thousand ways it could end badly and fracture their fragile fellowship before they'd even taken the first swing at figuring out what Tranquility was, let alone taking it down.

He threw on a sweatshirt and went out to the main room. He heard a soft whimper coming from the kitchen. Ellie was at the table, silhouetted in shadow. Her hands were clasped together, and her body trembled as she wept. He froze, unsure of whether he should approach her, see what was wrong. Before he could settle on a plan, the decision was made for him.

"I'm sorry," she said, her voice thick with the congestion of depression.

"Sorry for what?"

"Just having a bad night."

"Everyone's entitled to a bad night every now and again."

"I try to avoid having them when I'm a guest in someone else's home."

He took a few steps toward her, slowly, not wanting to come on too strong, startle her.

"Weird times," Ben said. "Everyone gets a new set of rules to play by."

She tapped the table.

"Have a seat," she said. "You're just in time for tonight's meeting of Insomniacs Anonymous."

He smiled, hoping the darkness of the room concealed some of the goofiness that he was sure was evident on his face.

"How about some tea?"

"Sounds good," she said.

He set to work in the kitchen, and, after a bit of trial and error, found a pair of mugs and an old box of teabags in a cabinet high above the stove. Walt had many skills, but kitchen organization was not one of them.

He carried the mugs back to the table, setting one in front of Ellie. As the steam swirled from the cup, it caught a bit of the moonlight streaming in from the skylight overhead. The vaporous curtain shimmered in front of Ellie's face, and Ben couldn't remember the last time he had seen something so beautiful. He looked down at the dark cylinder of his own mug, suddenly self-conscious of everything.

"Couldn't find the sugar," he said.

"I don't use it anyway," she said.

He sat down across from her. The room brightened a bit as a full moon shone down through the skylights.

After the disastrous end to dinner, they'd all stayed out of each other's way. Ben and Ellie cleaned the table and the kitchen while Walt smoked his pipe in silence, no one in a hurry to revisit Ben's request for Walt's assistance. They left things in a state that could be best described as an uneasy détente. Ben didn't quite understand the man's sudden reticence, but he figured he needed to leave it alone, let Walt stew on it overnight. If he was going to help them, it would be because Walt had decided to, not because his fancy lawyer son-in-law had talked him into it.

"I'm sorry about earlier," Ben said.

"No need to apologize," Ellie said. "Thanks for trying."

She sat quietly, picking at a ragged fingernail.

"So what's your big plan?"

"Well, our best bet is finding Mercury and seeing if we can't use that as a way into R&R headquarters," he said.

Her eyebrows popped upwards as she heard his plan.

"Your own personal Mission: Impossible?"

He softly hummed the opening bars from the famous theme song.

"Pretty crazy, eh?"

"It's loony," she said. "But I can't say we have many other options."

"I've been racking my brain, and there just doesn't seem to be another way."

She nodded.

"Hey, let me ask you something," he said.

"What?"

"Are there other Havens?"

She sighed, and took a sip of her tea, a wan smile on her face.

"Supposedly."

"Supposedly?"

"Thompson occasionally mentioned other groups, but he always talked badly about them. Never trusted them, thought they were weak, corrupt. There was supposed to be a meeting of the leaders of the various Havens, but it never happened. What made you think to ask?"

"Whitmore asked me. One of the questions I was able to answer truthfully."

He took a sip of his tea. It was weak and flavorless.

"So what do you think of my plan?"

"It's insane."

"Hear me out," he said, holding up a palm. "The world is basically a giant third-world country these days. Security is a mess. The Volunteers are badly trained and organized. There are more cracks in the system than people probably realize."

"But they're looking for you," she said. "That's a big problem."

"They're looking for a guy with long hair and a beard," he said, pointing his thumbs at his face. "I get rid of this before we leave."

"OK, say you get in," she said. "What then? Hope you stumble across a Tranquility briefing?" This he had no answer to. Of the skills listed on his resume, espionage was not one.

"I'm going to have to poke around a bit," he said. "It's a big place. If I have enough time, I might be able to dig something up."

She pushed the mug to the center of the table.

"You're going to get yourself killed," she said, her eyes boring into him. "I just don't know if it's worth it."

"I thought you said we didn't have any other options," he said.

"Doesn't mean it's a good option."

He laughed at that, and she smiled in return, and then he felt stupid because her smile made his heart race a little. It made him think of all the things that had once made him feel happy and safe. It made him long for a future similar to his past, where he had been a normal guy living a normal life and not a pseudo-rebel plotting a suicidal raid to accomplish a relatively hazy and undefined mission.

"So what about you?"

"What do you mean?"

"Why are you still at it?"

"What do you mean?"

"Luke wasn't crazy about you being part of the Haven. And you don't need to risk your life for this. You could still have a life."

"Luke," she said, a sad smile sweeping across her face. "He wanted me to go live my life. He thought I owed it to him and the other Reds to live my life the way I wanted to, the way that they wanted to themselves. His point was that no one wanted to be a Redeye. Sort of like that old dumbass argument that being gay was a choice as opposed to how you were born. Like why would someone choose to be gay in our society?"

"Anyway, I'm rambling. The point I want to make, the thing I need you to know, is that I couldn't just keep living my life."

"Why not?"

"Because of what I did."

"What did you do?"

"I killed my husband."

A chill rippled through him. He wrapped his hands

around the mug, letting its good heat seep into his fingers. He said nothing, figuring that she would tell him whatever she was going to tell him in her good time and no one else's. She leaned over and blew across the top of the mug, diffusing the steam across the table. The scent of the tea filled his nostrils, and he felt tired all of a sudden. Not sleepy. Worn out.

"His name was Mark," she said. "He was an English teacher."

She kept talking but in a disconnected and distant way, almost as if she were telling someone else's story.

"He was a very sweet man," she said, her voice softening with each successive word. "We'd only been married a year when the Panic began. He'd actually been married once before. It was my first."

Ben lifted the cup to his lips and took a sip. It tasted weak and old and he wondered how long the bags had been kicking it under the cupboard, absorbing pipe smoke and mildew.

"He was infected on April 24," she said. "A bunch of us had hunkered down in the biggest house on the block, eight adults, four or five kids. For a week, ten days, we holed up, twenty-four-hour watch, supply runs in pairs. We started to think we had a pretty good handle on things, started to talk about where we would go when things died down."

Ben nodded while she paused to take a sip of her tea.

"A small group of them came at us just before dawn. They were so fast. That was something I think we forgot. Maybe we'd seen too many zombie movies. I don't know."

Ben nodded. He knew what she meant. As the crisis deepened, people seemed to have a hard time separating fact from fiction. The Internet was rife with tips and tricks to surviving a Red attack, mostly drawn from the slew of zombie movies and novels that had been all the rage, and nearly all of which conflicted with the advice from the Centers from Disease Control to avoid infection. People wasted time trying to kill Redeyes with head shots, forgetting that they weren't undead, they were just sick. They bled and died just like anyone else.

The infection's most unique characteristic was that the aggressive behavior only manifested itself in the presence of another living creature. Alone, Redeyes acted relatively normal, scrounging for food and water, looking to get home. Many experienced short-term memory loss. But the sight of an uninfected mammal activated the virus response in a way that scientists had never quite understood, and it remained a mystery that had never been unlocked.

"They overran the house," she said, her voice barely a whisper. "I'll never forget it. They must have seen someone in the window because just like that, they came crashing through. There must have been a dozen of them. One little boy, Evan, was asleep on the couch, and they just tore him to shreds. He was seven years old."

Ben heard a faint *plip* noise; Ellie was crying, the tears splashing against the worn wood of the tabletop. She cleared her throat before continuing.

"The fighting was just horrific," she said. "In this nice suburban house. Blood everywhere."

The depth of the Reds' rage was the hardest thing to adjust to. People simply could not fathom the violence the Redeyes were capable of, often to their fatal detriment. Ben closed his eyes as she continued recounting her tale.

"We lost nine people that night. Six were killed outright, the other three were bitten or scratched and became symptomatic overnight.

"Mark was bitten by our neighbor during this terrible

scrum out in the yard, a retired Army colonel who didn't do much but run marathons and drink whiskey. It was such a little thing, the bite. Just above his elbow."

She fell silent for a moment, undoubtedly playing a *what-if* game in her head. Ben knew what she was thinking about, and he let her run through it. A million little decisions stacked one on top of another, each domino toppling over until it reached its coda, his right leg on the business end of that woman's teeth. Ben had gotten good at training his mind to keep the *What-If* door closed, because behind it was nothing but trouble. But sometimes, the door creaked open, giving him an unobstructed look inside.

Behind it he saw a different life, one with Sarah and Gavin, one where they'd survived the Panic together, one where he and Carlos had had a bad feeling about the baseball complex and they had passed it by. Maybe in some parallel universe, another version of Ben had done just that, and he and Sarah and Gavin had survived. Maybe in that parallel universe, the Panic hadn't happened at all, and Parallel Universe Ben knew nothing of the horrible thing that begotten this version of Ben Sullivan.

"Yeah," she said, wiping the tears from her face with the heels of her hand. "Didn't even realize he'd been bitten at first. We took off, we just ran like hell. We'd made it a few miles before he started complaining about his arm throbbing. I looked at his arm by the light of the goddamn moon.

"It was just a little flap of torn flesh, right here," she said. She folded her arm, like she was flexing a bicep, and pointed to the thin bolt of flesh right at the tip of the elbow.

"At first I didn't think anything of it. Just a scrape from the battle. When I went to put the antibiotic cream on it ... that's when I saw the teeth marks. It was like getting kicked in the stomach."

She pressed a hand against her lips and shut her eyes tight; Ben's heart broke as the memory played back in her head again. No matter how many times she saw it, he knew, it would be as crisp and clear as the first time.

"And the worst part was that I had to tell him. He couldn't see the bite."

"I'm sorry," he said.

"He just kept saying, 'are you sure?' over and over, his voice getting higher and higher each time.

"I hugged him as hard as I could," she said. "He begged me to leave him there and run away. I just kept telling it was going to be OK. That was when the seizure hit."

Ben felt cold. The seizure. A violent *grand mal* seizure that killed one percent of the virus' victims and constituted the pathogen's final stage direction in the terrible play of converting its human host into mindless killing machine. He'd long wondered how about his own conversion, and he supposed that hearing Ellie's recollection was as close to it as he would ever get. He didn't know if hearing this play-by-play made him feel better or worse.

"I rolled him on his side while it was going on, trying to get him through it. I knew I should have taken off, but I just couldn't leave him there in the woods. I don't know what I was thinking."

"You were thinking about your husband," Ben said.

"Probably thinking he wouldn't come after me," she said, laughing, a cold, terrible giggle. "Stupid. Like I was a special little flower. Idiot.

"Once the seizure ended, his fever had broken, and I thought he was OK. He stumbled to his feet, and as soon as he saw me...as soon as..."

Her voice cracked and the last of her words trailed away like the sound of a car racing away in the night.

"He came after you," Ben said.

She nodded.

"Believe me," Ben said. "It wasn't personal. It was like every thought in our heads had been shut off, save one."

She nodded again.

"That's what people tell me."

"I suppose I was lucky that he had staggered away from me before he realized I was there," she said. "It gave me the few seconds I needed."

She took a deep breath and let it out slowly, as if keeping her personal horror locked up had been weighing her down, preventing her from putting it behind her.

"One shot, right in the chest."

"You had no choice," Ben said. "He would have killed you. And it wouldn't have been as merciful as a bullet in the chest. You did him a favor."

"A favor."

"Yeah."

"Know what else?"

"What?"

"After he died..." Then she stopped. "You know what really sucked? I hated myself."

"Why?"

"I was happy to be alive."

"Of course you were."

"How did that make me different than the Reds? Killing to survive?"

He shook his head.

"I don't know."

"That's when things really started going to shit," she said. "And I really didn't care all that much. I holed up in an abandoned hotel for a couple weeks, did what I had to do to find food and water. A front-row seat for the apocalypse."

"And then..."

Ben sat stone still, knowing what she was thinking. About a world where Mark was still alive.

"When I heard the first reports of folks recovering, I couldn't believe it. I didn't want to believe it. At first, no one believed them. Crazy rumors, the desperate hopes of a civilization on its last legs. But then I saw that Army colonel, the one who'd bitten Mark, back at his house, sweeping up debris, trying to get his shit back together. He tried to apologize, but he just couldn't. He didn't bother asking where Mark was."

She paused, took a sip of her tea. It had long since cooled off, but she didn't seem to care.

"When were you infected?" she asked.

"May sixteenth."

"Late May, early June, that was the worst of it."

Ben knew this, but he let her talk. This had been building in her for a while, pressure building up like in a helium balloon and she was finally getting a chance to vent it. The longer she talked, the more relaxed she became. The clench in her jaw, forever present since he'd met her, seemed to loosen, and her face softened a little, like twilight taking the edge off a harsh summer day.

"So there you go," she said. "My own dark secret."

She chuckled softly to herself.

"What's so funny?"

"A billion people out there with the same sad story."

"True. But it doesn't make it any less shitty. I'd tell you not to beat yourself up, but I gather you already know that rationally."

"Seeing you, you know, it's hard for me. You remind me of him a little. Sorry I was such a jackass to you on the HARD crew."

"No worries," Ben said.

They finished their tea in silence, each on a private island of contemplation and reflection. He couldn't imagine having to put down a loved one.

"So you really want to carry the torch for the Haven?" she asked.

"Yeah. Yeah, I really do."

20

Ben finally grabbed a few hours of much-needed sleep on the couch in Walter's small office; it wasn't much, but it was a high-octane snooze. When he woke up, his head felt clear, as though a terrible afternoon storm had blown through and left clear blue skies in its wake. He was full of purpose for the first time in a long time. It reminded him of his days playing soccer in college, and later, his days in the courtroom. The adrenalin, the fear, the way the world felt bigger and more alive, almost as if he could feel the pulse of the world, a current of good strong electricity buzzing along underneath the surface. He flung the curtain opened and took in the vista, a bright sunny morning greeting him.

After a quick shower, he trimmed his hair down to the scalp and wrecked one of Walt's razors removing his beard. When he was done, he barely recognized the man in the mirror. A fresh start.

He went out to the main room, where Walt and Ellie were watching television. Their backs were to him, and they didn't seem to hear him approach. Walt had his hand on the rabbit-ear antenna, holding it just so to catch the signal, enough to keep the picture from snapping out of focus. Ellie was sitting on the loveseat that was perpendicular to the screen, her elbows propped on her knees, her hands clasped at her lips.

"Morning," he said.

Ellie looked up at him, and immediately Ben knew that something was wrong. The clench in her jaw was back, and her eyes looked pained. He looked to Walt and saw in his face the same look he'd had the day his wife Nancy, Sarah's mother, had been killed in a car accident a decade earlier.

"Again, our top story this morning," a soothing female voice was saying on the screen. Ben blinked and turned his focus to the screen, where he saw a pretty blonde Freedom One anchor delivering a report. A BREAKING NEWS banner was striped across the bottom of the screen. But that wasn't what really caught his eye. The thing that had his undivided attention, the thing he had zeroed in on like a heat-seeking missile, was the thumbnail photograph over the anchor's right shoulder. It was a photograph of Ben, a passport picture, snapped long ago. The photo was at least ten years old, his face smoother and free of the lines that had later carved themselves in like riverbeds on the surface of a rapidly maturing planet.

"A massive manhunt is underway this morning for this man," the anchor said grimly. "Department officials have identified Ben Sullivan, a forty-year-old former attorney from Raleigh, North Carolina, as the prime suspect in an early morning bombing at an R&R job site in Norfolk, Virginia, that's left a dozen people dead, including six Volunteers. A Department official, speaking on the condition of anonymity, has told Freedom One that the Department has credible evidence that Sullivan, who was previously infected with the Orchid virus, had been acting erratically and may be showing signs of an active infection."

Ben gasped, a quick sharp breath, as though the F-One anchor had reached through the screen and punched him in the sternum. He felt dizzy, like he had stood up too fast, and he grabbed the top of the couch as his legs began to give out underneath him.

"If you have any information regarding the whereabouts of this man, Department officials are requesting that you notify your local Department office. He is considered armed, dangerous and infectious, so officials are asking that you do not attempt to make contact with Mr. Sullivan."

"What is this?" Ben said, not really to anyone. He heard the pitch and alarm in his voice, and he could only imagine what it sounded like to Walt and Ellie.

"What is this?" he said again, the sight of his photograph on television difficult to comprehend.

"I guess they got tired of waiting to see what you're going to do," Ellie said.

"This is bad," Ben said. "Why would they do this?"

"Because we found the transmitter," she said.

Ben cursed himself; they should've held onto it a bit longer.

"They still see you as a threat," she continued. "Now that they know there's no chance you'll lead them back to other Havens, they can just make you radioactive to everyone, Pures and Reds alike."

"So whatever Tranquility is," Ben said, "it's a big deal."

"Yeah," Ellie said. "It would appear that way."

Walt was staring at him, and he had a terrible thought. Sarah would see this. Gavin would see this. He would think his father was a criminal, a diseased criminal, a walking time bomb, someone who could singlehandedly unravel the fragile progress the world had made. If there had been a flicker of hope in the back of Sarah's mind about reconciliation, undoubtedly, this little news report would snuff that out like a sharp puff of breath on a lit match. He wondered if he should try getting a message to her, letting her know it was just a lie, but he wasn't sure he'd built up enough goodwill capital to spend. His words could fall on deaf ears. Ben turned his attention back to the screen, where the anchor was wrapping up the story on new celebrity Ben Sullivan.

"The Department is offering a reward for information leading to the capture of this dangerous fugitive. Again, if you see him or know anything about his whereabouts, we encourage you to call the Department."

Ben threw up his hands in disgust as the anchor moved onto a secondary story about his terrorist attack, something about how lucky everyone was to have the Department there to take care of things for everyone.

"I won't last a week out there," he said. "Every mercenary and bounty hunter from here to the moon will be looking for me."

"We need to get out of here," Ellie said.

"Do you want to hide out here?" Walt said.

"What?" Ben asked, surprised by Walt's offer.

"I want to help," Walt said after a long pause. "I was up all night thinking about it. If I turned my back on you, I don't think I'd be able to look at myself in the mirror. All my life, I tried to teach my kids the importance of doing what was right. Sarah would want me to."

"No," Ben said, shaking his head firmly. "I can't stay here. I'm sure they'll come knocking at your door before too long. I can't put that on you."

"The hell with them," Walt said. "I dare them to come here."

Ben smiled, not doubting for a moment that Walt would welcome a squad of badly trained Volunteers traipsing across his land, mainly for the opportunity to tell them to kiss his wrinkled old ass.

"We need to try and find Mercury. I don't know if it will make a difference. Hell, maybe it will make things worse, although I'm not exactly sure how that would be possible at this point."

"Are you sure? I thought this was a bad idea last night. Now it just seems like suicide."

"No, I'm not sure, but now I really have nothing to lose," he said. "Six weeks ago, my life was shit, but at least it was mine. I was on my own, anonymous, no different than any other poor Redeye trying to eke out a life in this brave new world. But now, what choice do I have but to try and figure this out?"

He looked at them, and he knew they were trying to come up with reasons why he shouldn't, why it was too dangerous, why he should just slip away somewhere, perhaps to Mexico or Canada, but he knew they weren't stupid. The Department had effectively made him a pariah, a man without a country. This was the path that fate had laid out for him. It had all led to this day, to this moment.

Walt was focused on his hands, which were engaged in a complicated bit of choreographed wringing.

"I'll be fine," Ben said. "Thanks for putting us up for the night."

"Yes, Walt," Ellie added. "It was a huge help. You're taking a huge risk just having us here now."

"You know me, Ben, before the Panic, I never had much use for the government. Look, I understand taxes and the need for somebody minding the store a little, but I always thought it had gotten out of control. Government studies on whether red cabbage or green cabbage is healthier. Gimme a break. And that's what this is. It's the same damn thing, just dressed in different clothes."

An idea bloomed in Ben's head.

"Walt, do me a favor," he said. "If they ask, just tell them we were here. It's easier to hide a lie under layers of truth."

"Way ahead of you, son," Walt said, his face brightening, if just for a moment. "I'll take any chance I get to screw these guys over."

A lull settled over the conversation like a dark cloud, and it seemed like there was nothing left to say, nothing left for Ben and Ellie to do but hit the road and simply try to do it. That was the way it was with anything, really, be it a big pile of laundry that needed folding, a banker's box full of documents that needed reviewing or a totalitarian regime that needed screwing. You just rolled up your sleeves and got to it.

"I'll start loading the car," Ellie said. "Give you guys a chance to say farewell."

"Nice to meet you, Ellie," Walt said. "I hope I haven't been rude to you. It's hard, you know. Seeing Ben. Not the way you expect things to go when you walk your little girl down the aisle."

"Not at all, sir," she said.

She grabbed their packs and stepped out the door.

"In some ways, you're lucky," Walt said.

"How's that?"

"You're smarter than these assholes. The Department uses cruelty and terror to cover its incompetence. This government has no idea what it's doing, and that scares me more than anything."

"Well, at least some things haven't changed," Ben said.

Walt chuckled, which exploded into a throaty laugh they

shared, and when the laughter had died down and drifted away, Ben was left coated with a profound sense of sadness, like the salt residue after a wave has crashed across the beach and retreated back into the sea.

"I guess this is it," Ben said.

He extended his hand, and Walt took it; then he squeezed Ben's shoulder with his free hand, a gesture of intimacy Ben had seen only twice before – the day that he had married Sarah, and the day that Gavin had been born. There were no hugs from this man, not even on an occasion like this one. Sarah had always said he was a hard man, and it was this hardness that had made him a good father, if not the most loving.

"You take care of yourself."

"I will," Ben said. He looked for the right thing to say to end things on, something deep and profound and moving, something that would penetrate Walt's soul and be amplified back to his wife and son tenfold and bury itself deep inside them so they would know for the rest of their days how much he truly loved them.

"Why did you come here?"

Ben pinched his lips between his index finger and thumb, looking for the right words.

"When you talk to them again..."

His throat began to close up.

"I'll make sure they know," Walt said.

Ben turned and just made it to the front porch before his eyes spilled over with tears.

THE BLACK SUBURBAN made its way down Walter's driveway a little after noon that day. Whitmore rode in the back, leafing through the thin dossier on Walter Clark. He was sixty-five, a retired Boeing engineer, a widower. He was the registered owner of two handguns, so they would need to be careful. Clark probably had more they didn't know about, as was often the case.

Whitmore wasn't entirely sure what he was looking for in coming here. He knew Sullivan would ultimately discover and discard the tracking device, but he hadn't expected him to do it so quickly. And there was no way to know whether he had found it or if he had just gotten rid of the backpack. Better to assume the former. Sullivan was a bright guy and would likely be suspicious of Whitmore's decision to release him. He didn't want Sullivan establishing a foothold anywhere. He wanted him to remain a ship without a port. It was a bit of a risk, providing him with the kind of name recognition he now had, but it was done. He just had to make sure that Ben Sullivan didn't metastasize into something bigger than Ben Sullivan.

Walter Clark was sitting on his porch in an old rocking chair, sipping a tumbler of something or the other. All he needed was a pipe to complete the watercolor painting. Whitmore told his security detail to wait for him in the car and got out.

"Mr. Clark ?" he called out, holding up a friendly hand as he approached the porch. "Might I have a word?"

"Be my guest," Walt said, gesturing to the empty second rocker on the porch.

Whitmore sat down, crossed one leg over the other, reached into his pocket for his billfold.

"My name is Alexander Whitmore," he said, flashing his credentials. I'm with the U.S. Department of Reconstruction & Recovery. I'd like to ask you some questions."

"About Ben."

"Yes."

"What do you want to know?"

"What he's planning."

"What he's planning?" replied Clark mockingly, his voice dripping with contempt. "He's planning to stay out of history's way. You good folks have ruined his life. He's a good man, you know."

"I'm sure he is," Whitmore replied. "I just want to make sure he's not getting into any trouble. Desperate times can make a man do damn near anything. Has he been here?"

"You know he has."

Whitmore smiled.

"Just wanted to be sure we were on the same page."

Clark took a long swig of his drink. The oaky scent of bourbon wafted into the air.

"Look, I don't care what you do to me, but you leave my daughter and grandson alone. They've had a rough enough go of it as it is."

Whitmore shifted uncomfortably in his seat. Jesus, some days, he really hated this job. He wanted to shout at the man. He wanted to stand up and scream and ask Walter Clark if he thought that Whitmore actually enjoyed doing this. If he thought that Whitmore actually enjoyed his new role as a latter day Gestapo foot soldier. Only a lunatic would like this job. But that didn't mean the job didn't need to be done. And better him than some no-necked backwoods ex-Sheriff's deputy who would get off on busting Redeye heads. Not because it needed to be done but because he would enjoy it. Because he would be afraid of them and he would blame them for his shitty life, as though his life would not have been shitty if the Panic had never happened. That's what Clark didn't understand. That's what most people did not understand. You did it because you loved your country and you wanted her to be safe. You wanted everyone to be safe. That's why they had come up with Tranquility in the first place.

It was to keep everyone safe.

Safe from once again having to go through what they had all gone through.

From having to again go through what Alexander Whitmore, husband to Lydia, father to Michele and Emma, had gone through.

The fourth of June. The date was indelibly marked into his soul like a cattle brand. Everything had unraveled by then. Everything. As an FBI agent in the Richmond field office, he'd known early on how much trouble they were in. Whitmore, his wife, and their two daughters had tried to make it to a military base offering refuge to law enforcement officers and their families a month earlier, but they'd encountered a flock of Redeyes on the road and had taken refuge in an old barn in Goochland County, about twenty miles west of Richmond. Redeye activity was high in the area and he called in for help; they had hunkered down, waiting for a rescue. They ran out of food and water, and things became desperate.

Then the worst kind of luck hit them. Emma developed a bad cough and could not stop hacking. The noise drew a steady stream of Redeyes toward the barn; for days, Whitmore kept watch from the cupola, where they slept, hoping beyond hope that the chopper would come. Finally, on the fourth day of June, a chopper, a dozen Marines on board, armed to the teeth. The soldiers lay down cover fire as the Whitmores made for the chopper. A dozen Reds followed them; the snipers could not shoot, as the family was in the line of fire.

They were so close.

Michelle stumbled and fell to the ground. Whitmore's focus was so set on the chopper that he didn't even notice the girls weren't ahead of him anymore until he heard Emma scream. The Redeyes were on the girls in seconds. Lydia went back for her daughters, a decision for which she paid with her life.

A pair of Marines jumped from the helicopter and hustled Whitmore back to the safety of the chopper, literally dragging him as he bucked to free himself and go back for his girls. He could not leave them there to die, but that was exactly what he had done. They had died there and he had lived, and every day since then, he had looked for a reason not to slide the barrel of his Glock into his mouth and pull the trigger. As the helicopter rose into the sky, he looked down at the swarm of Redeyes on his family, so many of them that he could no longer even see the three people he had loved best in the world.

Clark cleared his throat, loosening Whitmore from the grip of his walking nightmare.

"You okay, Mister Whitmore?"

Whitmore cleared his throat.

"Your daughter and grandson don't have anything to worry about," Whitmore said. "We're watching the house and we're aware that Mr. Sullivan is not welcome there."

Clark nodded.

"So where is he headed?"

"I don't know."

"Surely he must have told you his plans."

"He did not."

Whitmore pointed at Clark's tumbler of whiskey.

"May I?"

"Be my guest."

Whitmore took a sip, hoping that Clark did not notice

his hand was trembling. The bourbon burned down his throat and filled him with warmth.

"I don't think you're being honest with me."

"Okay."

"Would you like us to pay your daughter a visit?"

"She knows even less than I do," Clark replied. "She won't even see him. Too afraid."

Clark finished off the bourbon, using it to fill the empty moment between them. The old man was right; there was no evidence Sullivan had tried to contact them.

"I still think you're holding something back."

"You believe what you want," he said. "Will there be anything else?"

"Yes," Whitmore said. "You'll be coming with us."

Walter chuckled.

"Like hell I am."

Whitmore uncrossed and re-crossed his legs. Just two guys sitting on an old country porch having a drink. He poured another finger of bourbon; as he did so, Clark lunged at him.

A single gunshot rang out, courtesy of Whitmore's security detail.

The impact blew Clark out of his chair and onto the porch.

Whitmore drank the bourbon.

21

They considered using the back roads, skipping to and fro through the underbelly of Virginia on their way to the capital, but ultimately, the decision was made for them. They didn't have enough fuel for such a detour, and there was none to be had with barely a dollar between them. They'd have to press north on the main highways, risking entanglements with the Department and its Volunteers, and even then, there was no guarantee that they'd make it before the old Jeep ran dry.

Most of the drive was uneventful; as they approached the I-95 checkpoint just south of Washington, D.C., Ben drummed the steering wheel nervously with his fingers. Here the highway splintered into a tangled web of concrete threads that ran west toward the mountains, bypassed the District entirely, or speared toward the ruined metropolises in the northeast. After two hours of painstaking stop-and-go progress, the busy checkpoint came into view.

"I just don't see the purpose," Ben said, breaking a long silence. They'd been quiet for most of the trip, the pair steeping in tension like a pair of teabags in hot water. He felt antsy, edgy, right on the edge of trouble.

"Of what?" Ellie said, her eyes constantly scanning the road ahead, the mirrors.

"These checkpoints," Ben replied, jabbing a thumb over his shoulder. "What good are they? They can't watch every road in every state."

"Well, if they catch us, they'll have done plenty of good."

"True," he said.

"It's about control. The perception that Big Brother is watching."

Ahead of them, a pair of Volunteers were showing a fair amount of interest in an ancient blue pickup truck. One of the soldiers wrestled an elderly black man out by the lapels of his blue work shirt and shoved him against the driver's side door. A pale-skinned soldier, young, his face still a bright-red relief map of acne, spread the man's legs apart with the barrel of his rifle and patted him down. He was a big guy, corn-fed and Midwest-born, the sun glinting off his closely shorn scalp, his skin red with sunburn. He outweighed the driver by a good hundred pounds and was obviously not afraid to use it. As he finished palpating the man's lower legs, he stood up and gave the driver a little forearm shiver, ever so subtle, but enough to bang the man's forehead into the frame of the truck. Other than press his hand to his forehead, the driver did nothing to respond.

Ben cracked his window, just enough that the voices of the Volunteers snapped into focus, as if he'd hit just the right spot on the radio dial on a late summer night. As the driver turned around, Ben saw his red eyes shining back at him; even from a dozen yards away, they virtually screamed their color at the world. Ben shook his head. Black and a Redeye. Quite the combination in this new America.

"What are you doing?" Ellie whispered.

"Shh, I want to hear what's going on."

"So where you headed, old man?" the Volunteer said, his voice loud and empty and suggestive of a man who quite frankly wasn't particularly interested in where this man was headed.

Ben couldn't make out the response.

"He said he's just headed home," Ellie said.

Ben looked at her.

"I can read lips," she said. "My mom was deaf."

"Good to know."

The Volunteer slung his rifle over his shoulder and gestured to his colleagues.

"Search the car," he barked at them.

A pair of soldiers spent five minutes digging through the vehicle; behind them traffic continued to pile up like hair clogging a sink drain. They didn't seem to find any contraband, although they did confiscate a six-pack of bottled water and a box of protein bars.

"Your country thanks you for your contribution," he said, grabbing one of the bars from the box.

The pale soldier tore one open and took a bite.

"Ugh," he said, spitting the bite out on the pavement. "These are disgusting."

He flung the remainder to the ground. The man's face collapsed; all supplies were precious, moreso to Redeyes than anyone. Perhaps the man had been hoping that he could get through unmolested, or that maybe they'd just give him a hard time and then send him on his way.

"I'll keep these for my men," the soldier said. "No way I'm eating this nasty shit. But these guys are animals. They'll eat anything. Now get the fuck out of here while I'm still in a good mood."

The man climbed back into his truck, no doubt wondering how he was going to explain the absence of the food and water. Ellie tapped Ben on the shoulder.

"Hold your right arm against your chest and lean forward," she said. "Rock back and forth like you hurt it and you're in a lot of pain. Quick, do it now before they see us. Don't overplay it."

Ben cradled his right arm close to his body, partially shielding it with his left. As Ellie pulled forward in the queue, he focused on a spot of dirt on the top of his shoe, paying no mind to the soldier who would be delighted to learn that he'd detained a wanted fugitive, the catch of a lifetime.

Ellie wasted no time, taking the upper hand as soon as the soldier was in earshot.

"Oh, you're not going to believe what my idiot husband did," she said, her words coming like machine gun fire as the Volunteer bent down to talk face-to-face. The barrel of his rifle rested on the doorframe; Ben caught the black O of the muzzle eyeing them like a quiet but alert guard dog. "Climbing on the roof, trying to clean the gutter, and I told him to be careful, and of course, he slips."

"Papers, ma'am," the soldier said, his voice clinical and disinterested.

"And I'm there in the kitchen, thinking that he's going to get himself killed just to get a few leaves out of the goddamn gutter and leave me a widow, and then all of a sudden…"

"Pap-" the soldier said, unable to get the complete word out before Ellie was on him again.

"I hear him yell, 'Oh, fuck!', excuse my language, but my husband's not a cusser, you understand and then there was this huge bang, and I swear to God, I thought he was dead. That was it, he'd fallen off the roof."

"Ma'am, what is it you need?"

Boom, Ben thought, as he continued to rock back and forth. She'd struck a blow.

"Can you guys treat him? I think he broke his arm real bad. Is there a medic here?"

Ben froze. What was she doing?

A second soldier had drifted over, this one taking position outside Ben's window. Ben maintained his metronomic movement, keeping up appearances. He didn't have to do much, as Ellie was drawing all the attention from the soldiers.

"We got a medic here?"

Ben glanced in time to see the second soldier shrug his shoulders and shake his head.

"No? Jesus, he hit his head real bad, and I think he broke his arm, too, and you guys don't have a goddamn medic? We gotta get to the hospital. Isn't there one up the road a piece?"

The soldier, the name Spivey stitched over his shirt pocket, nodded his head enthusiastically.

"About a mile," Spivey said. "Hey, why didn't you guys get out of the car earlier? We could've helped you sooner."

Ben tensed up, like he'd been hit with a stun gun.

"I don't know!" Ellie barked, her voice saturated in hysterics now, cracking. Damn it if she wasn't crying a little now. "I wasn't thinking. I try to follow the rules. I didn't know what to do."

Ben began to relax as Ellie's gambit came into focus. It was brilliant. She was using their authority against them. It was their fault. What else was she supposed to do? She didn't want to get shot. She'd put the integrity of the system ahead of her husband's well-being. And they would reward her for it.

Spivey stood up and spun his finger around in a circular motion.

"Open the barricade," he barked. "Now!"

Like a well-trained housefly, Spivey fed from the pile of bullshit that Ellie had just dumped at his feet. Just as she knew he would. Ben figured he probably would have gone for it as well. It was hard to resist a pretty woman, especially when she was making you feel like a big important man.

A pair of Volunteers raised the gate and waved them through. As Ellie lifted her foot off the brake, Spivey leaned down again.

"You folks take care," he said.

"Thank you," she said, her voice as syrupy sweet as he'd ever heard it. He found it unnerving and irresistible. "Thank you all so much for keeping us safe."

Spivey smiled, stood up and banged the roof of the car twice. Ellie eased through the barricade and continued north. In his rearview mirror, Ben watched the next car in the queue pull forward and await its own personal drama with the Volunteer detachment assigned to the checkpoint.

ELLIE STARTED HYPERVENTILATING within a quarter-mile of clearing the checkpoint, just as the Key Bridge came into view, providing a panoramic vista of Washington, D.C.

"Hey, are you OK?" Ben asked.

"Yeah," she said. "No, I'm not OK. I gotta pull over."

She eased over to the shoulder and brought the car to a ragged stop, half on the shoulder, half on the embankment that gently sloped down to a thicket of trees lining the highway. She crossed her arms and took several deep, cleansing breaths. Ben gave her a moment, as much privacy as he could afford her in the cramped compartment. He looked out the windshield toward the northwest, where the sun had begun its slow descent for the night. It cast a soft orange glow across the city, and if he tilted his head just right, he could still see Washington the way it once was, before it had been shredded by war.

"That was a hell of a thing you did," Ben said.

"I didn't think we'd be able to get through without some kind of scam. I just had this terrible feeling in my gut."

"It was brilliant."

"You were right," she said. "We have to get to that apartment. No clue what we're going to do when we get there, but you were right, we had to get inside the city, and this was the only way, short of swimming across the Potomac."

"I wonder if it's still mined."

"Beats me."

At the peak of the Panic, the Army Corps of Engineers had strung nets of floating mines up and down the river after a herd of Redeyes had swum across and overwhelmed a squadron of Marines protecting this edge of the capital. They were able to repel the onslaught but lost dozens of Marines in the battle. It had never occurred to anyone that the infected could still swim; the mines made it much easier to hold the city's southern perimeter and kept D.C. off a list of cities marked for disinfection.

"How are we on gas?"

She tilted her head to check the gas gauge.

"Unless we can score some in D.C., this is going to be a one-way trip."

Ellie was quiet a minute, picking at a jagged thumbnail. She started to say something and then stopped. She seemed to be struggling with some internal debate.

"There's something I haven't told you," she said.

"What?"

"There was a reason I was working on that HARD team."

Ben was not entirely surprised by this. If the Haven was engaged in some struggle with the Department, an uninfected ally like Ellie would have been a tremendously useful resource, especially if she could get inside the Department's operations.

"And what reason is that?"

"Not all of the bodies that the crews recover are disposed in the incinerator," she said.

"How are they disposed then?" Ben said.

"We'd noticed that the Department had been taking custody of certain remains before they're incinerated. Each of the processing centers has a refrigerated unit where fresher bodies are kept until they're transported off site in unmarked tractor trailers."

"Fresher bodies?"

"Bodies that haven't degraded much. A fair amount of meat on the bones. We found quite a few like that. Especially folks that died later in the Panic, indoors. Especially the recent suicides."

"Weird," Ben said.

"Thompson was obsessed with it," she said, giving up on the thumb and laying her hands in her lap.

"Maybe they just wanted bodies for medical research."

"I don't know what they wanted them for."

"Did you ever try following the trucks?"

"Yes," she said. "Once. But I got the feeling they spotted me, so I pulled off. The next day, they seemed to watch me really close at work. I never chanced it again."

"Did you all think it was related to Tranquility?"

"Thompson must've thought it was," she said. "I think he believed it was part of some larger plan."

"It could have been something less sinister," he said. "I would expect that medical research is pretty high on the government's priority list these days."

"True."

"And fresh bodies, I expect, would be most useful, especially where organs, tissue, blood, are still intact." Ben yawned. "I don't know. I could be totally talking out of my ass here. Hell, maybe they're trying to re-animate them, like zombies. You know, we did get a little shortchanged on the whole zombie part of the zombie apocalypse thing."

Ellie laughed at that, but Ben barely heard it. The door in his mind was opening again, and he couldn't keep it closed. It was as if he were inside the ruptured hull of a ship, trying to hold back the ocean from pulling him down into the depths of his mind, where his darkest secrets remain trapped, like cargo aboard a ship lost to the depths.

IT WAS dark out when Ben regained consciousness, the seizure having knocked him clean out. The pain in his calf had faded to a dull throb, but it was manageable. It felt like there was something he should be doing for such an injury, but for the life of him, he couldn't remember what it was. It was too complicated to think about, and everything in his head felt very simple.

1 + 1 = 2

The cat. Sat. On a hat.

He needed to urinate (*Piss!*) and so he unzipped his pants and relieved himself where he stood. And then he was done and that was out of his head, in the rearview mirror of his consciousness like a billboard for a decrepit motor lodge advertising *FREE CABLE* and *POOL!* slipping by on the highway.

I + I = 2

He was hungry. He looked around. It was a forest. The moon was fat and round, God's flashlight shining down on a dark, dark world. The shimmery coin hung proudly in the sky, cutting a channel of white light across the clearing.

A noise.

A noise!

Ben's body tensed up, and he began scanning his surroundings for the target. For his prey. Again, this felt wrong in some way, deep down inside him, but everywhere else, it felt right.

There! In the trees!

A small deer traipsing through the woods stopped to look at him, eyeing him through the branches spreading out from the trunk of an old oak. And Ben didn't know anything else at that moment other than the knowledge, burning through him the way spent uranium would burn through an un-cooled reactor core, that he had to kill this deer and he had to kill it now or it would kill him first and he started running at it, full bore. The deer was so startled by this aggressive move, one usually not seen in the humans it had previously encountered, that it staggered and lost its footing on the humus covering the soft forest floor.

An instant later, Ben lowered his shoulder into the muscular flank of the doe as it struggled to regain its footing. With everything else forgotten, the Ben of yesterday gone, he wrapped his arms around the deer's neck and squeezed tightly as he could, cutting off the animal's air supply. It thrashed about like a bucking bronco, stunned by the ferocity of this unimaginable offensive, unable to break free of Ben's rage-fueled inferno. As he strangled the deer, he began kneeing the deer in its right flank over and over and over, eliciting a pathetic hooting sound from the doomed animal. Then Ben lost his grip, and the animal broke free of his grip; it crashed into the brush, barely escaping with its life. Immediately, his heart rate decelerated like a racecar entering pit row. His mind, apparently unable to multitask, cycled over to a single new thought, that the threat had been neutralized.

THE STRUGGLE HAD TAKEN its toll on Ben; he collapsed to the cool forest floor and fell asleep. He woke up an hour later, and another new thought snapped into place. It was like having a compact disc changer in his head, each slot holding a single discrete thought.

He walked until he was too tired to walk anymore, and he slept in the front yard of an abandoned house. After a few hours of sleep, he woke up covered in dew. It was still dark, but the concept of going back to sleep was beyond the scope of what his infected mind could comprehend, and so he got up and continued walking. He was on the west side of Raleigh, but that didn't mean anything to him. He didn't care where he was. He didn't even care that he was.

He cut through a park and came upon a small creek, swollen with the heavy rains from an earlier storm. He licked his lips and found them dry and cracked. New thought. Thirst. Ben bent down and scooped up water with his cupped hands, enjoying the cool liquid splashing against his lips at an almost primal level, until his thirst was quenched, and he continued his walk to nowhere. As the bright boiling sun traced its ancient course across the ancient sky, his skin began to feel hot and when he looked at it, the skin was flame-red. It had no bearing on his survival and he so gave it no thought. The survival disc continued to spin in the great compact disc player of his mind.

The creek petered out at a short ramp connecting two thoroughfares, and he climbed up the embankment. A vehicle, a green sedan, passed by, and each time, he felt the threat level ramp up into the red and then back down almost instantly as they pulled clear of his location. It was getting dark and he was hungry for the first time since he'd become infected. A commotion to the south caught his attention and he went in that direction because although there wasn't necessarily any reason to, there was no reason not to.

He came across a low fence and climbed it because it was as easy to climb it as it was to find some other way around. This put him in a large square backyard, the grass long and shaggy. A fresh bed of mulch covered a semi-circular flowerbed in the corner, still waiting for its first seedlings. Opposite that, an expensive-looking playset sat unattended, the swings drifting back and forth in the early spring breeze.

Another pang in his stomach reminded him how hungry he was, and he set his sights on the back door, which stood open invitingly. The house was abandoned. He scavenged the kitchen, ate crackers and moldy roast beef and drank orange juice and flat, lukewarm ginger ale.

His first encounter with another person happened late that afternoon, just as the sun had started to dip low in the late spring sky. He felt the bullet whiz by, like a puff of hot breath across his cheek, before he'd even heard the report of the gun.

Click. Spin.

Survive.

He dropped to the ground and scanned the area around

him. He was in an old neighborhood of Cape Cods and small ranchers, and again, this meant nothing to him besides the context it provided. Nothing. His heart was racing, racing, racing. It was out there, this thing that would kill him. Unless he killed it first. There was no want, no joy in this decision. It was survival.

"I'll kill you!" the voice boomed through the quiet neighborhood.

Ben's head swiveled to the left. His would-be killer poked his head around the side of a large pickup truck that was parked in the driveway. He was heavyset, shirtless, wearing dirty jean shorts. Several bodies lay strewn about the yard, and these posed no threat.

Ben rushed him the way he'd gone after the deer, but zig-zagging, making it difficult for the shooter to get a clear shot. He didn't think about this, he just did it, but it seemed like the most natural thing in the world and it was going to get him to his would-be killer and he would be safe again.

The man's eyes filled with terror as Ben drew on top of him. His weapon ran dry, leaving him to fumble with the ammunition, but before he could get the chamber loaded, Ben tackled him to the ground. The man got one solid blow, connecting against the side of Ben's head with the butt of the gun, but that was it, and it wasn't enough.

Ben grabbed the man by the ears and slammed his head against the concrete, once, twice, three times. The back of his skull collapsed like the wall of a coal mine giving way, and his body went limp. Ben got up and stood over the man for a moment. Empty, dead eyes looked up at the bright blue sky, seeing nothing. Dark red blood began pooling under the shooter's head. Ben turned to find a group of other infectees, about a half dozen of them, behind him. He gauged them carefully and decided they posed no threat.

The group, five men, and two women, absorbed him into their ranks, and they moved on as one unit until they linked up with other smaller packs.

The group dynamic among the Redeyes had never been fully understood, even after hundreds and thousands of hours of interviews with recovered Redeyes. One never consciously acknowledged the fact that other Reds posed no threat to him; it was simply something he understood at a deep primal level. Together they became something bigger and more powerful than each of them could be alone, a great machine of death and destruction, a snowball of horror rolling down a hill. It was a bond that couldn't be broken, bought, or compromised in any way until the final seizure; coming ten to twelve weeks after the initial infection, it marked the human body's ultimate victory over the Orchid virus, except for the one percent that succumbed to the second seizure.

Ben's flock swelled in size as it drifted northwest, picking up men, women, and children. The tsunami of infected humanity swept him along, the mass undulating, stretching, contracting, but never breaking. Victims wore the clothes that had been on their backs when they'd become infected, three-thousand-dollar suits and nightgowns and Little League outfits, dirty and torn, stained with the sickly stench of filth and waste, the stink of a full garbage can that has gone over. Some wore nothing at all, their clothes ripped from their bodies, or worse, having been infected in the nude, karma's ultimate slap in the face. A wave of rage and violence, sweeping over the land and leaving death and ruin in its wake. There was no limit, no cap, no restrictor plate on their ferocity.

At six o'clock on a Wednesday evening, two days after he'd become infected, Ben's flock reached the intersection of

Interstates 40 and 85 just west of Durham, North Carolina. An Army unit dispatched from Fort Bragg was embedded here to hold the line at these two major arteries so they could protect the state capital and pin down flocks to the east until they could be firebombed by attack helicopters. The strategy had proven effective in some areas across the country in the early stages of the Panic, but as the numbers of infected ballooned into the millions and the flocks grew in size, it was becoming a losing proposition. A hundred nervous soldiers, tucked behind a wall of sandbags and flanked by a pair of tanks, watched as Ben and nearly three thousand Redeyes closed in on them on full bore.

When the squads opened fire, the flock spread itself thin, making it difficult for the guns to bring down large numbers in a single fusillade. The first wave of fire brought down a hundred. Even now, Ben could still see the chests and heads exploding in a tempest of blood, showering the cracked asphalt and weed-choked median grass with fresh blood and brain matter. And the soldiers did not discriminate between their targets, as their orders were to terminate everyone – men, women, children, the elderly, the infirm – exhibiting signs of infection with extreme prejudice.

Ben and a breakaway group moved from tree to abandoned car to concrete barrier for cover; they did not speak or communicate in any way. As the soldiers fired their .50-caliber machine guns, spitting nearly two thousand rounds per minute, focused on a frontal assault, Ben and two dozen Reds overwhelmed the western flank of the unit. As they broke the defensive perimeter, they swallowed up the unit with a ferocity that the soldiers simply could not comprehend. Many of these soldiers had fought in Iraq and Afghanistan but they had never encountered an enemy whose morale and resolve could never be broken. No religious or ethnic or geopolitical fervor had ever matched the biological drive to kill that marked infection with the Orchid virus.

Ben stripped a bowie knife from the hand of a young soldier and jammed it over and over into his right flank. Blood coated his hands like a red rubber glove. The mating of knife and flesh, like two lovers who've found one another after a long and desperate separation, was the scratch of a hard-to-explain itch, of a mosquito bite on his soul. The fear in the young private's face had no effect on Ben, his eyes wide and virtually erupting from their sockets in terror as this monster, this thing from every child's nightmare world, drove the knife home while scratching at his face. It was not Ben's place to know or think about the soldier's mother, handwringingly worried about her son, or his girlfriend, already a refugee from Des Moines, where the infection was rampant and which had earned a bright red triangle superimposed on a large map displayed on the White House Situation Room's eighty-inch monitor.

He scratched the itch over and over as the Redeyes overran the barricade. The surviving soldiers abandoned their posts, streaming to the four points of the compass as the Army lost yet another pinch point in the increasingly desperate war against an enemy that didn't know it was an enemy, that didn't know it was fighting a war, that didn't know it was at the mercy of the virus that had hijacked its humanity. Ben's memory of the night grew hazy from that point, and the last thing he remembered was bringing down a quartet of retreating soldiers with a dozen Reds.

And that's the way it went for Ben. They drifted through the streets and neighborhoods like viruses attacking healthy cells, embedding themselves into uninfected areas, creating copy after copy until they overwhelmed the defenders brave enough to fight to the end even as they refused to believe that yes, this was actually happening, that the apocalypse was inside their perfectly manicured, meticulously planned subdivision.

And the blood. There was always so much blood.

22

Ben hadn't been to Washington, D.C., in years, not since he and Sarah had taken Gavin up for a weekend to visit the National Air and Space Museum. The boy's eyes were wide with wonder as he ran from biplane to commercial jet to space shuttle. That had been a good trip. Now he and Ellie inched across the I-395 Bridge, the urban nightmare sprawling before him nothing like the carefully organized metropolis he'd seen back then, with its precise grids and sparkling monuments, this shining symbol of the greatest nation on earth. It reminded Ben of Elvis Presley in his later years, the jowls, the cloudy eyes, the worn vocal cords. Before him, instead of the sparkly center of the free world, a tired, cautionary tale of urban warfare spread out toward the horizon.

The cityscape was a jumble of rubble, collapsed structures and scarred buildings with windows blown out, pockmarked with bullet holes. Off to the west, long rolls of yellow tape were strung around the perimeter of a pile of rocks that had once been the Jefferson Memorial, now just another thing on the government's very long to-do list. The rubble was still sparkly white in the afternoon sun, a reminder that this had once been something special, that this place had once meant something.

Ben wondered what had happened that day, at the moment that one of America's premier symbols had been rendered a reminder of the cataclysm that had befallen the nation. Had it been destroyed by vandals who'd finally realized that they could loot and pillage and plunder and destroy with impunity? By the military, which was desperate to turn the tide of the war at whatever cost? Looking at it was terrible and sad and yet he couldn't avert his gaze.

"Wow," Ellie said, as though she were reading his mind. "Rough."

"I didn't think it would look this bad," he said. "I'd heard the rumors, of course, but until you see it, you know?"

Something was amiss with the skyline.

"Where's the Monument?"

"Oh, you didn't know about that?"

He shook his head slowly.

"Some wacko jammed a bunch of C-4 at the base of the monument and blew it. They caught him and executed him right there in the middle of the Mall."

Ben looked at her with his brow furrowed.

"Sorry," she said, her cheeks flushing with embarrassment. "It happened on July 4."

"Oh," Ben said. He wouldn't recover from the infection until mid-July.

"Sorry," she said. "Sometimes I forget that..." Her voice trailed off.

"It's OK."

"You really think we can find Thompson's guy?"

"I hope so," he said. "We don't have much time. I know you know that. Everything the Department has done has been so aggressive. From the attack on the Haven to plastering my picture everywhere, it feels like the first dominoes are falling. It feels like things are about to change."

She bit the corner of her lip and looked away, and he knew she agreed with him.

As the car transitioned from bridge to terra firma, the hum of the tires growing more solid, more reassuring, a billboard caught Ben's eye, rising up over all entrants into the city. The red letters seemed to float above the jet black background.

ALL PERSONS SUBJECT TO SEARCH AT ANY TIME

"Remember the Constitution?" he asked.

"Yeah."

"Those were good times!"

He laughed heartily, and it felt good. There was nothing like a good laugh to drain the toxins building up inside one's soul. It was the ultimate flush of the mental toilet. It must have been contagious because Ellie began laughing too, and as they sat there in the braids of traffic that threaded back into Virginia and ahead of them into the heart of the District, they laughed about everything that was wrong with the world and right with the world and Ben tried not to think about the task that lay ahead of him.

EVENING. The sky had begun dropping its purplish curtain across the horizon. Ben was tired and hungry. The Jeep, which had performed so beautifully, was straining badly, its engine revving when it seemed totally unnecessary, bursting forward with a simple touch of the gas. They had begun looking for a place to hide it, somewhere out of the way so that they could use it for shelter as a last resort.

Ahead of them lay the baseball stadium, home to the Washington Nationals. When the Panic had hit, the city had been giddy with excitement about the team; it was coming off its first playoff appearance since the move back to Washington in 2004, and the Nats had been a favorite to represent the National League in the World Series. And had things gone differently, maybe that's what would have happened. Maybe on this very night, the team would have been hosting the first game of the World Series against the Yankees or the Red Sox, and this crisp evening air would feel much different than it did now. It would carry the scent of hot dogs and hot peanuts and a soundtrack of laughter and cheers.

It looked the same as it always had; even the bright stadium lights looked like he would have expected on the first night of the World Series, but it wasn't the same. There was no roar of the crowd, no buzz in the air, no steady stream of fans making their way toward the stadium from whichever dark corner of the District they'd found a parking spot, carrying their bright orange foam fingers and their vinyl seat cushions.

Now it was a military installation. A convoy of armored trucks ringed the perimeter, each guarded by a single soldier. Access to the lot was strictly controlled. Ben was happy to watch the stadium edge into their rearview mirror and he was reminded of the insanity of their plan.

In a crowded neighborhood of old brownstones and row houses, the Jeep sputtered one final time and died. Ben guided the car to the side of the road before its forward momentum abandoned it completely. This drew some attention from some of the folks loitering about in the growing gloom of the evening, looking for something, anything useful.

"I guess we're walking," Ellie said.

"Looks that way. You ready?"

"Yeah," she said. "Say goodbye to this car. They'll be on it like bugs on shit."

Both scoured the car for any useful supplies, loath to leave anything behind. They got out and joined the throng of humanity milling about. Immediately, a group of three young men swarmed the car and began working it over. One shattered the window with a hammer, and they were inside a moment later. They reminded Ben of a swarm of Reds attacking a helpless victim.

So much for using it for shelter.

They found the mailbox an hour later in front of an old brownstone, three stories high, the ground floor once home to a little bodega. Ellie casually struck the white mark across the side of the mailbox. It was done. It was after seven o'clock, full dark now. Ben's chest tightened with nerves as they passed the front stoop, where a group of young men were smoking cigarettes and sharing a bottle of liquor so strong that its aroma burned Ben's nostrils from where he stood. There were six of them, four white and two black, and Ben found that fascinating because in another era, these kids might not have been as friendly with one another as they were now. But now they found commonality and strength simply by being Redeyes.

"The fuck y'all doing?"

This was one of the white guys, one of the elders of the group. He was built like a side of beef; his hair was cropped close, his head sporting just a thin layer of red fuzz. The man's skin was splotchy red, almost as red as his eyes

"Just visiting a friend," he said.

"Is that right? Who's your friend?"

"You probably don't know him."

"Where's the other guy?"

Ben's brow furrowed in confusion.

"What other guy?"

"You think I didn't see you make that mark on the box?" asked the boy.

"You know the man who marked the box?" Ellie asked.

"Who's asking?" replied the boy.

Ben's skin rippled with gooseflesh; he flashed back to Danny and that terrible scene with Ellie in that house. They'd been lucky to escape that nightmare, but here, they were at the mercy of these men. It was one of those times where Ben found himself surprised at how quickly he'd lost control of the situation. He hated the feeling, especially the not knowing how he'd ended up there in the first place, when a million different decisions might have put him somewhere else. Like the day he'd become infected.

"Shut the fuck up, J-Bird," a second voice said.

This was a young, fresh-faced black kid sitting on top of the wide concrete railing, his back leaning the brick facade. He was skinny, not much more than a sliver. Despite the soft lilt to his voice, there was a certain cool confidence there; this was the little group's leader. The redhead was nothing more than a meathead, a lot of muscle but very little going on between the ears. Ben dropped his hands down to his sides and remained still, trading a long glance with the kid. The boy smoked a cigarette, slowly, deliberately.

"I seen your picture on TV," the kid said.

"Yes," Ben said.

"At least you honest about it."

"You going to turn me in?"

"To the Department?"

"Yes."

"Fuuuuck no," the boy said, his voice hard but laced with a bit of good cheer. Just enough to make Ben relax a little. "You think I want those assholes up in my business again?"

"You know there's a reward," Ben said.

No point in avoiding the obvious.

"Man, they ain't paying no mother-fucking reward."

Ben sighed loudly, his legs rubbery underneath him. The kid was wise beyond his years. Of course the Department wasn't paying a reward.

"Thank you."

"So where's the other guy?"

"Dead."

"You here for Mercury?"

Ben's heart began pounding. He felt like he was on a runaway train car, its ultimate destination seemingly predetermined but unknown to Ben. Maybe it would safely roll back into its wheelhouse, or maybe it would speed right off the tracks into a boiling, alligator-infested river. Part of him wanted to run screaming off into the night and hide in Brazil or Chile. It was bad enough that this kid had recognized him almost instantly. It was all fine and good that he wasn't planning to turn Ben in, but the next person might not be so altruistic. They were running out of time.

"Yes," he said.

"He's dead too."

The news was like a punch in the sternum. What little hope he'd had evaporated from his body like a puddle on a hot summer day. He'd put all his eggs into this basket not because he wanted to but because there were no other baskets. As it were, they were way out on the fringe, taking a hell of a chance because they didn't have anything else.

Eventually they would find him. They would find him and he would disappear and that would be it for the story of Ben Sullivan.

"Shit," Ellie said, just under her breath.

Dead. Dead. Dead. If he was dead, then Ben might as well be, too. He let out a long sigh and ran his hands slowly over his scalp.

"When?"

"Couple days ago."

"What happened?" he asked.

"Dude shot him on this porch. Broad daylight."

Ben did his best to maintain his composure. A headache was forming at the base of his skull, a byproduct of the stress and tension that had been building since they hit the checkpoint earlier. Their gossamer thread of hope was gone.

"You folks look like you could use a drink," the boy said.

BEN GAVE up on sleep around dawn. He was cold, his body shivering under the thin blanket, stiff and tight from a night spent on hardwood floors, but it beat the hell out of sleeping outside. The boy from the front stoop, Louis, had offered them shelter for the night, and Ben and Ellie were more than happy to accept his offer. They were in Louis' apartment, a tiny sliver of a thing, a one-bedroom unit. Ellie tossed and turned for most of the night, but she had finally fallen asleep on the couch, her breathing even and calm in the inky stillness.

It was all very clear to him now. With Mercury gone, there was really no other option. The plan had come to him in the dead middle of the night, a time once reserved for drunk dialing ex-girlfriends or online shopping. Nowadays, four a.m. decisions carried far more import; the one he'd just made would almost certainly get him killed. But the sad, sorry truth was that he was almost as likely to get caught trying to run away as he was standing up and taking one last swing. He could make up for siding with the Department, atone for the deaths of those Redeyes at the camp, the ones who'd shown true courage and bravery in refusing to give up without a fight.

He told himself that this was the brave thing to do, that he was doing the thing that might make Sarah and Gavin proud of him, that he could somehow undo the damage he'd done. But he was as scared as he'd ever been, as scared as he'd been while the virus percolated inside him. In some ways, he was even more scared, because he didn't know what might happen if the plan didn't work. The not knowing, that was the worst of all. At least this way, the outcome would be upon him sooner rather than later.

He'd gotten to the front door of the apartment when he heard her voice.

"You planning to leave without me?" Ellie said.

He froze, his hand on the doorknob.

"I didn't want to wake you."

"You really think I was sleeping?"

"I don't know."

She sighed loudly, and he could hear her disappointment in him.

"Where are you going so early anyway?"

"Something I've gotta do."

"Is it dumb?"

"Extremely."

"But it could work?"

"Probably not."

"And if it does?"

"It might be a good thing," he said. "It might help others like me."

"And if it doesn't work?"

"At least I tried."

"Is it worth dying for?" she asked.

He considered her question.

"I used to have this bad habit," Ben said finally. "When I was just starting out, years ago. If there was something I needed to do, I often found myself putting it off, putting it off, putting it off. There wasn't any reason why. Inertia, I guess. Body at rest and all that. Until I did it, and then I would think, 'there, that wasn't so bad, and now it's off your plate.' And I started reminding myself about the feeling I'd have once I did the thing. Eventually, it became a habit. If there was something that had to be done, I would force myself to do it, calling the vet, buying a birthday card for someone, reviewing a box of documents. I would just do it."

"And?"

"This, this is no different," he said. "It needs to be done. We can sit around and talk about all the reasons not to do it. Same as me driving home after work and not stopping to pick up my dry cleaning that's been there for two weeks."

"Yeah, but if you don't pick up your dry cleaning, you don't end up getting executed."

"Work with me," he said. "I'm trying to make a larger point here."

She held up her hands in playful surrender.

"Sorry," she said. "I won't get in the way of the great and wise philosopher."

"Thank you," he replied. "I'm having several very important thoughts here."

"Of course."

They held each other's gaze for a moment, long enough

for it to become a tad awkward. Ben Sullivan knew little about the machinations of the female mind, and he didn't know whether Ellie was staring at him because she wanted him or whether there was a rogue piece of food stuck in his teeth. It had never been his strong suit. He thought about Sarah and Gavin, and again, his mind replayed their last time together, a terrible, terrible show on a constant loop in his mind, like a crappy sitcom in syndication.

"It's been so hard," he said, breaking eye contact and looking down at the floor. "Just so goddamn hard."

He looked for the right words, the right thing to say, but he had never spoken of his infection period so openly. It felt raw, like skin scraped bare.

"I'm sure," she said. "I won't pretend to know what you went through."

"I'm a murderer."

"I know this won't be much help, but it wasn't your fault."

"You're right," he said, his voice hardening. "It isn't much help. And everything I've done since has made things worse."

"I haven't done one goddamn thing to help anyone but myself. And I couldn't even do that right. As if people haven't suffered enough because of me. This is my chance to do something. I've always believed that everyone gets a chance to do a good thing, to do something that matters."

"This isn't like running a soup kitchen," she said. "This is suicide."

"Something else I couldn't do right," he said, wincing as the words tumbled out of his mouth before he could stop himself. He glanced at her, hoping his confession had slipped by her like a hockey puck past an inattentive goalie.

"Oh, Ben."

Guess not, he thought. He sighed, thinking about the others that had opted out, the ones who had done the thing that he could not, and he often found himself jealous of their bravery. Hundreds of recovered Redeyes took their own lives every day, unable or unwilling to deal with their radically altered paradigms.

"It was about a month after I recovered," he said, his eyes cutting toward the floor again. His voice had dropped to a whisper, barely loud enough for him to hear. He didn't know if Ellie could hear; he looked up and noticed that she'd taken two steps toward him. They were just inches apart.

"I had just seen Sarah and Gavin, and that hadn't gone well. I couldn't eat, I couldn't sleep. Anytime I nodded off, even for a moment, the nightmares started. It was like reliving it all over again. You want to talk about hell..."

His throat tightened and his eyes welled with tears. He tapped a fist gently against his lips; breaking down in front of Ellie was not something he particularly relished. She placed her hand on his elbow and squeezed it gently.

"You don't have to do this," she said. "You don't."

He looked up at her. Her eyes were wet with tears.

"It was a Monday. I was wandering around downtown, hungry, dirty, and I suddenly stopped right in the middle of the street, and I thought to myself, 'what the hell am I doing?' What, precisely, was I trying to live for? Maybe if someone could erase my memories, I could've made a go of it, worked to win Sarah and Gavin back. But the memories.

"There was an office building, the biggest in Raleigh. Heavily damaged during the Panic. Just like that, I found myself walking up thirty flights of stairs. It seemed so natural. It was the first time I'd felt in control of anything since it started. Every few floors, I'd pass a body or a refugee.

I felt calm, like I was heading upstairs to grab a soda from the vending machine.

"I came out on the top floor. The wind was howling up there. A lot of the windows had been blown out, so it was like a wind tunnel. I marched right over to the edge. I guess in my head, I wasn't even going to stop. I was just going to walk right over the edge and that would be that."

"But you stopped."

"Yes."

He was crying now, the tears streaming silently down his cheeks. One dripped from his face and splashed onto Ellie's slender arm. She made no attempt to wipe it away.

"I stood there, like a fucking coward, grabbing the exposed girder, holding on so tightly I could feel the metal digging into my shoulder," he said. "I couldn't even get myself to the edge. I stood there for ten, fifteen minutes, crying like a baby, much like I am now, I might add."

"Because you wanted to live."

"I didn't know what I wanted. I just felt like a fool and a coward. I ended up spending the night up there. There was a nice, warm breeze. I actually slept that night. Not much. A couple hours. But a couple hours with no bad dreams. That didn't last. But it was nice for a night."

"You know, some people might say that the ones that go through with it, they're the cowards. You're the one that stayed, you're the one trying to do something."

"Yeah, they're really missing out on this brave new world of ours."

"This place, it's hard times for everyone."

He wanted to shout at her, tell her she didn't know the first goddamn thing about hard times. Had she brutally killed three dozen people, whose ultimate destiny had been merely to intersect with Ben Sullivan on a very, very bad day? Had they connected with him eight weeks earlier or eight weeks later, the extent of their interaction might have been something as simple and innocuous as a comment about the weather or those crazy gas prices.

He wanted to grab her by the shoulders and tell her she didn't know anything about what he'd gone through, but as he opened his mouth, the thought died away, like the flame on your last match in a brisk wind. Then he remembered. She'd had to kill the one person she loved most of all. He hadn't had to watch that person come at him like a rabid dog, he hadn't had to come to the terrible realization that Ellie had, that she would have to kill or be killed.

She had to live with that, the way he had to live with the memory of what he had done. The memory that each of those poor lost souls, dispatched from this life by Ben's feverish, infected hand, from his first victim to his last, had been someone's everything, and because of Ben, whether it was his fault or not, that everything was gone forever. He knew what she was thinking. That if she'd captured her husband, kept him locked away, she could have taken care of him until he recovered. He knew that telling her there was no way to know that anyone would ever recover from the infection would feel hollow and empty. And so he didn't try.

"Yeah," he said finally. "I guess we all know about hard times."

"Look at the bright side," she said, wiping her moist eyes with the tips of her index fingers.

"The bright side?"

"No one can ever tell us that we never had it rough."

He smiled.

"Goddamn right about that."

23

The U.S. Department of Reconstruction & Recovery made its home in the old Environmental Protection Agency headquarters in the Federal Triangle, around the Woodrow Wilson Plaza between 12th and 14th Streets; it had been one of the few federal complexes to escape the war largely unscathed. Although the Ronald Reagan building had sustained heavy damage, the remaining buildings were still functional. Much of the federal government's infrastructure had been destroyed during the Panic, and when the President had commissioned the new agency, it needed a home quickly. The powers-that-be quickly determined that protecting the environment was going to be pretty low on the national priority list for some time, so the EPA was disbanded and unceremoniously evicted from its digs. Its physical plant had only suffered minor cosmetic damage, and its proximity to the White House made it ideal as the agency's new home.

From here, Samantha Culver, the freshly anointed Secretary of Reconstruction & Recovery directed the nation's efforts to get back on its feet after the end of the

Panic. In an effort to centralize the recovery, the President and Congress eagerly gave her sweeping powers, simply happy that someone was willing to take on the mammoth challenge of rebuilding the free world. The Department's mandate was vast. The Secretary focused a great deal of attention on investigating reports of new outbreaks of the Orchid virus and monitoring the population for any evidence of relapses. Government health officials were not sure that the survivors wouldn't relapse. There was so much about the pathogen that they didn't understand, and that alone scared them senseless. Work on a vaccine continued unabated, but as there were no known active cases of Orchid, there was no way to effectively test it.

Suppressing civil unrest was another priority. By the end of the Panic, chaos and lawlessness reigned across the country. As the economy struggled to recover, food, water, and medicine were in short supply everywhere, leading to massive rioting and armed skirmishes in every corner of the nation. The Volunteers had been the Secretary's pet project; she believed that the National Guard was too fragmented to act effectively as the nation's civil defense unit. So the President dissolved the Guard at her recommendation and commissioned the Volunteers. The very existence of the Volunteer Corps itself rested on shaky legal ground at best, but very few people were in the mood to disagree with the methods chosen for the ugly work of nursing the badly wounded country back to health.

The third big item was the economy, which the war effort had left in shambles. China, which had seen minimal Orchid activity after closing its borders and had been the quickest to recover, was on its way to becoming the first post-Panic superpower. It began pumping money into the U.S., investing in infrastructure, buying controlling shares in

American trucking companies, snapping up land and buildings, buying U.S. debt.

With one eye turned inward, the U.S. kept its other one on the rest of the world. As the crisis had unfolded, the President had spoken daily with the leaders of the world's other nuclear powers, each blaming the other as the source of the virus, each assuring the other that they would not nuke the other in a wholesale disinfection attempt. For weeks, the U.S. military waited for inbound ICBMs to light up its radar, always making sure that the President was in a secure place to give a retaliatory strike order if needed.

Now a million active Volunteers were on patrol in the continental United States. Several hundred were assigned to the DRR headquarters, lining the perimeter of the vast complex, bracketed on the east and west sides by 9th and 15th Streets, to the north and south by Pennsylvania Avenue and Route 1. Tanks were positioned at each corner of the building's facade, anchors connected by a chain of armored personnel carriers.

When Ben and Ellie arrived at the southeastern tip of the complex, the place was already buzzing with activity. It was a bright, crisp morning, warm in the sun, a day custom-built for exploring an old city like Washington, D.C. The crowd was loud and ornery, shouting at the soldiers, who in turn, looked tight and on edge, their fingers wrapped around the trigger guards of their very powerful weapons.

Ben looked both ways across Route 1, but before he crossed, he froze. In the clarity of the day, amid the bustle of the protestors and the rippling might of the Volunteers, his plan seemed insane, not rooted in reality. But he considered the alternatives again; what those options lacked in mind-bending lunacy, they more than made up for in crappiness.

"Forget it," Ellie said. "I thought this was crazy when we

were just talking about it. But now that I see it in person -
there's got to be another way."

He looked over at her, numb. An icy bead of sweat cut a
trail down his back.

"There's no time for anything else," he said. "I feel it in
every fiber of my being. Something big is about to happen."

"What about cameras?" she asked.

"We're going to have to chance it," he replied. "We're
gonna need a little bit of luck on that front."

She ran her hands nervously through her hair, saying
nothing.

THEY WATCHED the building for the rest of the day, studying
patterns, traffic, shift changes, anything that they could
glean from their amateur surveillance. Sometimes they
patrolled together; other times they split up. A small group
of protestors had set up shop in a semi-circular driveway
across from the building right near the corner, drawing
significant attention from a small squad of Volunteers. They
were a haggard bunch, tired, dirty; some of them were
carrying signs. Ben was particularly fond of one that read:
Reminder: The Constitution Is Still in Effect! Another stated:
Down with R&R!

The Volunteers here worked eight-hour shifts, rotating
back inside when their shifts ended. Ben suspected that the
soldiers assigned to the complex were barracked indoors, as
most of them probably didn't have homes to return to.
Volunteers came and went; they were sloppy and lacked
precision. Rarely did the same soldier return to the same
post. They smoked and chatted and harassed folks who
passed by, especially Redeyes. The majority of them were

men, but a significant number of female soldiers were on duty as well. These women Volunteers had to work double duty, although they weren't compensated for the second job of resisting their male counterparts' constant sexual advances.

"How about that one?" Ben whispered to Ellie.

It was almost midnight, the sky cloudless, the air chilly. It was a new moon, and so that, along with the power restrictions in the District, left this section of the city swirling in darkness. Dim lights burned inside the complex, as the Department was, of course, exempt from the power restrictions. From his perch behind a rock wall, Ben focused on a dopey-looking fellow, guarding a loading dock on the north end of the complex. His partner was smoking a cigarette and eagerly sipping from a flask that likely contained something a little stronger than water. It seemed like a wonderful point of attack, a pair of less-than-focused soldiers guarding a decent access point to the complex.

"They don't think anything's going to happen on their watch," Ellie whispered back. "No one ever believes it's going to be them."

Ben nodded. Before the Panic, he was always fascinated by stories of ordinary people plunged into extraordinary circumstances. Spotting the kidnapper with the small child a hundred miles from home. Surviving a workplace shooting. That kind of thing. And here they were, spying on these soldiers the way a lion stalked a gazelle on the African prairie.

"Ready?" she asked.

"Yeah," Ben said. "Be careful."

"You too."

"So, if this, uh, works," she started, laughing a little, as if the idea of this plan succeeding was so ludicrous that they couldn't discuss it with a straight face. "What's the plan?"

He laughed too. He'd been so wrapped up in the insanity of the idea, its virtually guaranteed failure, he hadn't given much thought to the next step.

"Well," he said, deciding quickly. "I'll try to find out more about Tranquility."

"We know Mercury was assigned to Survivor Affairs," she said.

"The way I see it, this whole thing is going to happen quickly or not at all. I'll meet you tomorrow at noon at the Jefferson Memorial. Try and get us a car."

She nodded.

"So this is it," she said.

"Yeah," he said, hesitant to confess that "this" almost certainly included Ben throwing up sometime in the next thirty seconds.

"You got the walkie?" she asked.

He tapped his pocket; their new pal Louis had given them a pair.

"Channel 26."

He nodded. She leaned in and kissed him lightly, just a brush of her lips against his mouth. The kiss electrified him, as though he'd touched a live wire.

"Don't I feel like the little lady sending her man off to war," she said. "Damn, what a bad cliché this is."

"I'm not sure you're getting the easy end of the deal on this," he replied. "If this doesn't work, it's all going to be on you. You're going to have to come up with some new plan, something we haven't even thought of yet. Not only are you going to have to run Plan B, you're going to have to figure out what Plan B is."

"It doesn't feel right to just send you off like this."

"You saved me on that mountain," he said. "It's the least I can do. And no one is better positioned to do it than me."

Their eyes locked again. Hers were dry. The time for shedding tears was past.

Ellie slipped across the street, loudly singing a Beatles song and laughing to herself. She sounded positively tickled with life and the state of the universe, the kind of person you'd want to be around.

Especially if you were a bored, lonely soldier walking the midnight watch.

As she sashayed down the large sidewalk running along the front of the building, she popped up on the soldiers' radar almost immediately. Ben shook his head, reminded of the power that an attractive woman held over a man. There was something talismanic about a beautiful woman, something that tickled a man's core like a feather, an itch that needed to be scratched. No matter the price that would have to be paid.

"Hey there," one said, his voice booming in the still of the night. "What are you up to this evening?"

"Just looking for a good time," she said.

Ben cringed at the terrible cliché of it all; he was positive that they would sniff out her gambit, as though she were wearing a sandwich board announcing that THIS IS A SETUP!

"Hey, baby, we're looking for a good time, too," the Volunteer said. "Gets pretty boring up in here."

His partner, the one smoking, offered Ellie a cigarette, which she graciously accepted.

Ben almost felt bad for them even as he was stunned by their penis-driven foolishness. Their voices had dropped a notch, and he couldn't hear exactly what was being said, the night swallowing the specifics of their exchanges, but it was obvious that Ellie had focused her attention on the alpha male of the pair, the bigger guy with the booze and smokes. This was deliberate on her part, a bit of the old divide-and-conquer. She was the bait, and she'd be taking this guy on a little run, leaving the weaker link in the chain for Ben to deal with.

As the second Volunteer became increasingly aware of his third-wheel status, he began to disengage himself from the conversation. He passed under a security light mounted on the side of the building, revealing a pronounced pout on his face. A little bit of the green-eyed monster! He'd been the first one to interact with her, and Ben knew that this made him feel like he was somehow entitled to the first at-bat with Ellie.

Ellie was really laying it on thick now. The soldier said something, and she responded with her girliest giggle, her infectious laugh filling the night. With each passing minute, they drifted farther and farther away from his post, leaving the second soldier alone. He lit his own cigarette and smoked in sullen silence, oblivious to anything around him.

At the other end of the block, Ben slithered across the street like a snake, using the night to cover his move. Every muscle in his body was coiled up tightly, just waiting for the right moment to strike. Ellie and her new beau had disappeared around the corner; he strained his eyes, hoping to catch a glimpse of her, but he saw nothing. He would just have to hope she was okay.

The Volunteer still hadn't noticed Ben easing along the edge of the building, his back pressed tight against the cool cinderblock walls. Ben waited until the soldier turned away and then pounced. He eased up behind the man, who luckily was laying at least four inches and twenty pounds to Ben, and slid his arm around his neck. Before he could react, Ben had the man in a sturdy chokehold, the man's windpipe trapped in the crook of his arm. The soldier grunted and flailed, but his gasps died in the night breeze. Instinct prevailed over training, and instead of scrambling for a weapon, the soldier pawed desperately at Ben's arm-bar. After a minute, as Ben's arms screamed for relief, the fight in the soldier began to fade, and his legs turned to rubber. Sweat gushed from every pore, and he hated himself for what he was doing. He only hoped he wasn't inflicting permanent damage; he just wanted this fool to lose consciousness so Ben could let him go.

Finally, the soldier's knees buckled, followed quickly by the flop of the arms; Ben held tight for another minute or so, just in case the guy was faking his demise. He lowered the subdued man gently to the ground. Ben placed a hand on the man's chest, which rose and fell rhythmically, and felt a steady heartbeat, thumping away rapidly. He'd managed not to kill someone. A good first step, he decided. After a quick check of his surroundings, he dragged the unconscious soldier away closer to the building, where he could work in shadow.

Ben stripped the man down to his briefs, carefully taking inventory of his standard-issue gear. After securing the rifle, Ben began searching for the man's most valuable possession – the access card they'd watched the soldiers use to enter the building. His panic was off the charts almost instantly. It felt like his insides were up in his throat as he pawed through one deep pocket after another.

Then: *Success!*

It was gray and plastic, about the size and dimensions of a credit card. The soldier's image and name – Goodale – was superimposed on its surface.

Then he dressed the soldier in his civilian clothes, which

were a bit tight on him; after a brief but intense struggle, Ben gave up trying to zip up the man's pants. Then Ben got busy squeezing himself into the man's BDUs. The pants were a bit short, but they fit pretty well around the waist. The boots were a perfect fit. They were lightweight, airy, but they were as sturdy as the ground he stood on.

As he finished buttoning the gray urban camouflage shirt, Ben's thoughts turned to Ellie. He looked down the street in the direction they'd gone, but he saw nothing but a swirl of blackness and street mist. Dammit, he thought. The first step of a journey that had something like thirty-four steps, and it felt like they were already off track, unmoored, each alone.

He counted to sixty, his eyes focused on the dark sidewalk ahead of him, willing her to drift out of the darkness like some ghostly apparition. Then to a hundred. Still nothing. It was time to go. He slung the rifle over his shoulder and dug through the soldier's lightweight pack. There was an energy bar in it, which he greedily gobbled down.

He waved the card across the access panel. The tiny red light toggled to green and a hidden lock disengaged. Somewhere, Goodale's name was being logged in a computer. He stepped inside and gently guided the door closed. The electronic lock re-engaged, a loud *ka-chunk* echoing in the quiet corridor, causing him to jump.

Here we go.

HE ENTERED the building on the north side. A long hallway stretched out before him. Part of him couldn't believe that he was actually inside. But it hadn't been dumb luck. They'd planned as carefully as they could, found the weak spots in the system, and exploited them. The soldiers simply hadn't been expecting a threat. They'd gotten lazy and sloppy.

And the federal government, never a bastion of efficiency before the Panic, was still a mess. So much institutional memory had been wiped out during the crisis that they were making things up as they went along. This gave them their best opportunity for success. Things wouldn't be like this forever, that much was certain. Not when they had men like Mr. Whitmore in their employ. Mr. Whitmore was a machine, an instrument, an engine that could drive a place like this, continue to make it the thing that a scared, tired populace would simply accept as long as he took care of all the icky stuff. Ben wondered if Whitmore had been at the Haven on the night of the raid. That would have been right up his alley.

He made his way down the corridor, carefully but not too cautiously. He needed to act like he belonged here; the longer he could blend in, the better chance he would have at figuring out what Tranquility was and how he could, per Calvin Thompson's final request, stop it. After all, he was just another Volunteer, another worker ant scurrying about the anthill.

Tranquility.

That word again.

Haunting him. Mocking him. Daring him to get himself killed. Doubt crept in, an impossible-to-reach itch under his new camouflaged collar. He pushed it to the back of his mind and refocused his attention on the building.

As he made his way deeper into the building, the activity level increased, getting his hackles up. He turned a corner, bumping into a pair of soldiers laughing and joking about something or the other. His heart froze, the fingers on his left hand curling around the barrel of his new rifle; he took comfort in the strength and chill of the steel. But they paid him no mind and kept going. With each passing minute, he saw more and more Volunteers. Every now and again, he'd see someone dressed in a suit.

He passed by a series of small offices, the doors shut, the blinds drawn tightly. Nearly all of them dark but one, a thin sliver of light shining from underneath the door of the last office on the left. This one creeped Ben out more than the dark ones. It made him think of men in dark suits scheming and plotting. Experimentation. Human subjects. The Orchid virus.

A small sign hanging from the ceiling at the first intersection of corridors highlighted routes to the Department's various divisions, including Disease Monitoring, Infrastructure, Refugee Affairs, Debris Removal, and of course, Ben's favorite, Human Asset Recovery & Disposition. They all led in different directions, depicted by a confusing tangle of arrows that were difficult to decipher.

Panic began to ripple through him as the magnitude of his mission began to sink in.

He was going about this all wrong. He hadn't thought this through at all, and it was going to get him killed. As he wound through the building, he began to feel flush, heat crawling up his neck like kudzu inching its way up the side of a dilapidated shack. He ran a hand across his scalp, which was damp with perspiration. Time to regroup.

At the end of a short hallway connecting two longer corridors, he found an unlocked storage closet and took refuge inside. Metal shelving, stocked with all manner of cleaning supplies, lined the walls, leaving just enough room for a stepstool. Ben took a seat, resting his elbows on his knees, his head in his hands, to get his bearings. Get a hold of this panic attack before it consumed him and left him unable to think straight.

This strategy was ludicrous. As though he would just stumble across a door marked TRANQUILITY, conveniently left unlocked, where all the answers would be waiting for him. It was stupid and naïve. This would have been hard enough with a *good* plan, and here he was, flailing about like a small-time thug trying to rip off a Mafia don. These were serious people he was dealing with, he reminded himself, and they were not to be taken lightly.

He thought about the single lit office he'd seen earlier, and about the machinations and dealings of the men who ran this place. About their dark suits and how men in suits, men like Mr. Whitmore, ran things. They'd run things before the Panic, from their back rooms and aboard their private jets and multimillion-dollar compounds. They ran things now. Not much had changed. It still came down to power. The ones who held the power could do the things they wanted. Because men like Mr. Whitmore had cast off the Redeyes, people like Ben faced a bleak and uncertain future.

And that's when it hit him. His head popped straight up, his mind cleared of the tangled knot that had been crippling him. He needed to find one of these power players. He needed to take the fight to them directly. One of these suits.

He took a long cleansing breath, the air redolent with the scent of pine floor cleaner and antiseptic. It smelled sharp and clean and healthy, a stark contrast to the real world. It was time. He opened the door and stepped back out into the corridor.

24

He marched down the hall with purpose, passing one Volunteer after another, none of whom took any interest in him. Ben had long ago learned that acting like you knew what the hell was going on, even if you didn't know up from down, went a long way. Most people lived their lives in perpetual states of self-doubt, so going against that grain merely reinforced those folks' belief in their own shortcomings while convincing them that you knew what you were doing.

He didn't know how long it would last, or how quickly someone might recognize him, but for now, he was holding the upper hand in this match. He reviewed the informational signs when he saw them again and decided that the Office of Survivor Affairs, which was housed on the second floor, was probably his best bet. Whatever Tranquility was, Thompson believed that it affected the Redeyes. Nothing else would really make sense. It was his life's work, his reason for being. It was what had gotten him killed.

Ben took an elevator to the second floor. He could almost hear a countdown timer ticking toward zero. The car slid gently to a stop, and the doors swished open. A large reception desk manned by a Department volunteer greeted him. The Department kept strange hours; amazing how busy the place was. Then again, building a totalitarian regime from the ashes of the greatest democracy the world had ever known wasn't exactly a nine-to-five gig. A lot of overtime and cheap takeout.

Serious men wearing serious suits.

He saluted the Volunteer crisply and then pointed to the locked door, his heart leaping into his throat as he did so. He had no idea if he was supposed to salute this Volunteer or if these mercenaries even saluted each other at all. Time stopped for a moment and then he relaxed when the soldier returned the salute. The door buzzed, followed by an audible click, the sound of the lock disengaging.

The floor's outer perimeter was lined with larger offices; it was these he focused on. The air was alive with the clickety-clack of fingers flying across keyboards, the gruff and official-sounding voices of soldiers speaking in flat, robotic monotones. Still, no one paid him any attention.

Ben spotted a single lighted office at the end of a long row of dark ones. The blinds were open; a middle-aged black man sat at a desk tapping away at his computer, eating a snack. He looked to be about Ben's age. Ben approached the office with cautious confidence. The name Robert Bowen was stenciled on the door. The DRR man had his nose to his screen, oblivious to his surroundings. He didn't seem to notice Ben or really anything else around him. Ben's heart felt like it might burst through his chest and get all over this guy's nice suit.

Ben knocked on the door twice and stepped in the office without waiting for a response. The man looked up from his computer screen, startled. He looked tired.

His short-cropped hair graying at the temples. His reading glasses sat perched on the tip of his pointed nose.

"Can I help you?"

"Agent Whitmore sent me."

Bowen's eyes widened at hearing Whitmore's name.

"Yes?"

Ben rolled his eyes and sighed.

"He said you'd be expecting me?"

"For what?"

"Jesus," Ben whispered. Then louder, with more heft:

"He asked me to see you for the file."

"What file?"

"I don't know," Ben said, exasperated. "Hang on. I wrote it on my hand."

Ben glanced at his bare palm.

"The Tranquility file."

Silence. Like the oxygen had been sucked right out of the room.

"I wasn't told about this."

Here Ben had to take charge to keep the ruse alive.

"I don't know what to tell you," Ben said. "Whitmore told me to see Robert Bowen."

"Okay."

"You are Robert Bowen, right?"

"Yes."

"Are there any other Robert Bowens here?"

"No."

"So there we go."

Bowen removed his reading glasses and set them on his keyboard. He tugged at his beard, which made a faint hissing noise.

"This is highly unusual," he said.

"Look, man, I just work here," Ben said in a sigh, patting his hand against his chest.

"I'm gonna call this in," Bowen said. "I don't know who you are."

Fear blistered Ben.

"You really gonna call Whitmore?"

"There are strict protocols when it comes to Tranquility," he said, lifting the phone from its receiver. "Someone fucked up. They're not gonna bust me for this."

"Fine," Ben said. "Wake up, Whitmore. You know how he loves being called at home."

"What the fuck are you talking about?"

Ben's stomach dropped. His gambit was collapsing.

"He's gonna be pissed," Ben said.

"Then he can be pissed," Bowen said. "I'm not risking a treason charge because I'm afraid of getting yelled at."

He started pushing numbers on the keypad.

Then he stopped and glanced right at Ben.

"Wait. I do know you."

Well, Ben thought. That was that.

He swung the business end of the rifle up.

"Give me the fucking file."

"Security breach!" yelled Bowen as he dove to the floor, behind the desk and out of range of Ben's weapon. Not that it mattered; Ben didn't think he had the stomach to murder an innocent office jockey. Bowen's scream echoed through the floor, leaving Ben no chance but to flee. He grabbed a file from Bowen's desk and bolted from the office as others began turning their attention toward the commotion.

Footsteps behind him.

"Lock down the building, lock it down," a voice behind him called out.

"In the fatigues!" called out another voice.

Ben raced through the cubicle maze, his eyes tracking the Exit signs. There was a door at the end of the corridor. A glance across the floor confirmed that another chase group was closing in. At his current pace, he would probably make it to the door a step or two ahead of them.

He burst through the door a few seconds later, spilling into the stairwell. He slammed the door closed behind him and started down the steps. Sweat lacquered his panic-stricken body as he took the steps two at a time. As he reached the second floor landing, the stairwell echoed with increased activity, more soldiers joining the chase. The boot-falls on the metal steps sounded like a herd of elephants stampeding through a minefield.

One floor to go.

Now he took the steps three at a time, figuring the reward of a quicker descent was worth the risk of a broken ankle. He safely made it to the first-floor landing, where two doors awaited him. The emergency exit and the door back to the first floor. If they were expecting him to vacate the building, he could shake them by going back through the main lobby. He might even blend in with other Volunteers.

He waved the identification card over the access panel and waited for the red light to switch to green. The panel beeped once, alarmingly, but the tiny lamp continued to shine red. He tried not to panic, remind himself of all those times his access card at work hadn't taken the first time and waved it a second time.

BEEEP!

Red.

A third time.

BEEEP!

Still red.

"Oh, shit," Ben whispered.

Out. He had to get out now. With the file tucked securely under his arm, he crossed the landing to the exit. The door was stenciled with the words EMERGENCY EXIT ONLY – ALARM WILL SOUND.

He scanned the access panel with the card one last time, but again, the box beeped its unhappy beep.

Screw it, he thought. He turned toward the emergency exit and depressed the lock-release bar, steeling himself for the chaos of the klaxon alarms howling in his ear but anticipating the sweet breath of fresh air. As he pressed the bar, he kept moving, not wanting to break stride as he made his way outside.

And so it was to his great surprise when his shoulder connected with the very recalcitrant door. He pressed the release bar again, and then a third time, but the door remained shut. Fear bloomed into full-blown panic, the likes of which he hadn't felt since the moment that woman's teeth had sunk into his calf so many moons ago. He rattled the door, he kicked the door, but it held firm. He was trapped in the stairwell.

Well then.

At least he could finally find out what he'd come here to learn. Even if it wouldn't do anyone else any good. He sat down and opened the folder that he'd purloined from Robert Bowen. It wasn't a huge file, maybe half an inch thick. He could get through a little bit before they took him back into custody. Like a hungry man eyeing an all-you-can-eat seafood buffet, he flipped the file open and began to read.

The first page was a cover memorandum, titled *Eisenhower Interstate Highway Reconstruction Protocol 2027-2030*. Confused, he flipped through the rest of the report, looking for any reference to Tranquility, something that might pull the curtain back a little, but he found nothing. Instead, he came across maps of the interstate highway system marked with little red crosses indicating areas needing repair, bid sheets from highway contractors, civil engineering reports. He closed the folder and set it in his lap, fully aware that this file he'd stolen didn't have the first goddamn thing to do with Tranquility.

He laughed out loud at himself, first an insane-sounding high-pitched giggle, quickly escalating into a belly-shaking, body-trembling roar of laughter, as though he'd seen the holy grail of keyboard-playing cats on YouTube.

Had he really thought that he would accomplish anything? That had been silly. A lie he'd told himself to make himself feel useful. A lie so convincing that he'd managed to pull Ellie along in his wake of naïve stupidity. He felt stupid and small, his wasted life lying before him broken and ruined, like a crime scene, waiting for a seasoned investigator to roll up in a dark brown sedan and sort through the mess that was left behind, to make some sense of how things had gone so terribly wrong.

He was nothing. A nothing man. Just another statistic, another sad story from humanity's biggest sad face. When they taught the Panic in history books fifty years down the road, Ben would be just another one of the faceless millions who were lost, another anonymous soul in a sea of them. One day, Gavin would tell his future wife that his father had died in the Panic, and maybe she'd have a similar story about her father or mother or uncle or best friend. And that would tie them together, the way it tied them all together.

The sound of a door clattering open broke him from his trance; a stampede of boots and shouts filled the stairwell in a tsunami of chaos barreling down toward him. He looked at the automatic rifle leaned up against the step and wondered if he should just eat a bullet right now; it would probably be preferable to the fate that certainly awaited him once they arrived. Or maybe he should just hunker down and take out as many Volunteers as he could before he ran out of ammunition. At least he would have done something to make these assholes pay for the carnage back at the Haven. But it seemed like more trouble than it was worth.

They'd locked down the stairwell.

They'd caught him.

And he had nothing.

He lifted the gun, aimed it at the landing.

He rested his finger on the trigger.

25

I n the end, Ben did not make a suicidal last stand in the stairwell. They'd found him on the landing, his hands on his head in the universal language of surrender. He debated turning to face the wall to show how little a threat he posed, lest a Volunteer with an itchy trigger finger mistake his decision to face them head on as an offensive maneuver, but he decided against it. He wanted to look them in the face, and he wanted them to see his red eyes and be a little bit afraid.

They confiscated his weapon and cuffed him. A quartet of Volunteers escorted him to a holding room on the third floor and guarded him until Whitmore arrived. Ben sat with his cuffed hands folded on the square table in the center of the room while Whitmore took report from one of the guards.

"Your carriage has turned into a pumpkin, Mr. Sullivan," he said, taking the seat across from Ben.

"Meaning what?"

"You'll be held pending a detention hearing."

"What's the charge?"

"Same ones from before," Whitmore said. "Plus six counts of murder."

Ben laughed out loud at this and wondered if Whitmore actually thought that Ben believed he would see an ounce of due process before they remanded him to a detention facility or, more likely, shot him in the head and dumped his body in a landfill.

"I didn't realize I'd said something funny, Mr. Sullivan," he had said.

"This idea of a detention hearing is funny," Ben had replied. "This whole goddamn thing is funny."

"I don't think it's funny at all, Mr. Sullivan."

Ben hated being addressed as Mr. Sullivan, even when it wasn't coming from a self-righteous douchebag like Whitmore. It stank of insincerity and it stank of contempt.

"Too bad."

And so Whitmore had left him there for another hour, or maybe it was two, or maybe it was three minutes because after a few seconds, it quickly became difficult to gauge the passage of time, and Ben spent the rest of his time in that holding room pondering the difficulty of marking time. It kept him from having to think about Sarah or Gavin or the Haven or Ellie or the millions of Redeyes that the Department seemed hell-bent on screwing over.

After a while, he needed to use the bathroom, but they ignored his pleas for a restroom break, and so he ended up peeing in the corner of the room. Then he'd had to sit in the room stinking of urine for yet another indeterminate period of time. By the time they came and got him, he no longer gave a shit what they did.

They marched him down the hallway, through a series of corridors and onto a loading dock, where a white box truck emblazoned with the Department logo awaited them.

His two escorts followed him up the truck's ramp, and Mr. Whitmore joined them a few minutes later. The truck had been retrofitted with hard metal benches bolted to the wall of the cargo bay and leg chains dangling from each bench. Each of Ben's ankles was fastened to a cuff, but being the good sport that he was, Whitmore had left Ben's hands free. Ben wore an orange prison jumpsuit and baby blue paper booties, the point of which were completely lost on him.

Whitmore, of course, was immaculately dressed, his suit neat and ironed, his shirt a brilliant white, virtually crackling with starch. It was warm in the truck, but the knot of his expensive tie, of course, was perfect and uncompromised, an unspoiled field, because Mr. Whitmore was a serious man doing serious things, whereas Ben was simply old gum stuck in the treads of the struggling country's shoe.

Time dragged by, more slowly and maddeningly than Ben could ever remember feeling in his whole life. The combination of not knowing where he was, where they were going, and how much longer he had to live was warping his ability to assess the passage of time. The two soldiers sat ramrod straight, one on either side of him. Whitmore sat across from him and seemed to enjoy studying Ben's reaction to the circumstances in which he found himself. He smoked a cigarette, and then another and then a third. The smoke smelled rancid and acidic and burned Ben's eyes.

"That was pretty clever what you did back there," Whitmore said. "Bowen's a pretty smart guy, one of our brightest. You stroll into just about anyone else's office, you probably walk out with what you're looking for. I think it was just dumb luck that we caught you."

Ben didn't reply; instead he returned Whitmore's gaze, tracking the man's eyes with his own. However long this took, he wanted Whitmore to know that he wasn't afraid of him. Whatever they did to him, he wasn't afraid anymore. He was in no hurry to die, but he was not afraid.

"I blame myself, actually," Whitmore said, leaning back in his chair. "I guess I didn't really expect you to show up here. That took guts, Mr. Sullivan."

And the bitch of it was that Whitmore probably did respect him a little for his dumb-ass move.

"Although for the life of me, I can't imagine why you would take such a risk."

You and me both, brother.

"Care to share?"

Ben continued to sit stone still.

"Let's make a game of it," Whitmore said, a delighted grin blooming on his face.

Ben couldn't bear to look at him anymore so he picked out a spot on the floor of the cargo bay and stared at that instead.

"You really don't know what Tranquility is, do you?" Whitmore said.

Ben looked up at him, and he sort of wished he hadn't, because Whitmore's grin had evolved into a full-on smile, full of sparkling white teeth, the mouth of a man who didn't struggle for basic necessities. He probably continued to use one of the electric toothbrushes with the spinning heads, his middle finger to the rolling blackouts that continued across the nation.

Whitmore had the look of a man who knew he'd won, who knew that he'd gotten his man. The last thread that needed to be snipped. The final piece of the puzzle. He looked back at the floor, back at the tiny spot in the shape of a crescent moon, and wondered about its origin. A coffee stain. Maybe dried blood.

"Mr. Sullivan," Whitmore said. "Aren't you the least bit curious where we're taking you?"

Ben looked back up at Whitmore, annoyed with the man for distracting him from the stain on the floor.

"No. Not particularly."

He looked back down at the stain and thought about Ellie. He wondered how long she would wait for him before she realized he wasn't coming back. He wondered how long it would take her to start the next chapter of her life now that this one was drawing to a close. He hoped that she would find some solace. She hadn't been any more to blame for killing her husband than he had been for trying to kill her. He hoped that she would be able to move on and that she wouldn't stay rooted in the past, anchored by the memory of a terrible thing she had had to do. Because eventually life would rise around her like floodwaters, and if she couldn't rise with it, she would drown. He didn't want that to happen.

He still wasn't afraid. He could control it. He could hide it from them. If he could hide that from them, by ignoring them, not rising to the bait, he'd be okay. It was hard to fear a situation that you controlled. That's why it was easy to be afraid of the dark or that strange lump or that weird noise late night, just loud enough to wake you up. Beyond your control. And so he sat there, quietly, letting Whitmore and his lackeys think whatever they were going to think.

Ben went back to the spot on the floor.

HE MUST HAVE FALLEN asleep because the sensation of the truck hitching to a stop startled him, and for a moment, he couldn't remember where he was. But then he saw the two

Volunteers and Whitmore's stupid face, and it all came rushing back. He sighed softly. At least he'd gotten some sleep. It was, in fact, the first decent snooze he'd had in a while. His head was clear, and despite a bit of a kink in his neck, he felt remarkably refreshed. Amazing how well one could sleep when the mind was unoccupied with a bunch of useless clutter.

Whitmore stood up and stretched. As he did so, his cell phone began to chirp.

"Whitmore."

He listened intently for a moment.

"We'll disembark here and walk the rest of the way," he said.

Another pause as he listened to the party on the other end of the line.

"Excellent."

He ended the call and slipped the phone inside his jacket pocket.

"We're here," he said.

A moment later, Ben heard the squelch and squeal of the truck's metal door as it rolled open, revealing the early evening gloom beyond. The driver, a third Volunteer, extended the metal ramp from a hidden slot under the floor of the truck. The other two unhooked Ben's leg chains and escorted him off the truck.

The air was fresh and clean, as though it had been laundered. After years of the post-Panic miasma, he'd forgotten what fresh air smelled like. The scent was a shock to the system. It was so fragrant and crisp that he sneezed twice. He looked off to the east, back in the direction they'd come from and saw nothing but undeveloped land, the road they were on the sole concession to human development, cutting through the land like a black vein.

"That air is something, eh, Sullivan?" Whitmore said as he followed Ben down the ramp.

They'd stopped in front of a small building. A Department banner, rippling in the breeze, had been strung across the structure's façade. The road they were on plunged away from them into the falling twilight. Behind him, tall barbed-wire fence stretched away in either direction, following the slope of the land. About a half-mile off, the fence lines suddenly ended, and in the dim twilight, he could just make out the fence turning north. There were a dozen watchtowers spaced apart along the perimeter fence. Dozens of buildings dotted the complex.

It was quiet here, the silence magnified by the white blast of the spotlights. It felt like the calm before the storm. As though the place was now ready for whatever it had been designed for.

A feeling of unease began to nibble at Ben like a lost puppy scratching at a back door.

"Where are we?"

The question got away from him like an unruly child. He wished he hadn't asked, because he wasn't particularly sure that he wanted to know the answer, and he didn't like giving Whitmore that kind of power over him. But there it was, hanging out there for Whitmore to return however he saw fit. There were so many ways he could return serve. He could lie, he could mock, and he could refuse to answer the question at all.

Or, and this was what scared Ben most of all, he could tell the truth. And Ben wasn't sure he wanted to know it.

"Ben, this is your new home."

It was the first time Whitmore had ever addressed him as Ben, and it sounded twisted and awful, and he now hated the sound of his own name. It was tainted now, corrupted, anathema to hear the name that his parents had chosen for him, the name of his maternal grandfather, uttered by this piece of human garbage.

Ben bit his lip so he wouldn't rise to the bait. He ignored the mystery of his new surroundings and stared at his captor, this anonymous agent of the Department. He really looked at him for the first time. Ben was terrible at deducing how old someone was, but Whitmore looked to be about his age. In another life, they may have been contemporaries. Maybe even friends. Who was this man? What had he done before the Panic? Did he have a wife? A husband? Kids? A dog? Did he like to read fiction? Did he go to dogfights? Did he drink too much? Why did he hate Ben so much? Why did he hate the Reds so much? How could he derive so much pleasure from Ben's suffering? Had Redeyes murdered his family? Or had his family become infected?

Did any of that matter?

Whitmore had said something.

"What was that?"

"Jesus Christ, I said if you need to take a piss, now would be the time."

"I'm fine."

Whitmore stepped up to the side of the building and relieved himself. "I'm getting to that age I gotta get up in the middle of the night to piss."

No, Ben didn't have to use the bathroom because he hadn't had anything to drink in the last twenty-four hours.

Ben was suddenly annoyed with Whitmore and his little slice-of-life tale of middle age. He was rubbing Ben's face in the wonder of the ordinary, the little checkpoints that every man expected to face on that long journey to old age.

Ben scanned the quiet landscape, dotted with old farmhouses and dead cornfields, and briefly considered making a run for it. He wouldn't make it far before the grind of the M4 rifles cut him down, leaving him a bloody mess on the ground. It might be worth it, though, just to screw Whitmore's life up; he'd probably be in a lot of hot water for failing to deliver the prisoner to wherever the hell they were going.

On the other hand, Whitmore would probably enjoy ordering these yahoos to gun him down; for him, it might actually be worth the dressing down he'd get back at DRR headquarters. They could always find another Redeye troublemaker. Overhead, a flock of geese streamed south, squawking in the evening air. Ben looked up, watching the birds fly in perfect formation. It was things like this, little subtle things that popped up out of nowhere, like an apocalyptic jack-in-the-box, to remind you that holy shit, the world nearly came to an end.

As Ben turned back to face his captors, Whitmore punched him in the stomach, leaving him doubled over, gasping for air. Despite the sudden burst of agony, Ben couldn't explain the joy that was coursing through his body as he listened to Whitmore dress him down. He'd never been religious, and what all with the Panic and everything, he was hard-pressed to think that he'd been wrong about it, but he thought this ecstasy he was now feeling must have been something like finding God. Never in his life had anything brought him the kind of joy like pushing Whitmore's buttons.

After taking a minute to catch his breath, his hands on his knees like a winded basketball player, Ben rose back up to his full height.

"Where were we?" Whitmore asked.

"You were going to tell me about what we were doing here."

"Of course."

Whitmore's phone began to ring again; he held up a finger and excused himself, right at the gates, just out of earshot. He chatted for a few minutes, hung up and slid the phone into his jacket pocket. He motioned for the Volunteers, and that earned Ben another tip of the muzzle in the small of his back. Ben winced, surprised at how much that hurt. It didn't seem like it should, but it did. As soon as he got close enough to see Whitmore's face, he knew he was in trouble.

Big trouble.

Whitmore was smiling, ear to ear, almost as if he were trying to get his lips to stretch around the circumference of his head and touch in the back. He looked like a man with a secret he couldn't wait to share. Some juicy, juicy gossip.

"Mr. Sullivan," he said, his voice positively dripping with glee. "I was just on the phone with the Secretary herself."

Ben felt dizzy, and he found himself having to concentrate on breathing, and as he did so, he wondered how he had made it this far in his life without making sure that he was always breathing. He thought about his eighth-grade science teacher, Mrs. Martin, and how she had taught them that it was an involuntary reaction, and he was sure that had been a gigantic lie. Each breath seemed to get stuck in his throat.

"What did you talk about?" Ben said, his voice sounding small and far away, barely making its way over the stream of wind blowing by.

"Why, we talked about you, my good man!"

Ben didn't reply. He couldn't think of anything to say.

"Mr. Sullivan, would you like to know what Tranquility is?"

26

Ben found himself nodding stupidly, like a game-show contestant offered the chance to peek behind the Mystery Door #2. He did want to know what Tranquility was. He wanted to know what he'd sacrificed his life for.

"Well, I'm going to tell you," Whitmore said, stepping closer and clapping Ben on the shoulder. "After all, you have worked so hard to find out. You've been quite the little eager beaver!"

More dizziness ensued, the feeling that Ben had gotten up too fast, faster than he'd ever gotten up in his life; his knees buckled underneath him. The Volunteers hoisted him back onto his feet.

"Why tell me now?"

"Because, Mr. Sullivan, after I tell you all about it – and trust me, I'm not going to leave out any details – I'm going to blow your brains out."

~

BEN'S second seizure hit at 6:18 p.m. on July 26, some seventy-one days after he'd become infected with the virus. According to numerous studies conducted since the Panic, the mean symptomatic period for infection was approximately sixty-nine days (and hadn't that been a source of amusement online). The quickest recovery on record had been fifty-four days; the longest, ninety-one. He'd been inside a Dumpster foraging for his dinner, when his body seized up and everything went dark. He flopped around the stinking trash container for nearly a minute; he fractured his right wrist and sliced his bicep on a shard of a broken beer bottle, but other than that he emerged from the seizure none too worse for the wear. He was lucky; about one percent of Redeyes died during this second seizure.

When it was over, Ben sat up, confused but alert. At some primal level, deep down, he knew that his body had prevailed over the infection. He was in disbelief; in those horrific hours after he'd been bitten, it had never occurred to him that he would recover. There had been no documented cases of recovery by then. The assumption had been that infection with Orchid was permanent, and the government's sole objective had been to wipe out the Redeyes. He didn't know why they had thought that; it just seemed weird that a disease that would push humanity to the brink would simply fade away like the common cold.

He was sitting atop a mound of damp, sweaty trash, cloaked in an invisible cloud of the stink of rotting garbage. As his insides curdled from the stench, he scampered over the side of the Dumpster and dropped down to the ground below. The ruins of an apartment complex, consumed by fire, stood before him.

He didn't know what month it was, let alone what day it was. He certainly didn't know where he was. Instinctively, he checked the bite wound on his calf and found that it had healed; a faded semi-circular scar of jagged dashes remained, a ghostly reminder of his attacker's teeth marks. The sun had burnished his sleeveless arms to a dark brown hue, and he felt the stinging tightness of more sunburn on his neck and face. He was wearing filthy, loose-fitting jeans; these were the same pants he'd been wearing the day he'd been bitten. They were terribly loose around his waist, and that gave him his first clue that it had been a while since that terrible day. The pants had been snug back then, maybe a little too snug. A pat of his stomach revealed his paunch was gone.

And then it all came rushing back to him, a flood of blood, of beatings and wild rampages, like a hungry lion let loose on a roomful of wounded baby gazelles. His legs gave way underneath him as the faces of those whose lives he had ended slid by, like one of those *In Memoriam* photo montages from the awards shows. Except this wasn't any black-tie affair, movie stars mourning the loss of the giants of the business who'd died after long, happy lives. No, this was a terrible slideshow through hell.

He screamed, a bellowing howl that originated deep in his soul and roared out of him like a runaway express train with evil as the conductor. And yet the faces of his victims continued to scroll by. Seven, eight, nine. Ten. Twelve. Sixteen before he lost count. No. It was impossible. He hadn't killed those people. Hallucinations. From the fever that accompanied the virus. Psychotic visions that had anchored themselves in his head, like weeds taking root, making it difficult to discern what was real and what was imagined.

But he was just kidding himself.

He started running, running as fast as he could. Perhaps

if he ran fast enough he could stay ahead of the horror show looping in his mind. He ran behind the ruins of the complex into a woodsy area choked with pines and oaks and maples. The canopy provided good coverage from the sun, keeping it cool, the air ripe with summer pine. At the far edge of the trees, he crashed into a tent, knocking it flat, stumbling over its occupants like a bowling ball clearing a spare. Cursing and yelling ensued, and as they emerged from the tent, Ben scampered to his feet and continued running. The sound of gunshots cracked the afternoon. A round whizzed by his head and splintered a young sapling not ten feet to his left. But no matter how far or how fast he ran, he couldn't get the images out of his mind.

He spent that first night under an overpass, huddled in a little recess between the metal railing and concrete wall, unable to control the flood of tears, the trembling, the never-ending loop of the images of his victims. He ran the gamut of human emotion, from fear and terror, to depression and melancholy, to joy and glee. One hour he wept, another he laughed hysterically, a third he spent quiet, almost catatonic.

As dawn broke, he was hanging onto a single frayed thread of sanity. He'd figured out where he was, some sixty miles north of the home he shared with Sarah and Gavin. It took him three days to cover the distance and slalom around scores of abandoned vehicles dotting the landscape like dead bugs. As he drew closer to the Raleigh metro area, the scope of the devastation came into ever-sharpening focus, as though he was adjusting the lens on the camera in his mind. The more he saw, the more he remembered about his time in the grip of the Orchid infection. The denser the population grid, the worse it got.

Things appeared to be dying down; the very few

Redeyes he saw paid him no mind. He would later learn that Redeyes did not attack individuals carrying antibodies to the virus, even those who had kicked the infection. Yet another quirk of the virus that scientists were trying to unravel. By this point, most were injured or emaciated, usually both, and there were far fewer with an active infection. Food was particularly hard to come by in the latter half of that summer, as the distribution channels that had fed America before the Panic had been all but destroyed. It was nothing like the absolute chaos that they'd all become accustomed to in the weeks preceding his infection.

He made it back to his neighborhood just as the sun had begun its slow descent to the horizon. The twilight was still but for the sounds of the cicadas and crickets. The power was out, but when he saw the lantern burning in the bay window at the front of his house, his heart began to race, but in a good way. Not like the terror-fueled jackhammer that had been thrumming away since springtime. For the first time, he began to feel like things might work out, that he'd made it, that he'd survived this horrible thing. As he made his way up the front walk, checking out the lawn that he'd once lovingly cared for, long since choked with waist-high weeds, he began to think about the things he'd need to do.

But first, he needed to put his family back together.

He climbed the four brick steps to the front door, and before he could stop himself, he knocked firmly on the door.

And so when Sarah answered the door, looking thin, tired, like she'd been to hell and back, he was most surprised to hear her utter a blood-curdling shriek and raise a gun to his face.

THE VOLUNTEERS ESCORTED Ben behind the building, Whitmore trailing close behind. In a clearing about fifty yards north of the truck, they stopped and formed a triangle around him. The soldiers had their rifles trained at him, and Whitmore joined in as well, pointing a large-caliber handgun at Ben's face. A brisk wind had picked up, and Ben was cold. Ben worked very hard not to shiver in front of Whitmore, lest the jackass think that he was afraid of him.

"So what now?" Ben asked.

"Now you find out everything you wanted to know."

"Kind of Scooby-Dooish, isn't it?" Ben said. "Telling me the master plan?"

"You know, I thought about that," Whitmore said. "But I so desperately want you to know. I want you to die here knowing what's about to happen. Otherwise, killing you is almost pointless. And besides, things are already in motion."

"Tell me, don't tell me. I really don't give a shit."

Whitmore smiled. One of his stupid smiles that Ben had come to associate with Whitmore sitting on a juicy bit of gossip that he was just dying to share with Ben. He was worse than a teenage girl.

"How did you ever make it as a covert operative?"

This earned Ben the butt of Whitmore's hand cannon across his face. His field of vision lit up with white-hot pain, and his legs buckled underneath him. He tried mightily to stay on his feet, but the sudden burst of vertigo dropped him to his knees.

"The Department estimates that approximately one hundred eighty million people became infected with the Orchid virus during the Panic," Whitmore said, with all the verve of a college professor who truly loved his subject matter. "As you know, these people…"

He paused, as though looking for just the right way to put his next thought.

"You people…"

There.

Now he looked satisfied.

"…caused untold devastation and carnage."

"I'd tell you it wasn't our fault," Ben replied, "but I'm guessing you don't care about things like facts."

Whitmore ignored him and continued.

"There are about thirty million Reds still alive in the continental United States," he said, "mostly concentrated along the East and West Coasts. A good chunk in Texas and around Chicago. The rest scattered through the less densely populated regions.

"And I have to be honest with you, Mr. Sullivan. The country is still in bad, bad shape. The economy is not coming along like we had hoped. The infrastructure is still a mess. The military is a shell of its former self. Luckily, the rest of the world is in the same shape we are. For now. But the race is on, Mr. Sullivan. The race to become the world's first post-Panic superpower."

Ben was trying to parse meaning from his words, but he was missing something. Something that Whitmore hadn't shared yet. Or maybe Whitmore was just screwing with him.

"But we can't reclaim our spot at the top with this drag on our progress," he said. "We did a survey a couple months ago. Asked people how things were going, their concerns, what they thought the country needed to work on. You know, we're pretty far afield here. Uncharted waters. We thought the input would be useful."

"Do you know what the respondents' number one answer was?"

"Let me guess," Ben said. "The Redeyes."

"Precisely," he said. "They're afraid, Ben. They're afraid it's all going to start up again. You remember what it was like, don't you? Before they got you?

Ben did remember.

"You really don't know how close we came to going under," Whitmore said. "Some projections said that we had another week. Maybe two. You know what happened on the West Coast?"

Ben shook his head. The news had been filtered, sanitized and spun until it was as clean as an operating room.

"The Redeyes outnumbered us eight-to-one, ten-to-one in the metro areas. San Diego, Los Angeles, San Francisco. Fifteen million infected in California by the beginning of June. That's more than the goddamn Chinese Army. The President authorized a tactical nuclear strike on each of the cities. To disinfect."

"Millions of people, vaporized in the blink of an eye. The West Coast, it's uninhabitable for the next fifty years. And it didn't help. Y'all absolutely destroyed the Midwest. They were too scattered for the military to make an effective campaign against, especially since they were having such a hard time here and farther north.

"We can't go through that again," Whitmore said. "It could finish us off. The Secretary meets with the President daily. This is all they talk about. They review reports of suspected outbreaks. They review pathology reports, looking for any sign that the virus could make a comeback. Like shingles."

"You're comparing the Orchid virus to shingles?"

"You know what I mean. The point is, Mr. Sullivan, is

that if the virus ever reactivates, we've got to be able to get a handle on it quickly. And so the administration has decided that for the safety of your people-"

"My people?" Ben repeated. "Do you have any idea how stupid that sounds?"

"Spare me your judgment," he said. "For the safety of this country, this is what we're going to do. This is Camp Alpha. If the Secretary hadn't decided that you were too dangerous, this would have been your new home. There are nineteen other camps like it."

"Nineteen more?"

Ben was confused.

"Why do you need twenty camps this size? How many people do you plan on arresting?"

"Why, Mr. Sullivan, I'm surprised that you haven't picked it up yet."

Ben's gaze bounced between the look of satisfaction on Whitmore's face and the empty camp that lay before him like a brand-new subdivision, awaiting the influx of young families and minivans and bottles of Pinot and golf bags. Behind the camp, the sun was dipping toward the horizon; the approaching darkness bothered Ben at his core, and he silently pleaded with the sun to stay aloft a little longer, to not abandon him with these monsters.

And then it came to him in a flash, all at once.

"Jesus Christ," Ben said, stumbling backwards away from Whitmore. His feet tangled together and he fell on his ass, hard; the shock of the impact fired a bolt of pain through his spine. They laughed at him, and as they laughed, he was more certain than ever of what they were doing.

"You finally figure it out?"

Ben stared at him, his eyes wide with horror.

"You're starting up camps. Permanent camps."

"You're a bomb just waiting to go off," Whitmore said. "And if it does, we can keep it under control."

"But there haven't been any outbreaks since the end of the Panic."

Terror fluttered in his chest, a can of butterflies tickling his insides.

"We cannot take that chance," he said. "We don't understand how the virus works. We still don't even know where it came from. For all we know, it could be fatal next time. Or more easily transmitted."

"Even if that were true, this isn't how you do it. This is what the Nazis would do."

Whitmore slapped Ben hard across the face. Rage rippled across his face, which was flush and tight.

"We're doing this to save the country," he barked at him. "This goddamn thing was nearly the end of everything!"

Ben took the slap in stride. He didn't even raise a hand to check on his cheek, which felt warm and numb. He poked Whitmore in the chest and shook his head violently.

"It'll never work," Ben said. "The American people aren't going to stand idly by while you guys start up a bunch of concentration camps."

"Very good, Mr. Sullivan," Whitmore said, his tone changing course dramatically, as though they were a couple of political science graduate students, kicking back in a Starbucks, sipping a little organic free trade coffee. Wearing thick sweaters and discussing the dynamics of a totalitarian regime.

"You're right," he said. "The people probably wouldn't stand for it. I think they'd have a very hard time accepting the permanent internment of their fellow citizens. That is, unless you win their hearts and minds. If you do that, the people will follow you anywhere, because they'll believe that you're looking for out for their best interests.

"And you believe that, don't you? That we're looking for out for your best interests?"

"Like it matters what I believe," Ben snapped.

They were quiet a moment as Ben considered the ramifications of Whitmore's confession.

How do you win their hearts and minds?

They were still Americans. They'd been to hell and back, sure, but would they be so eager to turn on millions of their fellow citizens? On their neighbors, their friends, their families, their children's teachers and pastors and pizza delivery guys and nice ladies who cleaned their teeth?

They wouldn't.

Unless they felt there was no choice.

And what would lead them to believe there was no choice but to intern millions of American citizens? What could the Department possibly tell them to believe that there was no choice?

Tranquility. Tranquility. Tranquility.

He looked up at a sliver of moon, looking back down on him like a smirk. Alone in the indigo sky. Men had walked up there. More than half a century earlier, America had put a man on the moon, and now they were ready to start up a new version of Nazi Germany. Quite the cultural progression. He wished he'd been alive to see the moon landing. He couldn't believe that he'd lived his entire life and never seen a man go to the moon. He couldn't believe that one of mankind's great achievements had occurred before he was born. It seemed backwards.

Tranquility. Tranquility. Tranquility.

He began to feel a nagging ache inside his mind, like a

song lyric that was just out of reach, the name of an old classmate that had slipped away over the years.

"Well, Mr. Sullivan, I have enjoyed our little discussion, but I'm afraid that our time is up."

What was it?

Tranquility. Tranquility. Tranquility.

Houston, Tranquility Base here. The Eagle has landed.

Those amazing words, cloaked in static. He could still hear them, having watched the clips from the moon landing over and over and over, a reminder of what mankind was capable of.

Tranquility. Tranquility. Tranquility.

And now they'd poisoned the word with their monstrous vision.

Why?

Had it been some automatically generated code word, ruthlessly spit out by some Department computer in that building back in Washington? Or was it something more? Perhaps the Department felt that once they'd locked them all up, the people would feel tranquil again. They could start focusing on reality television and college basketball and hot yoga again.

"On your knees," Whitmore said, his voice flat and devoid of emotion.

Ben was barely listening now; he stood there, ignoring Whitmore as he tried to scratch the itch in his brain.

No. There was something else at work here. He was sure of it.

He looked back up at the moon; now it looked like the smirk of someone who'd told a joke you hadn't quite understood. Possibly a joke at your expense.

Unless you win their hearts and minds...

Then it hit him like a ton of bricks.

You won the people's hearts and minds in the simplest, cruelest way possible.

You made them think that the Orchid virus had come back.

And Ben knew how they were going to do it.

27

He had just seconds to execute his plan.

He waited until the two Volunteers pushed him to his knees and then he set his irreversible plan into motion. He fell to his knees and flopped over on his side before he could change his mind. He thrashed about the ground as violently as he could, fluttering his eyelids but keeping them half open so he could keep an eye on things. He didn't know if people moaned during the seizure, so he kept as quiet as he could. As he flailed about like a marlin on a charter fishing boat, he waited for the report of a rifle, for the sudden extinguishment of light, of hope, of everything that had once been or would ever be Ben Sullivan.

"Grab his legs!" Whitmore barked.

"Fuck this," a Volunteer barked. "I'm going to shoot him!"

"Don't you dare," Whitmore yelled. "Put the gun away or I'll kill you myself. Get him into the truck. Now!"

This was what Ben had been counting on. Whitmore would be beyond excited that his prisoner, his fugitive, had relapsed. Ben had to hope that the man's fear and contempt of the Redeyes would mask the coincidence that the relapse had hit just as Ben was about to be executed. And regardless, he couldn't take a chance that Ben was faking it. Best to secure him, whisk him away to some secret government lab and let the doctors sort it out.

A pair of powerful hands slid under his armpits and lifted him off the ground. He kept twitching as best as he could as they dragged him along the compacted dirt. His body began to ache from fatigue; he was running out of time. Now. It had to be now.

He dialed back the convulsions as he positioned himself to strike. He lolled his head to the side toward the Volunteer on his right. When the soldier stopped to adjust his arm under him, Ben snapped his head at the man's bare arm, the sleeves of his Volunteer uniform rolled up to just below the elbow. His teeth sank into the fleshy muscle halfway down the arm, and he bit down with all his might, feeling the sudden burst of blood in his mouth as his canines tore down into the man's epidermis and subcutaneous tissue. The sensation repulsed him instantly, triggering dry heaves. He forced himself to keep it down, telling himself he had to get through this. He absolutely had to.

The soldier howled in agony as he let Ben go. Ben righted himself just as he began to lose balance, and he turned toward the other soldier, who was now frantically unslinging his rifle, his face locked in a rictus of terror. Behind him, Whitmore chambered a round, the sound of the metallic click unmistakable even against the backdrop of the wounded soldier's wails. Ben rushed at the second soldier's legs, and they crashed to the hard-packed ground in a heap.

His insides were still recoiling at the horror of what he'd

just done to the other soldier, and he couldn't bring himself to bite this guy as well. Instead, he scratched at the man's face, his hands trembling as they tore at the guy's flesh. Blood from the first soldier's arm now smeared against the man's cheeks and lips, and he whimpered in fear. As he waged his surprise attack, the man's eyes widened with horror, Ben seeing in them the same thing he'd felt the day he'd been bitten.

"No, no, no," he pleaded.

A burst of machine-gun fire crackled around him, and he looked up to see the driver rushing at them with his rifle blazing at him, just along the side of the truck. Ben rolled off his second victim just before the driver drew a bead on his target; the machine gun roared a second time, but the fusillade only found Soldier Number Two, riddling his prone form with bullets.

Ben scrambled across the ground toward the dead soldier's gun, which had fallen to the ground in between him and the bullet-pocked corpse. He tucked the stock under his shoulder and fired a wild burst at the driver. His first burst missed badly; he fired again, and this time, his salvo found purchase in the driver's legs and abdomen. The soldier crashed to the ground like a puppeteer had cut his strings, and he lay still.

As he looked around for Whitmore, the sky echoed with the report of another gunshot and his leg lit up with pain. He looked down and saw a dark stain spreading across his right pant leg, just as Whitmore crashed into his flank. He went down again, hard, his world filling with white light of pain as the small of his back collided with the unforgiving ground.

Whitmore was on top of him now, the gun in his hand, but the barrel not quite centered on Ben's face. Ben wrapped his fingers around the burning-hot muzzle and pushed it away even as Whitmore pressed the heel of his hand into Ben's throat, reducing his intake of air to no more than a whistle. He grunted in pain from the scald of the gun's muzzle and the gunshot to his leg burned like liquid fire. But those were the least of his problems; if he couldn't break Whitmore's grip on his throat soon, he'd black out. Already, he could feel things going fuzzy.

The gun. He had to get control of the gun.

He slithered his free hand between their bodies, jamming it through a tiny crevice where Whitmore's ribcage was pressed down against Ben's chest. His left shoulder burned with fatigue, but he refused to let go of the gun; he'd come too far to give up now. With all the strength he could muster, he pushed the barrel back toward Whitmore's midsection as his right hand inched ever closer to the trigger guard. The periphery of his vision began to darken and fade away as his body screamed for more oxygen. Whitmore was so hellbent on strangling Ben that he couldn't quite detect the tide turning beneath him.

Ben's finger slipped around the trigger guard moments after he'd gotten the barrel turned 180 degrees away from his body. His sweaty hands fumbled with the trigger for a moment before finding their grip. He pulled the trigger one time, the muzzle pressed flush against Whitmore's rib cage, and the pistol roared.

Immediately, Ben felt the hand on his throat go slack. Ben rolled onto his side, and Whitmore slid off, his hands laced together in a protective cocoon on the bloom of blood that had appeared in the middle of his abdomen. He lay on his back, groaning. Ben pushed himself off the ground, and then his legs turned to jelly underneath him. He crumpled back to the ground and looked at the scene before him. It was carnage. Total carnage.

The soldier he'd bitten was still there, cradling his wounded arm and muttering to himself. He seemed uninterested in the goings-on around him, focused as he was on what he believed was the imminent end of his life as he knew it. Ben watched him wander around, scanning the ground, like he'd dropped a contact lens. He stopped, and Ben followed the soldier's line of sight. The soldier bent down to pick up his rifle, jammed the barrel in his mouth and pulled the trigger.

"Nooooo!" Ben yelled.

But it was too late. The back of the soldier's head disintegrated; he was dead before his body finished crumpling to the ground. Ben stood there in the shadow of blood, amid the dead and dying. He turned back toward Whitmore, who was crying and whimpering; his breaths came in ragged bursts, as though the act of respiration was pure agony.

Ben looked at him with equal parts pity and disgust. He couldn't help it. Part of him was glad the man was dying. The world was in a shitty enough place as it was. The last thing it needed was a man like Whitmore.

"So when is it going to happen?" Ben asked, crouching next to the doomed man. It made him feel cold and callous and uncaring to question this man in his dying breath, but he had to know.

Whitmore groaned and pressed his hands to the wound, perhaps believing that pressure would relieve some of his pain. Instead, it just accelerated the blood loss, and the crimson liquid seeped through his fingers.

"Fuck off."

"I know what you're going to do," Ben said. "You might as well tell me when it's going to happen."

"I said fuck off," he replied, his voice softer and more muted. He didn't have long. "You haven't stopped anything. You got lucky tonight. This is all going to happen whether I'm here or not."

His eyes closed as a wave of pain washed over him. His face tightened and he rolled onto his side, toward Ben, curled into the fetal position. Ben didn't need to examine it to know there was nothing he could do for Whitmore, even if he wanted to, which, he had to admit to himself, he most certainly did not.

"Jesus," he said. "Fucking hurts."

Ben stayed low, his eyes locked on the man's face, rocking back and forth on his heels as the life drained out of Whitmore. The Department operative didn't speak again, and he died without telling Ben what he wanted to know.

He stood up, his knees popping like muted gunshots as he did so. He scanned the scene before him, stunned by the sight of so much blood. It was like the Panic all over again, a microcosm of the world around him, the world that they all called home. He couldn't believe he'd survived. To them, he was the boogeyman, a specter, the evil clown from *It*, and instead of treating him like an out-of-control prisoner, they'd panicked. A one-in-a-million shot if ever there was one, but it had worked.

As the adrenaline drained away from his body like dirty bathwater, he became aware of a dull throb where the bullet had clipped him. Fortunately, it had grazed Ben's leg, leaving a short shallow channel of devastated flesh running along his right knee. It burned like hell, but the good news was that the bleeding had stopped. He'd need an antibiotic, and he didn't know where the hell he would find that. Medicine was hard to come by these days. He hoped that the heat of the bullet had disinfected the wound on its way through his flesh.

His entire body ached. Apocalypse or no, time continued its never-ending assault on his body, and the aches and pains were showing up right on schedule. His back was tight and stiff. He could only imagine the pain he'd be feeling tomorrow.

What now, he wondered. What now?

The camp was empty now, but it wouldn't be for long. And certainly, when Whitmore and his team didn't check in, they'd send reinforcements to find out what the hell had happened. He hustled over to Whitmore's corpse and took the wireless phone. Part of him felt strange about violating the man's personal effects, but he had to do what he could to survive, right?

He slipped the phone into his pocket and scanned the area for anything else useful. The guns were next, which he scooped off the blood-soaked ground like stray branches before an afternoon mowing of the lawn. The soldiers each had daypacks, stocked with protein bars, first-aid kits, bottled water. And first-aid kits. This stuff was gold.

Ben was so engrossed in scavenging the scene to outfitting himself that he didn't hear the vehicle boring down on him until it was too late. He was in the wide open, some thirty yards away from the truck, as the headlights bounced down the road toward him. He dropped all the rifles save one and brought it up into a firing position. It was nearly full dark now; there was nowhere for him to go. The DRR truck was the only way out of here.

The headlights, initially bright and fixed and ominous like some terrifying sea creature, began flashing wildly, as though someone was trying to signal him. He could hear a voice shouting; he primed his ears to cut through the night chatter and the sound of the car's engine revving, trying desperately to isolate the voice itself.

"Ben! Don't shoot! It's me!"

Ellie.

BEN AND ELLIE spent ten minutes clearing the scene of anything useful, during which time she explained the story as to how she'd managed to tail them all the way to the camp given that they hadn't had a car when they'd last seen each other. After Ben had slipped inside the DRR building, Ellie had flirted with the other Volunteer for another quarter hour and then disappeared into the darkness.

"I'm sorry," she said.

"For what?" Ben asked.

"I should've bought you a little more time," she said. "But he was starting to get a little aggressive."

Her voice was stern and tight.

"He looked for me a little while, which gave you a little more time. But eventually he found his partner unconscious back at his post."

"Brilliant infiltration on my part," he said. "It was an idiotic plan anyway."

"He wasn't the brightest bulb in the drawer, but he did seem to piece together that I was probably in on it, and that I'd lured him away from his post. I gather that's a big no-no among these idiots. He didn't call it in right away, and I could see him there, thinking it through, trying to figure out how he was going to explain the mess he'd made.

"Eventually, he called it in," she said.

They continued picking through the scene, conscious of a clock in their minds, that they would have to be quick about it, but careful not to overlook anything that might come in handy. They were pretty far off the reservation now, with no backup, no support, and no one to count on but themselves. She told him the rest of the story in the truck, as they chugged away from the now deathly quiet camp.

"A van showed up about two minutes later," she went on, "and an entire squad of Volunteers poured out. They were in riot gear, loaded for bear. That's when I knew you were in trouble."

Ellie had watched the building entrance for an hour, skulking in an out of the shadows like an alley cat, waiting to see if there was anything she could do to help Ben, quickly realizing how long a shot this would be. After an hour, she spotted a small Honda sedan idling across the street, its door swung open, its headlights shining in the dark like a rabid beast. A man stood in the V between the door and the chassis, partially illuminated by the car's interior dome light; his arm was draped across the roof of the car, and he was arguing with a woman standing on the sidewalk. Ellie couldn't hear the specifics of the discussion, but the woman must have said something he didn't like, because he slammed the door, chased her down and began beating the ever-living snot out of her, right there on the sidewalk.

Ellie froze, unsure if she should intervene and risk getting caught, or simply stand there while this man violently beat this woman. He was really getting into it, and Ellie had finally decided to get some help when she saw two Volunteers approach from the west and drag the man off in handcuffs. The woman pleaded with them to let him go as they dragged him down the street. A swirl of smoke from the car's exhaust pipe revealed that the man had left it running.

The Volunteers disappeared around a corner with their detainee, the woman in tow, leaving the car abandoned. A car with the keys in the ignition, the engine running quietly. Ellie waited one minute, then two, and no one came to recover the car. Seeing it just sitting there was pure agony, an itch just begging to be scratched. Ellie took a quick glance toward the building perimeter, where the activity level had begun to increase.

"That's probably when they sounded the alarm for me," Ben said.

Ben, driving the first shift, checked the gas gauge, praying that he'd have enough juice to get back to D.C.

"I got lucky," she said. "I happened to drive by just as they brought you out of the building. Another five seconds later or earlier, and I would've missed you."

"Lucky," Ben said, whistling softly.

"So what's this all about?" she finally asked.

"We need to get to the Freedom One Network building," he said.

"Jesus, why?"

"The Department. They've filmed a fake outbreak of the virus. They're going to broadcast it. They're going to make it look like the Panic has started back up again."

"What?"

Her voice cracked with incredulity.

"That's what Tranquility is all about," he said.

"I'm not following you."

"It was actually something you told me that started the train rolling," Ben said. "When you told me about the trucks from the processing centers. I figured out what those were for. For the fresher bodies."

"Fresher bodies for what?"

"I'll get to that," he said. "First I need to tell you what Tranquility is."

He nodded over his shoulder back toward the direction they'd come from.

"That place back there. It's going to be a permanent detention camp for Redeyes," he said.

"What do you mean permanent?"

"They're going to round us all up. Whitmore told me the government has decided that's how it's going to solve its Redeye problem. Remember, I'm really lucky. I broke a few bones, a got a few scars. But a lot of us have extensive medical needs. This is how the country is going to get beyond the Panic. By sweeping us under the rug. Out of sight, out of mind."

"Jesus Christ," she said. "So this is the end game."

"Yeah," he said. "And it's all bullshit. The people that run the Department, they like the way things are. Before the Panic, our republic was messy. Hard to manage. Price of democracy and all that. You were right. Things are so fucked up that people are willing to follow anyone that can keep the trains running on time. That becomes easier when it's more about survival than enlightenment."

"I don't quite understand this fake outbreak you're talking about. Why go to all the trouble?"

"Honestly, I think it actually makes a sick bit of sense," Ben said. "Not sure what that says about me as a person. Anyway, they figured people wouldn't feel comfortable with these government-run camps. It feels too Nazi-ish. When you get right down to it, we still believe in the Declaration of Independence and the Bill of Rights and apple pie and equality and all that. The only reason the people put up with the Department is because of how screwed up things are right now. But to sell the camps, they need something special. Because it's a paradigm shift. It would be a fundamental change to how our society works. Turns out not everyone is created equal after all. And the only way the people would go along with it is to make them believe that there is no choice. And how do you do that?"

She thought about it for a moment, and he could see her working it out.

"You make them think the virus is back," she said.

"Exactly."

She sat quietly for a moment, picking at a fingernail.

"And they told you this?"

"More or less," he said.

"How did you figure it out?"

"Since the Panic ended," Ben said, "I've spent a lot of nights outside. Especially during the warm months. I would look up at the moon. It helped calm me down. Plus, I've always been a bit of a space nut. So there we were, back at the camp. Whitmore had just told me that he was going to kill me. I looked up at the moon, just a little sliver of a thing up there, and it helped calm me down a little. And staring at it, it all kind of fell into place for me.

"Anyway, how much of your NASA history do you remember?"

"A little, I guess."

"What did they name the spot where they made the moon landing?"

She thought about it for a moment and then chuckled softly as her mind made the connection.

"The Sea of Tranquility."

"Exactly."

"But how did you make the leap from that to a fake outbreak?"

"I've always been a bit of a conspiracy nut," Ben said. "You know the theory that NASA faked the moon landing, right? That it was too important to the American psyche that we deliver on Kennedy's promise, that we take the lead from the Russians in the space race. So, the theory goes, when they realized they couldn't make the moon, the government decided to perpetrate this hoax. Now, I believe a lot of crazy shit, but I never bought into that one. But that's all I could think about as Whitmore told me about winning the hearts and minds of the public."

"Yeah," she said softly. "You're right, it does make sense."

"They have to win their hearts and minds," he said. "Whitmore's own words."

"But how will they pull something like that off?"

"That's where the bodies come in," he said. "They were harvesting them for use in the hoax. They'll be able to show footage of fresh bodies, victims of a recent Redeye rampage."

"Jesus. I think I'm going to be sick," she said.

"And now?"

"We have to stop it," he said. "Just like Calvin said. We have to stop Tranquility."

"How are we going to do that?"

"We have to get to the F-One Network building and get on the air somehow," he said. "We have to plant enough doubt in the public's mind to make them scrap the plan."

"What if they don't buy it? We'll be branded as terrorists and liars."

"You can count on that. All we can hope for is that we reach enough of them before it's too late. That we appeal to their better nature. Truly, I think this idea will repulse most people to their core. But when it comes down to internment versus the threat of a new Panic, I think the public will fall in line pretty quickly. They may not like it, but they'll probably agree that it's for the greater good. To be honest, even if we succeed at exposing the truth, they might go ahead with the plan anyway."

"It makes sense," she said softly. "I'm just having a hard time wrapping my head around it. Even after all that's happened, I can't believe it's come to this."

She was crying softly. Ben looked away, letting her deal with this revelation in her own way. It was a hard thing to accept. The Panic had been one thing, a truly terrible catastrophe that had been thrust upon all of them, forcing the world to change. He had hoped that after enough time had gone by, the world would emerge from the shadow of the Panic a stronger and greater if somewhat sadder place. But this was something else, a dirty, sordid affair, exploitation of the weak, not much different than a predatory adult film producer feeding on a starving waitress just dying to catch a break in Tinseltown. And now it seemed that the Panic was just a step, a big step, on the highway toward the final dismantling of what once had been good.

"I know," he replied, his voice tight, as though he were speaking while holding his breath. "I know."

"Back to D.C.?" she said.

"Freedom One Network, here we come."

28

Camp Alpha was in Buchanan County in southwestern Virginia, a rural chunk of the state that had known plenty about hard times long before the Panic. Unemployment, poverty, and drug addiction were rampant long before the Panic, and the area had been all but abandoned in its aftermath. The towns were small and far apart, and many had since ceased to exist.

Ben and Ellie rolled through one ghost town after another, dark and empty. They were quiet as they passed by the spectral storefronts and under dead traffic lights, gently swinging in the breeze, the emptiness of the towns huge and sentient. They saw one car in the first two hours on the road; it seemed ghostly as it passed them by, and Ben felt a chill as he watched its rear taillights recede into the darkness.

In Roanoke, Ben turned over the driving to Ellie and tried to get some sleep as they winged northeast toward D.C. They'd been on the road for about four hours when the call came in. Ben had all but forgotten about the phone that he'd pilfered from Whitmore's body; its rhythmic buzz caused him to jump. He'd been sleeping hard, and it took him a moment to pinpoint the source of the vibration.

"What is it?" Ellie asked. She began decelerating.

"Oh, shit," Ben said, digging the phone out of his pocket. "It's Whitmore's phone. I snagged it from him."

"Does it say who's calling?"

"Restricted."

The phone buzzed again.

"I'm going to answer it," he said. "I heard him take a couple calls. I can probably skate by. Maybe we can get some something useful."

His hand was trembling as he pressed the button to accept the call and held the phone up to his ear.

"Whitmore," he said, in as flat and unemotional voice as he could, the way the man had answer the phone on two separate occasions.

"You were supposed to call an hour ago," a female voice at the end of the line said. It was dusted with a hint of a southern accent. "What the hell is going on? Is Sullivan dead?"

It felt like a million volts of electricity ripping through him. He pulled the phone away from his ear and activated the speakerphone feature. He looked over at Ellie and pressed a finger to his lips. She nodded.

"Yes," he said. "It's all taken care of."

A brief pause. Nausea rose in his belly, like he'd just eaten some bad shrimp.

Jesus Christ, this was such a bad idea.

They're on to you.

The phone has a tracking device, and they'll be on you before you can say boo.

"Excellent," she said finally. Her voice sounded tinny and small echoing in the passenger cabin. "We've been listening to the chatter. No martyrdom for our good friend Sullivan. He's a pariah. He turned out to be quite the asset. We took something that could have been a serious problem and turned it to our advantage."

Ben's heart was pounding so hard he could feel the rush of blood in his ears. An idea bloomed in his mind like the first spring flower, unfurling its petals for a rush of sunlight and life and growth. It was the sum of all the inferences and deductions he'd made recently. He needed one more piece to the puzzle, and if he could get it on this phone call, he was confident that the full picture would become clear.

"Are we still on for the broadcast then?"

Silence. Fear coiled itself around his heart as he waited for her to respond.

"What are you talking about?"

Undoubtedly, the woman's antennae were up now. She may not have known why yet, but already, suspicion was creeping in. Ben had to reel it in before it metastasized. There were a number of ways he could interpret her question, and he needed to respond with the precision of a cruise missile. There was zero room for error.

"I had heard a rumor that it was being postponed."

"Where did you hear that?"

Relief flooded through him like water from a hydrant on a sweltering summer day.

"It doesn't matter," he snapped back. "Is it still on?" He put a little mustard on each word, lacing them like a fastball pitcher reaching back for his best stuff.

Silence again, but far less ominous. It seemed almost subservient.

"Yes, of course it's still on. The broadcast is still scheduled for tomorrow morning at 9:03. They'll interrupt the morning show with a breaking news alert and cut to footage of the rampage."

"Glad to hear it," he said, dialing back the tone of his voice and trying to contain a swirl of fear, horror, shock, and excitement. He turned on the charm again, now that he was hearing what he wanted to hear. He suspected that the woman was Whitmore's professional equivalent, perhaps assigned to a different department. Either way, he needed to end this call quickly. Eventually, he'd make a misstep, and that would be that.

"At six p.m. tomorrow, the President will address the nation and announce the opening of the internment camps."

He'd heard all he needed to know. Staying on the phone any longer was foolish.

"Very good," Ben said. "I'm looking forward to it."

He ended the call and let out a large sigh. He was sweating heavily; his shirt was soaked through, stuck to the small of his back. His stomach felt tight, as though he'd spent the last fifteen minutes doing crunches.

"Holy shit," she said. "That was unbelievable."

A laugh burst out of him, a loud, sharp explosion that seemed aware of the ridiculousness of what had just happened. He slid the phone back into his pocket and tried to regulate his breathing.

"I figured that my execution would be closely tied to Tranquility," he said. "That if someone knew about one operation, they'd be likely to know about the other. Once the loose end that was me was snipped, there'd be nothing to stop them from proceeding. There's one thing I can't figure out, though."

"Which is?"

"The camps. They already exist. Won't it be suspicious that they have these camps ready to go?"

"I can answer that one," she said. "The government began building the camps in mid-May. They were supposed to be camps for us. For the uninfected. They built them in the extremely rural areas, away from the biggest Redeye concentrations. That was when everyone thought the battle was lost."

"How many would they hold?" he asked.

"Millions," she said. "Truly, it looked very bad."

"Yeah, that's what Whitmore told me. Repeatedly."

"He wasn't lying about that," she said, her voice trailing off.

Deep down, part of him that was glad he'd been spared the darkest days of the Panic. He'd never admit it to Ellie. He could barely admit it to himself, but he didn't want to think about what it must have been like when all seemed lost. He couldn't bear to think about the despair and horror that Sarah and Gavin had felt, knowing the end was near, wondering when a pack of Redeyes would corner them in a convenience store while they scavenged for food. Being there for the end of the world.

"Anyway," she continued, "they began making arrangements to transport survivors to the camps. When the first reports of the recovery began to go national in late June, plans for the camps were abandoned, and that was pretty much it for them."

"And there they were, just sitting there for when they hatched their little plan."

"You got it," Ellie said softly.

They drove on.

❧

THEY HIT their first checkpoint around dawn. The day was breaking grey and overcast and a fine mist was falling. Twin threads of city-bound traffic curled back toward them as Ben downshifted; Ellie looked up from a map and pointed toward a shorter stub of traffic on the far right edge of the highway. A banner strung across the overpass read Government Use Only.

"Look," she said.

Ben looked over and saw a string of Department vehicles – SUVs, pickup trucks, and larger trucks lined up at the government-use checkpoint

"Think we should risk it?" Ben asked.

"It would be risky not to."

"You're right," Ben said.

He jerked the truck across two lanes of traffic, drawing no objection from the civilians he was cutting off. He fell in behind a troop transport truck, its cargo area full of Volunteers. The bright orange points of their lit cigarettes in the gloom of the morning looked like strange constellations.

He studied the Department vehicles ahead of him carefully. The checkpoint guard lazily waved each vehicle through, the only apparent prerequisite being a Department logo stamped on the driver's side door. Ben let his foot off the gas, slowing the big truck to about five miles per hour, but he didn't stop, nor did the guard indicate that Ben should stop.

And just like that, they were through. Inside the District again, a path to the Freedom One Network headquarters open before them. It was a strange feeling, operating outside the bounds of the law. He was suddenly ashamed. Would he be fighting for the rights of the Reds if he'd made it through the Panic unscathed? Would he fear and judge them for bringing the world to the brink of ruin? He wanted to think he'd be their champion, demanding equal rights, but he knew better.

He'd have supported men like Mr. Whitmore.

Because he'd have listened to Freedom One, and he would have decided Mr. Whitmore was right. He'd think back to the darkest days of the Panic, paralyzed by the feeling that there was nothing that he could do to protect his family. He'd have accepted the reprieve they'd all been given, and he would do his level best to make sure that nothing like that ever happened again. There was no way to know if or when the virus would suddenly re-appear. No, it didn't seem fair.

But hell, life wasn't fair.

The needs of the many outweigh the needs of the few.

And many other important clichés in which he could have wrapped himself in the bleak cold of the world after the Panic.

MUCH OF THE world's communications network infrastructure had sustained heavy damage during the war, and so the government had commandeered SpaceRock and established a fierce perimeter around the building housing the world's biggest satellite radio operation. Relying on a series of satellites deployed high above the earth, the company had been the last worldwide media outlet broadcasting during the Panic.

From the relative safety of SpaceRock headquarters, the government broadcast news and propaganda to those satellite radio subscribers and counted on word of mouth to spread news or some facsimile of it to the rest of the population. Throughout, the calm, steady voices of their deejays bubbled across the nation, reassuring the rapidly dwindling population that the tide was turning.

When the Panic was declared over in mid-November, the government moved quickly. The President ordered the Federal Communications Commission to seize all available bandwidth and enjoin all media outlets from broadcasting or printing all news until the state of emergency was lifted. The country was too shell-shocked to raise too much of a fuss, and it all went down like a perfectly mixed glass of chocolate milk. The Army Corps of Engineers reprogrammed the SpaceRock satellites so that they'd reach terrestrial radio and television.

On October 1 of the following year, about eleven months after the cessation of hostilities, Freedom One came to life, beginning with an evening news broadcast during which the beautiful anchors discussed all the progress the country had made in the previous year. A new routine was created, and slowly, the world began adjusting to its new paradigm.

Ben found the trendy brick building just after eight in the morning. Less than an hour to go.

"Maybe we go with a different approach this time," Ben said as he guided the truck down Florida Avenue and toward a driveway at the back of the monolithic building. He turned right down a wide alley ran alongside the structure. A series of rollaway doors lined the rear of the complex; two were closed, but the other three were wide open, which made the façade of the building look like a large mouth missing a few teeth. Two men, both wearing dark coveralls, were on a loading dock at the end down the alley, tossing bags of garbage into the back of a Department pickup.

"Agreed," she said. "This truck ought to help us."

"I wish we had uniforms," Ben said. "Might help us blend in a little more."

"On the other hand," Ellie said, "we can be anything in these clothes. Cleaning crew. Undercover Department operatives. Production staff."

Ben hadn't considered this.

"Good point. OK, let's go over our tremendously complicated plan once more," Ben said.

She grinned, and he felt warm, like the sun had slipped out from behind a cloud that had been hiding it all day.

"OK," she said. "Let's hear it."

"We storm the set and spill as much as we can before they grab us."

"Sounds like a plan."

"I was never much for complicated schemes anyway," Ben said. "Too many moving parts, too many things can go wrong. I think this will be more effective. We know where the camp is."

"Let's move."

Ben backed the truck into the spot farthest away from the workers, but they paid him no mind. The metronomic beeping of the truck pierced the morning calm, but Ben found it reassuring. Just another truck driver getting shit done. Refuge in the cocoon of the ordinary. He and Ellie slung the rifles over their shoulder and dropped down to the concrete dock, jutting out some ten feet from the building.

They stared at the gaping maw of the open door, revealing little of the dark warehouse beyond. Ellie reached over and squeezed Ben's hand. He returned the squeeze. It felt good knowing they were in this together. It didn't seem quite as lonely or loony. If you were by yourself, how would you ever know that you were crazy?

"Here we go."

29

I t was ten minutes to nine.

The day's installment of First Cup, the cleverly named morning show that aired from seven to ten each weekday morning, was airing on the television screens mounted throughout the building. Rob Simpson, one half of the First Cup morning team, was interviewing some Department official or another. The sound was muted, but the closed captioning was active. Simpson's pixie-like partner, Jill Daniels, was currently off-screen. The two hosts made Ben's skin crawl, and he welcomed the brief reprieve from at least one of them before he encountered them in person. Daniels was so goddamned bubbly that it wasn't entirely clear that she was aware that the Panic had happened at all.

"And I think, in another year, you're going to see some real progress in our country," the official was saying as he and Ellie passed under the ceiling-mounted television. Ellie hadn't even looked up at the screen, and Ben decided that was the wiser course of action.

"I did an internship at one of the local news affiliates

when I was in college," she said. "So I have a vague idea of how these places are set up. The studio will be at the center of the building, so as long we keep moving toward the middle, we'll be there in a couple minutes. When we get there, I'll take the booth, and you-"

"Hey!" a voice boomed down the hallway behind them.

"Go with it," Ben said. "Just follow my lead."

He stopped and spun to face the interloper, a heavy-set man wearing khaki pants and a short-sleeve dress shirt. A walkie-talkie clipped to his belt caught Ben's eye; this worried him. With a word or two, this guy could have a lot of help here in a flash.

"What are you two doing here?" he barked. "There aren't supposed to be any weapons inside the building."

"Special operations, sir," Ben said gruffly. "We've been assigned here for the morning." He maintained as stiff a pose as he could manage. Just following orders.

The Freedom One man eyed them carefully, thinking it through.

"Perhaps you'd like to contact my superiors," Ben said.

"No," he said. "No, that won't be necessary."

The man sighed loudly and pinched the bridge of his nose.

"So they're really doing this," the man said softly, more to himself than to Ben and Ellie. "Jeeeeesus Christ."

Ben's eyebrows popped at that one; he cut his eyes over to Ellie to gauge her reaction. She was one step ahead of him, and he found her eyes waiting. Ben wondered how much the man knew.

"Sorry for jumping all over you like that," he said. "Name's Jerry Cooper. I'm an associate producer here. I haven't slept much. A lot going on, you know."

"Very good, sir," Ben replied. "May we accompany you to the set?"

JERRY COOPER LED the erstwhile rebels deeper into the bowels of the Freedom One building, negotiating each identical corridor like a veteran rat who knew where to find the cheese. He talked incessantly, about the Panic, about the Department, even about the Washington Redskins, who hadn't even played a damn game in three years. He talked so much that Ben was having a hard time concentrating. All he could think about was how easy this was. They'd be on set in moments.

How easy it was.

How easy it was.

"We're just about there," Cooper said, looking back over his shoulder. "Absolutely no weapons allowed on set, of course."

Sweat was beading on his head, glistening under the fluorescent track lighting.

Son of a bitch.

It had been easy. Way too easy.

It was a trap.

They'd known Ben and Ellie were here all along.

Ben grabbed the man by the back of his shirt and threw him up against the wall. He jammed the point of the rifle up against his reddening jowly cheeks. Ben unclipped the walkie-talkie from the man's hip and attached it to his own.

"You knew we were coming."

The man was crying now, nodding his head.

"They made me do it," he said, struggling to catch his breath. "They said they would kill my family."

"Why the set-up? Why not just take us at the loading dock?"

"I don't know! They wanted you inside the production booth. To see something. And they didn't want a gun battle."

"To see what?"

"I don't know, I swear to God!"

"Dammit!" Ben hissed.

"There's a back way into the production booth, right?" Ellie asked. "Through the floor, or a freight elevator?"

He nodded.

"Access panel in the floor."

Ben looked over at Ellie.

"Emergency exit," she said.

"Ah," replied Ben. "You're taking us in through there."

He shook his head violently, like a child refusing his vegetables.

"They'll kill me."

Ben drove the barrel of the gun deeper into the man's flesh. "I'll kill you."

"OK, I'll take you. Please don't hurt me."

Ben glanced up at a nearby TV screen.

8:59 a.m.

"Let's go, Jerry."

∼

THEY MOVED QUICKLY through another series of corridors, and then down a stairwell to another corridor. The walls were still decorated like they had been before the Panic. Signed band photos and posters, vintage guitars mounted in large Plexiglass cases.

"Next door down," Cooper said. "It's a service closet.

There's a panel in the ceiling. The stairs are built into the panel."

"Yeah, you're going to show us."

Cooper's shoulders sagged, as though he'd expected to be released of his obligation after leading them to the control booth.

"I'm going first," Ben said to Jerry. "Then you. She'll bring up the rear."

Ben went in first. He jimmied the panel open and released the latch, sending the ladder down. Its feet hit the floor with a loud thud. Before he had a chance to second-guess himself, he scrambled up the ladder and found himself in the back corner of the control booth. No one seemed to notice him, as the people staffing the booth were watching the broadcast, rapt. Jerry and Ellie followed him in a moment later, and still the crewmembers were oblivious. A large clock mounted at the top of the control booth read 9:04 a.m.

Ben looked up at the screen.

There it was.

A haggard-looking reporter was crouched down behind the dusty tracks of an olive green tank. It had already begun

"We've got very heavy military activity here," the reporter was saying. "Again, this is live footage we are bringing you from Wellesley, Massachusetts, less than twenty miles west of Boston. Unconfirmed reports of an outbreak."

"Pull back for a wide shot," he said, presumably to the cameraman.

A nice touch, Ben thought. Going off script added a bit of verisimilitude to the production.

The shot widened, pulling back from the close-up of the reporter and revealing more of the downtown area, where the supposed battle was underway. As the scene came into focus, Ben's heart sank. They had gone all out. At least fifty Redeyes were on the warpath, attacking the small squadron of Volunteers that had been called in to quell the disturbance. Were they actors?

Two cars were ablaze as was a building at the corner. At the top left corner of the screen, three Reds were mauling a soldier in the middle of the street, tearing him to pieces amid his howling pleas for mercy. They'd spared no expense. So visceral, so vivid that Ben began to wonder if this wasn't a hoax after all. He gave his head a quick, hard shake and re-focused his efforts.

"Everyone get your hands up!" he yelled. "Now or I start shooting!"

The crew had been so intent on the video they hadn't heard the intrusion behind them. They slowly raised their hands, many of them placing them on their heads.

"Who's the producer?" Ben called out.

No response. Ben put the barrel of the gun against Jerry's head and began to count.

"I am!" a woman called out. "I am. Don't hurt him. We'll do whatever you say."

"Where are they?" he asked.

"Who?"

"The fucking Department!"

"I don't know!"

"Hands on your heads! Lace your fingers together. Now!"

They did as they were told.

"Here's the deal," Ben said. "I'm going out to that set. When I give the signal, you're going to cut that video feed and come back to the studio. You'll keep the broadcast live. No cutaways to old footage of the Panic, no Please Stand By graphics. If you can't follow my simple directions, my friend here will start killing people until you do."

"Are we clear?"

Desperate nods.

He stepped over to Ellie and leaned in close to her ear.

"How can we be sure they don't kill the broadcast?" he whispered.

"Leave that to me," she responded, her eyes never leaving the dozen hostages. "I'll keep an eye on them."

"We're probably going to die here, you know," he said. "Really soon."

"I know, she said, her voice strong and dense, like concrete laced with steel rebar. "Go on before you chicken out. You won't have long."

As Ben kept the gun trained on the hostages, Ellie went over to the main control terminal and began fiddling with the computer. A few keystrokes later, and the onscreen image of the purported fighting in Wellesley snapped back to the studio, looking small and empty after the chaos of the riots. After another few moments at the keyboard, she turned back toward him and gave him a thumbs up.

He stepped outside the booth, closed the door behind him and descended the steps to the studio floor. The control booth must have been soundproofed, as the folks on the floor were going about their business as though nothing were out of the ordinary were occurring in the control booth.

Time slowed down around him as he lurked at the foot of the steps. He looked back up at the control booth, hoping beyond hope that Ellie could hold down the fort long enough for him to do what he needed to do. He swiveled his head back around to the floor, every tendon and muscle popping and crackling as he did so. He took a deep breath and let it out slowly, feeling his body settle as he did so.

They were long past the point of no return. He couldn't even remember where that point had been. Perhaps accepting the invitation to the Haven so many months ago had sealed his fate. This was just the last step in a long journey. And he was feeling the effects of that journey. His mind and body felt broken, a boxer who's rope-a-doped just long enough to uncork one, final, hopefully devastating blow to an overconfident opponent.

He raised the rifle and stepped out from the shadow of the control booth.

"Good morning, Rob!"

30

Ben took a seat on the couch next to Robert Simpson, his white teeth frozen in a morning television smile and sun-burnished skin provided a protective screen from the shock he must have been feeling.

"Is the camera on me?" Ben asked.

Robert nodded and continued to smile.

"Here's the deal," Ben said. "Keep the camera on me. I see the little red light up there. If I see it click off, or if anyone makes a move that my friend up in the booth doesn't like, people will die."

"Are we clear?"

Another smile-soaked nod of the head.

Ben turned to the camera.

"Good morning. My name is Ben Sullivan. I survived the infection with the Orchid virus. I am a Redeye. You've probably seen my picture all over the news."

He made a point to carve air quotes around the word news.

"I'm currently wanted by the Department, and I probably won't leave this building alive."

He began to sweat, the enormity of what he was doing settling in. He tried not to think about the fact that millions of people were watching him right now, wondering what the hell was going on.

"This government is lying to you. There is no outbreak of the virus in Wellesley, Massachusetts. It's a hoax. Perhaps the biggest lie in the history of our country. The people who run the Department, they like being in charge. They like the way things are now."

"Why would they do that?" Rob asked, suddenly finding his sea legs but conscious of the business end of the rifle pointed at him.

"Because, Rob," Ben said, suddenly feeling less alone and less insane, "they hate us. They want to sweep us under the rug and pretend we don't exist."

Rob fired off a fake laugh, the one that all television personalities had in their quivers.

"I find that hard to believe," Rob said.

"You believe what you want," Ben said.

"Don't you think people have a right to be scared?"

"Not when there's nothing to be scared of."

He turned his attention back to the main camera.

"They're doing this to justify the permanent internment of all Orchid survivors. In camps. Internment camps. The camps are ready. You'll be hearing an announcement soon. Camps. Our own concentration camps. Maybe just detention camps now, but how long before they decide we're too big a threat, too much a liability?

"This isn't what Americans do to make things better," he went on, his voice starting to crack. "This is what we do when we give up. When we don't want to deal with our problems."

He paused, conscious of how painfully inadequate it all

sounded. Everything he said sounded clichéd. As he'd mentally mapped out his speech, it had all sounded so grandiose and glorious, like Patrick Henry giving his speech to the Virginia legislature in 1775. Instead, it sounded small and pathetic, the ramblings of a crazy man.

A knocking sound broke him out of his trance. Ellie was pounding violently on the window of the control booth. She twirled her finger around as if to say, wrap it up.

He had to finish strong.

"Don't let fear be this country's new currency. We were great once. We can be again."

Jesus, that sounded stupid.

Everyone in the studio was staring at him. He scampered across the studio floor and back up the steps into the control booth.

"We've got company," Ellie said, pointing to a monitor in the corner.

A horde of Volunteers had surrounded the building. At least a dozen Army trucks were forming a perimeter. Soldiers scurried about, hunkering down for a standoff.

"Everybody out," Ben said.

The hostages were still a moment and then quietly filed out of the control room. When they were gone, the once-crowded control room seemed vacant and hollow. Ben scanned the studio floor, which rippled with activity as the crew members began whispering to one another, seemingly unsure of whether to stay or go.

"Now would be a good time for a cigarette," Ellie said.

"Yes, it would," Ben said, his forehead pressed against the cool glass of the control booth.

He laughed softly and looked over at her, standing there, her face sharp and full of resolve. The end was at hand. They were not going to survive this. Sarah and Gavin. Had they seen the broadcast? What would they have thought? He supposed it didn't matter. What he was doing was for them, even if they didn't know it.

"They'll be coming for us soon," she said.

"Yeah," he said.

Something on the monitor caught his eye. Something dissonant, out of step with the order and precision he expected to see as the Department tightened its noose around him. A large crowd was approaching from the northwest, the top left corner of the screen, drawing the attention of the Volunteers on that side of the perimeter. He blinked and the crowd seemed to double in size, almost instantly.

"Something's happening," he said. "Look."

A scuffle erupted between a group of civilians and a squad of Volunteers. Ben watched, unblinking, as the scuffle exploded into a riot, like a match to dry timber.

"Ben, now," she said, her voice suddenly crackling with life. And something else. Hope? "Now's our chance."

She made a beeline for the access panel in the floor, and he followed her down the ladder. They were back on the main level; yells and shouts echoed throughout the corridors. They zipped back the way they'd come, retracing the path that Cooper had led them on not thirty minutes earlier.

If only they'd had Hansel to leave a trail of breadcrumbs to follow on their way back out.

"Do you recognize this?" Ben asked.

They passed smaller studios. A suite of administrative offices. A small lunchroom, where a janitor was busy sweeping the floor.

"No," Ellie said. "But there's got to be more than one way out."

At a T-junction, Ben spotted an Emergency Exit sign, its

soft glow as inviting as any fireplace after a hard day playing in the snow.

"There!"

The door boomeranged open as they crashed into it. An alarm brayed wildly, freezing them in their tracks, but it was quickly washed out by the din of the commotion just outside. They were in a dead-end alley, looking north toward a sea of humanity, roiling like an ocean during a tropical storm. The air was charged with the tinkling of glass shattering and the buzz of automatic weapons fire. Then an explosion.

"What the hell happened?" he asked. "Relapse? Were we wrong?"

"I don't know," she said. "But let's not waste time trying to figure it out."

"Follow me," he said, taking her hand and gripping it tightly.

They bolted toward the crowd, which swallowed them up into its chaos. It was all-out war now, as hundreds of civilians took on the heavily outnumbered Volunteers.

Ben kept his head down, making sure that Ellie stayed close behind. He slipped around a Jeep that had been pushed over on its side. A dead civilian lay face down in a pool of his own blood.

Ellie squeezed his hand, hard.

"Look, look!"

From the corner of his eye, Ben watched a teenage boy deliver a fearsome right cross to a Volunteer who hadn't seen it coming. The soldier stumbled and then dropped to his knees. But far more significant was what the boy did next. He kept going. He didn't crash down on the helpless soldier and beat him to death.

"Jesus Christ," he said. "This isn't a relapse."

"No," she said. "It's an uprising."

Another burst of small-arms fire, this one much closer, broke them from their sociological study of the riot. Ben felt Ellie's hand in the small of his back, pushing him along, and he broke into a run. Another minute got them clear of the heart of the battle, to the outer edges, where the crowd wasn't as densely packed. People were continuing to stream toward the Freedom One building, and he felt like a fish swimming upstream, hoping they could make it through without being recognized. A hundred yards clear of the building, they ducked down an empty side street and took refuge between two old brownstones heavily damaged by fire.

As Ben bent over at the knees to catch his breath, Ellie's word cycled through his head like a hamster on a wheel.

Uprising.

EPILOGUE

"This really isn't a good idea," Ellie said.

"I just need to see them," Ben replied.

Ben swept the neighborhood before taking up surveillance of his old house in Raleigh. No out-of-place vehicles. It was a bit of a risk, but one he was willing to take. After today, he didn't know when or if he'd see his son again. It was one more reminder of what he was going to be fighting for. Whom he would be fighting for.

They were in an old Toyota SUV that Ellie had procured for them, parked about twenty yards down the street from Ben's house. They'd been there for an hour, Ben hoping to get a glimpse of Sarah and Gavin. He still hadn't seen them, and he wasn't sure he'd ever be able to see them again. At least not like he'd once hoped.

"Aw, they probably aren't even watching this place," Ben said. "They probably don't think I'm that dumb."

He glanced up in the rearview mirror, barely recognizing the chap looking back at him. He'd dyed his hair jet black and his beard had begun to thicken again. With a pair of aviator sunglasses concealing the upper half of his face, he looked virtually nothing like the man who'd crashed Morning Cup, the man who was the subject of a massive manhunt by the U.S. Department of Reconstruction & Recovery.

The Freedom One Riots, as they'd come to be known, had raged into the afternoon before the Volunteers were able to quell the unrest, but not before word of the rebellion had begun to spread in the underground. Thirty civilians had died in the battle, their sacrifices noted and respected and mourned.

The President's press conference, the one in which he would announce internment plans, never materialized. But the Department had come down heavily on any form of protest. Martial law had been declared, and the dusk-to-dawn curfew was strictly enforced. Disappearances had become commonplace, as the Department began branding various individuals as terrorists, in league with Public Enemy No. 1, Ben Sullivan.

The front door suddenly swung open, and Gavin emerged from the house, a friend of his trailing behind. Ben's throat clenched as he watched his son slip down the steps with the cool confidence of a boy just beginning the transition to manhood. His hair was blond and shaggy, hanging just so into his face. He looked tall and lean and Ben's heart shattered.

"He's so big," he said, his voice cracking.

"He's a good looking boy," Ellie whispered. "But seriously, we need to go. It wouldn't look very good if the leader of the rebellion got caught in the first place they'd look for you."

"Just another minute."

Gavin and his friend stepped out into the street and began throwing a football around, running routes, celebrating imaginary touchdowns. Gavin threw the ball with force and precision, zipping pass after pass to his buddy. Ben watched for a minute and then reached down to shift into Drive. Ellie was right. It was time to get going.

A pass got away from his friend, and the ball sailed well over Gavin's head, toward the Toyota. Gavin gave chase, loping easily down the street, a cheetah stalking his prey. As he bent over to pick up the ball, not ten feet away from the car, he paused. Then he scooped up the ball, stood up and looked straight at Ben and Ellie.

Ben's heart stopped as father and son exchanged stares.

Gavin tucked the ball under his left arm and nodded toward the car, ever so slightly. Ben nodded back, feeling a stupid grin spreading across his face, like butter across toast. Gavin looked over his shoulder quickly at his friend, who seemed oblivious to the event unfolding before him. Gavin looked back at the car and gave a quick wave.

That was more than Ben could handle. Tears filled his eyes and then streamed silently down his cheeks. He raised his hand and returned the wave, ever so briefly. Gavin nodded once more and then jogged back to his friend.

Ben felt Ellie's hand on his wrist. It was warm but firm.

"Time to go," she said. "We have a lot to do."

Ben nodded, wiping the tears away from his face. He eased out of the parking spot and gently pressed on the gas. Gavin and his friend stepped to the side of the road to let the car pass through.

"I'm ready."

ABOUT THE AUTHOR

David's first novel, *The Jackpot*, was a No.1 bestselling legal thriller and is available in print and e-book format. He is also the author of *The Immune*, *The Living*, and *Anomaly*.

His short comedy films about law and publishing have amassed more than 2.5 million hits on YouTube and have been featured on CNN, in *The Washington Post*, *The Huffington Post*, and *The Wall Street Journal*.

Visit him at his website or follow him on Facebook (David Kazzie, Author) and Twitter (@davidkazzie).

 facebook.com/davidkazzieauthor

 twitter.com/davidkazzie

 instagram.com/davidkazzie

Printed in Great Britain
by Amazon